DON

QUANTUM LEAP ADVENTURES...

QUANTUM LEAP

T

Sam's

W

After hi

Sam races a

Al must ma

PULITZER
Is Al a traitor to his country? Only Sam can find out for sure . . .

DOUBLE OR NOTHING
Sam leaps into two people—twin brothers who are mortal enemies . . .

ODYSSEY
Sam and Al must save a twelve-year-old from an uncertain
future—and himself . . .

INDEPENDENCE
In 1776, Sam's ancestor could have been a patriot or a Tory—
now he has to find out firsthand!

APR 06 1997

QUANTUM LEAP

OUT OF TIME. OUT OF BODY. OUT OF CONTROL.

QUANTUM LEAP

ANGELS UNAWARE

A NOVEL BY

L. ELIZABETH STORM

BASED ON THE UNIVERSAL TELEVISION SERIES *QUANTUM LEAP* CREATED BY DONALD P. BELLISARIO

BOULEVARD BOOKS, NEW YORK

Quantum Leap: Angels Unaware, a novel by L. Elizabeth Storm, based on the Universal television series QUANTUM LEAP, created by Donald P. Bellisario.

QUANTUM LEAP: ANGELS UNAWARE

A Boulevard Book / published by arrangement with
MCA Publishing Rights, a Division of MCA, Inc.

PRINTING HISTORY
Boulevard edition / January 1997

The Putnam Berkley World Wide Web site address is
http://www.berkley.com/berkley

Make sure to check out *PB Plug*, the science fiction/fantasy newsletter, at
http://www.pbplug.com

ISBN: 1-57297-206-8

BOULEVARD
Boulevard Books are published by The Berkley Publishing Group,
200 Madison Avenue, New York, New York 10016.
BOULEVARD and its logo are trademarks
belonging to Berkley Publishing Corporation.

PRINTED IN THE UNITED STATES OF AMERICA

10   9   8   7   6   5   4   3   2   1

ACKNOWLEDGMENTS

I gratefully acknowledge the hospitality, prayers, and support of the sisters and brothers at St. Scholastica's Priory and St. Mary's Monastery, Petersham, Massachusetts, and of the brothers of St. Benedict's Abbey, Still River, Massachusetts, upon which the fictional St. Bede's was modeled.

I must also acknowledge the particular "angels" who helped bring this book alive:

—Ginjer Buchanan, editor, who always has the right word at the right time.

—Charles and Stephen Willard, for their geographic and meteorological research.

—John, John, and Reverend John, who have given support and love during this past year, each in his own way.

—My sister, Patricia, in whose house the spirit of St. Benedict lives on. (Expletive deleted.)

—And above all, Malachi.

AUTHOR'S NOTES

On Benedictines

In the fifth century, a man named Benedict and his twin sister, Scholastica, founded an order of monks and nuns, known now as Benedictines. Lay persons who want to live the Rule of St. Benedict in their own lives take vows of stability to one particular Benedictine house, and are called oblates.

Benedictines are known for their expertise in Gregorian chant, their preservation of traditional liturgical practices, and their hospitality. Many Benedictine communities have guest houses to accommodate those who wish to leave the world behind for a time in order to regain, or refocus, their faith. While donations to support the community are welcome, they are not required.

No one is ever refused Benedictine hospitality.

On the Date of Sam Beckett's First Leap

According to *Quantum Leap* canon, Sam Beckett first Leaped in 1995. He found himself in the person of Tom Stratton, an Air Force test pilot scheduled to fly an X-2 four days later: a mission Tom Stratton did not survive. Al Calavicci reassured Sam that with him as "copilot," Sam could perform the mission and live. However, Al arrived late because he attended a Lakers play-off game that went into overtime.

On May 16, 1995, a Lakers play-off game went into overtime.

Coincidence?

Since the *Quantum Leap* Lakers game took place three and a half or four days after Sam Leaped in, I have (in this novel) calculated the date of Sam's first Leap to be May 12, 1995. It's not canon; but it *is* one heck of a coincidence!

This book is dedicated to
William C. Willard (November 20, 1994),
James O. Norton (December 7, 1994),
and
Katharine Postak (March 30, 1996).

May Light perpetual shine upon them.

Be not forgetful to entertain strangers;
For thereby some have entertained angels unawares.

—HEBREWS 13:2

PROLOGUE

Sunday, April 2, 1995   12:00 P.M.
Windy Bluffs, Massachusetts

And now she had nowhere left to go. She was out of time, out
of friends, out of family. And out of luck. The world had
turned into an ugly demon stalking her at night, haunting her
by day. And it had all happened so fast.

The world below her gaped and yawned, an ugly mouth
with rocks for teeth. She was falling, her fingertips slipping
on the precarious overhang she clung to, her body growing
heavier as each second passed.

"Oh, God," she whimpered. "Please! I'm not ready to
die!"

The rocks clasped in her bleeding fingers began to break
loose. She slipped downward, her feet scrambling frantically
for a hold on something, anything, to keep her from plunging
to the ground.

The cliff was dotted with trees, all too far for her to touch.
Below her, a hundred feet or more, the earth was waiting;
waiting to grasp her, cradle her, break her into a hundred
pieces.

The world turned, and she felt herself slipping further.

"Please! Please, don't let me die!"

Above her, at the edge of the cliff, was the man who had
brought her to this point.

"Got yourself into trouble?" a cool voice asked. The man
squatted down, and she could see his eyes, catlike and feral.

"Help me," she gasped. Her fingers were bleeding. She
could hardly breathe. Everything was going numb.

"Help you? Sure, girlie. When you tell me where you put
the stuff."

"Please!"

1

"Where is it, girlie? You brought it with you! It's here, somewhere."

"Help me!"

Darkness closed around her brain. She had been fighting the fall for nearly ten minutes now; her arms, her hands, her fingers were betraying her. She couldn't hold on any longer.

"Please," she whispered. A hand reached down and caught her wrist. For a moment, the weight of her body, hanging helplessly against the face of the cliff, was eased. Then the grip tightened, crunching the bones in her slender wrist, cutting off the circulation to her hand.

"Where is it?" the voice hissed. The man yanked her arm sharply, and pulled it out of the socket. She heard the snap as it popped loose.

She screamed.

"Where's the stuff, you frigging little whore?"

"Let me. . . ." *Let me go?* For a second she almost said it. Anything to make the pain go away.

He reached down with his other hand and grabbed her long, brown hair that had been tied in a braid earlier today. Now it was half undone, and he yanked it hard, half supporting her weight by the rope of hair on her head.

She cried out again, but her voice was almost gone.

"Did you give it to someone? Huh? Where is it, girlie?"

For a second, she considered telling him. Then she closed her eyes, and went back into her mind, into her memories, to a safer, more peaceful time.

She would not give him what he wanted. She couldn't. And she couldn't bear to die like this, flung over a cliff like an outgrown doll.

"Angel of God, guardian dear," she whispered.

She was a child again. For one timeless moment, she was five years old.

"I don't want you to go."

"I'm gonna come back. I don't know when—but I'll come back."

She could believe. She could hope. She could fear no evil. The world was reaching up for her, wanting to hold her. . . .

"To whom God's love commits me here. . . ."

"Screw you!"

The man let go of her wrist, and her arm dangled uselessly

at her side. Her other hand slipped on the rocks. Two finger-nails broke off at the quick.

"Ever this day be at my side," she whispered.

There was a doll she had slept with when she was little. She loved that doll, even though its head was always coming off.

She still had that doll.

"She's a little young, Al. . . ."

"To light and guard. . . ."

She scraped her fingers on the stones, clutching for a hold. But they tumbled out of her way, leaping from the cliff and joining the ranks of those that had gone before them.

"Say adios, girlie."

"—to rule and guide. . . ."

It was such a long way down.

The man released her hair, and the next second she began to fall. Falling through the air, tumbling against the rocks, against the few brave trees that crept out from the edges of the staggeringly steep ledge and lashed her with branches and pine needles.

She was bruised and battered as she fell. Every sharp edge, every jagged stone, struck some tender spot.

Only as she saw the ground, close enough to realize how the end would be, did she break out of her comforting memories.

"Oh, God! Don't let me die!"

As she screamed, the ground snatched her and broke her body into a shattered Picasso painting.

Then time began to twist in on itself . . .

Therefore, so that we may amend our evil ways,
the days of our lives have been lengthened. . . .
Let us ask God to supply . . .
what by nature is hardly possible.

—THE RULE OF ST. BENEDICT:
PROLOGUE

CHAPTER ONE

Friday, March 31, 1995   6:15 P.M.
Boston, Massachusetts

"You promised me you were going to stop!"

Friday night at Grendel's Den, the most popular dinner spot for college students and yuppies alike. It was crowded, as always, every table in the former hippie hangout taken. The place reeked of the tie-dyed sixties.

Across the citronella candle on the table between them, Teresa Bruckner stared at her dinner partner. Her voice, even to her, sounded whiny, nagging. It sounded that way because she was having the same conversation with George that she'd had a dozen times already. And she knew exactly what the man she was talking to would say next.

"And I am. Right after I make this last delivery. I swear, honey, honest. Just one more."

The man reached across the table and took her hand. His gray eyes sparkled in the candlelight, and like many of the men in the restaurant, he wore his hair long and tied at the nape of his neck. At twenty-four, George already had a craggy, weathered face that Teresa thought was very appealing. It made him look older, more mature. Somehow safe. He was a very sexy man, and when he turned on the charm, it was awfully hard to resist him.

But tonight was different. She pulled her hand back and crossed her arms. "No." She shook her head, glancing quickly around them. No one was listening. Nevertheless, she leaned closer and dropped her voice. "You promised me that the last drop was it," she reminded him. "You said you wouldn't work for them anymore."

"And I wasn't going to," George said, his voice smooth and seductive. He reached for her again, but she pulled back from the touch. He sighed and dropped his hand to the table. "Look, something came up. I just—I needed a little extra cash, all right? They gave me an advance, and I—well, I have to make this one more delivery to pay them back. It's no big deal," he continued when she started shaking her head again. "Look, Teresita," he whispered, using the intimate diminutive that turned her knees to butter, "you have my word. Just this one last delivery and it's over. I swear."

"You swore the last time," she reminded him, her voice still remarkably firm. Neither she nor George had touched their dinner; it had been sitting there for nearly ten minutes while they replayed what Teresa thought of as "conversation 131." "And the time before that," she continued, "and the time before that. George, you've broken your promise every time!" She felt tears of frustration gather and shut her eyes tightly.

He touched her arm gently. "I really mean it this time, honey. Really, after this, it'll be a clean start."

Teresa didn't answer at first. She sniffed, rubbed her eyes, and looked at him. "It's been eight months now, George," she reminded him. "Eight months, and you haven't stopped." She took a deep breath, picked up her fork, and toyed with her spaghetti. "It was so good before. . . ." She stopped short of saying anything outright. Not here, not in public.

"And it will be again," George soothed. He smiled at her, a disarming, almost childlike grin that, on his face, seemed to Teresa like a ray of sun on a cloudy day. God, he was gorgeous! "Look, I called Dad, he's sending me some more money. Once I pay off this one loan, everything'll be back to normal. I swear!" He pushed his salad plate away, and leaned closer. "Remember how much fun we used to have? Just going to the Gardens, or taking walks around the Fenway?"

"Yes." The spaghetti was tasteless. It could have been raw wood fiber for all Teresa could tell. She put her fork down. "That's the thing, George, it was—you used to be so much fun! Now . . ." She had a hard time putting into words the way George had changed. It had started shortly after they'd begun dating. Even before she knew what was causing the changes, she knew something was wrong. Then she discovered what it was, and their whole relationship had taken a turn down a dark alley.

She didn't want to abandon George: he needed help, and he

7

kept telling her how much it meant to him that she was standing by him. But she didn't want to go down that dark alley with him; she wanted him to come back.

"You have to make a choice, George," she said quietly. She glanced around the room again. In the corner, a group of three men with short cropped hair, T-shirts, and earrings glanced at them, then went back to their meal. They made her nervous; they looked like the kind of people George would be making his delivery to.

"I have, I told you. This is the last time. No more after this."

One of the men at the table looked up again and met her eyes briefly before turning away. Teresa folded her napkin and put it on the table.

"No. Not after this time. Now. It's over now, George. I'm sorry."

She got up quickly, before another glance into George's eyes, or another touch of his hand, made her change her mind. She started for the door.

"Teresa!" George was following her, but she ignored him until she got to the front door. Then she turned and put her hand out.

"It's your turn to pay the bill," she reminded him. "You don't want to get arrested here, do you?"

"Wait for me," he ordered. His voice was quiet and strong. Normally, she obeyed.

"I can't," she whispered. She turned and headed outside, into a night that had turned cool. A sidewalk threaded the park behind Grendel's Den. It was busy tonight, with college students on their way to or from the subway or the Galleria or the Coop. There was laughter and quiet whispering, and children running back and forth.

"Teresa! Teresa, wait! Come on, honey, wait!"

Teresa heard George close behind her; knowing him, he probably just dropped a twenty on the table and headed after her. She didn't turn. This part of their arguments was always the same, too; once he caught up with her and held her and whispered his promises to her, she'd be a goner.

She didn't know what it was about him that made her give in all the time; he always made her want to do things she never really wanted to do. And later, when she was alone, or back

8

in her apartment, she'd wonder at the kind of madness that overcame her when she was with him.

No, not madness, she told herself, walking a little quicker, but not wanting to run. Sickness. She was George-sick. She was addicted to him, like he was addicted to the coke.

She headed for the subway, determined not to give in again. Not to listen to his promises. Not to surrender.

But the moment she stopped to wait for a break in the traffic at JFK Street, he caught up with her.

"Teresita!" He took her arm and turned her around, not roughly, but forcefully. His strength made her feel small. It made her heart pound. And it scared her sometimes. "Honey, please! One more chance," he pleaded. His eyes were bright, almost as if he were going to cry. "Please, you don't know how important you are to me. You're—you're everything! Without you . . . God, without you . . ." He seemed to be at a loss for words. And for a moment, he seemed as vulnerable, as scared, as she felt.

"I want to believe you, George," she said. She tried to pull away, but couldn't quite find the strength. Something about his voice, his eyes, paralyzed her. She took a deep breath. "But if you were serious, you wouldn't have had all that— stuff—in your apartment."

He released her, ran a hand over his face, and shook his head. He looked at his feet.

"I know," he muttered. Then he looked at her. "Please, honey, just—let me have it back. One last drop, I swear! Look, I can't screw this up. These guys don't play games." There was fear in his voice. And in his eyes. Dark gray, they wrinkled at the corners, tightening. Maybe with fear, Teresa thought. Maybe with anger?

"I can't," she said. She looked away. The light had turned green, and she started across the street. George walked beside her. He was dressed more warmly than Teresa, in his new black leather jacket. He cut a dapper figure, if a somewhat anachronistic one with his long hair. It was one of the things that appealed to Teresa.

His "hobby" was one of the things that didn't.

"Teresa, I have to have the stuff!" He was quietly insistent, his hands thrust into his jacket pockets. He was watching the people around them, as Teresa was. She wasn't sure, but she

9

thought one of the men from Grendel's Den was following them. She decided not to look back to find out.

"Teresa, I swear on my mother's grave! I won't make another drop after this, never! But I've gotta have the stuff back!"

"Your mother's grave?" Teresa stopped and faced him. "Your mother's still alive!"

A sheepish grin formed on George's face, and he gave a half-shrug. "Okay, how about my Aunt Mabel?"

She didn't want to; she had no desire to; but she found herself smiling at the boyish charm that overtook him. And her.

For a moment, she just met his eyes, trying to discern how much sincerity was in them. Memories of how good things had been, of how much fun they'd had, of the wonderful sense of belonging and being needed that he'd given her, began to overpower her.

Maybe this time he really would stop. Maybe this was his last drop. Maybe, if she really made an effort, he'd find her more interesting than the coke.

She put a hand on his arm and felt the warm leather of his jacket. She could smell it in the brisk evening air, smelled his aftershave, smelled his warm breath as he waited for an answer.

Her mind took a brief vacation and her heart spoke. "Tomorrow," she said. "Meet me at the Coop, okay? I have to get a couple books for one of my classes. I'll—I'll bring it then."

"I *need* the stuff, Teresa," George said, impressing the urgency of his request by lowering his voice. He tilted her chin up with his hand. "I've got people who are expecting it."

Teresa pulled away. "I'll bring it to you tomorrow."

"I could pick it up now. Tonight."

"Tomorrow." She began to feel trapped. "I'll meet you at the Coop at lunchtime, all right? But don't push or I'll just throw it out, like I did the last time."

George's eyes glazed over for a moment. Then he focused on her again and took a deep breath. "Okay. Tomorrow." Then a wide, rapturous grin covered his weathered face. He pulled her close and held her and kissed her, a hard, passionate kiss.

10

She liked it when he kissed her like that; it reminded her of how strong he was. That nothing could hurt her while he was there, because he'd take care of her. He'd promised her that.

"I love you," he whispered when he let her go. He stroked her face and looked at her, a long, devouring look. "And I promise, honey. This is the last time."

"It better be," she murmured. But her heart was no longer in her threat; it was sinking down to her loins, aching for more of his touch.

"Noon," he said, running his hand along her arm. "Don't be late, okay?"

She shivered from his touch.

He was smiling as she walked alone toward the subway.

"Jou look like jou could juse a friend."

Teresa pulled out of her stupor, the strange euphoria she often felt after she'd been with George, and stared at the Hispanic woman who sat down next to her on the bench in the subway station.

"Are you talking to me?"

"Chore! Jou see anyone else around here that looks as bad as you?"

Teresa decided it would be impolite to point out that the woman who asked that question looked about as badly off as anyone *she* had ever seen. The portly stranger was dressed in a white outfit that was probably discarded from a bad stage production of *Thoroughly Modern Millie*. A matching white hat topped her short black hair, and she waved a fan in front of her, almost as if she were flirting. She carried a small clutch purse that couldn't have held more than a wallet and a lipstick, and her shoes weren't good for much besides doing the Charleston.

Teresa was torn between laughter and repulsion.

"Jou know, I just got here." The woman fanned herself and looked around the station as if she were a stranger to the town. "Jou got problems, jets? I can tell!" The woman smiled and twisted sideways to face Teresa, dropping her purse onto the bench.

"I don't know what you mean," Teresa said. "I'm just waiting for a train. . . ."

11

"Jou got a *big* problem!" The woman slid closer and lowered her voice, still smiling. "Jou see, I know! I'm jour angel!"

Teresa's eyes widened. "My what?" Only a few people in the station bothered to pay any attention, and after a quick survey of the two women, they turned away again.

"Jour angel! Jou believe in angels, don't jou?" Teresa hesitated, not sure how to answer. "Oh! They said this would be an easy one," the woman moaned, glancing toward the vaulted ceiling for a few seconds.

Teresa cleared her throat and glanced at her watch. The train would be there any minute. "Ma'am, I don't mean to be rude, but—well, I'd really like to be alone."

"No, no." The woman picked her fan up and toyed with it. "No, jou see, I'm here to help you. Only, they told me this would be an easy one, 'cause jou already believed in angels."

"My religious beliefs are my own business. If you say you're an angel, then fine, you're an angel. But if you don't mind, I'd like to be left alone.—Do you mind?" she asked, when the woman made no move to leave.

"Jou don't thin' we could talk about—"

"I'd really like to be alone."

"Oh, see, tha's no' a good idea, because bad men can get jou when jou're alone." The woman picked up her fan.

Teresa's stomach churned. "What?" she whispered. She took a quick look around: no one *seemed* to be watching her. But maybe she wouldn't notice if someone was.

"That man," the woman explained. "The one jou took something from? He has some very bad friends, jou know. And once they know jou have it, they're going to want to get it back. So, since jour roommate is off galvanizing around—"

"Galavanting," Teresa corrected her without thinking.

"Oh, well, whatever!" The fan waved in the air like an exclamation point. "They think they can get to you. Is no' safe to be alone this weekend."

Teresa ground her teeth. "Who are you?" she demanded, her words pressed through teeth that wouldn't part. "Who the hell are you?"

"Oh, jou couldn't talk to your angel like that!" The woman rapped her fan on the bench and several heads turned.

"I'm sorry, lady, but angels don't—they don't exactly—well—"

"Look like thees?" The woman swept her hands in front of herself. "Oh, chore, I know. Jou think angels chould look like that guy Clarence, right? Everybody says that, now. Well, let me tell you—"

"No, I don't think—who's Clarence?"

"Who's Clarence?" The woman's voice rose an octave and a decibel. Teresa winced. If she weren't so disturbed by what this stranger seemed to know, talking to a slightly deranged woman might have been fun. But this just felt too much like a setup. Her stomach was in a knot, her palms were sticky with sweat, and her feet tingled with the urge to run.

Had George not trusted her to bring the stuff to him tomorrow? Had he sent someone here to get it from her now, tonight? Someone to follow her back to her apartment, take the stuff, kill her?

God, what a mess she was in!

The woman opened her mouth, but before she could speak, a man not much older than Teresa came over to them. She recognized him from the restaurant: he was one of the three with cropped hair, T-shirts, and earrings. He had an eagle tattoo on his upper arm and he was twice the size of Teresa's uninvited companion.

"This woman givin' you problems?"

Teresa glanced from the flapper to the man, and back. Her choice of unwanted company was clear.

"Uh, no. No, she's—we're just having a theological discussion. Right?" she asked, turning to the woman for confirmation.

"Oh, chore. Right." The woman smiled easily and fanned herself.

The man stared at them for a few seconds, his breathing heavy and fast, as if he were working himself up for a fight. His small eyes glinted with a light Teresa had seen before. It wasn't a comforting glow.

Finally, without another word, the man turned and walked a few feet away, then stood by the edge of the platform, waiting for a train.

"God," she whispered when he'd gone, sinking her head forward into her palms. She wanted to cry.

13

"See, that's what I was saying!" The flapper interrupted the relief that washed over Teresa. "*He* sent me to help you out, hokay? So jou just listen to Angela, and she'll make everything all right."

"Angela," Teresa muttered. "That's your name?" She wondered if a drug dealer would really offer her name before killing her.

"*Si.*" The woman smiled. "Angelita Carmen Guadalupe Cecilia Jimenez. My mother, she called me Angelita; that means 'little angel.' But—I'm not." She shrugged, a little embarrassed.

"My mother. . . ." Teresa felt her eyes burning and blinked hard.

"Jou could juse jour mother right now, huh?" she said quietly. There was a very kind, very sympathetic look in Angela's eyes. Teresa turned away.

"She died. Five years ago. Ovarian cancer. . . ." At least, Teresa remembered, it had been quick. From the time she learned she was sick to the time she died was only eighteen months. It had only seemed endless at the time.

The woman nodded. "Jets, I know."

"How do you know?" Teresa asked. Her guard was back up, her stomach was clenching again.

"Oh, I was told many things about jou before I came here," the woman said. "Jou see, I'm supposed to keep anything bad from happening to you."

"You're with the police," Teresa concluded suddenly. Sure, that made sense. Somehow, the police had figured out what she had, and they were here to arrest her and get her to turn state's evidence.

"No! I told jou—"

"You're an angel," Teresa finished. Where was the train? "Look, don't take this the wrong way, but you're not exactly what I figure angels should look like."

The woman waved her fan back and forth in front of her face, as if she were hot. "Back to Clarence," she muttered.

"No, not Clarence—whoever he is. I mean—well, you're pretty out of style, aren't you?"

For a few seconds, the absurdity of her conversation struck Teresa. Here she was in the subway, discussing angelic fashion statements with a strange woman who looked like she'd stepped out of the twenties.

"Out of style? This was all the rage in my day!" The woman looked down at her outfit, fingered the white fabric and the pearls around her neck. "Jou know, I'm getting a lot of comments about it these days, though."

"Well, in my book, angels dress fashionably. You know, 'cutting edge' stuff."

The phrase came back to her mind, almost unbidden. And with it came a host of memories she'd long since relegated to a dark corner of her mind.

Quickly, Teresa grabbed her purse, got up, and walked several feet down the platform, away from the woman.

"Jou hoo!"

The woman was following. Teresa ignored her, ducked around the man who'd interrupted her conversation earlier, and stood stonily at the end of the platform. The man with the earring was watching her, watching the large flapper as she puffed, out of breath, to catch up with Teresa. But Teresa's only thought was to escape the painful memories.

The strange men weren't frightening. They were just big. One of them was wearing Mommy's clothes. And the other one was wearing a really yucky outfit.

"Where's my mommy?"

"Oh, your mommy?" The man with the yucky shirt hemmed and hawed for a second. "Your mommy. . . . Oh, your mommy had to go away for a little while. But she's going to be back very soon."

"Yeah. My name is Sam, and this is Al. And—for the next couple of days, everyone's going to pretend—that I'm your mommy."

"That's good, Sam."

"Thank you."

"Why?" Teresa asked.

"Why?" Both men repeated the question as if they hadn't expected it.

Then the man in the yucky shirt—Al—pulled a flat box from his pants pocket and crouched down to her level. The box made funny noises, and the man in Mommy's clothes looked over at it, trying to see what his friend saw.

"Oh, to help your big brother!"

15

"Do what?"

"Do what?" Sam asked, also curious.

"Oh, uh, to—to win the swim meet." He waved his hand in a circle as he said it.

"Are you angels?"

"No," Sam said. But at the same instant, Yucky-Shirt-Al contradicted him.

"Oh, yes," he said. *"Yes, uh, this is Angel Sam,"* he added, gesturing to his friend, *"and I'm Angel Al."* He pointed to his right shoulder.

"The truth, huh?" Sam muttered. He probably didn't think Teresa was paying attention. But she was.

"Here, I'll show you," Al said. He raised his hand, palm out. *"Try and touch my hand."*

She did. She lifted her hand as he had done and tried to meet his; but her hand slipped through him. Laughing, she stepped forward and jumped right through him.

"Come on back here," he ordered, twisting his head around. She obeyed.

What in the world made her think about that now, tonight? She didn't believe in angels anymore. She didn't believe angels lied to you and broke their promises.

Tears stung her eyes and she wiped them away.

"Jou scared jourself, huh?" the flapper asked calmly, standing next to her. She hadn't noticed the woman for the last few seconds, so strong had the memory been.

Teresa tried to walk around her, to put more distance between them, but the large woman grabbed her arms and held her gently.

"Let go!" Teresa squirmed, but the woman's grip paralyzed her.

"Hokay, maybe I don' look so fashionable—"

"Real angels don't look like flappers!" Teresa yelled. A few heads turned at her outburst. "And they don't wear halos, either. So, whoever you are, just go away and stop pretending that you're an angel!"

She finally wrestled free and started back along the platform, back toward the bench where she'd been sitting before. The seat was taken.

"Oh, jets? So what do angels wear, then?"

She couldn't quite help herself. Teresa stopped, closed her eyes, and tried to ignore the painful image in her mind.

"Fedoras," she said bitterly. She turned and faced Angela. "Teal-colored fedoras."

CHAPTER
TWO

Jackson's Java was, as far as Father O'Keefe was concerned, the only decent place in Charlotte to get a good cup of coffee. And without coffee, he often joked, there was no civilization.

"Check."

His chess partner, a former student from Harvard, had offered him a game while he drank his cappuccino. O'Keefe examined the board and made the only move open to him. His position seemed desperate, but he saw a solution he didn't think his opponent had.

"So what brought you down here?" the young man asked, moving his rook into an attack position. O'Keefe grimaced.

"Just—visiting." He captured a pawn but realized he was too distracted to play a really good game.

He'd flown in yesterday, hoping that delivering his news in person might ease its sting. But he had a distinct feeling that he had only made matters worse. Now, after a long search through the city for a decent cup of coffee, he'd found this small alcove near the university, a dark, quiet haven where, for an hour now, he'd nursed his cappuccino and engaged in a game of chess.

"What are you doing down here?"

"Just a—project I'm working on," the young man said. He seemed torn between wanting to discuss it and not wanting to say too much. It was the third time O'Keefe had asked him about it in the last hour. "They're doing a lot of work on holography here. I—had some friends I thought I'd talk to."

"Holography?" O'Keefe waited while the young man ex-

18

amined the board and made his choice. "Like the video games they have out now?"

"Check," his opponent said again, moving his queen. "Mate in three moves."

O'Keefe examined the board and drank the last of his coffee. Once again his opponent had decided not to discuss his reason for being here.

"Agreed." He moved his king, and smiled at his former student.

The young man chuckled and responded predictably. "Not bad," he muttered, an air of self-assurance weighting his words. He placed his queen just where O'Keefe had expected him to. The man had ignored one of O'Keefe's rooks. He'd ignored it for the last four moves.

"You going to be here long?" the former student asked, waiting for O'Keefe to consider his remaining options. O'Keefe pondered the board as if he weren't sure which move to make.

"I have an early flight back to Boston tomorrow," he said, and moved his rook. He looked up to watch the reaction on his opponent's face.

It took a moment; but as the realization of defeat hit him, the young man's face fell. He stared at the board, disbelieving, his mouth opening in a wordless protest.

"Mate in one move," O'Keefe said quietly. He smiled and waited.

Finally, with the grace of a good loser, the man shook his head and looked up. A wry grin twisted his face. "I should stick to playing with computers," he said. "They're not so sneaky."

He moved his remaining bishop and waited for O'Keefe to put his queen in place. Tipping his king over in defeat, the young man shook O'Keefe's hand.

"Next time you're in Boston, give me a ring," O'Keefe invited. "We'll have a rematch."

The man's crooked smile transformed his face. "I'm not used to losing," he said. "But on the other hand, I don't like to quit."

"Just as I remembered. You remind me of another of my students. Had her last semester. She's very bright." O'Keefe

19

started for the door, then turned and added, "You two would get along."

The young man grimaced. "I hope you're not trying to play matchmaker."

O'Keefe smiled as he collected his coat. "With you? Wouldn't dream of it! By the way. . . ." His former student looked up. "I heard about your Nobel. Congratulations. And— good luck on whatever it is you're doing now."

"Thanks."

O'Keefe headed back to the hotel in his rental car. It was almost 10:30 by the time he got back to his room and undressed. Late enough to sleep.

But the day wouldn't end. Memories of the unpleasant scene in Lillian Marco's living room, of the shouting and crying, of the disappointment and pain, came back to him as he closed his eyes. And the vision of the child Stephen, watching it all from the doorway, haunted him.

He'd had no choice, he reminded himself. He had a commitment, and he couldn't ignore that. He had work to do. And Lillian Marco had become a liability he couldn't afford. His editor wasn't going to give him an extension on his deadline. Harvard wasn't going to extend his leave. He had until July to finish his translation. And he couldn't keep making excuses any longer.

Sleep, when it finally came, was restless and troubled. In his dreams, he found himself trapped in a small room, surrounded by a blue-white light. A parade of former students passed through the room: his Nobel Prize-winning chess partner; the student who, last semester, had told him what she thought of his book without mincing words; Mother Mary Frances, who'd called and asked him to give the retreat at St. Bede's this weekend as a last-minute substitute.

And a hundred nameless students, many of whom he remembered only vaguely. Men and women who had moved through his lectures and his life over the years. Most of them had made no impression on O'Keefe. His linguistic work was what mattered, not the hordes of semiconscious drones who inhabited his classes.

But tonight, while he slept, it was the drones who wouldn't leave him alone. And Lillian and Stephen Marco.

There was no sign, as George climbed the three flights of stairs to his apartment, that he had company waiting for him. But then, there hadn't been any sign the last time, either. Three months ago, when Teresa had found his stash and tossed it, he'd been in the unenviable position of having to explain to his suppliers where the dope had gone. He'd done it then by claiming that someone in the building had warned him of a raid and he'd flushed the coke to keep from being caught. They hadn't exactly bought his story, but they'd agreed to give him another chance.

That second chance was what Teresa had endangered last night when she stopped by his place unexpectedly and found the coke in his bedroom. She'd taken off with it this time. Maybe because there was so much of it now, what with the new pushers he was supposed to be supplying, that she didn't dare just flush it. Or maybe she was just trying to make a point, scare him into stopping.

Problem was, he couldn't stop. Not just like that. Not with these guys, anyhow.

Besides, most of the people who got the coke he distributed were just recreational users, like him. They weren't addicts or anything. They just liked to take a hit now and then, mostly at parties. So what was the harm in getting high from time to time?

George was fairly certain that Teresa would show up tomorrow at the Coop. He wasn't quite as certain that she'd bring the stuff with her. But he knew how far to push her now, and when to back off. That had been the trouble three months ago: he'd forced her too hard and she'd dumped the stuff. This time, he'd be more careful.

But he *would* get the coke tomorrow, one way or the other.

His apartment door was locked when he put his key in, and the lights were off when he stepped inside and turned to close the door behind him.

"Hello, George." The voice from the darkness startled him, and he jumped. A light in the center of the room came on, and George saw the faces that had haunted him for the last three months. Mr. Belluno was dressed impeccably, as always,

21

in a handmade silk suit. The kind George's father liked to wear. Next to him on the sofa was the man George knew only as Nicky, a stupid-looking, hulking man who liked the leather and chain look. George had no interest in knowing anything more about him.

"You're late again, George," Mr. Belluno said, standing up while George stood dumbly in the doorway. "We missed you last night." Mr. Belluno was, by most accounts, closely connected with the Family in these parts; that, too, was more than George really wanted to know.

"I can explain." His gaze darted to Nicky, who also stood. The man moved slowly, as if his weight were difficult to carry. "I just—had a little—car trouble," he tried. He laughed nervously and felt his hands sweating. Nicky was still moving toward him. "See, my radiator—"

"Your radiator's not your problem, George," Mr. Belluno interrupted calmly. "Your problem is that this is the second time you've been late making payments. Last time, you lost the stuff. Where is it this time, George? Did you flush it down the toilet again?" As he spoke, his voice quiet and methodical, Nicky moved until he was behind George, his back to the door.

"I—I'll have it distributed tomorrow," George promised. But the moment he felt Nicky's arms grabbing his and holding him, he knew that tomorrow wasn't going to be soon enough.

"We did warn you, George," Mr. Belluno reminded him. He sounded so reasonable, so rational. George's mouth went dry. His armpits were soaked.

"Mr. Belluno," he started, but the man cut him off.

"Time for a lesson, George. And you'd better be sure that you *do* have the money to us by tomorrow night. You got that?"

George nodded; he had a nauseating feeling that he wasn't going to prefer this lesson to being killed outright.

Long before Nicky was finished, he was quite certain of it.

CHAPTER
THREE

Saturday, April 1, 1995   8:33 A.M.
Cambridge, Massachusetts

Teresa stared at the phone on the coffee table. It was ringing. It had been ringing off-and-on since 8:00 this morning. But she was afraid to pick it up, afraid that it would be George. Afraid he'd be calling to make sure she was still planning to meet him.

She sipped her coffee; it sank into her stomach and swam through her intestines and left her feeling nauseated. She wasn't going to meet George. She knew that now.

That's why she didn't pick up the phone.

She had called her brother last night for advice, but before she could get up the courage to tell him what was really going on, he offered his standard response to a call for help: "Look, Terry, we aren't going to keep coming to your rescue every time you get yourself into a bind. You've got to stop hanging out with those scummy friends of yours and start taking responsibility for your own life."

Well, hadn't she tried to do that? But things had gotten so confusing recently, especially with George. The world had become too demanding. And now everything was falling apart.

To hear him talk about it, you'd think Kevin had never had anything like that happen to *him!* No, Kevin was Mr. Perfect, and he knew it. He was a big-shot California lawyer, he had a wife and two children, and he had a house that was practically paid for, thanks to Mom's life insurance.

Teresa stared at the bag of cocaine she'd found in George's apartment two nights ago. It was the largest amount of the stuff she'd ever seen, certainly more than George had ever had before. And that was the problem. George kept promising that he'd stop selling the stuff. But each time she found another bag in his apartment, there was more than there had been the time before.

He wasn't going to stop. In the cold light of morning, away from the dark, hypnotizing eyes and the smile that melted her into a babbling idiot, Teresa realized that.

The phone kept ringing.

She couldn't answer it. She didn't want to hear George's voice, his pleas, his cajoling, his promises. They were all empty, all worthless.

If only she could bring herself to believe that George was, too, she wouldn't have any problem with what she knew she had to do.

Teresa screwed her eyes shut and tried not to cry. She was, after all, almost nineteen. She was an adult now. That's what everyone, even Kevin, kept telling her.

"If you want to go to college and live on your own, that's fine. But you live on your own. You may have gotten all the brains in this family, but that doesn't mean you got the smarts. You live like an adult, because that's what you're telling everyone you are. Don't come crying to me if you get yourself in trouble!"

But she *had* gotten in trouble. Big trouble. And now she had nothing to turn to. Nothing and no one. Kevin had made it clear that he wasn't going to help solve her problem. Not if she insisted on living in the East, going to school there.

And Susan. . . . Well, Susan was busy curing everyone's psychological troubles in Hawaii. She didn't even have time to answer her phone anymore.

So Teresa had nothing left.

Nothing except the dim, almost dreamlike memory that had erupted in her mind last night. The memory that once upon a time, in a galaxy far, far away, someone in the universe *had* cared. Someone who sent angels when angels were needed. Angels who wore teal-colored fedoras and sang, however badly, when you couldn't get to sleep at night. Angels who ran into the face of danger to save your brother—even if they couldn't cook a pot roast.

Kevin didn't understand anymore. It'd been so long, and even he had stopped believing. Angels? God? They were just stories or lucky coincidences.

"But what about the night Mommy saved your life?" she'd

ask. And he'd laugh, always so sure of himself, and say, "Mom had a moment of heroism, that's all. It happens all the time, munchkin. It doesn't mean she turned into an angel."

Teresa curled up on the couch and pulled her roommate's worn, green plaid afghan over her. She stared at the white powder on the coffee table.

The phone finally stopped ringing.

No, Kevin wouldn't understand. Not now. Kevin had the world by the tail; he knew everything, and everything made sense to him. She'd gotten herself into this mess. Trying to explain it to Kevin just wouldn't work. And running away from it wouldn't make it any better, either.

She was just going to have to deal with it on her own. She was going to have to figure out how to get herself out of this. Kevin wanted her to be responsible; Susan, whenever she *could* get her on the phone, said the same thing.

So, fine, she'd be responsible. She'd make it work. And she wouldn't need any angels to help her out.

She got up, straightened the afghan, and went to her bedroom to get dressed. Whatever else she did, one thing was sure: she couldn't stay here alone tonight. That flapper last night might not have been anything more than a crazy woman after all—Teresa hadn't been able to get rid of her until she got back to her apartment—but she did have a point: the kind of men George was dealing with weren't going to leave her alone if they found out she had his coke. And she couldn't exactly count on him not to tell them, especially if he was late in his deliveries.

So she had to go somewhere else. Somewhere safe, just until she could get up the nerve to go to the police.

She pulled her backpack out of the closet and realized she hadn't unpacked it from the last trip she'd taken. That had been to the North Shore, a trip with George. One of their first. She sat on the floor for a moment, remembering how good it had been back then. George had been funny and lighthearted. He had climbed rocks, and they'd rented a boat and taken a picnic lunch along. And when it got dark, they went back to their room at the romantic little bed-and-breakfast, and. . . .

She shook away the memories and gingerly opened the nylon pack, wondering if anything in there had mildewed.

She was pleasantly surprised. The few clothes were clean,

the toiletries were still sealed, and her favorite doll—her good luck charm—was still there. The head had popped off again, but Teresa just pushed it back on and put the doll on her bed.

There were some books in the pack, books she'd taken along to read for her classes. A philosophy text, a book of medieval literature. And a large, brown hardcover book she'd almost forgotten about.

Father Samuel Francis O'Keefe's famous tome, *The Secret Language*. A philosophy, a theory, a thesis, a textbook. It was all that—and none of it. She had read his book in two days, so impressed with the man's reputation that she'd devoured his words as if they belonged to God Himself.

"Linguistic studies provide us with a mirror to our own culture, our own formation. They provide us with a verbal justification for who and what we are."

Crap, crap, and more crap! She remembered getting back from that trip, walking into his class, and waiting through the tiresome lecture. Then, after class, she'd told him just what she thought of the book. Partly, she realized now, she'd been frustrated by a lot of other things as well. But she'd had to spend forty dollars for it, and at the time, it had seemed a monumental waste of money. And time.

But Father O'Keefe—it was odd. Last semester, he'd been a real sourdough in class, always putting her down, always criticizing her. Criticizing everyone. But one-on-one, the man was very different.

"If you're finding your school load too stressful," he'd told her, more than an hour later, when she'd finally stopped talking, *"why not take a break? Get a job for a semester. Take a breather. You're only nineteen, Miss Bruckner, and you're taking graduate-level courses. I had a student many years ago who was like you. Pushed himself too hard, in my opinion."*

"What happened to him?" Teresa asked. They walked together across campus. O'Keefe smiled.

"Well, he's still pushing. We'll have to see what happens in the end. But," he added, stopping for a moment and turning to her, *"you should keep something in mind. There are enough pressures in life as it is. You don't need to add to them."*

Teresa smiled and glanced through the book. She'd seen Father O'Keefe around the campus only a few times this semester. He was working on some sort of translation, and he'd taken the semester off from teaching. Last week he'd been in the library, working on his latest scholarly venture, when she'd caught his attention.

Still feeling the pressure of school and confusion over her relationship with George, she'd spilled her guts to him before she knew what she was doing.

"I'm sorry, Father, it's not your problem. I shouldn't have bothered you. . . ."

"I'm just sorry I can't offer any help." He closed his books and said, "I'm leaving Harvard for the rest of the semester. An old friend invited me to her monastery to finish the work." He'd smiled then, a rare smile. "Actually, it's a bribe, in exchange for giving a retreat there."

Teresa stared at the book in her lap and at the doll next to her. He had told her the name of the monastery. St. Bede's. Up on the North Shore, not far from Gloucester.

Impulse, more than rational thought, made her pick up the phone and call Information. Maybe there *was* a place she could go this weekend. Maybe she could even ask Father O'Keefe's advice. . . . Not that she'd interfere with his work, of course.

But it was a perfect place to go, to think, to figure out what to do. George would never think of looking for her there. No one he told would ever find her, either.

But what if there wasn't any room? Father O'Keefe had said they ran a retreat center, but he was giving a retreat this weekend. Maybe there weren't many rooms; maybe they were all filled up.

She got the number for St. Bede's in Windy Bluffs, dialed, and whispered a prayer she didn't really know was a prayer: "Please, let there be a place for me this weekend. Please!"

Saturday, April 1, 1995   11:45 A.M.
The New Jersey Turnpike

Stephen Charles Marco was asleep. His small head lolled to the right, straining against his seat belt, and his mouth was open. He'd fallen asleep with his glasses on, and when traffic on the turnpike slowed to a crawl, his mother leaned over and removed them.

Stephen took after his late father. Unlike his slender,

27

redheaded mother, he was built like an Italian linebacker, a hefty, compact, dark-skinned six-year-old. His brains, though—brains that kept every school psychologist and teacher in Charlotte hopping—he got from his mother.

Lillian Marco kept her eye on the traffic, fully aware that most accidents happen in this stop-and-go crawl when people let their attention wander.

It didn't surprise Lillian that Stephen had fallen asleep in the middle of the day. Since his father died, he'd stopped sleeping well at night. Bouts of sleepwalking, interspersed with nightmares about the accident that had killed his father, left Stephen restless and tired during the day. His sleeplessness kept Lillian up most nights, and she knew the strain had affected her work.

But Father Samuel had made a promise to her, and after he broke it last night, she wasn't about to sit still and let him have the last word.

And she was fairly sure the sisters at St. Bede's, if they found out, wouldn't be very happy about it, either.

But it wasn't just for herself that she was driving from North Carolina to Massachusetts. It was for Stephen as much as anything.

Lillian had known Father Samuel for years. He'd never gone back on a promise to her. Until last night. Last night, when he told her he didn't need her anymore, he had broken his promise. He said she should find someone else to take Jack's place and move on with her life.

But Lillian Marco wasn't ready to move on. Not without a fight.

Traffic sped up, and Stephen Charles snored. Lillian smiled fondly at the sound. He snored the way Jack used to, a deep rumble that came from the chest.

Yes, she told herself, she was doing this for Stephen Charles. Father Samuel had made a promise to her, and by God, she was going to make sure he kept it!

Saturday, April 1, 1995   12:49 P.M.
Boston, Massachusetts

"Welcome to Logan International Airport in the city of Boston. Whether you're here for business or pleasure, we hope

28

you enjoy your trip. Please remain in your seats until the plane comes to a complete stop. And once again, thank you for flying with us.''

The insipid voice of the chief steward on O'Keefe's long-delayed flight finally stopped yammering, and O'Keefe watched as the other passengers, blatantly ignoring the man's request, began unfastening their belts and removing their luggage from the overhead compartments, even as the plane taxied to a stop. He sighed, glanced at his watch, and stood, stretching his legs.

The flight was two hours overdue, and he was beginning to wish he'd had some breakfast before leaving North Carolina. In fact, he was feeling somewhat light-headed, almost dizzy.

He collected his luggage, slung his coat over his arm, and started down the aisle as the plane finally stopped. The swarm of men and women suddenly made him feel dizzier, and he paused to let the majority of passengers leave ahead of him.

The scene with Lillian Marco had left him more disturbed than he'd expected. He'd barely slept at all last night, and he woke feeling unsettled and irritable. He'd gotten to the airport an hour ahead of schedule, only to find his flight delayed. The delay lengthened, and he called St. Bede's to tell them. He'd only gotten an answering machine, however, and he'd left a message that was probably futile.

The delay, explained as "technical problems," dragged on longer than O'Keefe would normally have tolerated. Had he had a choice, he'd have canceled his flight and booked another. But the grant for his translation allotted only a limited amount of travel funds, and O'Keefe was stuck with the ticket he'd bought.

Now, on top of the delay and hunger, a crowd of irritated and disgruntled passengers was pushing anxiously down the too-narrow aisle, all of them feeling trapped and wanting to get off.

By the time O'Keefe risked putting himself in the midst of the crowd again, he knew that what he was feeling was more than simple hunger. He was feeling as if he were floating, removed from his body.

He barely made it off the plane before consciousness left him completely.

CHAPTER

FOUR

December 24, 1998
Stallion's Gate, New Mexico

"I'm not the enemy, Al."

Senator Joe Weitzman's last words, just before Admiral Al Calavicci prepared to hang up on him. It was the only insulting gesture Al still had open at this point. Punching Weitzman was out of the question: the bureaucratic nozzle was two thousand miles away!

"No, you're not the enemy," Al said, thinking of a better answer than a slamming phone. "Project Quantum Leap doesn't have enemies. Just too many people like you who don't give a damn!"

"Al. . . ."

"Save it! You got your message across. Now, if you don't mind, it looks like Sam's about to Leap in somewhere, so I gotta go."

"Al, the auditors will be there and back in two days. If everything's in order, I don't see what you're so bothered about."

"What I'm bothered about, *Senator*," Al said, chewing the man's title into a curse, "is that I've got less than a third of my staff still here, thanks to the fact that Christmas cheer seems to be catching. And the finance division wasn't prepared for an audit, so I've only got one guy in there playin' book-keeper! You wanna conduct an audit? Why the hell didn't you go through channels, huh? Or is this just another one of the committee's ways of lettin' us know we're not gettin' the up-grades you promised us for Ziggy?"

"Al." The man at the other end sighed. Loudly, melodra-matically. Al grabbed a cigar from the humidor on his desk and began unwrapping it. "Look, there were problems with the last audit. I explained it to you. And right now, you can't afford any problems. It's a new Senate, and they're cleaning house."

"And they're startin' out here? Why couldn't they wait a week for everyone to get back from vacation?"

"December twenty-fifth is not a holiday for everyone on the planet, Al. As I recall, you yourself always boasted that it was no big deal. Just a day like any other day. Right?"

Al grimaced and bit through the end of the cigar.

"Besides, we're under some pressure here as well." Weitzman paused. Al waited. "One of the committee members— Smallwood—is under the gun himself right now, Al. There are investigations, allegations—it's a political nightmare."

"The nightmare before Christmas, is that it?"

"I'm sending three independent auditors," Weitzman said calmly, ignoring Al's humor. "It's their first time in the field, so don't make it hard for them."

"Wouldn't think of it," Al muttered. The fire was going out of him. Weitzman had doused it very effectively in the last minute. "Unless you're sendin' a blonde, a brunette, and a redhead," he added, a pleasing fantasy suddenly coming to mind to halt the onslaught of depression.

"As long as you cooperate, they'll be out of your hair in no time. I'll have their clearances faxed to your security officer. The auditors ought to be there later tonight."

Al grunted and lit his cigar. Then he said, "You didn't answer my question."

"Which one?"

"We're not gettin' the upgrades, are we?"

The senator cleared his throat, and Al heard papers rustling. "Well, actually, there is a freeze in effect for some of—"

"Save it." His anger freshly stoked, Al Calavicci slammed the phone down. "Damn!" He stared at the phone for another moment, then sank back in his chair and lit the cigar.

Getting funding for Quantum Leap had always been a game, Al thought. But since the players—many of them—kept changing, so did the rules. Even the game itself. Sometimes it was poker; sometimes it was more like a crapshoot.

And sometimes, especially with Weitzman, it was nothing more than an elaborate Ping-Pong match. With Weitzman, the point was to get the ball back to him before he was ready to hit it again.

Al chuckled quietly to himself, suddenly realizing that Weitzman had given him all the ammo he needed to do just that.

"... their first time in the field ... don't make it hard for them."

"You wanna send gyrene auditors out here over Christmas?" he muttered to himself. "Fine. Send 'em out!"

Grinning around his stogie, Al Calavicci rose and straightened his jacket with a renewed eagerness, left his office, and rode the elevator to the main floor.

He was still grinning when he got off the elevator.

The Control Center was quiet. Much quieter than normal. The ornamented and tinseled three-foot-high plastic tree in the far corner of the room, near Verbeena Beeks's office, explained the quietness: everyone, including the psychiatrist, was gone, celebrating the holiday or just celebrating a chance to get away for a while.

Everyone, of course, except Al. And Gooshie, who was sprawled on the floor, his head half hidden under the multicolored console of a computer named Ziggy. Al had tried to get Gooshie to take a day or two off, had even promised to call him if Sam Leaped. But the head programmer was adamant: "I don't want to take the chance, Admiral. When Dr. Beckett Leaps, I should be here."

It wasn't so much that Al agreed with him. But he was afraid that if he pushed the issue, Gooshie would tell him the truth: that he had nowhere to go and no one to do anything with at Christmas. Being at work kept the loneliness at bay for both of them.

"It's just like any other day, isn't it, Admiral?" Gooshie had asked, not quite innocently. And Al had dropped the subject.

"Trouble?" Al asked as he moved next to the programmer and bent over to see what Gooshie was working on. He held his cigar away from the man's face, but the smoke drifted downward, blown by air from the vents above them.

"No, not really." Gooshie looked up. He was a typical redhead, with pale skin that flushed easily. "Uh, if you wouldn't,

32

uh, mind, Admiral?'' he asked, gesturing at the cigar. ''The smoke's not good for Ziggy's components.''

Al narrowed one eye, not believing the statement. It seemed to him that if Ziggy could stand Gooshie's breath, she could stand a little cigar smoke. But he backed away nonetheless. Why chance it?

After their last audit, a number of regulations Al had let slip had been tightened, including the ban on smoking in the Control Center. Al thought the rule was overly restrictive, but what the hell? With three auditors on their way out here for Christmas Eve, he didn't want anyone squawking about his cigar.

''So what're you doin'?''

''New routine,'' Gooshie grunted, his hands once more fiddling with the external ports at Ziggy's base. ''Every time Dr. Beckett psychosynergizes with someone, his brain waves change a little.'' He pulled a glowing pink tube from the console and handed it to the admiral. Al took it, puzzled. ''We have to keep recalibrating—would you hand me that extender on the console?—calibrating her for Sam's *new* brain waves. No, the green one,'' he corrected, as Al handed him a blue tube.

Al put the blue extender back on Ziggy's console and picked up the only green object on it: it was nearly three inches longer and three-quarters of an inch bigger in diameter. ''This one?'' he asked, handing it down.

''It'll help her keep in touch with Dr. Beckett if he psychosynergizes again. I hope.''

Gooshie took the tube, and it disappeared inside the console. The programmer stood up, brushed down his lab coat, and began studying the displays in front of him.

''Wait a minute,'' Al objected, waving his cigar toward Gooshie. ''You took out *this*,'' he said, holding the small, pink tube, ''and replaced it with *that*?''

Gooshie smiled, and Ziggy made a small noise. ''She's a female computer,'' Gooshie explained. ''Size really doesn't matter to her.''

Al was about to object to the logic of that—once he realized his mouth was hanging open—but Ziggy's self-satisfied voice spoke before he did.

''Admiral, Dr. Beckett is Leaping.''

"Let's hope for an easy one this time, huh?" Al said, and turned toward the Waiting Room behind him.

Gooshie's hands were already dancing over the console, his attention instantly and completely devoted to extracting information about the newest Leap, Guest, and cause. Saving the world never seemed to faze Gooshie.

The door to Verbeena Beeks's office opened, and Al stopped in midstride, the hand holding his cigar dropping quickly to his side and half behind him. The tall, black psychiatrist came out of her office, looked at Al, and smiled serenely.

"You thought I'd gone already, didn't you?"

"Uh, well, I sorta thought. . . ." Clearing his throat and determined not to be caught like a schoolboy with his hand in the—well, it had *never* been a cookie jar for Al!—he lifted the forbidden cigar and tilted his chin back a fraction of an inch. "What're you hangin' around for?"

Verbeena Beeks wore a cobalt blue pantsuit that had an especially flattering jacket with darts sewn into the bodice. In that outfit, with the red scarf tied around her head, and the red high heels, Al thought, she was quite a knockout.

She looked over the admiral, glanced at Gooshie, and extended her hand toward Al as she spoke.

"Heard Sam was about to Leap," she explained. "I told Donna and Tina to go on ahead so we wouldn't lose our reservations." She turned her gaze back to Al and let it rest on the cigar. "Thought I'd stick around long enough to make sure you didn't need a hand on this one."

"Nice o' you." Al kept the cigar defiantly between his lips a moment longer, ignoring the outstretched hand. She kept her eyes fixed on him.

"Aw, hell." He stepped forward and took the ashtray from Verbeena's hand, stubbed out the cigar, and sighed. "Okay. Happy?"

The woman smiled. "Just because everyone's gone, Al, that doesn't make Ziggy any less susceptible to damage from the smoke."

"Doesn't make you any less susceptible to a mistake on your next paycheck, either," Al snapped back. Then he wiped a hand across his face and muttered to himself.

"What did you say?"

34

"I said," he repeated, looking as forlorn as he knew how to, "I don't need to get it from both ends at once!"

For a second, Verbeena smiled. Then, seeing his face, she sobered. "What do you mean?"

"I mean Weitzman," he explained, waving his hand in an arc. "And three auditors who're gonna be here tonight to find some reason to keep us from gettin' the upgrades the committee promised us."

"Joe called?" Verbeena glanced at the ashtray in her hand and the cigar that was trying to smolder despite defeat. "You want me to—"

"Naw, don't worry," Al relented. "I just—" He stared at the stogie. "It's nuthin'," he told her. She didn't looked convinced. "Hey! If I thought it was, I'd have the whole damn staff back from Tinseltown so fast I'd make Scrooge look like Man of the Year." He flailed both hands, miming a gathering of the tribes for emphasis.

"Sometimes you *do*." Verbeena crossed the room and put the ashtray on the console. "Well, I hope you at least remembered to wish him Happy Hanukkah," she said.

Al scowled, pushed his hands into his pockets, and looked away. "Whaddya got, Ziggy?"

On the wall a dozen feet from where he stood, the luminescent plate that served as Ziggy's mouthpiece swirled with a hundred shades of sunset colors.

"Not much yet, Admiral." Superior female tones filled the Center. "Any information *you* might be able to obtain would be helpful."

Al narrowed one eye and ground his teeth. Fourteen billion dollars, and this damn computer still needed *him* to tell her who Sam had Leaped into!

"Pay *me* fourteen billion dollars and I could retire," he grumbled, turning back to the Waiting Room.

"Admiral?"

"Ignore him, Gooshie," Verbeena advised. "The grinch who stole Christmas Leaps into Al about this time every year. You know that."

Al stalked up the ramp, and Verbeena followed. The two-way mirror into the Waiting Room gave them both a first look at their latest Guest. But what each saw was quite different.

Verbeena saw Sam Beckett, physicist, astronomer, linguist,

35

musician, friend, and colleague lost in time. She saw the brown-haired, forty-five-year-old man who had left them one night three years ago. She saw the lock of silver hair, the strong jaw, the long nose, the muscular body of a man who, despite his intellectual gifts, had never neglected the physical.

What Al saw was harder to explain. If he had to put it into words, he'd say, "Yeah, that's Sam." But he saw more. This time, for instance, he saw a beard. It was graying, but still mostly black. He saw hair that, beneath the aura of Sam's presence, was dark as well, probably also black.

"Double vision," Al called it. It was disconcertingly like being drunk; one eye saw one image, the other eye saw something else, and they couldn't quite agree on what they saw.

"Male," Al said quietly. "Late fifties."

"Anything else?" Verbeena asked, her eyes fixed on the man who lay unconscious before them.

Al crossed his arms. "He's got a beard," he said shortly.

When the door slid open to admit them, their latest charge was just opening his eyes. They were dark eyes, Al saw, matching the expression on his face.

"Hi, there," Verbeena said. She moved slowly into the room, her steps carefully timed to indicate confidence without implying a threat. Al, as usual, waited just inside the door. Verbeena was the shrink: she was best at handling this "first contact" stuff, and Al was secretly grateful that she'd delayed her vacation a few hours to wait for this.

The man on the table looked around him, then quickly sat up and stared at the psychiatrist. His eyes took her in without much interest. Then they turned to him.

"I—I was on my way to Windy Bluffs," the man said quietly. His voice, as Al heard it, was sonorous and filled with authority. Al pulled himself up and tilted his head back. "This isn't—the monastery," the man continued. "And you're *not* a nun," he added, glancing again at Verbeena. "At least, not from St. Bede's."

"St. Bede's?" Verbeena asked. The man swung his legs over the table, stood, and eyed the white Fermi-Suit he wore.

"Odd," he muttered. "Did we crash? Is this a hospital?" He lifted his hands to his head, as if feeling for some trauma he hadn't yet noticed.

"Crash?" Al asked.

36

Verbeena ignored him. "Well, not exactly," she said, answering their Guest's last question and giving him her most professional smile. "My name is Verbeena. What's yours?"

Al listened and waited. Already, of course, Ziggy had more information than she'd had seconds ago. She already knew she had a middle-aged man. Now she knew he was on his way to Windy Bluffs, and while there might be hundreds of "Windy Bluffs," there couldn't be too many of them with a monastery called St. Bede's. And if Ziggy was as smart as she claimed to be, Al thought, she knew something else: wherever and whenever Sam was, it was later than the 1960s. It wasn't 'til after then that nuns began to dress in anything besides their habits. Before that, there would have been no question as to whether Verbeena was a nun.

St. Bede's, Al concluded, must be some throwback to the "good old days" of Latin Masses and dark confessionals.

"Bless me, Father, for I have sinned. It's been two days since my last confession."

"Two days?"

"Yes, Father. But Sister said that if I wanted God to hear me, I had to be free of sin. And—I really want God's attention right now."

"What have you done?"

"I dunno. But—well, maybe I did somethin' wrong and I don't know it, huh? Maybe that's why Poppa isn't gettin' any better? I mean, I'm goin' to Mass every day, and I'm prayin' as hard as I can, but he isn't gettin' better. So—I figure I must've done somethin' wrong and that's why God's not listenin' to me."

Al wiped a hand across his face.

"Who's he?" their Guest asked, turning piercing green eyes on Al. The admiral took a deep breath, feeling unaccountably attacked by the gaze and the question.

"The name's Al." He stepped forward and narrowed his own gaze. "And you are—?" He let the question dangle, with the implication that the man had somehow trespassed on a private party.

For seconds, the man met his eyes. Then he looked back at Verbeena. "Where am I?"

"Can you tell us your name?" she asked again.

The man looked away, looked around himself, stared at the

door, and then looked back at Al. "Samuel," he said slowly. Verbeena shot Al a look of surprise.

"Samuel—" he repeated. The way he ended the word, the look in his eyes just before he ducked his head, told Al enough. That was all of himself he remembered so far. The man's memory was Swiss-cheesed.

"Samuel," Verbeena said softly. "Don't be concerned. It'll come back to you."

"I'm—I'm on my way to Windy Bluffs," the man repeated quietly, latching on to what he *did* remember. But the haughtiness was gone from his voice. Al breathed a little easier.

"Windy Bluffs?" he asked. "That up in New England somewhere?"

"Massachusetts," the man snapped, looking up and regaining a measure of assurance. Al smiled thinly. "And you haven't told me where I am."

"You're safe," Al started. "Nuthin's gonna happen to you while you're here. But—there isn't a whole lot more we *can* tell you."

"Where am I?" the man asked again. His voice was practiced in patience. But that patience was about to end. "I'm supposed to give a retreat this weekend. And I have a translation to complete by the end of the summer. Now, whoever you are—*Al*—I suggest you tell me how I got here and where I am and what you intend to do to me."

"Samuel," Verbeena started. But before she got anything more out, the man whirled on her, his eyes dark and astonished with a new memory.

"Father Samuel," he said. "I'm—I'm a priest."

"A priest?" Verbeena shot a quick look at Al, then turned back to their Guest.

"Yes."

"A—Catholic priest?"

The man considered the question. Then he nodded. "Yes. I'm—"

He drew a deep breath, and as he did, his entire demeanor changed. He pulled his memories back, Al saw. He pulled himself through time, retrieving his own identity.

In that instant, Al knew he was in for trouble.

"I am Father Samuel Francis O'Keefe," the man announced, drawing himself up and glaring at Verbeena and Al in turn as if he were giving a lecture to a class of juvenile delinquents. "In case you haven't heard of me, I am one of the world's foremost linguists. I am returning to my teaching post this fall at Harvard. And I am expected at St. Bede's in two hours."

In the background, Al heard a muted squeal of delight from Ziggy as she located the beloved physicist who had traded places with this egotist.

"Now," their Guest continued, stepping toward Al, "I suggest you let me go at once. Or I assure you, you will be *very* sorry."

To those who are beginners in this way of life,
an easy entrance should not be granted.

—THE RULE OF ST. BENEDICT:
CHAPTER 58

CHAPTER
FIVE

Saturday, April 1, 1995   12:58 P.M.
Boston, Massachusetts

Airports, Sam Beckett decided, were decidedly *not* his favorite places to Leap into. Voices called out through crowds of talking heads. People moved in waves, and anyone not moving with them was drowned in the surge. Lights flared all around him: from glowing signs, from windows, reflected off planes outside, from flashing cameras, from expensive watches and fluorescent lights. It was a sensory overload to Sam, who wasn't yet sure what senses he had, much less which ones to trust.

Sighing, Sam closed his eyes for a moment, tried to gain his bearings, and decided to take stock of his situation.

In one hand he clutched a heavy black satchel and smaller overnight case; from the other, dangled a garment bag. Pushed upstream by the tug and press of the people around him, he moved along with the men, women, and children who, like him, were leaving the plane and scurrying toward friends, relatives, and business associates. He watched their frenetic activities, trying to isolate clues to his where- and whenabouts, hoping for someone to call out to him, recognize him, begin him on his new assignment.

What he gathered first—aside from the luggage in his hands—left him cautiously pleased. He knew this place! He'd been here before.

Logan International Airport. He'd flown in and out of this place at least half a dozen times during his years at MIT. The gentle "ah" that replaced the "r" sound in the New England babble around him reminded him of long, happy hours spent in the company of New England scholars and students and seekers.

The terminal was filled with sights and sounds and smells from all over the world. But what caught his immediate attention came from across the corridor by the arrival gate. His stomach growled: either he or his host was very hungry, and at the moment it didn't matter which. What mattered most right then, even more than finding out who he was, or when, or why, was answering an old, familiar yearning.

He wanted a hot dog. A cheap hot dog sold at an exorbitant price. A hot dog with mustard and onions.

Grinning, almost childishly happy, he began picking his way through the crowd, homing in on the familiar smell from the café. He looked around, still listening for other clues that might be important, and watching for anyone trying to catch his eye.

Then his gaze lit on the date flashing on a status board, and he shivered.

April Fool's Day.

"Father O'Keefe? Father O'Keefe!"

The clear, high-pitched voice at his shoulder startled him, and Sam turned too quickly. His garment bag flew outward and met resistance. The resistance grunted.

"Oh, uh, excuse me, I'm—I'm sorry. . . ."

Sam put his bags down and grasped the woman to steady her. As he did, three things registered almost simultaneously: he'd hit a nun; the nun was the source of the high-pitched call; and she'd been calling *him*.

"Oh, boy," he groaned.

She was young and identifiable by her black, floor-length habit. But she laughed easily as she pulled herself back from Sam's awkward grasp, smoothing her habit as she did.

"I'm so sorry," Sam began again, embarrassment heating his cheeks. It was bad enough to Leap in and not know what he was doing there; worse, in the first five minutes he'd inadvertently assaulted a nun! He had a bad feeling about *this* Leap already.

"Oh, don't worry, I get knocked around all the time." The young woman's blue eyes flashed a warm blue glow. "I'm Sister Mary Catherine. You're Father O'Keefe, right?"

"Uh, well, I—"

"I picked you out by your suitcases and the collar," the woman continued, oblivious to Sam's hesitation. "You look a lot younger than I expected!"

Sister Mary Catherine pulled a set of car keys from her habit as Sam glanced at the tags attached to his bags. Sure enough, they bore a clerical insignia and the name "S. F. O'Keefe, S. J." He wrinkled his forehead, tried to remember what "S. J." stood for, and realized that his companion was moving through the crowd ahead of him. He glanced longingly toward the scent of the hot dogs, then followed reluctantly, catching up with her in midsentence.

". . . since Mother Mary Frances is the only one who's ever seen you, and of course, now she's legally blind. But then, I thought to myself, even in a crowd, I'd be able to pick out Father O'Keefe, because, you know, I've read every one of your books, and—wasn't it in *The Secret Language* that you mentioned something about 'learning to know a people, or a person, through the writings they leave behind'?"

"I, uh, I did?" Sam cleared his throat, fell into step next to her, and said, more certainly, "I mean, I—I did."

"Anyway, so when Mother Mary Frances asked me if I'd come out to get you, since Sister Mary Clare has the flu—you know, it's going around the monastery; I hope you're not susceptible—I figured it'd be a great chance to meet you before the oblates all show up tonight, you know, just to talk about some of your works. I've always thought your theory on the development of linguistics and theology as dual indicators of a culture's sophistication was, well, I guess I'd have to say I didn't entirely agree. I hope that doesn't insult you."

For a split second, the small-child voice attached to the grown woman ceased. But only for a second. The nun stopped dead in her tracks, whirled, and squinted at Sam.

"You don't mind honest debate, do you, Father?" she asked. And in her smile was the answer she demanded: simple, undeniable acquiescence.

"Uh, no, of course not."

The young woman brandished her car keys like a sword in front of Sam.

"Oh, good, because, you know, there's Sister Mary Assumpta, she's from Peru, and she *really* didn't agree with your thesis in *The Secret Language*, either. Of course, she wants you to sign her book, though." The young nun began moving forward again, almost dancing as she walked. Sam watched, followed, and felt a peculiar sense of déjà vu.

Through the crowded terminal to the parking lot, and from there through a vast sea of cars, Sam followed his Host's hostess to a teal-colored Grand Prix. He stopped beside the car as she unlocked it, his expression one of honest surprise. The young woman met his gaze, then laughed.

"Oh, someone donated it," she explained. "Isn't it great? You know, we're *so* grateful for what God provides. Here, let me have that. No, really, I've got it."

The girl—Sam had a hard time thinking of her as fully grown—grabbed his bags from him and tossed them into the back seat of the car with the ease of a professional weight lifter.

"I'm sorry, I probably should have walked slower, I guess, but you seemed to be keeping up. Anyway, I just have to tell you, we're all *so* excited that you're giving the lectures this weekend. I mean, it's all so last-minute for you and everything."

"Uh-huh?"

Sam climbed into the passenger's seat, automatically taking in details as he did. Detail number one was the registration sticker on the car's rear license plate, which would expire in November 1995. Detail number two was the parking stub Sister Mary Who-Never-Stopped-Talking pulled out of her well-hidden pocket and thrust into his hand—"Here, would you hold this, Father?"—confirming that he had Leaped in on April 1, 1995, sometime after 10 A.M. And detail number three was that he was apparently scheduled to give these sisters some lectures, apparently on either linguistics or theology, about which (if he had ever studied them) he remembered nothing.

"Actually, your theory on the relevance of language in defining a culture's theological perspective isn't a new one, is it?" the young woman asked as she fastened herself into the seat. She started the engine with a gusto usually reserved for race car drivers.

Or jet pilots.

"I suppose you could argue that the whole idea of keeping the Mass in Latin had something to do with that, didn't it?" She half-glanced at him as she pulled through the lot, then turned and sped quickly up to the booth at the exit.

Sister Mary Catherine pulled the parking stub from Sam's

45

hand and gave it to the attendant, retrieved five dollars from her secret pouch, and paid the man. Then she slipped the Grand Prix into gear and sped out of the parking lot and onto the highway.

"Uh, Sister," Sam began as she swerved from lane to lane and accelerated to 70 miles per hour, "do you, um—well, do you get a chance to—drive much?" He tried hard to relax his grip on the handle above the door.

Sister Mary Catherine had a classic, lilting laugh. "Oh, Sister Mary Clare and I are the extern sisters, so we get to drive quite a bit. This is a nifty car, don't you think? What kind of car do you have, Father?"

"Uh, well—"

"Actually, I prefer a Porsche, myself, but this is okay. It was donated, you know."

"Uh, yeah." The fingers of his right hand were turning white with tension. He pried them loose with an effort and clasped the door handle instead.

Sister Mary Catherine passed the car in front of her, swerved right, then left, and hit 40 miles per hour around cars that were crawling along at 35.

"Frankly, we were concerned about the weather this weekend, since a lot of the oblates will be driving out here for the retreat and so many of them just hate driving in the rain, don't you? Personally, I don't mind it too much, depending on the kind of car you have, naturally, but I mean, after all, it's another chance to get out and see things, and you know, Mother Mary Frances—I'll bet you can hardly wait to see her!—she said to me the other day that she wasn't sure what she'd do with me if I weren't an extern sister, because I love being able to get out once in a while. Not that we don't have a lot to do in the monastery, of course, and I love the solitude and silence most of the time, but. . . ."

Sam continued to listen, but the scenery around him was suddenly too familiar to ignore. Without his realizing it, his grip on the door handle relaxed.

He had been here. He had lived here. This had been his home away from home. First MIT. Then, later, various apartments around the Boston area as he worked on his master's in physics, his doctorates.

Professor LoNigro had inspired him. Professor Chatham had

bored him to tears. Dr. Nestor had expelled him for streaking through the Sumner Tunnel at rush hour—then relented and let him back in.

Sam grinned to himself.

"Are we, um, taking the Sumner Tunnel?" he asked, testing his fragmented memories of Boston and interrupting Sister Mary Catherine's uninterrupted monologue.

"Oh, if you want to, sure. Sometimes I take the Salt-and-Pepper Bridge, you know, just for variety."

"The Salt-and-Pepper. . . ." His voice trailed off. The Long-fellow Bridge, nicknamed "Salt-and-Pepper" because of the small turrets along each side, resembling old-fashioned salt and pepper shakers.

Like the silver ones Mom used to pull out and polish every Thanksgiving and Christmas.

Sam smiled with the warmth of coming home.

How many years had he lived here? Two? Three? A dozen? It wasn't really how *long* he'd been here, though; it was all that had happened to him when he *was* here.

His first time away from home, away from the farm, halfway across the country. All the newness, the excitement of being on his own for the first time.

And all the college courses. The first interesting classes he'd ever taken, even if they did seem slow by his standards.

He could have breezed through the classes at a normal pace, spent the nights partying, carousing with friends. But as he stared through the window at the new, high-tech buildings spreading along the river, he thought he remembered having finished his bachelor's degree in less than the normal time; and he couldn't remember any wild nights.

"Did you—did you go to school around here?" he asked.

"Harvard," Sister Mary Catherine said, a classic Bostonian accent rounding off the edge of her word. "Mom and Dad wanted me to go on for a master's, but I wanted to check out the life of a religious. And, obviously, I stayed. Mother Mary Frances is sending me back for some more courses next fall, though. What would you recommend, Father? I mean, you're coming back to teach at Harvard again, aren't you?"

"Back to. . . . Uh, yeah, I—guess so."

Harvard? A sudden flash of memory shot through Sam's mind and blended into snippets of Sister Mary Catherine's

47

monologue. He fidgeted in his pants pocket and brought out a wallet, glancing quickly from the driver's license to the side mirror, and back.

Graying hair, tinged with the remnants of black that had once been a thick mop of waves, topped a broad head that narrowed at the cheeks. Small green eyes and a thin mouth gave the man a severe look, and a meticulously trimmed beard added to his image of highly disciplined austerity. He wore a clerical collar, but beneath the dark beard it was almost lost.

Father O'Keefe was just as Sam remembered him.

"Father Samuel Francis O'Keefe," he muttered to himself, shaking his head and chuckling softly.

"Glad *you* know who you are," his driver commented, more concerned with the traffic than his odd behavior. She slowed the car to 65 miles per hour, wove around two other vehicles to pass them, and sped back up. "You feeling okay, Father? Is it jet lag? Boy, I remember when I flew out to California to visit my family the last time, it took me two days to get over the jet lag. You know, I kept thinking it was ten at night when it was only seven there, and then when I got back—"

"Uh, yeah, no, I'm—fine. Must be—jet lag." Sam stuffed the wallet back into his pocket, smiling crookedly.

Ten minutes with Father O'Keefe, Sam remembered, was usually enough to turn a cucumber into a pickle. But twenty-some years ago, the radical Jesuit was also one of the world's most renowned linguistics scholars. A man Sam had felt privileged to be taught by when he was working on his doctorate in. . . .

"Ancient languages."

"Sorry, Father, what'd you say?"

"I, um, I said ancient languages are—really my specialty. So I'm not sure what other courses you might—want to take."

"Well, theology, of course. And some comparative philosophy. They have some classes at Boston College that I was thinking about, but Sister Mary Louise thinks I should stay at Harvard, you know, since I did my undergraduate work there."

Father O'Keefe had, as Sam remembered, been quite controversial back in the seventies when he "reinvented the noble savage theory," as one critic put it, by bringing previously postulated theories of linguistics and cultural development together.

But Sam had seen Father O'Keefe's work as a stepping-stone for something more, and prepared his own thesis: what he called the "unified language theory." In Sister Mary Catherine's Grand Prix, he had sharp memory of the fervor with which Father O'Keefe had received the 258-page thesis.

"Garbage," he shouted at his young student, tossing the work onto the floor of his living room and storming out as if he had been personally insulted.

Sam didn't remember exactly how old he'd been at the time; but he *did* remember that it was the first time anyone had scoffed openly at his ideas. And he remembered the sting of it, the embarrassment of having to pick up the papers from the living room floor while the housekeeper hovered in the background and tried to ignore him.

As they passed into the tunnel, traffic slowed. Sister Mary Catherine sighed good-naturedly and turned to him, her bright, round eyes still filled with a childish glee. "Must be an accident." She shrugged. "Anyway, the retreat center is all filled up, but after this weekend, we promise we'll leave you alone so you can finish your work. It's a translation, isn't it? Arabic or something?"

"Uh, yeah. Something." Sam nodded hesitantly and cleared his throat. The memory of Father O'Keefe's brusque teaching methods was beginning to diminish his pleasure in being here. So was being stuck in the Sumner Tunnel with a young woman who could talk endlessly about nothing.

Streaking through traffic at *this* point didn't seem to be an option.

"Uh, you mentioned the oblates?" Under the circumstances, the best he could hope for was to see how much he could figure out about the *why* of this Leap. At least until Al showed up.

"Oh, they're all really excited about your lectures. And I forgot to mention, one of your students called. She's coming up for the weekend."

Sam nodded, trying to keep up with the changing topics.

"Well, it's a good thing she didn't try calling before this, because we were completely filled up with oblates. But she called this morning, and you know what? The Mayfields canceled last night because their oldest son got sick. So we had room after all!" Sister Mary Catherine scowled. "You know, I wasn't the one who talked to her, actually, it was Sister Mary Michael, she's our portress, but she said the girl sounded pretty upset. Almost desperate. Is she in some kind of trouble?"

"Uh, well, I, uh. . . ."

Traffic sped up marginally, but nowhere near fast enough for Sister Speed: she kept inching her foot down on the accelerator, riding up behind the car in front of her, then inching back reluctantly.

"From what she said, she sure was in the doldrums, I can tell you that!"

Sam wrinkled his forehead. "Sister Mary Michael?"

"No, your student. Buckman, or something like that, right? Anyhow, she wanted us to tell you that she wasn't going to bother you while she was here, she just wanted to get away for a couple days. I sure hope coming here cheers her up some."

Sam glanced out the window. The tunnel traffic crept by at a steady pace. "Is it—very far to the convent?"

"Oh, maybe forty minutes once we get out of the city. You'll really like the drive. And—it's a monastery," she corrected him gently.

Once we get out of the city. Sam groaned quietly. Given the traffic, it could take an hour or more just to get through the tunnel. And once they got out? Nearly an hour more of non-stop talking by a nun who was obviously a repressed race car driver. No idea what kind of lectures he was scheduled to give, what or who oblates were, or whether the emotionally disturbed student Sister Mary Catherine had mentioned had anything to do with this Leap.

"Oh, and of course, there's Mass tonight for the oblates at five. That is, if we get back there in time. I know we've scheduled the whole weekend for you, but after the retreat, we're all going to leave you alone so you can do your work. Mother Mary Frances is so grateful for you filling in like this at the last minute. I don't know, we'd probably have had to cancel the retreat if you hadn't been able to come up here. It's really fortunate that you were free."

Sam stifled the urge to sigh, and stared at the monotonous

walls of the Sumner Tunnel, slowly inching past.

At least keeping up his end of the conversation wouldn't be hard. He could drop dead on the way to the monastery, Sam thought, and Sister Mary Catherine would keep right on talking.

CHAPTER
SIX

December 24, 1998
Stallion's Gate, New Mexico

"Admiral, your security chief wishes to speak to you."

Al shut his eyes momentarily and sighed. Ziggy's announcement, just as he was getting ready to visit Sam for the first time, was less than welcome.

"He says it's urgent," Ziggy purred.

It never rained. . . .

Al squinted at the glowing orb, then headed for his office.

"Al?" He stopped and turned to face Verbeena. "You want me to stick around?"

"Naw, piece o' cake." He waved her off. "Go skiing. Break a leg." He rubbed his eyes, started for his office again, then stopped and turned once more. Verbeena was waiting. "Better yet," he added, indulging another momentary fantasy, "have *Tina* break one. I'd *love* to have her laid up in bed when she gets back."

Verbeena shook her head and chuckled. "I'll warn her." She ducked into her office and returned seconds later with her packed bags. "See you next year," she called. He waved a distracted hand in farewell as she headed for the elevator.

Inside his office, with the door shut, Al pulled a new cigar from the humidor and sank his teeth into it as he picked up the security line.

"Calavicci."

"Admiral, I've got, uh, a little problem down here."

"If it's a bunch o' faxes from Weitzman. . . ."

"Uh, no, sir, not exactly. But you're close. Actually," the man continued, after clearing his throat, "I have three auditors here who claim their security clearances *have* been sent. But

I don't have any record of their arrival, sir. And no clearances."

Al let out a heavy breath and scratched the side of his nose. "Call Weitzman," he ordered, glancing at his watch. It was almost eight at night in the nation's capital. "And keep his penny-pinchers on ice until I get there. They're legit, but I'm not gonna let 'em have their way with my books 'til *their* visit is by the book. Got it?"

"Aye, sir."

Al hung up and debated calling Weitzman himself, just for the thrill of tongue-lashing him for his inefficiency. Actually, it was fairly standard for auditors to arrive before their clearances did. Through the existence of some perverse political time warp, it took less time to fly from the East Coast to the Project than it took to send a fax.

Al resisted the urge to call his favorite senator himself, deciding to let his security chief handle it. After all, Sam was waiting for word on his current existence; and there was something else Al needed to take care of before he let the auditors into the Project's administrative areas.

He left his office, the unlit stogie between his teeth, and crossed the room.

"Ziggy," he called. "What's Sam doin' now?"

"I can't be certain until you establish a lock with him, Admiral," the all-knowing computer began. "But I can predict with 78 percent accuracy that he is probably driving toward St. Bede's."

"Has anything changed?"

"Not that I'm aware of," Ziggy said sullenly. "However, I have yet to finish calculating the possible reason for Dr. Beckett's presence in Massachusetts in April 1995."

Al did a double take. So did Gooshie. They glanced nervously at each other, then back at Ziggy.

"1995?" Al repeated quietly. "That's damned close."

"April *first*, Admiral," Ziggy added. "1995."

Ignoring the slinking itch in his back and stomach, Al chewed nervously on the cigar. "That'd be about, uh—"

"Six weeks before Dr. Beckett first Leaped." Gooshie's somber conclusion took the admiral aback. It wasn't like Gooshie to finish his sentences for him.

"Yeah, well. . . ."

53

"I should have stopped him."

Al turned sharply. "That's history, Ziggy!" he snapped. He didn't like the way her voice had suddenly dropped half an octave. And he didn't like the train of thought his own mind had suddenly taken, either. "Look, you think I got time to get our auditors settled in before I go in there?" he asked, gesturing with his chin toward the Imaging Chamber Door. "I mean, is anything earth-shattering likely to happen in the next half-hour or so?"

"I'm unable to make that determination, Admiral."

Now, Al thought, she sounded downright depressed. "Well *try!*" he urged, impatiently waving his cigar in a circle.

For long seconds, the computer hummed. Then, with a deep blue glow in the center of her plate, she said, "I guess not."

"You guess—" Al bit off his instinctive response and took a deep, controlling breath. "Gooshie, I'm goin' over to Security. Seems our guests arrived without their invitations to the dance. Shouldn't take long to get it cleared up, but I figure, what with them pulling holiday duty, I might as well give 'em a personal greeting." He flicked his eyebrows and felt the first rush of adrenaline pouring through him. "I'll take a handlink so you can contact me if anything happens."

"Uh, right."

"And Ziggy," he added over his shoulder, as he started for the elevator, "either snap out of it or I'll have Gooshie replace that extender you seem so fond of with that teeny tiny blue one. Got it?"

If she did, she didn't bother to answer.

Captain Mark Davalos, Project Quantum Leap's chief of security, met Al at the door to the small building that sat just outside the Project's compound. He looked, as usual, a little anxious.

"They're inside sir," Davalos said as Al got out of his car. He gestured with his head at the building behind him. "I gave them some coffee and let them use the bathroom, but that's it. And I called Senator Weitzman; the clearances came through right after that."

Al grinned tightly. Knowing Weitzman, someone on his staff was having a less-than-cheery holiday right about now.

Al had gone first to his quarters to change; a little intimidation was always a good way to start, so he'd put on his dress whites, complete with every medal he'd ever been awarded. By the time he'd finished, he felt like a bowl of pasta primavera without the pasta.

"They givin' you any trouble?"

"Uh, well, not exactly, sir."

Al had known Davalos for over twenty years, now. They'd come up through the ranks together, though Al had been a lieutenant commander and Davalos only an ensign when they'd first met. But Al had seen two qualities in the kid, even then, that didn't come together too often: loyalty and trust.

Unfortunately, Davalos also had enough gullibility to make him entirely unsuited for his job in Naval Intelligence back in the seventies. So Al had him transferred out. Then, for the next two decades, he carefully monitored (and in some cases, arranged for) Davalos' assignments, watching as the kid gained experience and enough cautious skepticism to be worth something.

When Al had asked for Mark Davalos to head up the Project's security team, he'd gotten his request. And he'd gotten a damned loyal officer, with a fair amount of clout to boot.

"They just seem eager to get their job done and go home," Davalos explained, leading Al into the bare office.

The adobe building was a lonely squatter in the New Mexico desert. Inside, the building sported few amenities. It wasn't quite as cold or spartan as some government offices; Davalos had brought along enough paraphernalia to personalize his section with mementos of the academy, various assignments he'd been on, and pictures of his family. Each of the other three desks in the room was similarly adorned.

But the walls were largely bare, the lights were standard-issue fluorescent "day glow," and the puke-colored tile on the floor was some Army warehouse leftover. All in all, a perfect place to detain unwanted guests, and an efficient way station for nosy committee members who came to visit.

Al started for the door that led to the "holding pen," a slightly more comfortable room with an old sofa, two easy chairs, a vending machine, and a small bathroom.

"Uh, sir, before you—uh, there's something—"

Al stopped. Like Sam, Davalos hemmed and hawed only for a reason.

55

"What is it?"

"Uh, well, sir, they—"

"Come on, spit it out!"

"Well, sir, they—" The captain shut his eyes. "They're not—quite—what you'd expect, sir."

Al pulled his chin up and narrowed one eye, waiting. But Davalos was volunteering nothing more.

"Lemme see their clearances," the admiral ordered, shoving his unlit cigar between his teeth and holding out his hand. Davalos had them ready.

"C. Pike," he read aloud, looking over the faxed sheet. "Looks okay." He flipped to the next page. "K. Emerson. Fine." The third page. "J. Casper. Looks in order." He turned back to Davalos. "So what's wrong with 'em?"

Before Davalos could answer, the door to the back room opened and a new voice entered the conversation.

"Nothing's wrong with us. Except that *someone* won't let us get our work done!"

Al whirled.

Three women stood before him, crowded in the doorway. Three undeniably beautiful, incredibly voluptuous women! A blonde. A brunette. And a redhead.

Bingo, Bango, Bongo!

As the brunette stepped forward, Al had a flashing fantasy image of *Charlie's Angels*.

"We've been waiting half an hour for Admiral Calavicci to show up. I assume that's you?"

He smiled, a silly grin that slid all over his face before settling on his lips.

"I sure as hell hope so," he said.

Saturday, April 1, 1995   2:45 P.M.
Near Windy Bluffs, Massachusetts

For the last hour and a half, Teresa had almost forgotten her problem. She'd packed, left a note for her roommate, hidden the bag of cocaine in her things, and taken off for the North Shore.

The farther she got from Boston, the lighter she felt. The

56

farther she got from college and George, the easier she breathed.

By the time the first gray-brown encrustations of rock began to edge into view at the side of the road, she was happily tapping the steering wheel, listening to the music of the Electric Light Orchestra, and ignoring any possibility of disaster. She rolled down the window in her VW Bug, smelled the salty air, and smiled. She had a good feeling about this.

At least, she did for the next three minutes. Then a figure appeared on the road, a large figure, dressed in white. As Teresa closed on the lone pedestrian standing in the gravel at the side of the road, she groaned. The Hispanic flapper was signaling for a lift.

"God, what's she doing here?"

Despite her better instincts, Teresa pulled over to the side of the road as she approached the woman, and leaned across the seat to open the passenger door.

"How did you know where I was?" she demanded. "Or is this just a bad coincidence?"

The laughing woman scrambled into the seat next to Teresa and pulled the door shut. "Oh, jou don' know about coincidences! Ees no accident I'm here."

Teresa spared the woman a glance, then turned the car back onto the road.

"Look, if you followed me here—" she started.

"Chore, I followed you!" Angela cut in. She was still waving her fan as if to cool herself. "Jou think I'm out here in the middle of nowhere for my health?" She laughed. "I'm on this case, remember?"

"Case? What case? You're talking like a police officer or something." The calmness Teresa had been feeling moments ago dissolved. Once more, she remembered her fears from the night before.

"Jour case," the woman explained. She grinned and shrugged. "Jou know, that man who wants his bag back?"

Teresa glanced at her, then clenched her teeth and clutched the steering wheel. What was she going to do if the woman pulled a gun from her purse? Or made a move for the things in the back seat?

"What bag?" she stalled. She eyed the road ahead of her. It was deserted; there were tall pines, a few maples, but mostly

57

a barren highway that led from here to there, with nothing in between. There'd be no help along this road.

"That little bag with the white powder in it!" Angela exclaimed loudly. "Jou know! The one jou stole from him."

"I didn't steal. . . ."

Angela turned in her seat, staring at Teresa. "Why jou don' go to the police with it, huh?"

Teresa rolled her window up; the salty air was colder now, and the clouds above her were darker. It would rain soon.

She didn't bother to answer for a minute. Then, deciding that the woman could easily have pulled a weapon on her by now if she'd wanted the bag herself, she breathed a loud, long sigh and gave in.

"Because—Look, it's none of your business, all right? Where are you going? I'll drop you off."

"Oh, I'm goin' with jou. I told jou, I'm jour angel!"

"You don't even know where I'm going," Teresa snapped. She was getting tired of this woman.

"Chore, I do. Jou're going to the monastery, right? Ees a good idea, because, jou know, Father O'Keefe, he's there to help you out."

Teresa pulled off to the side of the road and stopped the car. She turned in her seat and faced the woman head on. "All right, look, I don't know how you know so much, but I think you'd better get out of the car. Now!"

"Oh, jou know these choes, they're not so comfortable to walk in," the woman whined, lifting one foot and rubbing her toes through the high-heeled shoe.

"You should have thought about that before getting stuck out here." Teresa wasn't sure where her anger was coming from; maybe just from the fact that if this woman knew where she was going, it was possible George would find her. Maybe his drug-dealing friends would find her.

She was scared again.

"If you're really an angel, you can fly to the monastery. So, good-bye."

She waited, and finally the woman opened the car door. "Hokey dokey," she said sadly, pulling her clutch from the seat and dropping her fan inside. "Jou chould be nicer to your angel, though," she added.

When the door was closed, Teresa got back on the road and

drove away. She was still a good twenty miles from the monastery, according to her directions. But as she turned the radio back up and listened to the music, the sense of everything being all right was gone. And the thought of leaving that woman—who might or might not be in need of some serious mental help—on the deserted road nagged at her.

If the woman had wanted the drugs, she'd probably have made a move for them by now. And if she was crazy, well, at least she seemed harmless. Even if she did know too much.

But if she was an angel, Teresa thought, maybe she knew other angels.

"Oh, what the heck," she muttered. Two miles down the road, she turned the car around and headed back.

Angela was waiting for Teresa, right where the girl had left her. She sat on a rock by the side of the road, and when she saw Teresa's VW coming toward her, she stood and waved.

"I knew jou'd be back," Angela said, climbing in. "I'll bet jou have a pair of tight choes, huh?"

Teresa looked at her for a moment, then shook her head and started back on the road.

Saturday April 1, 1995   2:48 P.M.
Cambridge, Massachusetts

Fortunately for George, his car was doing fine. There was nothing wrong with the radiator, or any other part. And it was a damn good thing, because without it, he'd be in shit so deep he'd never crawl out.

He'd phoned Teresa a dozen times this morning, and she hadn't answered. After last night, at least the part he remembered clearly, that scared him. Nicky, it turned out, loved his work, and he was good at it. George could barely stand to put weight on his right foot. The nails were gone, but the bones would heal. And he *could* still walk, which was better than he'd feared.

What scared him about Teresa not answering her phone, though, was only partly the thought that she'd taken off without giving him the stuff. Somewhere in the middle of last night's "lesson," George remembered that he'd cursed her for causing him this trouble. What he couldn't remember, once

59

the blinding pain had eased, was whether he'd actually said enough for Nicky and Mr. Belluno to find her on their own.

If he had. . . .

When he didn't get an answer by ten o'clock, he got dressed. It took him a long time; he had to bandage his foot in a thick wrapping of gauze and an Ace bandage, and then he had trouble finding a sock and shoe that would fit. The pain was intense, but most of the bleeding had stopped, and after downing a half-dozen aspirins, George set off for Teresa's apartment.

Her car was gone from its usual parking spot in back of the building, and when he knocked at the door, there was no answer. He used his copy of her key to let himself in.

The emptiness of the apartment was unnerving. He searched each room, hoping he wouldn't find her body in one of them. In her roommate's room, on the bed, was a note in Teresa's handwriting.

If I'm not back by Tuesday, call 555-3453. That's where I'm staying. But don't call unless it's an emergency, okay? See you.—Teresa.

He'd called the number, and the woman who answered told him he'd reached St. Bede's. He'd bluffed his way through the conversation, gotten enough information, and looked up the rest on the map.

It was well past noon when he left Teresa's apartment. He hobbled down the stairs and got back in his car. He had to get to Teresa. He had to get the stuff back from her now, today. And he had to get it to his dealers so he could get his money and pay Belluno.

He knew damn well that if he didn't pay them tonight, he'd lose a body part. He decided not to think about which one.

He set off for the North Shore, his foot throbbing, the pain creeping up his leg. He was distracted, so he didn't notice the Ford Taurus following him.

CHAPTER
SEVEN

Saturday, April 1, 1995   4:30 P.M.
Windy Bluffs, Massachusetts

"Great car, Sam!"

"Where have you been?"

Sister Mary Catherine's prisoner hissed the question over his shoulder as the familiar—and long overdue—sound of the Imaging Chamber Door opening and shutting filled his ears. After three and a half hours with Sister Mary Catherine, most of it stuck in the Sumner Tunnel, Sam was ready to take his chances and jump from a Grand Prix doing close to 80 miles an hour on a country road. *Anything* to get away from the ceaseless chatter!

"Sorry, Sam, I've been. . . ."

". . . fighting in the Crusades," Sister Mary Catherine was saying. "But then, I suppose you could make a case for the influence of the Moslems on Christian culture. . . ."

Glancing to his left, as if he were looking at his driver, Sam caught a pretty good glimpse of the hologram hovering behind the nun. Dressed in full uniform, Al looked a little flustered, but aside from that, Sam could discern nothing to indicate a terrible crisis at the Project.

". . . for Weitzman's surprise audit . . . ," the admiral said from the back seat. "Ziggy thought. . . ."

". . . since no one had ever been exposed to something like that. . . ."

Al began punching the handlink, and sucked idly on the unlit cigar between his lips. ". . . that you could handle it for a while. Anyway, you know how time flies. . . ."

". . . when you're carried away, virtually enslaved by strange people, and you're engaged in. . . ."

". . . a *really* good. . . ." Al glanced at the nun. "Audit," he finished, a sly grin beneath dancing eyebrows.

Sam had missed much of what both of them had said, but he suddenly caught enough of Al's expression and innuendo to feel irritated. "Don't tell me. The auditor is a woman?"

"A woman?" Sister Mary Catherine asked, catching only a word of Sam's muttered response. She laughed. "Oh, I suppose you're going to pin the Inquisition on Queen Isabella, aren't you? Well, I beg to differ, Father, but. . . ."

On closer examination, Sam thought, Al looked a little too happy. The admiral opened his mouth, then shut it in a sweet, guilty smile, and finally confessed. "Uh, well—three—women, actually."

Sam's eyes widened. He stared at the Observer, finally understood the uniform, and sighed with helpless frustration. The only thing harder than getting help from Al when he was having problems with women was getting help from Al when he was having no problems at all!

"And Sam! They are gorgeous!" Al added, squinting one eye and raising the opposite eyebrow. "There's this one, Jenna, and she has got the cutest little—"

"Al!"

"Calculator," Al said innocently. "The cutest calculator you ever saw."

"Did you say something, Father?"

Al turned, and Sam started to answer. He needn't have bothered.

"Anyway, it really was the Counter-Reformation, don't you think, that left such a sour taste in so many people's mouths for the Catholic Church? Yes, Queen Isabella could have handled it all a little more delicately, right? I know, you're going to tell me the Inquisition was her idea, but the point is. . . ."

The words faded into the background as Sam tried to concentrate on the gravelly voice from the back seat.

"Anyway. Let's see what we got." Al watched the pulsating glow in his hand for a moment. But when he started talking, the words of Sister Mary Catherine drowned him out.

"Your name. . . ."

". . . which most people don't believe anyway. . . ."

". . . is O'Keefe, and you've. . . ."

". . . proven, of course, that the number of people. . . ."

". . . in Massachusetts. . . ."

". . . acted in accordance with the lights of their own times. After all. . . ."

"Hey, Sam, it's. . . ."

". . . the early 1600s."

Sam shot Al a desperate look, shook his head, and pointed to his ear to indicate that between the two of them, Sister Mary Catherine was the clear winner. Half of what Al was saying was lost in the nonstop flow of history from the nun.

Al paused in midsentence and smiled thinly. "Beat by the competition, huh?" he asked drily. But the look he shot the nun was more paternal than irritated.

Fine, Sam thought: let *him* listen to her for three hours straight!

"Uh, Sister," he tapped her on the arm to pull her attention from her own words. She turned.

"I'm sorry, Father, were you saying something?"

"I, um, I wonder if we could—um, maybe find a spot along the road where I could—uh, you know." He grimaced awkwardly. It was always embarrassing to tell a stranger he had to answer nature's call; somehow, insinuating the need to a nun seemed, well, almost sacrilegious.

"Good idea, Sam," Al said, and before Sister Mary Catherine could agree to Sam's request, Al had punched out of the car.

"Oh, Father, I'm sorry, I should have been more thoughtful. After all those hours on the plane and all. And you *are* getting older. You know, Sister Mary Michael says one of the first things to go is bladder control, and she should know, she's in her eighties now, and—"

"Sister!" Sam interrupted. "Could you stop the car and let me out?" Despite his request, the woman had done nothing to slow the car.

"Oh, yes, I'm sorry." Several minutes later, she pulled off into a gravel ditch by the road. A small cluster of old pines huddled near the road, and Sam practically leaped from the car in his eagerness to acquire a few moments' respite from the nun.

"Father, watch your step. There are some rocks—"

Sam darted quickly into the grove of trees and found Al smiling at him with a devilishly pleased look on his face, his cigar now lit.

63

"Al!" Sam took a deep breath and leaned back against a pine tree. "Do you think it's possible for someone to be talked to death?"

"She like the sound of her own voice?" Al asked, enjoying himself a little too much.

Sam cocked his head to the side, impatiently. "What've you got for me, Al?"

"Hmm." Al shoved the cigar between his teeth and held it there, speaking around it like a ventriloquist. "Well, since you've gotten this far, you've probably got the basics, right? You're Father O'Keefe—"

"Yeah, I—I remember him." Sam rubbed a hand over his face, then looked around him. He could smell salt air and seaweed. But the ocean was still out of sight. It was cooling, though, and it looked like a storm was gathering for an early evening downpour.

"Remember him?"

"I—took a couple of classes with him. At Harvard," Sam explained.

"Oh." Al punched up more data from the box in his hand. "Anyhow, so you're Samuel O'Keefe—hey, you get to use your own first name!" Al pulled the cigar out of his mouth and gazed off into the distance again. "Not that that worked out so good the last time," he added.

Before Sam could ask him what he meant, he continued. "And you're a priest—done that before, too," he added, waving his hand in Sam's direction. Then he shifted his weight and said, "Not that that was such a hot one, either, was it?"

"Al—"

"And you're on your way to a convent—well, technically, it's a monastery, but it still boils down to staying with a group of nuns. Hey! That should be familiar, huh?"

Sam pulled his lips tight, waiting for Al's reminiscences to give way to something he *didn't* know.

"And it's—"

"April Fool's Day," Sam finished. He screwed his face into a grimace. "I don't think I like Leaping in on April Fool's Day, Al."

Al looked down on him for a moment, but didn't comment, except for a low grunt.

"Al. Please tell me Sister Mary Catherine has cancer of the

64

larynx.'' Sam started pacing nervously in front of his Observer. ''Because, you know, I've been thinking, and, with a couple textbooks and a little review, I could probably perform the surgery and remove it very cleanly—''

''The kid's really gettin' to you, huh?''

Sam sighed. ''I just—I don't think I've ever met anyone who could talk so incessantly, Al!'' He lowered his voice, afraid of being overhead. ''I mean, she never shuts up!''

A lopsided grin wrinkled Al's face, and he shrugged. ''Think of it as part of Father O'Keefe's penance,'' he suggested.

''Al!''

At the threatening tone in Sam's voice, Al sobered. ''Okay, okay, let's see what we've got.'' Sam waited, wondering how long Sister Mary Catherine would stay in the car before checking to make sure he hadn't stumbled on something and fallen.

''Well, it's not Sister Mary Catherine,'' Al announced after studying the handlink for several seconds. ''At least, not as far as we can tell. See, the problem is, Ziggy's got limited data on the nuns. I mean, they don't really get their names in the paper, they don't pay individual taxes, they don't really do anything at St. Bede's that gets into any public records. So until Ziggy can locate some more data—''

''Well, what about the Vatican?'' Sam asked.

''What about it?''

''Well, don't they have some kind of global database or something? You know, to keep track of everyone?''

The look on Al's face was close to a sneer. ''Global database? Geez, it's been a few years since I heard *that* one!'' He waved his cigar. ''No, Sam, the Vatican's got a lotta clout and a big membership roster, but there's no global database. Every parish keeps its own records, and the diocese keep theirs. And most of 'em—including this one—aren't even computerized. You wanna dig up information on Catholics, the best place to start is probably the political parties. Hey! There's a thought! Maybe some of these sisters are political animals.'' He punched the question into the handlink and waited. ''Nuthin'!'' he reported a moment later. Sam's forehead wrinkled; Ziggy seemed oddly quiet, he thought.

''What about this translation Father O'Keefe's working

on?'' Sam prompted. ''Sister Mary Catherine said something about it being in Arabic?''

''Yeah,'' Al muttered, still staring at the handlink, whacking it on the side and jiggling it. ''Here we go. Harvard's gonna publish it in a year.'' He sighed, exasperated, and shoved the link into his pants pocket. ''It was his swan song. You know, his final published work.''

''But it did get published?''

''Yeah, it got published.'' Al puffed on his cigar. ''Father O'Keefe may not be Mr. Personality, but he knows his Arabic.''

''You've talked to him?'' Sam asked cautiously. He'd wondered, since Leaping in here, how accurate his memories of the man were. But the grimace on Al's face told him they were pretty good. Sam smiled wryly and looked at the pine trees growing at the cliff's edge nearby.

''Did I ever tell you about the time he threw my thesis on the floor and stormed out of the room?''

Al's eyes widened. ''You're kiddin'! *Your* thesis?''

Sam chuckled: Al's incredulity was like a pat on the back.

''Geez, maybe the guy hasn't got as much up here as he thinks he does,'' Al suggested, gesturing toward his head. ''Anyway, until we come up with somethin', just keep your eyes open, and—listen a lot,'' he added, grinning. He pulled out the handlink and pressed several buttons without looking at them. ''I gotta get back to the auditors,'' he explained, a look of guilty pleasure on his face.

Sam let out a heavy breath and glanced back at the car. ''Sister Mary Catherine said the flu's going around. Maybe she'll get laryngitis.''

''I wouldn't count on it.'' The Door to Sam's future opened, and Al stepped into the glowing halo.

''Al! Al, wait! I'm—I'm supposed to say a Mass tonight.'' The thought of impersonating the priest at a task that involved more than just listening or working with ancient Arabic manuscripts left a cold feeling in the pit of his stomach. Or maybe that was just hunger gnawing at him.

''No problem,'' Al shrugged. ''They got cheat sheets on the altar.''

The illuminated future enveloped him just as Sister Mary Catherine came around the edge of the cluster of trees.

"Father? Were you talking to someone? Are you all right? It was taking you so long, and I was worried—"

"No, I'm—I'm fine." Sam turned away from the spot he'd been staring at, realizing he'd forgotten to ask Al about Father O'Keefe's troubled young student. Buckman, or something.

He started back to the car with the nun, only then realizing, to his dismay, that he really *did* need to "use a tree."

"I'll, um, I'll be right with you," he called, but she was walking on, her words still humming through the air.

"I just could have sworn I heard you talking to someone, though, so I thought. . . ."

He ducked back behind the trees, and when she was out of sight, he quickly unzipped.

"Father O'—Oh!"

Sam looked up, just as Sister Mary Catherine gasped, covered her mouth with one hand, and turned hastily away. She had come back for him—again.

"Oh, Father, I just—I'm sorry, I thought—when I didn't—oh." Her last word was a quiet moan, and Sam hastily zipped his pants and headed toward her, wondering which of them was more embarrassed. He tried to laugh it off.

"Don't worry, Sister."

The young woman wouldn't look at him. She ducked her head, her cheeks crimson, and turned away, heading wordlessly toward the car.

He followed her, sorry for her embarrassment, almost forgetting his own. He fastened his seat belt and waited as she started the car.

Her foot barely touched the gas pedal, and for the next thirty minutes, in a shroud of stunned, humiliated silence, Sister Mary Catherine drove a sedate 65 miles an hour along the back road that led to St. Bede's.

And the workshop where we are to labor . . . is
the cloister of the monastery. . . .

**—THE RULE OF ST. BENEDICT:
CHAPTER 4**

CHAPTER

EIGHT

Saturday, April 1, 1995   4:45 P.M.
Windy Bluffs, Massachusetts

Sister Mary Michael, portress at St. Bede's monastery, had had a full day. Since 7:30 this morning, oblates had been arriving for the retreat, checking in with her, getting towels and linens for their rooms, chatting and catching up on all the news since they'd last visited. She loved the oblates; they gave life to the place. Invariably, they brought their children, and Lord knew, Catholics loved children!

Sister Mary Michael loved them, too. It was her weakness that when the children started arriving, she always wanted to play with them. During the oblate retreat (and, of course, at Christmas and Easter), the sound of children filled the grounds of the monastery, reminding her of her days at the orphanage in Philly, years and years ago. She had been much younger then, more able to play with the children.

Today had been no different. She knew most of the kids, except, of course, the new ones, most of whom were still nursing.

From the first arrivals this morning, Sister Mary Michael had greeted each of them and seen to their needs. It was her job, after all. And if she *did* let Sister Mary Assumpta help her out a bit, well, that didn't mean she was getting old, did it? It was just that there were so many of them this year!

"Have Sister Mary Catherine and Father O'Keefe arrived yet?"

Mother Mary Frances was back, having left her office for the fifth time in the past two hours to check with the portress. She was just sixty, almost thirty years younger than Sister Mary Michael. But whereas Sister Mary Michael still went about without a cane or walker, Mother Mary Frances no longer had that independence. Her cataracts were so bad that there was very little she could make out clearly. And in the dark, Sister Mary Michael knew, the woman was almost completely blind.

"No, Mother. I'll let you know the moment they come walking through those doors, I promise," the elderly nun said patiently.

"I'd better tell Father Brenyzhov to prepare to say the Mass," the mother superior muttered, heading back to her office. "I'm sure it must be the traffic that's keeping them," she added. But in her voice, Sister Mary Michael heard concern.

It wasn't that anyone questioned Sister Mary Catherine's driving abilities; but it was always something they kept in mind whenever her return to the monastery was delayed.

How she'd avoided a speeding ticket all these years was anyone's guess!

This was, Sister Mary Michael decided, the strangest oblate retreat they'd ever had. Their original guest speaker had canceled at the last moment, and Mother Mary Frances had called in a favor to get Father O'Keefe to fill in. Even then, he couldn't make it on Friday, so they'd had to delay the retreat and reschedule it to go through Monday.

Now, here it was Saturday evening, and the retreat still hadn't begun. The lecture Father O'Keefe had been scheduled to give after lunch had been canceled, of course. Not that he could help the fact that his plane was delayed.

And now, Father Brenyzhov would say the Mass and apologize for all of them that their retreat leader still wasn't there.

It was almost, Sister Mary Michael thought, as if Someone didn't think there should be an oblate retreat this weekend.

Saturday, April 1, 1995   4:50 P.M.
Windy Bluffs, Massachusetts

Teresa Bruckner wasn't quite sure what to do with herself now that she was actually here. St. Bede's was such a quiet place. Even though there were children running around all over the grass (something she hadn't expected) and people gathering in clusters, talking and laughing, the whole place had an air of silence about it. Silence that came more from peace than from a lack of noise.

"Oh, this is a nice place, don' jou think?"

The woman in the car with her shattered that air of silence each time she opened her mouth, but Teresa was almost getting used to her. In fact, once she'd gotten the woman to talk about something other than Teresa's problems, she'd been a lot of fun. Certainly, she was mentally tipped; but she seemed quite harmless. And if Teresa had to have a traveling companion, she could have done a lot worse.

"Have you been here before?" Teresa asked. She pulled into the long, gravel driveway. Father O'Keefe had mentioned that the monastery was converted from an old New England farm, complete with several dependencies. The land had been donated to the Church back in the twenties, and set up as a monastery in the fifties.

"No, I—I did no' go to churches too much when I was alive."

Teresa smiled to herself. The woman told an amusing story of being a dead Puerto Rican singer who had come back to earth to help others. In this way, apparently, the woman also worked off her own vanity.

"I've never been around nuns before," Teresa said. She shut off the engine and watched the people outside; the black habits were everywhere, and she felt nervous, intimidated, like she used to when her mother took her to see Santa Claus.

"Oh, jou have nothing to worry about. They're just like jou."

Teresa glanced around her. She had a peculiar feeling that she was being watched, followed. She didn't like it.

"How would you know?" she shot back. "Thought you didn't go to church much."

"Jou think there are no nuns in Heaven?"

Teresa parked in the circular driveway, where a lot of other cars had parked. She got out, leaving her things on the back seat. She wanted to be sure that this was the right place, that no one had messed up her reservation. She just wanted to be careful.

She locked the car, watching everyone around her, wary and frightened.

"There's probably a place to check in, or something,

right?'' she asked, lowering her voice out of instinct. Angela got out and looked around.

"Try the big house," she suggested, waving her fan. "I'll bet that's where the check-in desk is."

Seeing no reason not to, Teresa walked toward the large farmhouse. Outside the building, several stone statues of saints, and one of a violent, avenging angel stabbing a serpent, stood guard. She climbed the three steps to the front, knocked, and hesitantly opened the heavy, wooden door.

The lobby was a large, open foyer, filled with Victorian furnishings. Saints galore covered the walls, as did pictures of men Teresa thought looked like cardinals, or maybe they were popes. In the center of the room was an elderly nun, seated behind a dark, walnut desk. On the floor beside her, half hidden by the desk, Teresa saw large grocery bags, each of them stuffed with linens and towels.

"Uh, my name is Teresa Bruckner," she said, moving hesitantly forward. The woman behind the desk smiled, and the feeling of being on trial in front of God Himself lifted a bit.

"Teresa? You're the one called this morning, right? Father O'Keefe's student?"

"Uh, former student," Teresa agreed. She had brought her purse in, and she shifted it from hand to hand, not sure what to do. She wasn't even sure how you paid for these things. Did nuns take credit cards?

Behind the elderly nun, a door opened. Another woman in black stepped out and came toward them.

"Oh, Mother Mary Frances, this is Teresa. She's Father O'Keefe's student."

Teresa felt her cheeks begin to grow warm; she had a feeling that she would be watched over all weekend by these women, simply because she was Father O'Keefe's student. She wasn't sure that she liked the idea all that much.

"Uh, yes." Her voice sounded small in her own ears. Childish. She tried again. "I'm Teresa Bruckner. I called this morning."

The nun who joined them looked to be about fifty, the age her own mother would be, if she were still alive. She wore thick, black-rimmed glasses and carried a cane—things Teresa associated with old people. Maybe the woman was older than she looked.

73

"I'm Mother Mary Frances," the woman said. She extended a soft, pillow-like hand. "We're glad to have you. Father Samuel's mentioned you."

The woman's smile was contagious. Her eyes were half hidden behind the amplifying lenses, and her hair was covered by the wimple on her head. But her smile was genuine, and all the wrinkles of her face seemed to join in serene pleasure.

"He tell you I was impossible?"

She meant it as a joke; but Mother Mary Frances didn't laugh. She just took Teresa's hand in a warm clasp and said, as if welcoming a long lost daughter, "I'm so glad you're here."

It was silly, really silly; but Teresa bit her lips and closed her eyes tightly to keep from crying. There was something heartfelt and real in the woman's words. Something comforting.

"Well, let's see if you feel the same way after I leave," she said, pulling her hand away and taking a deep breath. "I'm not Catholic, you know. So—I hope you aren't going to try to convert me, or something."

"No, of course not." The woman let her hand go easily and took the cane in both of hers, leaning on it a little, but not as if she needed to. "You're awfully young to be taking graduate courses, aren't you?"

Teresa glanced around for Angela; the woman, oddly, had faded into the background. She was studying the pictures on the walls, apparently oblivious to Teresa's conversation.

"Well, I finished school early, so I started college early." She didn't bother to add that she'd finished her bachelor's in two years instead of four; it would sound too much like bragging. "I just—well, Father O'Keefe mentioned your place here, so I—thought I'd just—come out for a couple days. Just to get away from—school." She felt guilty, not coming clean with the woman; but she couldn't just launch into an explanation about George and the drug dealers and the bag of cocaine she had in her car, could she? Besides, now that she was actually here, that whole world seemed so far away, almost like a dream.

A bad dream.

The older woman laughed, quietly. "I know how that is! When I was working on my doctorate, I felt as if the whole world was watching me! Examining everything I did!"

Teresa shook her head, puzzled. "Doctorate?" she asked. "You—have a doctorate?"

"In philosophy," the woman said. "Tell me, what are you working on?"

The ground beneath Teresa's feet disappeared. Mother Mary Frances' question lifted the weight of the world from her, and sent her back to those wonderful, amazing days when every possibility was still before her.

"Archaeology," she answered. "I attended Father O'Keefe's seminar on Babylonian hieroglyphics last semester. It was great, but I wish I'd had more of a chance to study it. Have you ever taken any of his courses?"

"Oh, a long time ago. Back in the days of the dinosaurs." Mother Mary Frances chuckled and felt her way with her cane toward the front door. "Father Samuel tells me you're the first student he's ever had who came up to him and told him to his face that his book was a—how did you put it?—'a load of crap.' " She lowered her voice as she quoted Teresa.

Once more, Teresa blushed. It seemed Father O'Keefe had talked a lot about her. "I shouldn't have—I was just angry at everything that day," she muttered, studying the floor. A large, dark oriental rug was centered in the middle of the room, protecting the hardwood floor.

"He said you were right. He said you're a very smart, very courageous girl," Mother Mary Frances told her, her voice solemn and quiet. She released Teresa's arm. "He doesn't usually give out compliments, you know. That's not his style."

Teresa grinned, despite herself, remembering quite a few of Father O'Keefe's excruciating lectures. "I know."

"He's worried about you, Teresa."

Before Teresa could think of something to say—anything— Mother Mary Frances began walking away. "Mass is starting," she said over her shoulder. "But Father Samuel hasn't shown up yet. Sister Mary Michael will get you settled. I'll see you at dinner."

"Got you a room on the second floor," the elderly nun told Teresa, pulling her attention back. She reached down, picked up one of the bags, and handed it to Teresa. Then she glanced at Angela, who had resumed her place by Teresa's side. "Are you—together?"

75

"Oh, *si*."

Teresa turned to her companion. "I thought you had your own room here," she protested quietly. The last thing she wanted was to have to put up with this "angel" the whole time she was here.

"Oh, I don' need a room. I'll be fine."

The nun, who listened to the exchange, held out a bag to Angela. "There are two beds in that room," she said. "If you want to stay."

"Hokay," Angela agreed, smiling so brightly that Teresa had a hard time finding the will to be ungracious.

"Do you know where the guest house is?"

In the background, bells were clanging, Teresa realized. At first, it sounded as if someone were sending an alarm. Then, after a few moments, she realized it was a steady, slow ringing, not a fast call for action.

"No," the girl answered. "What are the bells for?"

"To let everyone know that Mass is starting." The nun smiled again. "The bells chime for each of the services during the day. There's a schedule posted in your room."

"I'm—I'm not Catholic." Teresa half extended her hand with the paper bag in it, expecting to be asked to leave.

But the nun just nodded and said, "Well, come if you're interested. Sister Mary Catherine, she's one of our extern sisters, will be having dinner with you. Assuming that she and Father O'Keefe get back in time. Anyhow, she'll tell you all about the library and the areas you might want to explore. And we have a bakery and bookstore, you might want to browse there. Just make yourself at home."

Despite the strangeness of the place, there *was* something homey about it, Teresa thought, as she and Angela left and followed directions the elderly nun gave them. The guest house was the next building over, to the right of the main house.

"Jou see," Angela exulted once they were outside. "I told jou is a nice place, jets?"

"Jet—yes," Teresa agreed. "I just wish Father O'Keefe were here." She looked around again; she felt eyes watching her. She was certain of it.

"Oh, he'll be here soon enough," Angela assured her. She sounded as if she knew that for certain, Teresa thought.

76

Lillian Marco had been coming to St. Bede's for at least five years, ever since Jack had taken his insurance job. He had to travel to Massachusetts twice a year, for a week each time, and when he did, Lillian and Stephen packed up and went with him, staying here at the monastery. Father O'Keefe had first told her about the place; he'd said she'd like the sisters here, and he'd been right. It was a curiously intellectual community, full of women her age who, like her, had been unsatisfied with a high school diploma.

It was the sisters who had encouraged her to go back to school to get her doctorate. She had a son, she explained, and a husband. And she was working part-time. When would she be able to fit in the work required for a doctorate?

But the sisters had persisted, and with their encouragement, and Jack's reluctant acquiescence, she had enrolled in two courses.

Jack's death five months ago put a halt to her studies; the life insurance he had bought was insufficient to live on. It barely paid for the funeral! And Stephen had had to leave the private school he'd been in; it wasn't fair for her to take what little they had and squander it on herself.

Nor was it fair for Father O'Keefe to pull the rug out from under her. After all this time, all she'd done for him, she deserved better. So did Stephen. And while Lillian didn't want to get into a battle here at St. Bede's, she was fully prepared to fight for what she deserved.

Sister Mary Michael finished checking in the young woman in front of them, then greeted them with her usual cheerfulness.

"Didn't know you were coming," she said, glancing quickly through the hand-scrawled roster of rooms she kept. There was nothing ungracious in her words, Lillian knew. It was simply a matter of space. "Let's see, there's one small room still open. The Mayfields had to cancel at the last minute, and that freed up two rooms. One of 'em's taken," she said, "but the other one's yours if you like."

"Thank you, Sister. I know this is unexpected. . . ."

77

"You know, Father O'Keefe's going to be here this weekend," the elderly nun informed her.

Lillian smiled tightly and nodded. "Stephen! Come back here."

"Oh, he won't get into anything," Sister Mary Michael said, watching the boy gallop through the large sitting room that fronted the old farmhouse. To the left, behind a heavy, maple door, was the chapel. The door was shut, but Lillian could hear the quiet chant through the walls.

"Mass?" she asked quietly. Sister Mary Michael nodded.

"Father O'Keefe was supposed to be here for it, but he hasn't arrived yet. Caught in traffic, I suppose." She leaned closer and whispered, "Sister Mary Catherine picked him up."

Lillian smiled. Almost punishment enough, she thought to herself. But of course, she said nothing. The glimmer in Sister Mary Michael's eyes was enough to know that the penance was well understood.

"Here you go." The nun pulled a bag of sheets and towels from under her desk and handed them to Lillian. "You know where room 224 is? Second floor of the guest house, go past the bathroom, turn right."

"Thank you. Listen, is there any way to lock the door? Stephen's been having trouble with sleepwalking ever since his dad died."

Sister Mary Michael glanced at the boy, who had latched onto a large coffee-table book. "Can't think that there is," she muttered. "Of course, you could always stop the door with a chair. Might keep him in at night."

"I'll try that." Lillian turned and found her son. "Stephen! Come on, we're going."

The boy brought the oversized book on monasteries of the world with him as he came back to the foyer. "Can I take this?" he asked, glancing first at his mother, then at Sister Mary Michael.

"No, Stephen, that stays here for guests."

"Aren't we guests?" the boy asked, moving toward his mother with the book tucked under his arm.

"Let the boy read it," Sister Mary Michael said. "You just bring it back when you're done."

Lillian sighed and smiled. "You're an old softie, Sister," she said. Sister Mary Michael's face wrinkled with a grin.

Lillian left the main house, and Stephen ran ahead of her. A few feet later, he tripped on the root of a large maple outside the guest house, and landed heavily on top of the book.

"Stephen! Be careful," Lillian chided him, pulling the child up and dusting him off. "That's an expensive book!"

"Is your book going to be expensive, too, Mommy?" Stephen asked, grabbing the volume tighter and staring at the cover photograph of an eleventh-century monastery that sat on a lofty mountaintop in France.

"I don't know that there's going to be a book," Lillian said quietly. "Not anymore."

CHAPTER NINE

December 24, 1998
Stallion's Gate, New Mexico

"We three auditors from Washington are,
"Bearing gifts to admirals afar...."

Admiral Calavicci hummed happily to himself as he left the Imaging Chamber, bouncing on the balls of his feet as he descended the ramp and gently laid the handlink on the console. Gooshie watched him, smiled, and said not a word.

"Anything new with our Guest?" Al asked, and shot a quick look at Waiting Room.

"He's bored," Gooshie reported. "So I found him a couple books. And we're getting him some food. He said he never eats before he flies, and he's been on a plane for four hours." Gooshie wiped a hand across his forehead and removed a trace of sweat. "He's a rather dour man, isn't he, Admiral?"

"Yeah." Al chuckled. "You should hear Sam talk about him," he added, moving away from the man and the console. "Ziggy got anything yet?" he asked. The elevator beckoned him; he wanted to go check on the auditors. Just to make sure everything was going well, of course.

"Uh, well...." Gooshie's hesitation stopped Al in his tracks. He turned.

"Well?"

"Well, uh, Ziggy's got a—sort of a theory."

"Has she got a theory on why this Leap is so full of co-incidences?" Al asked. "I mean, think about it. Sam's usin' his own name again, like he did at Havenwell." It was still hard not to wince at the name of the psychiatric institute Sam had Leaped into in the 1950s. "*And* he's a priest again, like that time in Philly. *And* he's stayin' with a bunch o' nuns, like the time he Leaped into Sacramento. Doesn't that seem odd to you? That there's all these coincidences?" His cigar swirled through the air, renewed regulations notwithstanding.

"Well, Ziggy was working on that, Admiral."

"And?"

"There is only one thing common to each of those Leaps, Admiral," Ziggy purred.

Al waited, but Ziggy was in a mood. A definite mood. "What's that, Ziggy?" Al finally gave in. He wanted an answer *before* midnight.

"Head trauma," Ziggy cooed.

Al narrowed his gaze and turned back to Gooshie. "I sure hope she's not suggesting that Sam's there to get his head bashed in."

"Uh, well, no Admiral, actually, she thinks. . . ." Gooshie's voice died.

"Well?" Al finally prompted. Gooshie was fiddling with the controls on the console, his face suddenly flushed.

"Well, she thinks Dr. Beckett may be there—"

"Gooshie!"

"To give himself a second chance." The redheaded programmer spat out the words quickly, as if they tasted bad.

Al stood where he was, grounded by a combination of surprise and irritation. "What?" he finally asked, his voice lowered to a growl. Gooshie cringed, and the computer whined quietly.

"She thinks," Gooshie repeated, a little more slowly, "that Dr. Beckett may be there to—well, to stop himself from Leaping prematurely."

It was several more breaths before Al could think of an answer. He stuck his half-finished cigar between his teeth as he looked at the programmer. Then he turned to the orb on the wall, its swirling colors hued in deep blues and grays.

"Ziggy," he said evenly, "that is *not* a possibility. You know damned well that we can't—"

"Why not?"

The question stunned Al. "Why not?" he repeated, pulling the cigar from his lips and closing the distance between him and the circular rainbow. "Why not? Quantum Leap Rule Numero Uno is why not: 'The time traveler shall not do anything to alter or improve his own life—' "

"A rule you've broken before, Admiral," the petulant

81

computer interrupted. Al glanced at Gooshie, who turned away. Obviously, the man didn't want to be in the middle of this discussion.

"Yeah, well. . . ." Al hesitated, still holding firmly to his irritation. "But if we give Sam any information that alters what happened in 1995. . . ."

"He might not Leap until the retrieval program works properly," Ziggy concluded. "If he is warned, he might not act so impetuously."

Al sucked on the cigar for a few seconds, safe in the knowledge that Verbeena really was gone and that the auditors were tucked away on another level.

"And if he doesn't?" he asked quietly. He took a deep breath. "What happens to all the people he's helped up 'til now, huh? What happens to Tom Stratton and Black Magic and Jimmy LaMotta, huh? What happens to all the other people whose lives have been helped by *them* because of what Sam did?"

Ziggy hummed for a second, her swirling thoughts taking on a wide spectrum of colors.

"I can predict with 50 percent accuracy that Dr. Beckett will still be able to help them."

"Fifty percent?" Al repeated. "Exactly?"

"There is a 50 percent chance that by the time Dr. Beckett perfects the retrieval program, he will also perfect a means by which to Leap without interfering with the original time line."

Al narrowed his gaze, and Gooshie cleared his throat. "Meaning that if this project works the way it was supposed to—Sam won't be able to do anything more than see the past. He won't interact with it, is that what you're sayin'?"

"That *was* the original plan, wasn't it?" Al didn't answer. "I believe that if he's warned—if Dr. Beckett warns himself—not to Leap on May twelfth, he may be able to convince himself to wait until the retrieval program works properly."

Al closed his eyes and sighed. "He Leaped because the committee threatened the funding," he reminded the hybrid computer. "They wanted proof, remember?"

"You *did* get the funding, Admiral," Ziggy said. Her voice was almost seductive.

"Yeah, 'cause Sam disappeared," Al protested, waving his

cigar in a circle. "We got funding 'cause it was the only way they figured they could get him back."

Ziggy's silence disagreed with him. He ground his teeth and turned to the elevator.

"We're not doin' it," he said.

He changed directions, no longer in the mood to see the auditors, and headed up the ramp to the Waiting Room.

Father O'Keefe paced. Sixteen paces from one end of his barren cell to the other; ten paces from side to side. He had been pacing for the better part of an hour now, having read all he cared to of the books that red-haired man had brought him.

He was not amused. Whatever was going on here, he found it neither interesting nor useful. And whatever was going on here, no one had seen fit to explain it to him.

So far, he had deduced little about this place. That it was a government operation seemed likely. Possibly with some military influence as well. His first thought had been that he was some part of an experiment; but if so, the only thing these people had done to "experiment" on him was to see how he handled being confined to a small room for a prolonged period of time.

He had discounted that theory about half an hour ago. Now, he was concentrating on the facts as he had them. To begin with, everyone he'd spoken to had seemed either surprised by his presence or uneasy, as if he hadn't actually been chosen by them for whatever they were going to do. The redhead was particularly effusive, offering him all the normal comforts of home—food, books, a drink—without letting him out of this cage. Or explaining where he was, or why.

The other man, the one called Al, had disappeared right after that first interview. He hadn't been seen since, and O'Keefe wondered what role he played in this organization.

Likewise, he wondered about the African-American woman he'd been quizzed by. She hadn't reappeared, either.

All supposition aside, however, a few things were clear. To begin with, these people intended to keep him healthy and wanted him to be happy. Or at least calm. In addition to that, he'd discovered, by talking to himself, that he could be heard from outside his room; when he wished aloud for something to do, the redheaded man with halitosis had come bustling in with a handful of old philosophy textbooks and an offer of food.

"I'm sorry we can't let you out," the man apologized. "But—those are the rules. If you need anything. . . ."

His words had trailed off under O'Keefe's angry stare, and the man scurried out of the room quickly.

Just as well, O'Keefe decided. Solitude was preferable to the endless chatter of those who simply talked without saying anything.

He was working on his twenty-fifth pace of the room's length when the door opened again. He expected the man with the mustache; he was rewarded, instead, with the one called Al. And this time, his preliminary theories were confirmed.

"So," he said quietly, stopping his pace to face the shorter man full on, "this *is* a military operation."

The man wasn't easily intimidated, O'Keefe noted. But then, given the admiral's uniform, he wouldn't have expected him to be.

"Not completely. But, yeah, the Navy's got a hand in it," the man acknowledged. He sucked a cigar and tilted his head back. The gesture seemed to add inches to his height. The priest pulled himself up, then leaned back against the bed. Behind him, on the pallet, were the books they'd brought him.

"Are you here to give me some answers or just to stare at your captive?"

The words hit a nerve, O'Keefe saw. Admiral Al pulled the cigar from his lips and narrowed one eye.

"There's only so much we're allowed to tell you," he started. His voice was low, and he spoke slowly, as if he were saying words he'd said many times in the past. "Basically, you're part of a government experiment."

"I figured out that much." O'Keefe regarded the medals on the man's chest; he knew how to read them. Purple Heart, Medal of Honor, several others that indicated the man who held him here had seen his own share of war and violence. He relented slightly.

"How did I get here?"

"Hmmm, that's a tricky one." The admiral put the stogie back between his teeth and considered how to answer the question. Or whether to.

"You don't happen to have another one of those, do you?" O'Keefe asked, pointing at the cigar.

The admiral cocked an eyebrow in surprise and slowly grinned. He pulled a fresh cigar from his jacket and held it out. O'Keefe took it, bit into the end, and tasted the fresh tobacco leaf on his tongue. It had been decades since he'd allowed himself the luxury, but it seemed to put him on firmer ground with his captor. So he indulged.

The shorter man held out a lighter and he took it, lighting the cigar slowly, sucking in the long-missed aroma, and finally handing the lighter back. For a few seconds, both men simply stood there, enjoying their cigars in companionable silence.

"So," O'Keefe began three puffs later, "how have you managed to explain my absence?"

The admiral glanced at his cigar; a doughnut of smoke escaped from the lit end and drifted upward. "Don't have to," he said. "See, you've traded places in time with—" The man hesitated, and when he spoke, he did so with half a grin. "Actually, with one o' your students."

"One of my. . . ."

"Yeah. The smartest one you ever had. Only it doesn't seem like you figured that out at the time." The man gestured with his hands and his cigar as he spoke.

"Teresa?"

The surprise in the admiral's eyes told him he'd guessed wrong. And yet. . . . "This has something to do with Teresa, doesn't it?" he asked. He moved toward the admiral, his eyes holding the shorter man's. "Is Teresa all right? What's happened to her?"

"Teresa?" The man pulled a colorful box from his pants pocket and punched several buttons into it. Clearly, O'Keefe saw, he had just given this man information he didn't have before.

"Teresa Bruckner," O'Keefe said, not sure now if he were helping or harming the girl. "She was my student last semester. She's—" he paused, seeing the look on the admiral's face. The man had turned white.

"What?" O'Keefe demanded. "Is she hurt? I knew something was wrong."

The man swallowed convulsively, his cigar dangling in his right hand, forgotten.

"Teresa," he whispered. His eyes were glazed, and for several seconds, he neither moved nor breathed.

"Yes, Teresa," O'Keefe repeated. He waited. For some reason, the name had affected this man deeply. "Do you know her?"

The admiral snapped back and finally focused on the priest. "Uh, yeah. Yeah, I met her—once. She was just a kid." Again the man turned his attention to the box in his hand. Apparently it was giving him information. He studied it as O'Keefe might have studied one of his own texts.

"Aw, hell!" Admiral Al shoved the glowing box into his pants and sighed. "Look, I gotta—I gotta go check on somethin'. Uh, Father."

And in that moment, O'Keefe knew something more about his captor. It was the way he said the word, the combination of familiarity and guilt he put into those last two syllables.

"You're Catholic, aren't you?" O'Keefe said as the man turned to the door and waited for it to open.

"What?"

"You're Catholic," O'Keefe repeated, a small grin of victory finding its way to his face. "Or—an ex-Catholic?"

He saw a faint red flush on the admiral's face. Then the man turned and strode toward the open door.

"No," he said. "I'm not."

O'Keefe smiled to himself when the door shut; after years of listening to people tell the truth in a dark confessional, he knew what the truth sounded like.

And the admiral's claim didn't have that sound to it.

CHAPTER

TEN

George knew he had a tail. A distant one, to be sure, but it was there.

He stopped on the way to the monastery, both to ease the pain in his foot and to get gas for the car. His foot was swelling inside the shoe, and when he took it off to examine the damage, a gray Ford slowly passed the gas station.

After rebandaging his foot and stuffing it painfully into the shoe, he got back on the road. A cup of coffee and some more aspirin for the pain were all he bothered to stock up on. If all went right, he'd have the dope in no time, and if the pain was really bad by tonight, he might just sniff a little coke to get him through.

When he resumed his route, he passed the Ford. It had gone by the gas station a good fifteen minutes earlier, and by all rights, it should have been long gone. But here it was, tootling along Route 128, heading in the same direction he was.

He slowed and deliberately waited for the car to pass him. He didn't recognize the driver. There were no passengers.

Ten minutes later, he caught up to the car again.

"Shit," he muttered, passing it in the left lane. The car dropped back, out of sight, and George lost it. He doubted that it had lost him.

He wasn't sure whether to continue to the monastery or not. If Belluno had sent one of his goons to get the dope, he doubted that a monastery full of nuns—or Teresa—would stop him from doing whatever he felt he had to do to get it.

Ten miles down the road, George made his decision. He'd call the monastery, talk to Teresa. Convince her to meet him somewhere. He knew she had the stuff with her. She hadn't

87

left it at her apartment; he'd searched it before leaving.

He found another gas station and pulled over, took out the slip of paper he'd copied the monastery's number on, and dialed from a pay phone.

"You have reached St. Bede's monastery," said a pleasant voice on the other end. A young voice. A recorded voice. "No one can take your call at this time. Please leave your message."

He hung up and limped back to his car. He pulled out a pack of cigarettes and lit one. Teresa hated the way he smelled when he smoked, so he was trying to give it up. But this was one time when he deserved a cigarette.

It would be getting dark soon. He wanted to get the dope and be back to Harvard before anyone started looking for him again. But he sure as hell didn't want to bring Belluno's man to the monastery.

He decided to wait. If the Ford was following him, it was probably up ahead, waiting for him to resume his trip. If he waited long enough, the man would probably double back, come looking for him.

But maybe the sisters at the monastery were at dinner. Maybe in a little while they'd answer the phone.

He'd wait a little longer and try again.

Saturday, April 1, 1995   5:22 P.M.
Windy Bluffs, Massachusetts

"Well, here we are, Father."

Sister Mary Catherine's first words in more than half an hour were still muted by her embarrassment. It occurred to Sam, at one point, to try to joke about the unfortunate "viewing," but Sister Mary Catherine's silence got the better of him, and he left her alone. After all, in the long run, it was easier than jumping from a moving vehicle.

The silence and the scenery along the road had let Sam drift back into his own memories. They weren't on the coast itself, but they weren't far from the ocean, either. The trees thinned as they drove, until few but the hardiest pines were left. Rocky ground, once captive to the ocean, began to show itself. The ground became harsher, less friendly to farmers who had struggled here for their livelihoods. And the clouded sky became a soft gray blanket that promised rain by the end of the night.

The familiarity of the land and the memories—however sketchy—of his years in Massachusetts filled Sam's thoughts and time. That and the eventual realization that they weren't going to make the five o'clock Mass he'd worried about having to say.

"It's not—quite what I expected," Sam said, as Sister Mary Catherine parked and climbed out of the car. He followed her and pulled his bags from the back seat. This time, Sister Mary Catherine didn't fight him for them. In fact, she still studiously avoided looking directly at him at all. He smiled to himself and followed his silent guide.

They had pulled up in front of what seemed to be an old stone farmhouse. A fairly large one, Sam noted, and from what he could see of it, it had been added on to over the years. The architecture was simple and practical, a typical New England home. Three visible dependencies—a barn to the right and two smaller buildings on the left—were obviously part of the monastery. A small congregation of waist-high, stone statues guarded the front.

A long, lush field spread out behind the farmhouse, and in the distance, crops were growing. Across the road, the land stretched toward the ocean. Sam could hear water dashing against rocky cliffs, foretelling the storm threatening from above.

"The guest house is over there," Sister Mary Catherine said, just before they entered the main house. She pointed to the barn. "But we should see Sister Mary Michael first. She's our portress." The young woman opened the heavy front door, scraped her shoes on a welcome mat, and stepped in. Sam followed.

In the foyer were occasional chairs and end tables arranged much like a doctor's waiting room, Sam thought. Except that the magazines and books on these tables weren't the sort you'd find in a typical medical office. One of them, a publication called *The Latin Mass*, made him wonder what sort of nuns these were: the last he'd heard, the Mass was in English now.

"Well, there you two are!" The elderly nun at the desk stood as Sam and Sister Mary Catherine came in. "Traffic bad in the tunnel?"

"Four-car accident," Sister Mary Catherine said, crossing herself as she had when they'd finally passed the remnants of carnage in the tunnel. Sister Mary Michael followed suit. "Anyway, I think Father O'Keefe's pretty tired. . . ."

She seemed eager to be rid of her charge. Sam couldn't entirely blame her.

"Father, good to meet you." The old nun extended her hand, and Sam took it. She had a firm grip, though her hand was little more than parchment over bones. When she smiled, Sam noticed the large gap between her front teeth.

"Uh, thanks, it's—good to be here," he said.

"I expect you're tired. Father Brenyzhov is saying Mass, since you were tied up." Sister Mary Michael reached under her desk and pulled out a bag of folded towels and bed linens. "Sister Mary Catherine can show you to your room. But Mother Mary Frances did want to see you when you got here. I suppose that can wait until after Mass, though. Sister?"

Sister Mary Catherine had been slowly inching toward the door when the elderly nun called her back.

"Show Father to his room, would you? I've given him 105. I'll tell Mother he's here." She turned her attention back to Sam as he hefted the bag of sheets and towels under his arm. "You look a mite hungry, too, Father," the old woman observed. "Sister, show him where the refectory is. Make sure he gets some food."

"Thank you." Sam's stomach growled audibly at the mention of food.

"I'll take care of it." With that, Sister Mary Catherine swept past Sam to the front door. She folded her hands under her scapular and stepped ahead of Sam down the walkway that led to the converted barn.

The few trees between the houses had thick roots that had worked their way to the surface. Sam wouldn't want to pick his way between houses in the dark.

"How close are we to the ocean?" he asked, hearing the sound of water lapping against rocks. Sister Mary Catherine turned and pointed across the main road.

"Over there," she said, "about a quarter-mile. That's where our property ends. It's a good walk. You can't see it from here, but on a nice day, you can sit on the cliff and watch the tide come in. It's beautiful. But you should watch your step.

90

It drops pretty steeply to the ocean. The rocks are unstable.''

"I'll be careful." He tried to catch her eyes and smile at her, but she ducked her head again and walked on. Sam sighed and followed.

The barn was larger than it looked from the outside; but then, as Sam entered the converted building, he saw why. Like the main house, it had been added to in the years since it was built. The back, which Sam hadn't seen on their approach, was completely new. The front was used as a sitting room, with a baby grand piano in one corner and Victorian furniture filling the space with large, dark, overstuffed shapes. There were only a few people in the room when they entered: a teenager, with long brown hair tied in a braid down her back, who was trying to read a book; three boys and a plump, odd-looking woman playing Monopoly on the carpeted floor; and an elderly man writing in a notebook propped in his lap.

When Sam entered, the girl looked up from her book and smiled. So did the plump woman.

"Father O'Keefe!"

It was the girl who called out to him, and Sam and Sister Mary Catherine stopped as she leaped from her seat and came toward him. "I decided to come for the weekend," she said with a half-frightened grin.

This, he deduced, must be his troubled student. Only she didn't seem terribly troubled at the moment.

"Uh, yes, I see. That's—I'm glad you did."

"Joo hoo!" The woman on the floor was waving to him as well. He glanced at her, smiled, and turned back to the student. The large woman was getting up, coming over to them. The girl turned to her, then back to Sam.

"I met Mother Mary Frances," she said, blushing a bit. "You told her a lot about me."

"Uh, well. . . .''

"Hi, Sam!" The woman, in a white dress that looked quite out of date, came up to them, interrupting the conversation with almost the same ease as Sister Mary Catherine might.

"Uh, hello," he said. So far, she was the only person to refer to Father O'Keefe by his first name, and he wondered who she was. A relative, perhaps? Maybe an eccentric relative?

The young girl twisted her hands around the book she held,

as if she were afraid it would jump from her grasp. "Father, I know you're probably tired and all, and I promised myself I wouldn't bother you, but—well, do you think we could—could I talk to you?"

There was something familiar about the girl, Sam thought, something about her that reminded him of someone else. He just couldn't place who. But the look in her eyes, and the way she lowered her voice when she spoke to him, gave him a sudden insight that he hadn't had seconds ago: she was scared. Very scared.

"Uh, sure," he said, nodding and glancing at the other woman. She just stood there, happily smiling, and fanning herself as if she were on the verge of flirting with him. He cleared his throat. "Just—give me a few minutes to put my things away. And—I'm supposed to go see Mother Mary Frances," he added, glancing at Sister Mary Catherine for confirmation. "So—why don't you just wait here, okay? I'll—I'll be back in about half an hour."

The girl, who hadn't volunteered her name, since Father O'Keefe obviously knew it, nodded and went back to her seat. She opened her book again and pretended to read it. But her gaze darted here and there, looking nervously out the window, then back at her book, then to the door.

"It's me!" The plump woman before Sam smiled, and waited. Sam shook his head, still hoping for clues. "Jou don' recognize me, do you, Sam?" she asked quietly.

Sam shook his head, glad for the excuse. "Uh, I'm sorry, but—no, I don't." He did have a feeling about her, though. A feeling he couldn't quite put into words.

"Oh, that's hokay. That's the way it works, jets? But I remember you, Sam." The way she said his name was filled with fondness and familiarity.

"Father?"

Sister Mary Catherine pulled his attention away, and the overweight woman went back to the game on the floor. From the sound of it, she was winning.

Sam followed Sister Mary Catherine through the sitting room and halfway down the corridor that led into the building's extension.

"Room 105 is on the left," the nun told him, gesturing from where they stood. "The bathroom's on the right, at the end of the hall. And the horarium is posted in the bedroom.''

"The—horarium?'' Sam repeated. Once more, he was on unsure ground.

"Yes. Vespers is right after Mass tonight. Compline is at nine. If there's anything else you need. . . .''

"Uh, no, thanks, I—I think I'm fine.''

She nodded. "Well, okay. It was nice to see you—uh, I mean, meet you,'' she stammered. Her cheeks flushed, and she turned quickly away. Without another word, she was gone.

The corridor was lined on both sides with doors, much like a hotel. But the space between each door warned him that most of the rooms were quite small. He found 105—the third room down—and opened the door. It creaked on its hinges, and as he stepped in, the shades were drawn and the lights were off. The shadowed shape of a bed loomed from one wall, and Sam crossed to put his bags down before he looked for a light.

The door closed behind him. Purposefully. And in the darkness, someone moved behind the door. Sam turned and bumped against a small table. A lamp rocked precariously as he struck the table with his hip; he grabbed it, steadied it, and turned it on.

The person in the room with him was a woman. A young, attractive woman with dark red hair, green-gray eyes, and a lot of lipstick.

There wasn't a hint of a habit.

"I know what you told me,'' the woman began, before Sam could open his mouth. "But you can't get rid of me that easily. You've got to give me another chance. Please! After all these years, it isn't fair to just turn me away!''

"Uh, I think—I, uh, must have the wrong room.'' Sam reached for his bags, but the woman moved more quickly, stepping between him and the bed where his suitcases lay.

"No, this is the right room. You just tried to dump the wrong woman. I won't go away that easily. I've given you five years of my life!'' The woman's voice was escalating, and her hands had balled into fists at her side. "You can't call it off now. You can't find anyone else who can do for you what I do.''

Sam took a deep breath and looked into the woman's tearing eyes. "Oh, boy,'' he muttered.

93

December 24, 1998

Stallion's Gate, New Mexico

"I want answers, Ziggy, and I want them now!"

Admiral Calavicci strode through the Control Center, his head down, one hand shoved into his pants pocket, the other twirling his cigar between his lips. He was not a happy man.

"Answers to what questions, Admiral?"

"Why didn't you tell me Teresa Bruckner was at the monastery?"

Ziggy hummed, and Gooshie stared purposefully at the control console.

"Because," the hybrid computer finally answered, "it didn't seem relevant to Dr. Beckett's Leap."

"Not relevant?" Al stopped his pace and faced the hybrid plate on the wall as if he were making eye contact. "You just said she's gonna die! Now if Sam isn't there to keep that from happening—"

"I have no data to indicate that Dr. Beckett is there to assist her. I believe he's there to. . . ."

"I don't wanna hear that theory again, Ziggy, you got it? It's not an option."

There was no response for several seconds. Then, with a low whine, she said, "Why not?"

Al ground his teeth and glanced at Gooshie for help. There was none to be had from that quarter, though, he could see that. Gooshie was busy looking busy and staying out of this argument. He wasn't going to take sides.

"What happened to Teresa Bruckner in the original history?"

"She fell, broke her neck, and died."

"*How* did she fall?"

"I have no data on that, Admiral."

Al knew the sound of a pouting hybrid computer when he heard it; over the last three years, he'd heard it a lot.

"Well, let me tell you somethin'," he started, lowering his voice for effect. "You better get me some data in the next fifteen minutes, or I'm gonna auction you off to Bill Gates for parts! You got it?"

"Uh, Admiral?"

Al turned to Gooshie, who was staring at the telecom on

94

the console. "You've got a call from upstairs," he reported. "The auditors have a couple questions for you."

Al rubbed his eyes and took a puff on his cigar. "All right. Listen, get the Imaging Chamber on-line. This shouldn't take long." He turned once more to the colored plate on the wall. "And I want real answers and real information when I get back!" he said, jabbing the cigar at Ziggy as he left the room.

Three floors above him, in the administrative offices (most of which were unused at the moment), three lovely women waited in a small office set aside for the annual audits the Project Committee ordered. Al stopped and stubbed out his cigar in the ashtray attached to the wall just outside the elevator. It was a sad fact, but true, that most women hated cigar smoke. And if this Christmas was going to be any fun at all, he didn't want the auditors complaining about his cigar.

As Al entered, the women looked up from their desks. All three of them were tired, Al could see, and Jenna Casper's mascara was smudged under her eyes. All that did, though, was make her look even sexier.

Adding-machine tape curled in long waves from each of the desks, and notebooks and papers covered the floor. Fast food wrappers littered the desks and filled the trash cans. And the coffeepot Al had set up for them was empty.

"Admiral, we have a problem with our figures," Jenna said, the moment Al opened the door and stepped in. Despite himself, he smiled.

"Not from where I'm standin'."

"Admiral, please!" Kay Emerson, the brunette who had taken the lead earlier, stepped around her desk, picked up a hamburger wrapper from the floor, and tossed it in the wastebasket as she crossed the room. "Look at these numbers." She handed him a tablet of paper covered with figures from the various budgets she'd been working on. "Now, Jenna and I have compared the invoices you gave us with the spreadsheets, and the motor pool funds are way out of whack. Here, look."

She grabbed a stack of invoices from Jenna's desk. The blonde woman rose, and Al was momentarily distracted by the sight of her as she came around her desk and sat on the edge. Actually, he admitted to himself, he was distracted by the sight of all three of them.

95

"Someone's been moving money out of the motor pool fund and into something else," Jenna told him. She didn't look happy about it. "What we can't find is where the money's been moved to."

Al glanced over the familiar invoices and handed them back. Then he handed the tablet to Kay.

"Well, it doesn't seem like a big deal," he said, shrugging. "I mean, the motor pool's got enough money as it is, right? So. . . ."

"Where'd the money go, Admiral?"

It was Christine Pike, the redheaded goddess, who pinned him from behind with the quiet question. He turned and smiled at her, one of his most charming smiles.

"Well, if I had to guess, I'd say someone's invoices are just missing," he said smoothly.

"Two hundred thirty thousand dollars' worth of invoices?" Jenna probed. She crossed her arms over her chest, drawing Al's attention to her endowments. He cleared his throat.

"Well. . . ."

"That's not 'missing', Admiral," Kay said. "That's embezzlement."

"Hmm." He wished for his cigar.

Three pairs of dark, unhappy eyes were staring at him. Three sets of arms were crossed in what Al termed "female battle-ready." And from the looks on their faces, Al guessed that none of them was going to take an excuse very well.

"Well, now, see, embezzlement's a—well, it's not a real nice word. We don't like to use it around here."

"What do you prefer?" Kay asked. There was no humor in her eyes.

"How 'bout—'reappropriation of funds'?" Al suggested, smiling and waving a hand in the air. None of the frozen stares thawed. He cleared his throat again. "Okay, look, I got a situation I gotta take care of. So why don't you ladies just keep playing with the numbers and when I get back. . . ." He paused, trying to judge the temperature in the room. Cold wasn't enough. "We'll see what we can dig up then, huh? Maybe over a nightcap?" he added suggestively, taking all three women into the offer.

There were still no smiles.

"Admiral, the last audit showed $100,000 missing from the

motor pool fund. Now it's up to $230,000. This problem—''

"There *is* no problem," he said, his voice sharper than he'd wanted. "Look, the guys in the motor pool are happy. There's more 'n enough to keep us all in our saddles. So why worry about . . . ?''

"The committee's also concerned," Jenna said quietly, "that there seem to have been various unreported alterations made to your control computer in the last three years. Alterations the committee did not preapprove.''

Al narrowed his gaze and tilted his chin back. "Just who're you workin' for, anyway? The GAO doesn't have any authority to—''

"We aren't working for the GAO." Al turned to see Christine rise from her desk. She joined her two companions at Jenna's desk and leaned back against it. "We're working for Senator Weitzman. And for you.''

"For me?" Al wasn't entirely sure how to take that, and he wasn't sure he wanted her to tell him, either; the fantasy was too much fun.

"There was a big stink after the last audit, Admiral," Jenna explained. "One of the senators on your committee said the GAO auditors had proof that you were embezzling money from the Project. And—he's threatening to have you shut down.''

A cold fist tightened around Al's stomach.

It didn't look like Christmas was going to be a whole hell of a lotta fun this year, after all.

CHAPTER

ELEVEN

Saturday, April 1, 1995   5:47 P.M.
Windy Bluffs, Massachusetts

Sam Beckett had escaped. The first few minutes in his room with the woman who claimed he was ''dumping'' her for someone else had been tense. But when she'd started crying, he'd urged her back to her own room, to calm herself, and had promised they'd talk later.

''Later'' was the key word. For Sam that meant after Al found out who this woman was and why Father O'Keefe was having an affair with her. And more important, what he was supposed to do about it.

Sam remembered going to church—Christmas, Thanksgiving, Easter—when he was little, but he didn't remember a lot about it. He did know, with as much certainty as his Swiss-cheesed memories ever allowed, that he hadn't been brought up Catholic. All the little rituals and signs of Catholicism—from the statues and pictures of saints, to crossing themselves and genuflections—were strange to him. Foreign. He wasn't even sure he'd known any Catholics. Except, of course, Al, who was probably not the best authority to ask in this case.

One thing Sam did know, however, was that Catholic priests took vows of celibacy. If Father O'Keefe was breaking that vow, Sam had a feeling the problem of this Leap was going to be a lot bigger than he'd counted on.

Once Sam had convinced the woman—whose name he hadn't gotten—to leave, he'd spent a few minutes rummaging through Father O'Keefe's bags, desperate for help from his former instructor. What he'd found left him less than enthusiastic.

The man's garment bag held two more suits like the one he wore: clerical garb. There was a pair of blue jeans, a couple shirts and sweaters, but it was obvious the man normally went about in uniform, so to speak.

The suitcase held only some of what Sam had been really looking for. The Arabic text Father O'Keefe was working on was incomprehensible to Sam; it was photocopied from some large, ancient volume, and the writing itself was hard to distinguish. The pages were worn badly, and the ink, in many places, had faded into the paper on which the text had been written. Four large, spiral notebooks, each numbered, were filled with the translation of the Arabic work. After glancing through the first three volumes, Sam realized the man was working on an Islamic record from the fifteenth century that claimed to be a recording of supernatural occurrences, most of them surrounding angelic appearances.

"Great! The fifteenth century's answer to *Unsolved Mysteries*."

Several computer disks and a laptop computer were also tucked into the suitcase, as were books on the Arabic language, Islam, and the history of various ancient texts recovered in the Middle East.

What he couldn't find were any notes or writings that indicated what he had planned to lecture on this weekend.

"You've got it all in your head, and your head's in the future," Sam muttered, putting down the last of the books Father O'Keefe had stuffed into the case. He sighed and glanced around the room. Though sparsely furnished, it contained all the things a man needed to complete a scholarly work. There was a small desk, large enough to hold his computer. A twin bed. Two chairs: one for reading, one at the desk. And pegs on the wall with empty hangers, indicating that that was where he should hang his clothes. A dresser at the foot of the bed filled the last space. All the furniture looked like it had been donated to the monastery in the early fifties. It was plain and ugly, but functional.

Posted on the wall next to the door was a schedule of the various services held daily at the monastery, from Lauds to Compline. Apparently this was the horarium Sister Mary Catherine had mentioned. He wondered which, if any, of them, he was supposed to attend. Or worse, preside over.

On the wall over the bed was a picture of a saint. This one, a very young woman in black, carried a bouquet of roses. She

99

smiled down at Sam, and for a second he smiled back.

Suddenly remembering the girl in the sitting room, he got up and opened the door. And then an unpleasant new thought struck him: what if Father O'Keefe was dumping the older woman in his room for the girl who was waiting for him in the sitting area?

With a sigh, Sam glanced upward. "If You're there," he said quietly, "it sure would be nice to have some idea what I'm supposed to be doing." He waited. There was, of course, no response.

The sitting room, when he returned to it, was filled with music. One of the boys who'd been playing Monopoly was now playing the piano. The old man was still there, and so were the other boys, still working on their real estate ventures. But both the woman and Father O'Keefe's student had left.

"Uh, excuse me." Three heads turned toward him as he stepped into the room. The boy at the piano continued to play. "Did any of you notice when that girl left?"

"What girl, Father?" the elderly man asked.

"The one sitting there?" the taller of the two would-be millionaires asked, gesturing with his head toward the seat she'd been in. "Yeah, she split about five minutes ago."

"Did she say where she was going?"

The boys shrugged; neither one thought the question worth a verbal response.

Sam headed for the front door. It wasn't yet dark, and as he stepped out, he saw a long row of nuns leaving the farmhouse and walking to one of the smaller buildings at the left. He started to follow, wondering if the girl had joined them. Then the sound of the Door opening behind him stopped him in his tracks.

"Al!" Relief broadened his lips into a grin at the sight of the admiral, still in uniform, glowing with the light behind him. "Al, I think I know why I'm here."

"You saw Teresa?"

Sam's forehead wrinkled. "Teresa? Is that her name?"

Al looked irritated. Irritated, frustrated—and bothered. Maybe there was trouble with the auditors after all.

"Yeah, that's her name. Don't you remember her, Sam?" The admiral's cigar was nearly gone. It glowed a bright red at the end, and Al studied the oddly silent handlink in his palm.

"Remember her?"

"Ziggy can be such a putz," the Observer muttered, swatting the link with the side of his hand. It let out a small groan.

"Al, all I know is that—well, it looks like Father O'Keefe and she. . . ." He couldn't say it.

Al looked up sharply, and his eyes were darker than they had been a second ago. "Father O'Keefe and she *what*?" he demanded.

Sam grimaced. "Well, it seems like they're—well—you know."

The storm clouds overhead were reflected in Al's eyes. "No, I don't know." He shoved the handlink into his pants pocket and stared at Sam with a look that made him distinctly uncomfortable. "Are you sayin' that you and Teresa are—"

"No, not me! Father O'Keefe!"

"And Teresa?" Al repeated, incredulity spilling into his words. He waved his hands in negation, and cigar ash flew from the tip of his stogie. It disappeared in thin air. "No," he said. "No, not Teresa!"

In the distance, several of the nuns who were leaving the Mass that Sam had missed turned to watch him. Sam gestured Al to follow him, and they walked into the relative privacy of three pines that hedged the building.

"All right, look, who is this Teresa? I mean, is she someone on the Project, or what? I don't—I don't remember her, Al."

Al shut his eyes and let out a heavy breath. "She's just a kid, Sam." He shoved the cigar between his lips. "She's only nineteen. And I don't think Father O'Keefe would go after a student. He just doesn't seem like—"

"Nineteen?" Sam interrupted. He leaned one hand against the trunk of a tree and shook his head. "Al, I think we're talking about two different people here. The woman I met was in her thirties."

"What?" Al pulled the handlink back out and punched it. He waited, staring at the display that Sam couldn't read, and shaking his head. "Sam, who're you talkin' about?"

"I'm talking about the woman in Father O'Keefe's room," he said, one hand waving toward the building he'd come from. Around the corner, several of the nuns were still watching him. Seeing them, he moved further into the trees. "She's got red hair and she is *definitely* not nineteen."

"Huh." Al slammed the link against the side of his hand, shook it, and grunted again. "Damn thing!" He looked up. "Sam, we think we know why you're here. And it doesn't have anything to do with a thirty-year-old redhead. Much as you might want it to," he added.

"I don't want—Al, Father O'Keefe is having an affair with someone," Sam repeated. "And—he's going to dump her for someone else."

Al shook his head. "That doesn't sound right," he said quietly. Then he looked back. "Sam, don't you remember Teresa Bruckner?"

"Teresa. . . ." The name tingled in Sam's brain, a memory he knew he should have but didn't.

"You saved her brother a couple years ago. She was just a kid." Al let out a breath and rubbed his eyes. Then he sucked the cigar back between his lips. "Actually, a couple years ago for us, but about fourteen years for her. She's nineteen now, Sam. And she's here. And—she's gonna die."

"What? When?"

"Sometime in the next twenty-four hours," Al said. He wouldn't meet Sam's eyes. "She falls and breaks her neck. They found her body on Monday morning. Autopsy couldn't tell exactly when she—died." He looked back then, and his face was twisted with torment. "You're here to save her, Sam. You gotta save her."

Sam met the Observer's gaze for only a second. Then the memories began to return, and he looked away.

Squabbling teenagers. . . . A "Queen" T-shirt ripped in two. . . . A dog named Wookiee.

"Kevin, right? Her brother's name—was Kevin?"

"Yeah."

"That's not my mommy. That's a man."

"And Teresa could see us," Sam remembered. He looked back. "She saw us, didn't she? And you—you told her we were angels."

Al shrugged, a little too complacently. "Well, it was either that or try explaining the subatomic agitation of carbon quarks to a five-year-old," he said. For a second, he tried to look Sam in the eye. Then he turned away and stared at the handlink. "I let her down, Sam."

"How did you . . . ? We saved her brother, right?"

102

"Yeah. We saved *him*." Al looked up. "But I promised her I'd come back, Sam. And—I never did. She died in 1995."

"Al, if she died in 1995, you couldn't have gone *back* to her. I didn't even Leap until—" And as he spoke, the world tumbled around a new memory. "I—I first Leaped in 1995, didn't I?"

Al looked back. "Uh, yeah. So?"

"When in 1995, Al? Was it—was it before April first?" Something in his voice or expression must have communicated his thoughts to Al, because the Observer immediately became wary.

"Sam," he said, his voice lowered, pulling the cigar from his mouth, "you know I can't tell you that."

"Al, all I want to know is—have I already Leaped?"

A long, dark stare met his question, and for several seconds Al said nothing. Then, with a deep breath, he closed his eyes and said, "No."

Sam felt dizzy. Almost light-headed.

Here he was: Massachusetts. The Back Bay, the Boston Public Library, MIT, and Harvard Square.

His first home away from home.

His first chance to prove himself, away from Indiana, away from those who believed in him just because they knew him.

His first step from the cradle.

There were other steps that followed, a lot of them. And finally, they took him to New Mexico and his last home away from home: Project Quantum Leap.

555-2231.

The Project's main phone number came back to him, a small hole in his memory suddenly and sharply filled in.

555-2231.

He needed the area code. What was the area code for New Mexico? He could find that out, make a call. . . .

One phone call. Just one, and he'd be home!

Home! Indiana was only a few hours from New Mexico, right? He could board a plane, fly out, taste Mom's cooking. . . .

There was always a pie cooling in the window.

"Al," he said, his own voice dropping in volume, "I could—I could. . . ."

The look in Al's eyes stopped him from completing the

103

thought. There was something dangerous, angry in the Observer's gaze. Something that told Sam, without words, not to make the suggestion.

"Sam, I know what you're thinkin'. But you *can't* do it."

Why not? Why not make one call, warn myself not to try it yet . . . I'd be back home as soon as I hang up. . . .

"Sam, you don't remember, but I do," Al continued quickly. "You wouldn't have listened to yourself any more than you listened to me. If you're thinkin' of tryin' what I think you're thinkin' of tryin', you could really screw things up.—Sam! Hello! Are you listening to me?" Al waved his cigar hand in front of Sam's face, and the Observer came back into focus.

"Al, I was just—look, you don't know that for sure. Maybe if I'd waited—"

"Sam, listen to me. You've done a lotta good for a lotta people. You don't wanna undo all that, do you?"

For a long minute, Sam held Al's gaze, and the Observer stared evenly back.

"I want to go home, Al."

Al shut his eyes and rubbed a hand across them. "Sam—"

"I *want* to go home!"

"It won't work! It doesn't—" He stopped his words abruptly and turned away. "Look, don't you think everyone else wants you home, too?"

"Maybe." Sam swallowed and felt his muscles tighten. "Maybe not. I mean, you're saying that all these other people I've helped—they count for more than getting me home."

"If you try to stop yourself from Leapin', Sam, you won't 'get home,' because you'll never have left!" Al flailed his hands for emphasis. "Sam, look, we're doin' everything we can to get you back. But—well, God or Time or Fate thought you could do some good in the past, right? I mean, isn't that what this is all about?"

Sam said nothing. From Al's standpoint, the leap from altruism to selfishness was pretty small.

"Look, let's focus on why you're here for now, okay?" the Observer went on. "There'll be time later to think about—this other thing." He ended his words with a deprecating wave of his hand. When he looked back, Sam sighed.

"Is Teresa—is she Father O'Keefe's student?"

With a glimmer of relief in his eyes, Al nodded and pulled the handlink back out. "Yeah." Despite a few hard knocks on it, though, it apparently gave up little information. "She was. But since Father O'Keefe only gives graduate-level courses, she must be up there in your league." He looked up. "According to Ziggy, she was workin' on her master's already. She graduated from high school when she was fifteen and got her bachelor's when she was seventeen. Some kid, huh?"

Sam nodded, thinking back to the girl in the sitting room. She had seemed familiar; now he knew why. She still had the large dark eyes that had, as a child, captured the heart of a man who'd never wanted children. He remembered seeing, for the first time, a side of Al that he'd never imagined before. A gentle, paternal side that had, in the midst of Sam's confusion about saving Kevin Bruckner, made an impression on him.

And had apparently left a deep impression on Al.

"I saw her, Al. Sister Mary Catherine said something about her being troubled. Is that—does that have something to do with why she died?"

Al studied the link, sighed, and shrugged. "Dunno," he admitted. "Ziggy's having trouble finding out what happened."

"Well, go back and see what you can find out."

"Yeah." Without hesitating, Al punched open the Door behind him.

"Oh, and ask Father O'Keefe about—that other woman, will you? Find out who she is. Okay?"

"Yeah, sure." Still obviously troubled, Al stepped through the Door and disappeared.

555-2231.

In his mind, Sam heard the phone at the Project ringing as he turned and headed back toward the guest house. And, he hoped, something to eat.

Saturday, April 1, 1995 5:48 P.M.
Windy Bluffs, Massachusetts

Sister Mary Catherine knew what she'd seen. And from the looks on the other sister's faces, so did half of those who had

105

been leaving the chapel with her to go to dinner.

"I didn't imagine it, did I?" she whispered. With the others, she was still staring at the spot where the apparition had been. There, in the trees, near Father O'Keefe. It looked to her as if Father O'Keefe could see the apparition as well. It seemed he was talking to it, or listening to it.

"You mean—the bright light? And—a man, dressed all in white?" Sister Mary Assumpta asked, also whispering. Awe had quieted their voices.

"Was it a man?" Sister Mary Gerard asked. She wore glasses that didn't entirely correct her vision. "It was— blurred."

"Yes, it was," Sister Mary Catherine agreed. "But—I think it was a man. And—he had something in his hands. . . ."

"He kissed it reverently," Sister Mary Joseph said. She crossed herself, and the others followed suit, all of them standing immobile on the path between the farmhouse and the refectory. "A crucifix?" she guessed.

"He had something else, something that glowed with an inner light—"

"A rosary," Sister Mary Assumpta suggested. "It was hard to see, but—perhaps each of those colors was—a bead touched by Our Lady."

"Yes," three others agreed, nodding and watching Father O'Keefe head back to the guest house. The priest had finished his interview with the apparition, and Sister Mary Catherine was surprised that he hadn't adopted a more prayerful attitude. After all, it wasn't every day that a messenger from Heaven came to St. Bede's!

"Perhaps," Sister Mary Gerard suggested slowly, "that was his angel."

The others murmured possible agreement.

"That's it!" Sister Mary Assumpta jumped in, her voice returning to a normal pitch. "Father O'Keefe once wrote something about the language of angels being a prototype of all human language. I'll bet he knew that from personal experience!"

The explanation seemed a little far-fetched to Sister Mary Catherine. She chuckled. "Then he must be on better terms with his angel than we are with ours," she said. The others laughed nervously. "Should we tell Mother Mary Frances?"

For a moment, the sisters stood staring at each other. This wasn't a matter to be taken lightly.

"Father O'Keefe kept moving into the trees when he spoke with his angel," Sister Mary Assumpta pointed out. "Perhaps, we weren't meant to see it."

"A private revelation?"

"Hi, sisters."

The cluster of habits turned at the call. Behind them, coming up the path, was Stephen Charles Marco. The boy was dancing along, running over the lawn and around the statue of the Blessed Mother.

"Hi, Stephen!" The boy glanced at Sister Mary Catherine and continued running around them. "Where's your mom?"

"She's in there," the boy said, pointing toward the refectory.

"Well, why don't we go join her?" Sister Mary Catherine tried to take his hand and guide him back. Stephen might have been left alone to play, with the understanding that the nuns would look after him; or he might have gotten away from his mother without her knowledge. Knowing Stephen as she did, Sister Mary Catherine suspected the latter.

"She said I could play outside," Stephen pouted, pulling his hand free and darting around the first available tree. With a glance at her sisters, Mary Catherine followed him.

"Well, it's starting to get cold," she cajoled him. "Why don't we go back and at least get you a coat, OK?"

She grabbed the boy's hand and pulled him gently along with her.

With that, and with an unspoken understanding to say nothing yet, the sisters moved off.

But Sister Mary Catherine kept remembering all the time Father O'Keefe had spent earlier today at the side of the road. How certain she'd been then that he was talking to someone. Now, she was even more certain.

An angel had visited St. Bede's. There was no choice but to tell Mother Mary Frances what she and the others had seen.

CHAPTER
TWELVE

"I just feel bad about it, that's all." Teresa heard in her voice, once again, the sound of a whining child, and she tried to change her tone before she spoke again. "Look, Angela, I—I shouldn't have bothered him. You could see how tired he was! He didn't want one of his students following him up here like a groupie!" She stopped, picked up a rock, and tossed it in the direction of the ocean. "He's a busy man, he's got more important things to worry about than my problems."

"Oh, see, that's where jou're wrong!" Angela tagged along as Teresa wandered toward the rocky coastline. The clouds obscured the evening sunset, threatening rain, and a wind blew across the land. Angela's dress billowed, and she had to use both hands to hold the skirt down.

"Father O'Keefe is here to help you, Teresa. Jou gotta give him a chance, jets?"

Teresa ignored her. After throwing herself at her former instructor, she'd left the guest house, ashamed and embarrassed by her actions. She hated herself when she did that, assuming that someone else would help her out of her problems, provide the answers for her.

She stopped at the edge of the road, waited until three cars had passed, then crossed. The wind blowing from the ocean had picked up, and the temperature was dropping. She shivered and kept walking.

"Jou should go back there," Angela called, scurrying after her as quickly as she could in her high heels. "He's looking for you."

Teresa turned, waited for her overweight guardian to catch up, and asked, "How do you know him? I mean, if you died

108

when you said you did, you couldn't possibly know Father O'Keefe!''

For a second, just a heartbeat, the woman looked uncomfortable, as if Teresa had discovered her lie. Then she laughed and pulled out her fan, waving it in front of her face.

''I am an angel,'' she reminded the girl. ''Angels can go anywhere they want to, jets?''

Teresa wasn't sure about that, but she wasn't in the mood to argue. Or to worry about Angela. She turned and started for the cliffs.

She loved the water: she and George had had some of their best times in this area, on the water, in the water, by the water. Her problems, like the coastline itself, might seem insurmountable; but in the end, the water would claim the rocks. And in the end, her problems would—somehow—work themselves out.

''Teresa!'' She hesitated long enough for Angela to catch up again. The woman picked her way across the rocky stretch of land, her ankles twisting with each step. Clad in more practical loafers, Teresa had no such difficulties.

''Teresa, I gotta go check in on someone else for a little while, hokay? I'll be back later.''

''Check in on someone?'' Ahead, Teresa could see the edge of the ocean, just creeping onto the horizon. Closer, the ground began to dip downward, a slow slope toward the water. There were few trees growing this close to the water, but Teresa saw a few hardy pines here and there, jutting up like nature's skyscrapers, dark and immense in the growing shadows.

''Jou go talk to Father O'Keefe, hokay?'' Angela persisted. She put a hand on Teresa's arm. ''He's looking for you,'' she repeated.

Teresa wanted to sit by the ocean's edge, find a rock, and wait until she didn't feel quite so foolish for having accosted Father O'Keefe the moment he'd come in. But something in Angela's eyes made her change her mind. Maybe the ''angel'' was right. Maybe Father O'Keefe really wouldn't mind listening to her problems—assuming she could bring herself to tell him about them.

''Okay.'' She surrendered halfheartedly, and picked her way back toward the guest house, Angela following her, muttering each time she twisted her foot on a rock.

"Jou chould stay away from the cliffs," Angela instructed. "They're dangerous, jou know."

"Yeah, right." Teresa turned to see how close her companion was. Angela was standing her ground now, not moving. She smiled at Teresa, a bittersweet smile.

"I gotta go now," she said. "But jou don' worry. I'll be back later."

Teresa started to respond, but a voice across the road called out to her.

"Are you Teresa Bruckner?" A woman with red hair was waving frantically at her, calling out. "Is your name Teresa Bruckner?"

Puzzled, Teresa quickened her pace. "Yes," she called back. Two cars whizzed past her, and she waited to cross the road. "Yes, I'm Teresa."

"There's a call for you in the refectory," the redheaded woman yelled back. "He says it's urgent."

Feeling her stomach tighten in fear, Teresa crossed the road. There could be only one person who would be calling her here. And that had to mean he'd gone to her apartment and found the note she'd left for her roommate.

And that meant his friends might have done the same thing.

She crossed the road in a daze, and came to the woman who had signaled her, her mind numb with anxiety.

"Sister Mary Michael asked me to come get you," the woman explained. "My name is Lillian, by the way. Lillian Marco."

The woman walked with Teresa back to the smaller building, where the refectory—whatever that was—was apparently housed. The woman chatted companionably as they walked, but Teresa heard nothing but the sound of her heart beating in her chest. A sound she wasn't sure would continue for long if George and his suppliers had followed her here.

December 24, 1998
Stallion's Gate New Mexico

Admiral Al Calavicci remained in the empty Imaging Chamber several minutes after the images from the past had faded. The stark blue walls and floor were a peaceful sea in which he floated, his eyes shut.

110

Unlike Sam's, Al's memory was sometimes too good. At times like these, he'd have traded a few Swiss-cheese holes with Sam if he'd been able to.

April 1, 1995, was a day Al was never going to forget.

Unless it never happened.

And at the moment, there was a distinct possibility that it *would* never happen. He wasn't sure why, since he hadn't given Sam any information. But according to the readout in his hand, it was now 38 percent probable that the time traveler remembered enough on his own to alter his own past.

On April 1, 1995, the committee's threats to cut funding had come to an ultimatum: either prove the theory or lose the Project. They had two months to present unequivocal proof that it worked. Two months.

But it wasn't just the committee's threat that had driven Sam to his reckless act. It was the coincidence of the threat and the upcoming anniversary Sam spent in mourning every year: the anniversary of his brother's death in Vietnam.

Originally, Sam's presumptive Leap had been driven by desperation: a desire to keep the Project alive, mingled with a secret desire to try to change the past. To save one very important life.

On April 1, 1995, after an abruptly foreshortened trip to North Carolina, Sam had confessed that forbidden wish to a very angry admiral, who reminded him with chapter and verse about the Committee's—and their own—rules.

"I thought we settled this."

"No. You just gave me the odds. But I'm placing the bet."

Al stared, unblinking. *"You'll die!"*

"The Project's going to be shut down," Sam countered.

"Not if we show 'em it works!"

"Not if I try to Leap!"

"So your Project is more important than your own life?"

"I won't die, Al."

"You can't Leap!" Al stepped closer, very close. *"You can't save your father, Sam. You can't keep Katie from marrying the wrong guy!"* Sam looked stubbornly at him. Al shut his eyes tightly. *"You can't save Tom,"* he whispered.

That day had ended in one of the most heated arguments Sam and Al had ever had. Al had left knowing that Sam understood the reasons for the rules, the inconceivable damage

111

that could be caused by fiddling with past events. But he'd also left feeling—knowing—that the committee's ultimatum had come at just the wrong time for Sam Beckett.

He knew Sam pretty well: he knew that all Sam wanted was one chance. Just one chance.

But that had changed now. And in dreams, in memories he tried to forget, Al remembered Sam's first Leap in two variations. Once upon a time, after Tom's life *had* been saved by Sam, the premature Leap had been driven by yet another secret wish. The need to save his Project was still there; but so was the need to save someone else he knew he *couldn't* save.

Al leaned against the wall of the Imaging Chamber and sighed, the handlink playing its mechanical song in his palm.

It was history now. All of it.

From the moment of the first Leap, all history had been open to change. And so many things *had* changed. But history had not yet changed one thing, the thing that had kept Al Calavicci fighting for the Project's survival night and day for three years.

The fact that, no matter what, Sam Beckett still Leaped.

He still Leaped before the retrieval program was ready to bring him home.

And he still Leaped into other people's lives and made them, somehow, better.

It had taken three years, but Al had finally come to believe that Whoever or Whatever was Leaping Sam around would, one day, bring him home. When he'd fixed all he could fix. When he'd done all he could do.

Or when the retrieval program finally worked.

What Al had trouble with now was the thought that Sam might never do any of it. The thought that Sam might never Leap, never help Jimmy LaMotta, never save Tom Stratton's life, or his daughter's. He might never save his own brother.

And now, he might not save Teresa Bruckner from dying at the age of nineteen.

"Um, Admiral?"

"Gooshie's unwelcome voice pierced the silence of the Imaging Chamber."

"Yeah, Gooshie, what is it?"

"Uh, your security officer wants to speak to you. He says—you've got another guest."

Al wiped away the memories with a swipe of his hand and

started for the Door. The present and the future were calling. "On my way."

Three gorgeous women wanted him to account for $230,000. Someone on the committee wanted the Project shut down. And Ziggy still had a lot of explaining to do.

It'd be a while before he really had to worry about none of this ever happening. In the meantime, he had more than enough to worry about.

... the works of our hands are reported to Him night and day by the angels appointed to watch over us.

—THE RULE OF ST. BENEDICT:
CHAPTER 7

CHAPTER
THIRTEEN

December 24, 1998
Stallion's Gate, New Mexico

Mark Davalos tapped his pen on his desk, smiled at the grinning woman across from him, and hoped to hell the admiral would get his ass over here. Now!

This wasn't what he'd expected when he'd volunteered for Christmas Eve duty. Normally, nothing much happened on Christmas Eve. Even spies generally took the night off to be with their families. Davalos had signed up for this shift for one reason: an intuitive feeling that, despite all protestations to the contrary, Admiral Calavicci really didn't like to be alone on Christmas. Hell, he'd heard the man's "same as any other day" speech for years now. And invariably, the man's words were less than convincing. At least, to those who knew him.

Mark would never have presumed to think of himself as one of Admiral Calavicci's friends. But he'd known the man for twenty-some years. That probably counted for a little more on Christmas Eve than spending the night with a couple of gyrenes.

Besides, he owed the admiral a lot. The man had pulled his butt out of the fire years ago and had taken a personal interest in the success of Mark's career ever since. Some debts were worth pulling holiday duty.

But this Christmas Eve had turned out to be more than Mark had bargained for. The surprise audit had been the first odd occurrence of the day. He smiled to himself, remembering the conversation with Senator Weitzman earlier.

"Charmers, aren't they? I hope Al appreciates all the effort I went to to find them. By the way," the man added, *"they're also qualified to do their jobs. Make sure he doesn't forget that. I'll send their clearances."*

Knowing Admiral Calavicci as he did, Mark doubted that he appreciated Senator Weitzman's efforts; but he was probably enjoying the results.

Now, however, a new guest had shown up. This one had no clearances, no identification, nothing. A call to Weitzman—one the senator obviously didn't appreciate at that hour—confirmed that this woman was not one of his.

Not that she claimed to be.

The problem was that what she claimed to be put her in a status Mark would prefer not to deal with: loonies.

She said she was a friend of Al's. That was fine, but Mark doubted it. She was, well, rather more amply endowed—all over—than the admiral usually preferred. And much older. The woman had to be in her forties, and in all the years he'd known him, Mark had never seen the admiral go out with anyone over thirty-five.

Added to that was the way the woman dressed: not eccentric, as the admiral often dressed, but—well, out of date. Old-fashioned. And if there was one thing the admiral wasn't, it was old-fashioned.

And then came the clincher. The woman claimed, with a perfectly straight face and no hint of a joke, that she was an angel.

Right.

That's when he'd phoned the main compound and risked Admiral Calavicci's wrath. Anyone out here, this far from civilization, who knew Calavicci was here and who claimed to be an angel, was a definite security risk. And even if he did get a tongue-lashing from Calavicci—God knows, he was immune to them by now—he wasn't about to deal with this woman without backup. Not on Christmas Eve.

"Jou don' believe me, do jou?" the woman asked him, after he'd called the Project office. "Jou think I'm loco, right?"

He smiled at the woman. No need to get her angry.

"Would you like a soda? Or some coffee, maybe? It—it could be a while until the admiral gets here."

He stood, moving toward the back room. The woman seemed harmless, but these days, he wasn't taking any chances. Best bet was to keep her happy and calm.

"Oh, no, I don' eat. Thank you, though." She gave him another dazzling smile and fanned herself as if she were hot.

117

Next to her, on the overfilled seat, her small clutch purse was crushed between her hip and the arm of the chair.

"You sure you don't have an ID of some kind?" Mark asked again, eyeing the purse. He had put it through the security scanner earlier: nothing had registered. Not even the purse itself.

He had to get the scanner repaired.

In the meantime, he couldn't exactly demand that the woman turn her purse over for a manual search. That would have to wait for Admiral Calavicci's presence. And authority.

"Oh, no, I jus' have my lipstick," the woman said. And then, as if she'd read his mind, she laughed, stood, and opened her purse for his inspection. "See? No bombs. I told jou, I'm jus' a friend."

Mark peered into the small bag: as she'd claimed, there was a small lipstick in there. That and a compact.

Either one, though, could conceal a bomb. Mark knew that. And he knew that until Calavicci arrived, he wasn't letting the woman anywhere near the Project compound.

It seemed an eternity before the monitor on his desk beeped to let him know a car had entered the perimeter of the security field. He punched up the specs, saw with relief that it was the admiral's car, and sighed.

"Well, Admiral Calavicci is here now," he reported. "So we should be able to get this straightened out without much trouble. Wait here."

He rose and walked past the woman, heading for the door. He grabbed his coat: nights in New Mexico were as cold as the days were hot.

He met the admiral on his way from the car, as was his habit.

"Who've you got in there for me this time?" the man asked drily. "And don't tell me it's a reporter."

"Uh, no sir, she—says she's a friend of yours."

The admiral raised an eyebrow in surprise. "A friend, huh? She cute?"

"Not—really, sir."

He stepped aside to let the admiral into the building first. He decided to follow at a safe distance.

"What the hell?"

As Admiral Calavicci entered the room, the plump woman

stood up. Shock and dismay covered the admiral's face: pleasured glee suffused the woman's.

"Hi, Al! Jou remember me, huh?"

It occurred to Mark that he couldn't remember having seen the admiral struck utterly speechless before. Well, maybe once or twice. But it was a dramatic—and frightening—sight. The man stood with his mouth half open, lips moving soundlessly around words that wouldn't come out.

"Now, jou jus' tell this nice young man that jou know me, and we can go get to work. Hokey dokey?"

The pleasure of the woman, born of a childlike oblivion to everything around her, spilled through the room. Mark couldn't help smiling back at her.

"What the hell are you—Where did you—What are you—?"

Admiral Calavicci regained his voice, but not his power of speech. He stammered incoherently for a few more seconds as the woman watched. Then she moved forward.

"Jou're surprised to see me, jets?"

"Angela—"

"Jou see?" The woman spoke again to Mark. "I told jou he'd know me."

"What are you—How did you get—?"

"*He* sent me," the woman said, glancing quickly upward. "Jou know, this is the first time I ever got to go back to someone who remembers me!"

"This is a serious breach of—" Again the admiral was at a loss for words. Mark stepped forward.

Calavicci had turned pale. Whoever this woman was, she was obviously unwelcome. A hundred scenarios ran quickly through Davalos's mind, but none of them really made sense. He decided not to try to figure it out.

"Sir, I'll be happy to escort her out," Mark offered.

"Oh, that would no' be a good idea," the woman said, waving her fan for emphasis. "See, I'm supposed to help you."

"Help *me?*" the admiral repeated. He drew himself up and said, "I don't need any help! Especially not from you!"

"Oh, chore you do! Jou just don' know it yet," the woman protested. "Jou see, jou canno' be in two places at once. That was the same problem I had." The woman's grin was growing.

"What?"

119

"Oh, I screwed up the first time and—well, things didn't turn out so good." The woman lowered her eyes, momentarily embarrassed. "So now I'm going to help you make it right." She chuckled. "Jou and me, we get to work together again!" She grabbed her purse and prepared to leave with Admiral Calavicci. "Is fun, no?"

The admiral took a deep breath. "Fun," he said, in a tone that made Mark wince, "isn't exactly the word I'd use."

Saturday, April 1, 1995   6:15 P.M.
Windy Bluffs, Massachusetts

"Teresita, listen to me." George's voice was low, melodic, calmly urgent. Teresa knew the tone, and she didn't like it.

The refectory, where the woman named Lillian had taken her, was one of the smaller dependencies, set off to the left of the main house. As old as the original farm, the building had a large dining room, an industrial-size kitchen, and yet another sitting room furnished in Victorian castoffs. Outside the dining room, off the hallway just inside the front door, was a small room that housed the phone Teresa was using. The room offered a modicum of privacy, but Teresa was cautious about saying anything too specific.

"You followed me!" she accused. She was shaking inwardly, looking around outside the doorway for some sign of Father O'Keefe; but the priest hadn't shown up for dinner yet.

"You said you were going to meet me at noon," George reminded her. "In case your watch is broken, it's well past that!"

"I know what time it is." Teresa pulled her braid around her shoulder and fingered the end. It was a nervous habit she'd tried for years to break. "Look, George, I don't think I can—meet you. I'm sorry, but I can't—I can't turn that stuff over to you. I've been thinking, and if I—"

"If I don't have that stuff by tonight, Teresa," George interrupted, his voice growing louder, "I'm going to get another visit from two guys who've already delivered their message once!"

Teresa felt an icicle slide along her spine. "What do you mean?" she whispered. Her hand began shaking. "George, are

120

you—are you all right?'' Even as she asked, she knew he wasn't. She could hear it in his voice; he was scared. And he was hurting.

God, what had she done?

"Teresa, I don't have any time left. I *need* the stuff! I need to pay these guys, and I can't do that until I get this stuff to— where it belongs,'' he finished. "Teresita, please! These guys aren't joking around. They were in my apartment last night, and—'' He took a deep breath and Teresa swallowed a taste of bile.

"Where are you?'' she asked.

"A gas station, off 128,'' George answered quickly. "If I give you directions, will you—will you please get the stuff to me? Teresa, this isn't a game!'' She didn't answer right away. "Teresita, honey, please! I'm begging you, please! I've learned my lesson. I'm going to stop as soon as I can pay these guys off. Please, for God's sake, bring me the stuff!''

"Will you be much longer?''

Teresa looked up; in the doorway was one of the other guests.

She covered the receiver and shook her head. "No, I'm almost done.'' The guest nodded and disappeared around the corner. Teresa took her hand from the receiver and sighed. "Give me the directions.''

"Um, excuse me, Sister, could you tell me where can I find some food?'' Bluntness, Sam had decided, was about the only thing that worked anymore. He caught up with one of the sisters who straggled out of the chapel after the others, and cornered her with the question. Sister Mary Catherine had not, as Sister Mary Michael instructed, told him where to eat. And after searching through the guest house, he hadn't found one room that looked like it was set up for food preparation or ingestion.

The nun turned, startled at first. Then she looked more closely at him and smiled. "Father Samuel? Sister Mary Catherine told me you were freshening up. She said you'd be over to see me after Mass. Come along, let's talk in my study.''

It didn't take the mind of a genius to realize that he'd found Mother Mary Frances, and not someone who would direct him toward nourishment. At least, not the kind his body needed.

121

His stomach growled loudly. He grinned weakly and followed her to the main house, through the lobby, and into a spacious office off the back corridor.

She closed the door behind her as Sam entered, and gestured him to a seat. He sat, smiled, and hoped this reunion interview would be brief. According to Sister Mary Catherine, the mother superior was the only person here who'd actually met Father O'Keefe. So his first big hurdle—convincing her he was who he claimed to be—was about to be faced head-on.

"You know, I can't thank you enough for coming here like this. It was such a last minute thing." Mother Mary Frances sat next to him on the large, green, camelback sofa. She settled her cane next to her, and Sam saw that she really wasn't very old. Apparently, her failing eyesight made the cane necessary.

"It's really—no problem," Sam said, smiling back. She reminded him of his own mother. He wasn't sure why. He tried to keep in mind that Father O'Keefe was probably about a decade older than she.

"It was a miracle," she said, resting a hand familiarly on his. She patted it. "You've saved the weekend, I'm sure. Everyone is so excited. I think," she added, dropping her voice conspiratorially, "that a lot of the oblates went out and bought your book so you could sign it."

Sam smiled, trying to think which book that would be. And whether he had any idea at all what was in it.

"Lillian Marco came up unexpectedly," Mother Mary Frances continued. "Weren't you just down there? Anyhow, it's always nice to have her visit."

"Lillian," Sam repeated. The woman in his room? It would help to have a name.

"And Stephen has grown a lot, hasn't he? Of course, it was lucky we had room for her this weekend. How's she doing with the translation?"

"Uh, the translation." Sam's repetitions were beginning to sound lame, even to his ears. "Well, uh, you know, as well as possible, considering." It seemed a safe answer, and Mother Mary Frances nodded understandingly.

"I know it must be difficult for her these days. Jack's death hit her hard. Not to mention the financial problems he left behind for her to deal with."

"Uh, yeah."

"She was so depressed the last time she visited, but—well, she seems much more like her old self now, doesn't she?"

Sam nodded and felt the smile freeze on his face, wondering how long Lillian's 'old self' and Father O'Keefe had been having an affair. At least now, though, he had a name to give Al. Maybe the Observer could help him out with this problem.

"I met Teresa," Mother Mary Frances continued. "Lovely girl, but she seems troubled."

"Uh, yeah, well, I think she's—got some problems."

"Maybe the weekend here will help her sort them out. Sister Mary Michael talked to her when she called this morning; she got the impression the girl was coming here to see you."

"Uh, probably," Sam agreed helplessly. He glanced at his watch. "You know, I—told her I'd talk to her after I got my things settled, so I should probably. . . ."

"Oh, of course." Mother Mary Frances rose. "I just wanted to thank you again for coming on such short notice. You're a lifesaver. If you hadn't made it, I'd have had to give the retreat myself, and we both know how effective that would be!"

The woman laughed at her own deprecating remark, obviously not taking herself very seriously. Sam smiled, and she let go of his hand. "Well, I'll see you at Compline."

In the lobby, Sister Mary Catherine was waiting, her hands folded beneath her scapular, out of sight. She nodded at Sam as he passed, then turned to Mother Mary Frances.

"Mother, do you have a minute? There's something I need to speak to you about."

Sam left the two women to talk.

Outside, the night air had taken on a moist chill. Small drops of rain had begun to spatter the ground, but it was no more than a sprinkling yet.

Compline, Sam remembered from the horarium, was at nine. That left him a little more than two hours to talk to Teresa, stall Lillian Marco, and, most important, eat.

The scent of food wafted through the cool air, coming from one of the smaller buildings. With any luck, food—real, honest-to-goodness food—was only a few yards away.

CHAPTER
FOURTEEN

December 24, 1998
Stallion's Gate, New Mexico

"Admiral Calavicci, who is *that?*"

Gooshie's face wrinkled in puzzlement and concern as Angela followed Al into the Control Center. Even the auditors weren't allowed in here, so it was natural for Gooshie to question the presence of a woman whose outfit alone could get her sent to the nearest psych ward. But Angela, despite her outfit, was unflappable.

"Her name's Angela," he told Gooshie, shooting an unhappy look at the angel. "And since I'm too old for Santa to put coal in my stocking, I guess this is his way of punishing me for being a bad boy this year."

"Oh, no, I'm no' jour punishment," Angela protested. "I am an angel!" She looked around the large room—at the lights, Ziggy's console, the orb—her eyes opening as if she were a child on Christmas morning. She went over to Gooshie and stared at the console. "This is very pretty," she observed.

When she put her hand out to touch it, Gooshie practically swatted it back, his protectiveness of the hybrid computer coming out in an unthinking, almost paternal gesture.

"Don't touch."

Al raised one eyebrow; not that they'd ever faced the problem before, but he was surprised to see the sudden fire in Gooshie's eyes.

"Um, Angela," Al said, "let's talk, huh? Somewhere a little more *private!*" He moved forward, grabbed the woman's soft upper arm, and started dragging her—an impossible task if she hadn't been willing—toward his office.

"Jou know, I was wondering—" she protested halfheartedly, waving her fan toward the orb on the wall.

"You can wonder later!" he snapped, slamming his hand on the Identiscanner and waiting for the door to the office he had on this level to open.

Privacy. That's what he needed right now. That and some time to think. And a fresh cigar.

"What are you doing here?" he demanded, releasing her arm sharply once the door closed. "Aren't you supposed to be on assignment somewhere? Like Bosnia or the Middle East?"

Angela narrowed her black eyes. "Jou chould be grateful that *Someone* cares enough for *you* to keep making *my* life miserable!" Her voice rose up and out as she answered him, and Al winced.

"For me?" Al repeated.

"Jets! How would jou feel if Teresa died again?"

For a moment, he said nothing. Without knowing it, the woman had, indeed, hit a nerve. A raw one.

Or maybe she had known.

"All right," Al said, his voice lowered. "Just tell me what the hell you're doing here."

The portly woman moved closer and stuck her fan out, jabbing it at him angrily. "Jou stop using that word when jou talk to me!" she scolded. "This don' have nothing to do with *that* place!"

Al sighed, shut his eyes, and sank into the chair behind his desk. It was bad enough that Teresa was going to die sometime in the next twenty-four hours; but if Angela *had* to show up again, why, he wondered, couldn't she have shown up in Massachusetts, instead of here?

"Jou're wondering why I'm here instead of with Sam, huh?" the woman said. She turned to the bookshelves against the wall and looked over the titles, as if even one of them would make sense to her.

"Hey!" she exclaimed after a minute. "Jou were an astronaut?"

Al rose, grabbed the commemorative book on the Apollo space program from her hands, and put it back in its place.

"Don't touch that," he ordered. "Look, first you said somethin' about bein' in two places at once. Which," he added drily, "would be twice as many places as I'd like to see you." She glared at him. "Then on the way back here," he

125

continued, not giving her a chance to break in, "you said you wanted to see O'Keefe. So what exactly *do* you want?" he asked, narrowing one eye and lacing his words with sarcasm.

Angela fanned herself and bent over at the waist so she could see the books on the lower shelves. In most cases, when a woman leaned over like that, Al tried to sneak a look. This time, he didn't even try.

"Oh, jou were a chet chock too!"

"A what?"

"A chet chock!" She stood and looked at him. "Jou fly around in those big *planes!*"

"Jets," Al corrected her quietly.

"Chore, I thought so," she said.

"No, the word is—never mind." He ran a hand across his face and let out his breath.

He needed another cigar. He opened the humidor and pulled one out. Angela was still examining his bookshelves. He sliced off the tip of the fresh cigar, lit it, and began puffing on it until it was smoking nicely.

He could grill Angela for the next four months and still not get any answers, he thought. Or he could try not to panic, sit back, and wait for her to tell him what she was doing there.

Angela had proven a proverbial thorn in the flesh the last time she'd shown up, which hadn't been that long ago. But she *had* been instrumental in helping to keep Sam from being shot.

The memory of that Leap was still fresh in Al's mind. So was the last time he'd seen her, walking into an alley, ready to go to her next assignment. She had turned when Sam called to her, her face wet with tears, something Al had hardly expected. And, as she reminded them, Sam would not remember her when she was gone, but Al would, thanks to the fact that he wasn't technically "in" 1958, as she and Sam were.

And it was then that they realized she wasn't just a strange, possibly unbalanced woman. Somehow, she knew Sam's name; his real name.

"Who do you think I was really here to protect?" she'd asked, and smiled sadly as her mission ended. She reached forward and kissed Sam, leaving a large imprint of bright red lipstick on his right cheek. Then she turned to Al, smiling and looking sad at the same time. She held his gaze for several

seconds before she turned and walked alone down the deserted alley.

Angela was still perusing the bookshelves, his walls, the entire office, as if she'd never seen anything like it. Finally, Al's patience wore out.

"Look, what did you mean you screwed up the first time?" he asked.

She turned around and noticed the empty chair across from Al's desk. She dropped herself into it, none too gracefully. "Teresa died."

Her gift for the obvious was instantly apparent. "Yeah, she died. And you were supposed to stop that, right?"

"Oh, *si,* but I—got a little distracted." She flapped her fan and didn't quite meet his eyes.

"Distracted? By what?"

"Admiral?" Ziggy's sulking voice intruded, and Angela let out a small squeal of surprise. She turned to the small orb, a copy of the one that hung on the wall of the Control Center.

"Jou're very rude!" she scolded, waving her fan at the circle. "Jou should no' interrupt like that!"

Al raised an eyebrow, watched the monitor, and waited. No one had ever talked to Ziggy that way before. Except him.

"I should inform you, Ms. Jimenez," Ziggy responded coolly, "that according to my data, you're dead. Therefore, you cannot be 'interrupted.' "

Despite himself, a grin formed on Al's face.

"What is it, Ziggy?"

"I believe Dr. Beckett may be in need of your services, Admiral. Teresa has disappeared."

"What?" He rose quickly, crossed the room, and slapped his hand on the Identiscanner, only half aware of Angela behind him. "Where the hell did she go? Did this happen in the original history?" By the time he'd finished his verbal barrage, he was back in the Control Center. Gooshie, as he had expected, was putting the Imaging Chamber back on-line, his attention only momentarily diverted to Al's unwanted companion.

"I have no record on Teresa Bruckner's activities at the monastery in the original history," Ziggy explained calmly. "But I can predict with 45 percent accuracy that she has left the monastery to rendezvous with her killer."

127

That stopped Al in his tracks. He turned his gaze first to Gooshie, then to Angela. Then he glanced at the faceless computer. "Killer?" he repeated. "You never said anything about a killer!" He grabbed the updated handlink Gooshie handed him, still battling a renewed sense of frustration with the computerized ego Sam had doomed him to live with. "I thought you said it was an accident!"

"I never said it was accident, Admiral. You assumed that."

"So where did you get the idea that there's a killer?"

"Although the police never found any direct evidence of foul play," Ziggy began, sounding a little too much like an extract from an Agatha Christie novel, "there were several persons at the monastery that weekend who were strangers to all the sisters. Two of them were never identified. It's possible that someone wished her harm," the computer finished, her voice lowered. "Leaving the monastery so soon after having arrived seems odd."

"Yeah, especially if you're going there to get away from someone," Al snapped.

Angela was following him up the ramp, but he stopped her. "Later, Charo. I gotta help Sam find Teresa."

"Jou choold listen to—"

Al didn't wait to hear the end of her sentence. The Door opened and he stepped in, waiting for time to swirl around him and take him back to Sam.

Saturday, April 1, 1995   6:35 P.M.
Windy Bluffs, Massachusetts

Food, glorious food! There was *nothing* quite like it!

Ravenous and almost giddy from hunger, Sam Beckett opened the door to the second of the small buildings next to the main house. Feeling more like a bloodhound than a physicist, he'd followed the scent this far, and he was looking forward to ending his inadvertent fast.

"Father O'Keefe?"

It was the urgency in the young nun's voice that made Sam grimace and shut his eyes, praying silently for a miracle: make it go away.

He turned, reluctantly, to face the woman who was coming

toward him from the dining room—he could see the food inside, it was that close!—and tried to smile.

"Uh, yes, Sister?"

"I have a message for you. From your student, Teresa?"

Sam's stomach, already growling from hunger, began to knot. Years of Leaping had taught him to instinctively dislike a message left by the person he was there to help. It was never, ever good news.

"What about her?" he asked, trying to still the disappointment in his voice and concentrate on the task at hand. It wasn't easy with the aroma of lasagna and garlic bread wafting toward him from the next room.

"She said to tell you," the woman began, pulling a slip of paper from under her scapular and reading from it, "that she had to go meet someone, but she'd try to talk to you tomorrow." The young woman looked up and handed Sam the scrawled message. "She said she'd be fine. And not to worry."

If Sister No-Name hadn't added that injunction, Sam thought, he might not have. Or at least he might have ignored the worry until *after* he'd eaten. But the otherwise unnecessary reassurance, coupled with a look in the nun's eyes that told him more than he wanted to know, destroyed all hope of being fed.

"Why—did she say that?" he asked slowly.

The nun shrugged. "I don't know, Father, I figured you'd understand."

Sam sighed and shut his eyes. So close. . . .

He turned and left the building, glancing again at the handwritten note. On it, the nun's words came back to him: "Please tell Father O'Keefe I'll be fine. Tell him not to worry about me."

The message had slightly less urgency in written form, he thought. Maybe, after all, it was just a common reassurance: "Don't worry, I'll be back soon."

But Sam knew better.

He crossed the grounds, went back to the main house, passed Sister Mary Catherine—sitting at the desk in the lobby, silently studying a prayer book—and knocked on Mother Mary Frances' door.

"She's not in there, Father," Sister Mary Catherine said, turning to face him. "She's in the chapel."

A heavy breath escaped Sam's chest. He crossed the room. "Do you think you could interrupt her, Sister? I think—I think Teresa's in trouble and—I need to find her."

"In trouble? Did she leave?"

"Yes, and she's—I don't know where she is," Sam finished. "I need to find her!"

He couldn't remember a time when he'd been without a means of transportation when he needed to go after someone. He was frustrated and hungry and tired. And he didn't want to have to argue his point with anyone right now.

"Here." Sister Mary Catherine may or may not have understood what he was feeling. But she pulled the keys to the Grand Prix from her secret pocket and handed them to him. Her eyes never quite met his. "Mother said that whatever you needed while you were here—we were to make sure you had it. I'll tell her when she comes out."

"Thank you, Sister!"

He was halfway to the door when Sister Mary Catherine called out to him.

"Father O'Keefe!" He turned. "I'm sure your angel will help you find her," the young woman said, a conspiratorial look in her eyes.

He nodded. "He'd better," he muttered, realizing that without his "guardian angel" he didn't have much chance of finding Teresa.

CHAPTER
FIFTEEN

Saturday, April 1, 1995   7:05 P.M.
Rte. 128, Northern Massachusetts

The pressure of the leather shoe around George's right foot was growing. His foot was swelling, throbbing, and he knew he had to take the shoe off soon. He just didn't want to take it off when he might need to get away fast. His leg was propped on the passenger's seat next to him to ease the pain, but it hadn't helped much.

He'd finished a lousy hot dog and a Coke the clerk in the convenience store had sold him, and was working on his fifth cigarette. The combination of the impending sunset and rain was making it hard to see. But about half an hour after he'd called Teresa, he saw a pair of headlights slowly approach the service station and pull in.

It was a false alarm. The car, not Teresa's VW Bug, pulled up to one of the pumps. A teenager got out and started filling up. George sighed, relaxed a little, and tossed his cigarette butt out the window.

It shouldn't take Teresa this long to get to him, he thought. He was only about ten miles from the monastery, according to the directions he'd been given. He looked at his watch. He was toying with the idea of going after her when another pair of headlights slowed and pulled into the station.

''Shit!''

Swiveling quickly in his seat, George started the car. The Ford that had just pulled in was the one that had been following him earlier. His tail must have been doubling back, checking every stop and pull-off along the way, looking for him.

George had parked his car at the side of the station, out of direct view, and now he drove around the rear of the building and onto the road without being seen.

131

He hoped.

"Damn it all!" he muttered to himself, slamming his hands on the steering wheel and watching his rearview mirror. He drove west on 128, away from the monastery, a route he'd already decided on in case this very thing happened. He'd wait down the road, at another service station he'd passed earlier. Give it fifteen minutes, then go back.

If Teresa showed up, the man who was following him wouldn't recognize her. He just hoped she'd wait there for him.

He glanced at his watch again. By now, Belluno and his goon were going to be pretty damned anxious for their money. And all George had to show for his efforts was a promise from a woman who, twice before, had changed her mind at the last minute.

He couldn't let that happen again.

The crushed, nailless toes of his right foot reminded him of that.

Sam Beckett was, according to Ziggy, in a car, heading out Route 128 in what she considered was probably the most likely direction Teresa would have gone.

"Center me on him," Al ordered from within the Imaging Chamber. Almost instantly, time swirled in a violent vortex as his brain waves and Sam's came together at a moment three years in the past.

"Sam!" Al adjusted his image so that he appeared to be in the seat next to the physicist, who jumped with alarm at the sudden sight of the hologram.

"Al! Thank goodness you're here. Teresa's in trouble—"

"Teresa's in trouble, Sam," Al said, his words tumbling over Sam's in his haste. He stopped, as Sam had, and for a moment each waited for the other to continue.

Finally, Sam turned the windshield wipers on and said, "Go ahead, Al, what've you got?"

"Not a lot, unfortunately," the admiral answered, punching the handlink for any further data—or conjecture—Ziggy might have. "Just that it's possible it wasn't an accident after all. She thinks someone was responsible for Teresa's death. And—that she may be on her way to meet him."

"Or her," Sam pointed out.

"Yeah, maybe."

"She acted nervous earlier," Sam muttered, more to himself than to Al. He watched the road, trying to see through the rain. The area wasn't well lit. "Where does Ziggy think she's going?"

Al shook his head, feeling worse than useless at the moment. Ziggy was still spitting out percentages relating to Sam's attempt to keep himself from Leaping in the first place. He slapped the handlink.

"Ziggy hasn't got any data on anything Teresa did while she was at the monastery, Sam." He glanced up from the handlink in time to see them pass a well-lit service station on the other side of the road. Pulled in front of the store was a Volkswagen Bug.

"Sam! Isn't that Teresa's car?"

Sam turned to him, frustrated. "I don't know what kind of car she's driving, Al!"

"It's an old yellow VW Bug. That could be it, over there. Turn around, Sam, turn around. Let's see if she's there." He waved his hands in circles, waiting for Sam to turn the Grand Prix.

The rain had picked up. Sam had the windshield wipers on high now, and as he pulled into the station, Al saw the car more clearly.

"That's it, Sam. That's Teresa's car." He punched out and waited for Sam outside the store. There were three cars at the pumps and two parked in front of the convenience store. Al began running the license plate numbers and makes of the cars through Ziggy, searching for any correlation between them and Teresa.

"Al," Sam whispered as he got out of the car, "there she is. Talking to that guy over there."

Al looked up, turned in the direction Sam was pointing, and saw her. In the front of the store, near the newspapers, a young girl with a long brown braid and large dark eyes was talking to someone. Her companion had short-cropped blonde hair, a ring in one ear, and a tattoo on the opposite arm. He didn't, Al decided, look at all like Teresa's type.

"You think that's him?" Sam whispered. Al didn't answer at first; for a few seconds, he just stared at the girl, his first look at the child who had grown to womanhood.

133

"I'll sing you to sleep, honey. . . ."

"Al! Is that him?"

"Oh, uh, let's see. . . ." He shook the handlink, wiping the refreshed memory from his mind. "Ziggy doesn't know. Face it Sam," he said, putting the handlink in his side pocket, "until we get some information from Teresa herself, we're not gonna know a whole lot about what happened to her."

"Well, at least she isn't anywhere near where she died," Sam muttered, still watching from just beside the car. "Is she?"

"No," Al confirmed. "She dies at the monastery."

Sam wiped rain from his face. "Check her school records, Al," he suggested. "Maybe someone she knew who got into trouble, or—"

He stopped, and Al turned back to the girl. She was moving away from the man, her conversation over. Perhaps, Al thought, it had just been one of those "chatting in the store with strangers" conversations.

The man left and got into one of the other cars parked at the store. He had purchased some chips and a soda, and he sat in his Ford munching and drinking as if he were waiting for someone. Al pulled the handlink back out and checked Ziggy's records for the license number, but she came up empty.

"No data on him," he reported. "At least, not on the car. Ziggy's having trouble getting through to the Massachusetts Division of Motor Vehicles."

"I'm going to go talk to her, Al," Sam decided. He glanced at the admiral. "If that wasn't the guy she was here to meet—"

"Or girl," Al quipped.

"Or girl," Sam conceded, "then she may still be waiting for him." He started forward, then stopped, just before he put his hand on the door. "Al." The Observer looked up from the link. "Does Teresa—does she—well, have any—record? I mean—has she ever been in trouble before?"

Al shook his head and smiled reassuringly. "Nada," he reported. "Zip, zilch, zero. Far as we can tell, she's clean as a whistle."

Sam let out a heavy breath and went into the convenience store. Al followed.

"Father O'Keefe!"

Teresa, Al decided, was as lovely grown-up as she had been adorable as a child. She was, in fact, exactly the kind of girl Al would have had a hard time resisting—under vastly different circumstances. At the moment, all he felt for her was a kind of protectiveness he'd felt for only a few other people in all his life: people like his sister, Trudy, and Jimmy LaMotta.

And, on occasion, Sam Beckett.

"What are you doing here?" Teresa Bruckner was nervous. Scared. She looked around the store, her gaze flitting to the door, to the side window, behind her. She had picked up a magazine and was browsing through it when Sam came up behind her and touched her on the shoulder. That magazine was being twisted into a tube in her hands now.

"I got your message," Sam said. "And—well, I've been—doing this job for a while now." He grimaced slightly and shrugged. "It sounded like you needed help."

"Sam, the poor kid's scared out of her mind," Al informed him. "Whoever she was here to meet, my guess is he's likely to cause some trouble if he finds you here."

"Father, you shouldn't be here," Teresa said, before Sam could say anything further. "Please, everything's fine!"

Sam shook his head and smiled gently. "If everything were fine, you wouldn't have bothered with a message. You could have just gone off and come back whenever." He put his hands on her shoulders. "You left that message because you *weren't* sure everything was all right." He waited, and over the next few seconds, the young woman's eyes began to fill with tears. "What's wrong, Teresa?" Sam asked quietly.

"Nothing," she whispered, looking away. Al watched helplessly as she wiped her face and rubbed her eyes. "Nothing's wrong."

"You came to the monastery to get away from—someone, didn't you?" Sam guessed. Teresa stared at him, her hands twisting the magazine violently. "Who is it, Teresa?"

Something in the girl broke then. She shut her eyes tightly and took a deep breath; a tear trickled down her cheek.

"Oh, Father O'Keefe, I've messed everything up! I'm so messed up!"

Sam put his arm around the girl and held her close. He began to guide her toward the door. "Come on," he urged, "let's get back to the monastery." She pulled free, gathering

135

her composure once more. "We'll talk there," Sam promised. "I'll bet—well, maybe all you need is—another perspective."

With no need for further urging, and without another word, Sam led her outside. She pulled her keys out and unlocked her car door. Then she stopped and looked at Sam.

"I don't think another perspective's going to help much," she said. She pulled her braided hair around her shoulder and bit the end. "I think this one's going to take a miracle."

"Well, that's what we specialize in." He smiled encouragingly at her.

So did Al; but she couldn't see that anymore. She was too old, Al realized. Now that he *had* come back to her, as he'd promised, she'd never know it.

Saturday, April 1, 1995   7:17 P.M.
Windy Bluffs, Massachusetts

"I understand from one of the sisters," Mother Mary Frances began, "that you and some of the others have seen something here this evening. Something—that you could not explain by natural causes."

Mother Mary Frances was in the process of her third interview on the subject of Sister Mary Catherine's reported apparition. It was a process she would not normally have begun on the basis of one nun's word; however, there were, now, extenuating circumstances.

To begin with, Sister Mary Catherine had informed her, when she'd left the chapel earlier, that Father Samuel had requested (in a manner of speaking) to borrow the sisters' car in order to locate his student. When questioned about it, Sister Mary Catherine—a verbose but generally sensible woman— had told her that Father Samuel seemed frantic. But when Mother Mary Frances questioned Sister Mary Assumpta—who had given Teresa's message to Father Samuel—the sister said that the girl had seemed calm.

Father Samuel Francis O'Keefe would *never* jump to conclusions. He would never act panicked. And he would not, between here and his eternal reward, risk any activity that might not seem proper, cautious, and well thought out. Not Father Samuel.

Either Father Samuel knew more than he had let on about what had brought the girl to the monastery this particular weekend, Mother Mary Frances concluded, or *someone* had told him to go after the girl.

"Well, Mother, it was—odd," Sister Mary Joseph said. "We were just leaving Mass, and most of us were still meditating on the Holy Mystery. . . ." She dropped her gaze to her lap. "I can't explain what I saw, Mother. It was—it appeared to be a man, dressed all in white. A blue glow preceded his arrival, and—and he spoke at length with Father O'Keefe. He carried a rosary, I think. And a crucifix, which he devoutly kissed." The woman looked up. "While they spoke, they moved away from us, as if we weren't supposed to see them. Or hear them. And then another brilliant light appeared and—the man disappeared."

What Mother Mary Frances had secretly hoped for was a case of mass hysteria. It wasn't that she didn't believe in angelic apparitions, or visitations by the Blessed Mother.

She just didn't want them happening here.

So far, all the stories had been the same, despite the fact that each of the sisters had sworn that she had not talked to the others about the apparition after they had gone to dinner. And Mother Mary Frances had no reason to doubt any of them.

"Thank you, Sister, that will be all." Sister Mary Joseph rose. "But I will enjoin you, as I have enjoined the others, that you are not to speak of this among yourselves without permission."

"Yes, Mother." Sister Mary Joseph turned toward the door.

"And if you see anything else," Mother Mary Frances added, "please come and tell me at once."

"Yes, Mother."

Once Sister Mary Joseph was gone, and before Sister Mary Gerard came in, Mother Mary Frances indulged in another desperate prayer.

"Dear God," she whispered, "protect us from publicity!"

Saturday, April 1, 1995   7:25 P.M.
Rte. 128, Northern Massachusetts

By the time George returned to the service station where

Teresa was to meet him, the man in the Ford was gone. There was no sign of Teresa.

He pulled his car off to the side of the store, in the shadows, and limped over to the pay phone. His stomach hurt from all the aspirin, and his foot was gouged with pain. But above all, fear was still guiding him.

He dialed the monastery and waited for someone to answer the phone.

"St. Bede's monastery."

"Yeah, look," he started, shifting his weight to his good foot. "Is Teresa Bruckner there?"

There was a pause. A very long pause.

"I can take a message for her," the noncommittal nun on the other end said. "May I have your name?"

He hung up. "Bitch," he muttered under his breath. "Bitch, bitch, bitch!"

He swore for the next three minutes as he crept back to the car, pulled out a cigarette, and lit it. He smoked, cursing Teresa and the nuns and Belluno and Nicky. Finally, when he ran out of people to curse, he cursed his own stupidity for having gotten involved with cocaine in the first place.

And then, with the fiery pain in his foot driving him on, he began to plan the next step.

CHAPTER
SIXTEEN

December 24, 1998
Stallion's Gate, New Mexico

"All right, I don't care which one of you has them, I want some answers. And I want them now." Al stalked down the ramp, slammed the handlink on the console, and ignored Gooshie's wince. He glared at Angela, who stood there fanning herself. "Let's start with you."

"Oh, I don' know too much—"

"You said you screwed up the first time through," Al interrupted. He wasn't in the mood for Angela. Not the first time he'd met her, and certainly not now.

"Jets," she said, obviously not in the mood to elaborate now. She glanced at the Waiting Room. "Jou still haven't let me see Father Samuel," she added angrily, poking her fan toward him.

"You'll see him when—and if—I decide you'll see him." He turned away from her. "Ziggy, what have you got?"

"As I've told you, Admiral," Ziggy said, her computerized voice tight with irritation, "there are almost no records of Teresa's original accident."

"Have you run the license plates from the convenience store?"

"Three of them were from Massachusetts," Ziggy explained. "And I cannot gain access to the Massachusetts—"

"Yeah, yeah, you told me," Al interrupted. "What about the others?"

"None of the owners of the vehicles seems to have ever come into contact with Teresa Bruckner."

"Great." Al swiped a hand over his eyes. He was, he realized suddenly, very tired. It was late, and it had been a long day. And unless Sam got some sleep, Al was unlikely to get any. The curse of being an Observer was the need to be on duty as long as there was a chance Sam needed him.

"How 'bout students in her classes?" he tried. "Any of 'em involved with her?"

Ziggy's quiet hum filled the room for a moment. Angela stood next to Al, still fanning herself, though the room was far from hot.

"Teresa was taking graduate courses, Admiral," the computer reminded him. "She had four lecture classes this semester—quite a heavy load—with a total of 1,345 students registered for those classes. That number does not, of course, include students from last semester who might be involved with her now."

Al glowered at the orb for a moment, then turned to Gooshie. He started to order an overhaul of the apparently useless $14 billion machine when he got a better idea.

"Father O'Keefe," he muttered, glancing at the Waiting Room window. "He was afraid she was in some kind of trouble. Maybe he knew who she hung out with."

"Oh, *si,* that's a good idea," Angela commented, moving closer. "Jou and I can talk to him—"

"*I'll* talk to him," Al corrected her. He narrowed his eyes. "You just stay put and stay outta trouble, all right?"

"Jou don' understand," Angela protested, following him up the ramp. "I gotta job to do, too, jou know. And I can't get back to Teresa until I finish with *him!*"

Even Gooshie winced as her voice ascended.

"Get back. . . . Whaddya mean 'get back'?" Al demanded.

"I gotta help save Teresa," she explained. "I told jou, but jou did no' listen to me!" She slapped her fan at him. He pulled back.

"Are you tellin' me," Al started slowly, "that you're workin' both sides o' this Leap?"

Angela gave a low, guttural laugh. "Ees more fun that way, no?"

Al climbed the ramp, and Angela followed.

"Jou see, I got Teresa to go to the monastery, but now I got to help Father Samuel, because, jou know, he's going to do something very bad!"

"Really? What's he gonna do? Give someone a smaller penance than they deserve?"

"Jou don' know nothin' about penance, so jou better not talk!" the angel advised him angrily.

Al turned to her, his eyes narrowed. She'd hit a nerve. Another one. And despite his better judgment, he decided it was time to give Angela a taste of reality.

"Oh, I don't, huh?" he started. "Well, how 'bout losing your mom when you're just a kid and being put in an orphanage? You think that's kinda like penance?" He took a step toward her. "Or how 'bout losing your sister, 'cause some bureaucrat decides she'll be better off in an institution for the insane?" He took another step, heedless of the fact that Goowhie was watching him with horror. "And how 'bout losing your father when you're ten, 'cause no matter how hard you pray, it doesn't make a damn bit of difference 'cause no one's listening anyway?" He walked the rest of the way down the ramp and lowered his voice. "And how 'bout having your best friend trapped in time because *He*—" Al added, gesturing toward the ceiling with his finger, "thinks it's fun to Leap himself around from here to there and doesn't give a damn about how *he* feels about it!"

"That is no' penance," Angela said calmly. "That's just life!" Her fan moved back and forth in front of her face.

Al stared at her.

It was Christmas, he reasoned. That's why he'd blown up like that. Christmas was a hell of a time to begin with. But having an old-fashioned priest in the neighborhood, and an angel he'd just as soon forget hanging around, seemed to make it worse.

Christmas was bad enough. No need to make it worse by digging up old memories.

Al walked back up the ramp, focused his thoughts on saving Teresa, and pressed his palm against the scanner in the wall.

Father O'Keefe was resting on the bed, hands behind his head, his eyes shut. But he opened them and turned as Al entered, then swung his legs over the side of the bed to sit.

"Was Teresa involved with anyone?" Al had neither time nor patience for subtlety right now.

Father O'Keefe stood and looked past Al; Angela had followed him in, and was waving her fan and smiling.

"Who's she?" he asked, a bemused expression on his face.

141

"She's here to torture you if you don't tell me what I need to know."

Father O'Keefe cocked an eyebrow. "Ah. The interrogation at last," he muttered. He crossed his arms over his chest. Then he turned to Angela. "Are you Catholic?" he asked calmly. The woman glanced nervously at Al, then returned her gaze to the priest.

"Well, I was bap*tized* a Catholic, *si*, but—well, it didn't take so good, jou know?" She shrugged.

A slow, triumphant grin slid over Father O'Keefe's face. "It always 'takes,' " he said. "That's the problem." He shot a quick look at Al, then turned back to his primary target. "It's like a bloodstain. You can't wash it out. You can't bleach it away. The best you can do is try to find a scarf or a brooch to cover it up and hope no one notices."

The analogy, Al thought, was an odd one. But Angela blushed; and for the pleasure of watching her squirm, he might almost have stayed to chat a while longer.

But information on Teresa was at something of a premium right now. And Al wanted information.

"Teresa?" he asked, recalling the point of the conversation. Father O'Keefe turned back to him. "What kinda trouble was she havin'?"

"Her schoolwork," he said. It wasn't the answer Al had expected. "She'd been taking heavy loads the last two semesters. It was beginning to stress her."

"What about boyfriends?" Al prompted. "Or someone else who might be—"

Father O'Keefe shook his head. "Teresa never spoke to me about any of her friends," he said. Then his face wrinkled in puzzlement. "Or at least—if she did, I don't remember."

"All right, look, here's the deal," Al said, breaking rules he knew he'd have to answer for later. At the moment, he didn't really give a damn. "Teresa's gonna die in the next twenty-four hours or so. Sometime between now and Monday morning. And the only way we can stop it is if we know why she died to begin with!"

Father O'Keefe's eyes tightened with understanding. His gaze drifted away, trying to recall details that time traveling might have hidden from his conscious memory.

"I didn't know her that well," he apologized. There was genuine concern in his eyes.

"Do you know if she was—involved—in anything illegal?" He hated himself for asking.

"Oh, *si*, but only because of her boyfriend." Angela waved the fan, as if by doing so, she could dismiss all suspicion against Teresa.

Al's frustration with the woman mounted. "Why the hell didn't you tell me that when I asked you five minutes ago?"

"Jou didn't ask nicely," she said, narrowing her eyes.

"Oh, so manners are real important in Heaven, huh? What happens if you're rude? They kick you out?"

"Jou never gonna get there, so jou never gonna know!"

Rage overcame frustration. Al narrowed his gaze and opened his mouth. Then he remembered that he was still in the presence of a priest, and closed it.

"Who's her boyfriend?" he asked. He lowered his voice for control.

Angela shrugged. "Oh, some kid che met last year," Angela said. "He's got a big-shot father, and he thinks he chould have as much money as he wants. So—he started selling drugs."

"And Teresa knows what he's doing?" Al asked.

"Of course che knows!" Angela's voice rose. "Che's got the dope!"

"What?" Father O'Keefe and Al asked the same monosyllabic question together.

"Che has the dope," Angela repeated slowly, as if she were explaining it to a child. "Che found it and took it away. Now he wants it back."

"So her boyfriend's after her for the dope?"

"Chore, he's after her. That's why che went to the monastery. Che thought che'd be safe there."

"Well, obviously," Al said, his words spiked with sarcasm, "she isn't. He knows she's there!" He glared at the chubby cherub, then started for the door.

He left, deciding he might as well keep Angela locked in the Waiting Room, too. So far, she hadn't exhibited any angelic ability to walk through walls. But she *had* exhibited a strong desire to torment Father O'Keefe. And that, Al decided, was fine with him.

A very unhappy head programmer was waiting for him when he came back down the ramp.

"What is it, Gooshie?" he asked, dreading the answer.

"Uh, the auditors called again, sir," he said. He wasn't quite sweating, but he was definitely nervous. "They said—they were expecting you back to explain the, uh, little problem they found in the books?"

Damn! Al pulled a fresh cigar from his pocket. "Tell 'em I'll be there as soon as I can." He bit off the end of his cigar and lit it, then grabbed the handlink. "Better yet," he said, starting back toward the Imaging Chamber, "tell 'em I'm on vacation in the Bahamas spendin' the $230,000 I embezzled from the Project."

He stepped through the Door, never dreaming that Gooshie would take him literally.

CHAPTER

SEVENTEEN

The rain was gentle, a spring rain that fell in a soft sheet. It hadn't been difficult to drive through, and it wasn't bad for a walk.

After returning to the monastery, Sam and Teresa had searched in vain for a place to talk in private. But the guest house was full, the other dependencies had been locked up—and, Sam noted, the food was gone—so Sam suggested a walk.

"In the rain?" Teresa asked, surprised by the suggestion.

"Sure." Sam shrugged and grinned. "Didn't you ever take a walk in the rain?" The girl shook her head, disbelief mounting in her expression. "Well, let me tell you, it's great for clearing your head. And if you want to have a good cry—well, no one will ever know."

Teresa laughed quietly, and they parted to change into more appropriate clothes.

Now, with Sam wearing Father O'Keefe's windbreaker over his clerical garb, and with Teresa dressed more warmly in an Irish sweater, raincoat, and hat, they walked companionably over the rocky land that bordered St. Bede's, picking their way carefully in the dark. Sam had brought a flashlight that he had found in the bedroom. It lit their way dimly.

In the distance, the ocean sound was a soothing lullaby. And over the last half hour, Teresa had slowly begun to unfold her problems, laying them out like so much dirty linen, waiting, with each revelation, for rejection.

Instead, what Sam heard was more like a replay of his own days at MIT and Harvard. Not with quite the difficulties Teresa had managed to get herself into, but with much the same basis.

A lot of pressure. Intelligence without the experience to deal

145

with all the opportunities that presented themselves. And a lot of homesickness.

"So you went to the gas station to give George back the dope," Sam finally concluded. They had gone quite a distance from the monastery, and, as Sister Mary Catherine had promised, it had been a nice walk. But Sam was leery of getting too close to where the ground dipped toward the water. Even from a distance, he could see that the bluffs were steep and slick with rain.

Teresa hugged herself and looked up at Sam. "I think—I think the people he got the drugs from—hurt him when he didn't give them their money." She took in a shaky breath. "But he wasn't there when I got to the station—" She didn't finish the sentence, but Sam understood.

"You think they got to him before you did," Sam said quietly. Teresa was shivering, but Sam doubted that it was from the chill.

"I never wanted anything bad to happen to him!" Teresa protested. "That's why I never went to the police, Father, I—I didn't want him to go to jail!"

"He's a drug dealer, Teresa. Jail might be the only thing that convinces him to stop."

Teresa said nothing. She stared into the night, toward the cliffs.

"Who was that guy you were talking to at the store?" Sam asked.

For a moment, he wasn't sure she'd heard him. Then, very quietly, she said, "I don't know. He started chatting with me, you know? About the weather? I don't think he knew I recognized him. But I've seen him before." She looked back then, and her face was wet. It could have been the rain, Sam thought. "At Grendel's Den, last night," she explained. "He was there. And then, later, when I was waiting for the T, he showed up again."

"But you don't know his name?" Sam pressed. Teresa shook her head.

One of the men following George, Sam guessed. Maybe someone waiting for him there, at the station.

"If he was waiting for George to show up," he theorized aloud, "then maybe no one's gotten to him yet. Maybe," he suggested, only half believing himself, "he's still all right."

Teresa sniffed and wiped her face. Her braided hair was tucked under her coat to keep it dry, but she tried to finger it all the same. A nervous habit, Sam realized.

"Then where was he?" she demanded. "He called me and told me to meet him there. He wouldn't have just taken off before I got there. I've got what he needs!"

Sam let out a deep breath. He didn't have an answer. The rain was beginning to pick up now, and a wind had started to blow. "Look, let's go back to the guest house. We could both use a good night's sleep, right? First thing in the morning, though," he said, his voice firm, "you and I are going to go down to the local police and turn over that stuff."

"No, no, Sam, she can't do that!"

Sam half turned in surprise, his foot catching on a rock as he did. He caught himself, and Teresa put a hand out to help him.

"Al," he muttered.

"What?" Teresa asked.

Both the admiral and Sam opened their mouths to answer. But Teresa got the next words out first. "Did you say—Al?"

"I said," Sam covered quickly, "*I'll* think about what we should do." He grimaced at the inanity of his words and waited for Al to provide some more information. He hated having the Observer show up without notice. Not only did the sudden appearances often startle him, but he had to cover his outburst when he was with others.

"Sam, we gotta talk. Angela says that Teresa's boyfriend is dealing dope on the streets."

"What about George?" Teresa asked. Her eyes were on him, studying him. As if she suspected he was not the man he appeared to be.

"George!" Al exclaimed. "That's great, Sam. You got a last name?"

"Well, uh," Sam hesitated, starting back toward the guest house. "Look, the guys who're after George," he said. "If he hasn't paid them yet, they're probably not going to kill him until he does. Or until—they get their drugs back, right?" he added. Al, he realized, was walking back to the monastery with them.

"What about the guy from the store?" Teresa asked. "Maybe he followed us back here. . . ."

147

"The one that—was probably working for the drug dealers?" Sam glanced at Al for an answer, but it was obvious that the handlink—and Ziggy—were being less than helpful.

"No data," Al reported his face a picture of frustration.

Ahead of them, across the road, the lights in the monastery were almost all off. The porch light at the guest house was still on, and so was the one outside the main house. Sam could see several people leaving the chapel, and he realized he'd missed the final service of the day. He wondered, halfheartedly, if he'd been slated to officiate at that, too.

"If he did," Sam said, watching a few of the nuns follow the oblates out of the main house, "he's not going to be able to get to you anyway. He'll have to wait until tomorrow. You should be safe in the guest house."

"*Should* be," Teresa repeated bitterly. "If they got to George, they can get to me."

They crossed the road, and Sam scanned the parking area for any car that resembled the Ford from the convenience store.

"I don't see his car," he reported to both Al and Teresa. The admiral punched the handlink again, then shook it.

"Ziggy says there's less than a 10 percent chance Teresa dies tonight." He looked at the girl who shivered beneath Sam's touch on her arm.

"Why don't you go on back to your room and get some sleep," Sam suggested. "I don't think anything's going to happen tonight."

Teresa nodded and started for the front door. Then she turned. "Aren't you coming?"

"Uh, yeah, in a minute." Sam waved her on, waiting for her to leave so he could find out what Al had. Or, perhaps, supply information he was lacking.

But Teresa lingered another minute, staring into the distance, her hands thrust into the pockets of her coat. Finally, she looked back at Sam and said, "Do you ever wish you were a kid again? And—well, that someone was there to—make things right?"

Next to him, Sam heard Al let out a long, low breath.

"Lots of times." He cleared his throat. "You know, when I was—well, when I didn't know what to do, sometimes, I'd—call my family." Teresa's face wrinkled in a spasm. "Have you

148

tried calling your brother, Teresa? Have you told him—''

''Mr. Perfect?'' Teresa cut in. ''The one who never screws up, never gets into trouble, always knows exactly how much is in his bank account, and takes his car to Quicky Lube exactly every three months? You know, I visited him at Christmas, and he even had a schedule worked out for when to wrap the presents!''

''Kevin?'' Al's incredulity matched Sam's. He couldn't help it: he started to laugh. Remembering the awkward sixteen-year-old, trying to envision him at almost thirty, the contrast was too sharp. Kevin Bruckner had been a lot of things as a teenager: anal-retentive hadn't been one of them. He'd learned that somewhere along the way.

Teresa, he noticed, had the grace to smile.

''Teresa, I'm sure he'd understand. If you explained it to him. Have you tried?'' he asked.

The answer came after a long silence. ''Well, not exactly.'' She cleared her throat. ''You don't understand! He's—he's so *right* about everything! And he keeps telling me that if I want to be grown-up, I have to take responsibility for my own life. And that I shouldn't—''

''Come crying to him to fix things if they don't work out?'' Sam finished. Teresa's words sounded painfully familiar. He stared ahead, avoiding the curious look Al was giving him.

''Yeah!'' She looked at him. ''How did you know?''

Sam pulled his lips together, then said, quietly, ''I—had an older brother, too.''

555-2231.

Like a mantra, the phone number came back to him again. In his mind, he heard it ringing. He was at the Project, in his office, and the phone was ringing. If he picked it up. . . .

''Sa-am!'' Al warned quietly, almost as if he could read Sam's thoughts. Sam hunched his shoulders and avoided the older man's gaze.

''Was he Mr. Perfect?'' Teresa asked bitterly.

''He was to me.''

One phone call. Just one call, and he'd be home. He could see Tom again, talk to him, hug him. He could see his mother, and Katie. . . .

''Do you believe in angels, Father?''

The question took Sam off guard. He shot a furtive glance

149

at Al, wondering if his inadvertent exclamation earlier had, indeed, given them away.

"Uh, well, I—guess so. In a manner of speaking."

Teresa pondered his answer for a moment. Then, quietly, sadly, she said, "I never told anyone. But when I was little— I had an angel. Well, two, actually."

Sam held his breath. He heard Al sucking on his cigar.

"An angel?"

"They—they said they were there to help my brother win a swim meet. But—later on, I found out—they'd saved Kevin from being kidnapped."

She stopped and turned to him. Still, he didn't breathe. "They promised they'd come back. . . ."

She stared at him, her gaze moving back to the road from time to time, almost meeting Al's eyes, as if some aura of his presence were visible to her. But mostly her gaze was locked on Sam's face. A long, penetrating stare.

"Sometimes," she finally said, looking down at the ground, "I wish—I just wish things were that simple again. I wish it was that easy to believe." Then she turned and went inside.

As soon as she was out of sight, Sam turned to his holographic companion. "Al, do you think—do you think she suspects who I am?"

Al was staring at the spot where Teresa had been standing. It took a moment for him to shrug and answer. "Dunno." Al shook himself free from whatever thoughts Teresa's memories had dredged up and turned to him.

"So who's Angela?" Sam demanded, asking the first question that came to mind. The admiral's earlier reference had made absolutely no sense to him.

"Oh, uh, Angela's, uh—" The admiral squirmed and shrugged, then finally met Sam's eyes. "Never mind," he said at last. "The thing is, Sam, Teresa's got herself into a bad situation here. Angela says she's got drugs that her boyfriend's supposed to be peddling on the street."

"From what Teresa said, he's the middleman," Sam said. "He sells the stuff to the local dealers, and they get it out on the street. Problem is," he added, pushing his hands into the pockets of the windbreaker to warm them, "this is the second stash of coke Teresa's found and—well, apparently, George's suppliers aren't too happy with him right now."

150

"Aren't too happy?" Al repeated drily, narrowing one eye as he tilted his head back. "Sam, if George is the local supplier for the street scum, then that means his suppliers are right up there in the cartel! They're not going to be unhappy; they're going to be dangerous! Big time dangerous!"

Sam winced as Al's hands flew outward as exclamation marks. "So what are we supposed to do? Teresa went to the gas station to meet George, and he wasn't there. She thinks they already got to him."

Once more, with an air of defeat, Al punched, jabbed, shook, and slapped the handlink. But nothing came through.

"Damn!" he swore quietly.

"Al, what's wrong with Ziggy? I mean, normally she's a little hard to deal with, but—well, this is ridiculous."

"Oh, it's nuthin', Sam. She and I are just havin' a little—difference of opinion!"

"Yeah, well, that difference of opinion is leaving us without much information about this Leap."

"Don't worry, Sam," Al said, pushing the colored box back into his pocket. "I think I got an alternative source of data." The look in Al's eyes made Sam decide against asking for more details.

In the distance, Lillian Marco and a young boy—undoubtedly her son, Stephen—were coming toward them from the chapel. She saw Sam and waved. He nodded to her and held a hand up in a half-greeting.

"Al, what have you found out about Lillian Marco?" Sam asked under his breath as the woman neared them. Al looked up, caught sight of the woman, and gave her an appreciative gaze.

"Well, she's not bad looking," he commented. "A little less makeup would be nice. . . ."

"Al!"

Al tilted his head. "Look, I'm sorry, I haven't had a chance to grill Father O'Keefe," he snapped. "I've had a couple other things to worry about besides who the man is shacked up with!"

"I'm not sure anymore that that's what's going on, Al," Sam said. He was speaking more quickly; the woman was almost in hearing range. He turned to Al. "Mother Mary Frances said her husband died a little while ago," he explained. "And—she

151

asked me how her work on the translation was going. Al, I think—I think she works for Father O'Keefe.''

Al gave him a sour look. "Well, that takes all the fun out of it.''

"Al! Just see what you can find out, all right? About *anything*.''

Wordlessly, Al punched open the Door and stepped through. It closed with a sigh, and Sam found himself mimicking the sound; he hadn't meant to be sharp with Al. He was just frustrated. And a bit concerned about being stalked by drug dealers.

And he was very, very hungry.

He wiped the rain from his face and smiled at Lillian Marco as she and her son closed on him.

"Missed you at Compline," the woman said as she came over to him. She had taken her son's hand, presumably to keep him from running off.

"Uh, yeah, I—something came up.''

"Let me put Stephen to bed," she said. "Then we can talk.''

"Uh, well, actually," Sam said, "I'm kind of beat right now. How about—tomorrow?''

Already, he realized, he was booking himself a busy day.

"Tomorrow," Lillian repeated coolly. She took in a deep breath that came out very slowly. "Fine," she agreed. Icicles dangled from her voice. "We'll talk tomorrow. At *your* convenience. Never mind that I spent all day and part of last night driving up here to talk with you. Never mind that all I have to count on right now is what you're taking away from me. Never mind any of that! *You're* tired, so we'll wait until tomorrow!'' She turned to Stephen. "Come on, honey," she said. "Let's go to bed.''

Without another word, the angered woman went into the guest house.

Part of Sam wanted to call her back, to apologize. But the rest of him was bone-weary. So he kept his mouth shut. He gave her a moment's head start, then followed her in.

CHAPTER EIGHTEEN

December 25, 1998
Stallion's Gate, New Mexico

"They said *what?*"

Al Calavicci, still in full dress uniform, stalked from the Imaging Chamber, glancing only once in passing at the Waiting Room. Inside, it appeared that Angela and Father O'Keefe were playing cards. As he passed the room, Angela looked up, as if she could sense him, and put her cards on the small table that Gooshie had taken into the Waiting Room.

"Uh, I'm sorry, sir, they—well, they were very insistent." The redheaded programmer was sweating profusely, barely able to make eye contact. His hands were moving over Ziggy's main console: Al doubted they were doing anything but keeping Gooshie from crawling out of his skin.

"*They* were insistent?" Al slapped the handlink on the console, ignored Ziggy's protesting whine, and maintained his unbroken glare. "Since when do three green government CPAs take precedence over a Leap?" Gooshie made a small sound, not really a word. "Look, Sam and Teresa have drug dealers chasing after 'em. They're in a monastery full o' nuns who aren't gonna be able to do a damn bit of good if some Colombian drug lord shows up with a semiautomatic. And as far as Ziggy can tell," he added, waving at the useless orb on the wall, "Teresa's still gonna die! Now how in the hell could that be any more important—"

"They—they said you have twenty-four hours to account for—well—for—uh—" Gooshie's excuse died in his mouth.

"To account for *what?*"

"For, um, your—vacation, sir."

Al waited vainly for reality to check in. But the misery in

153

Gooshie's eyes and the long silence after that last statement told him reality had taken a hike.

"Vacation?" he repeated quietly. Another set of Gooshie's sweat glands burst open. "What vacation, Gooshie?"

"Uh, well, sir, I guess—um, I guess the auditors—didn't realize I was—I mean, that you were—" The man stopped and, as bravely as he could, tried to meet the admiral's glare. "They took me seriously."

"About what?"

Gooshie winced, ducked his head, and stared at the disco lights in front of him. "Uh, well, I guess about you going— on vacation with the $230,000 you—They gave you twenty-four hours to account for the money before Senator Weitzman closes us down."

For a moment, Al could think of nothing to say or do.

Gooshie stood there, drenched in sweat. Ziggy hung silently on the wall, depressed over her inability to convince Al that Sam had returned to 1995 to undo all the good he'd done since he'd stepped into the Accelerator.

Three years in the past, Sam was dodging drug dealers and cocaine addicts. A five-year-old child Al had promised to return to was waiting for him to keep that promise before she died at the age of nineteen. Six levels above them, three lovely sirens had just sung their song. And Al, ever the seaman, knew what happened to sailors when the sirens sang.

Then, with the fate of Project Quantum Leap, and the lives of Sam Beckett, Teresa Bruckner, and who knew what else hanging in the balance, Ziggy suddenly pulled out of her self-induced depression. From the orb on the wall and from the console caressed by Gooshie's touch, a song burst forth. A song Sam must have programmed into her long ago, before anything like *this* night had ever occurred to him.

Oh, Holy Night,
The stars are brightly shining. . . .

"Obscene" was the only word that came to Al's mind to describe her sudden joviality.

"Gooshie!" Al yelled, "shut that damn thing off!"

Instantly, Gooshie tried to respond. But Ziggy had a mind of her own at the moment. A perverse, calculating, manipulative mind.

The song was apparently carried into the Waiting Room: Al

saw both Father O'Keefe and Angela stare around them, wondering at the source of the familiar carol.

Oh, hear the angel voices.

Al waited only a moment longer. Then, convinced that Gooshie wasn't able to override the computer's determination, he moved toward the elevator.

He had to get out of here. Away from the carol. Away from the past.

"It's after midnight, Admiral," Gooshie said quietly as the door to the elevator opened.

Al turned and met the man's wistful gaze. And from the corner of his eyes, Al saw Angela in the Waiting Room. She was grinning from ear to ear.

"Merry Christmas, sir," Gooshie said.

Al couldn't bring himself to answer.

Of all the things Father O'Keefe had expected since waking here in this strange, blue room, two of the furthest from his imagination had just happened. He hadn't expected to hear a Christmas carol, and he hadn't expected to be visited by an angel. Or a woman who claimed to be one.

As the recorded music played through his cell, he and the woman stopped their card game for a time. It was the woman who recovered first. She grinned, then gave a deep, throaty laugh, and turned back to him.

"Jou see?" she said lightly. "Jou get to be here for Christmas this year after all!"

"Christmas?" he repeated drily. "In April?"

"No, is no' April in *this* year!"

It was the second reference to a time displacement that Father O'Keefe had heard. The first he'd discounted: after all, if the admiral had been anywhere near serious, the repercussions for humanity would be inconceivable. Certainly the man wouldn't be talking about it as if he'd just discovered a new restaurant!

On the other hand, here was this stranger, someone who claimed not even to work on this Project, now making the same reference.

Christmas in April. A woman who claimed to be an angel and had a gift for poker. A man who claimed to be an admiral, who claimed to work on a top-secret time-travel project. . . .

155

Suddenly, Father O'Keefe began to wonder just what was going on here. Perhaps it was some kind of mental experiment, designed to disorient people. Perhaps the government, aware of the current trend in paranoia fiction, had concocted a test to see what a normal subject did after being subjected to a staged kidnapping such as his.

"So what year is this?" he asked. He leaned back in the chair, watching the woman carefully.

"1998," the woman responded. "But that does no' matter right now. What matters is what jou are doing to Lillian Marco!"

He narrowed his gaze and pulled his lips together in a fine line, a technique that often made graduate students start to sweat. The woman seemed unimpressed. He rose from the card table to stretch his legs.

"Lillian Marco," he said slowly, "was a top-notch research assistant until her husband died. But ever since then," he explained calmly, "she's been given to bouts of depression, and her work has suffered. I can't afford to keep her on as my assistant any longer. I have a deadline." He paused and shook his head. "And besides, it's no business of yours."

"Oh, *si,* it is. I told jou, I'm—"

"An angel, right," he cut in. He crossed his arms over his chest and nodded. "According to the admiral," he said, gesturing to the door through which the man had left a few minutes before, "you're here to torture me. Now, which is it?"

"I told jou, jou chould no' listen to him," the woman ordered sternly. "He's just jealous of me."

"Jealous?" This was getting better every second.

"He likes to think he's the only one looking out for Sam, but he don' know what angels do. Right?"

O'Keefe nodded. "Right." He uncrossed his arms, still moderately uncomfortable in the strange suit he wore (it was somewhat immodest in certain aspects), and leaned his hands behind him on the table. "In all my years as a priest, I've never heard of any apparition of angels in which they appeared—well—"

"Jou say one word about Clarence, and I'll—"

"Clarence?" In a moment, the reference became clear, and her story began to crumble in his mind. "You mean the angel in that movie?'' He could see by her eyes that she did. There was a dare in her expression. But for O'Keefe, it only confirmed his first theory: this was some kind of mind game they were playing here.

"Clarence was a fictional character. And besides," he added pointedly, "even in the movie, technically he wasn't an angel."

That took his would-be tormentor aback. "What jou mean, he was no' an angel? Chore he was! He came back to save—"

"If you'd studied your theology a little better before trying this," he said, "you'd know that angels aren't people who die and come back to earth to help others. Angels are pure, bodiless spirits. *Not* reincarnated humans!"

Both a sense of victory and a sense of irritation punctuated his words. He saw Angela's face twist in puzzlement, confusion, dismay. Then she regrouped and strode closer to him.

"Jou don' know everything about angels," she said. "I *am* an angel. And I used to be alive. So, jou see? Jou're not always right!"

"You used to be alive?" He was relaxing again: whatever manipulation these people were trying, they hadn't done a thorough enough job on their homework to make it work. Now, he could just stand back and watch them try to recover.

He wondered, detachedly, if they'd try another game, now that this one had failed. Or would they just send him back and try again with someone else, someone more gullible?

"*Si*," Angela said. She stood, animated by the prospect of talking about herself. "I was a singer in New York in the twenties. Then I got a part in a *big production*—" the volume and pitch of her words went up, as did her hands, "and when I was in rehearsal, I fell off the stage and went esplat."

"Esplat?"

"*Si*. I died."

She seemed to take that well, O'Keefe thought.

"Only when I got up there," she went on, gesturing to the ceiling, "they said I was too vain. So, now I have to help other people. And—"

"Wait a minute." He put his hand out. This wasn't what he'd expected her to pull. "You died, but you were too vain? So you were sent back to—what? Help others?"

157

"*Si*. And—to learn humility," she confessed, her eyes cast down in a doleful manner.

O'Keefe watched her for a minute, putting together a new scenario.

"You said earlier that I won't remember you when you finish your work here."

"No. That's how it works."

"Why?" he pressed. This could be a bit more fun than simply staring at the blank walls. "Is that part of the—humbling experience?"

"Jou know," the woman said slowly, "jou could be right."

If he hadn't still been holding onto his "paranoid government's antigovernment paranoia" theory, he might have thought that this idea really *had* just occurred to her for the first time.

"Jou see, no matter how much I do for someone, as soon as I leave, they forget I did any of it. So—"

"You never get credit for it."

The woman looked pleased, as if he'd given her the answer to a test question. She came over to the bed and leaned one hand on it, facing him at a right angle. "Jou know, maybe if I'd gotten that at the beginning, I'd be done by now."

"But that's my point," O'Keefe said. He wasn't sure why he was taking an interest in this conversation. "You see, real angels never 'get done' with their work. Because their work isn't what they are."

"What jou mean?" Angela asked, bordering on anger again.

"I mean that angels don't stop being angels, any more than human beings stop being human beings. It's like—"

He didn't have a chance to finish. The door to the Waiting Room opened, and the admiral appeared again. He looked very tired, O'Keefe thought. And not very happy. In one hand he carried an unlit cigar, and in the other, a manila folder crammed with papers.

"Sorry for the interruption," he said, not looking in Angela's direction. "Just thought I'd see how you're doin'."

His voice was quiet, almost defeated.

"Oh, him and me, we're having a good time!" Angela volunteered. O'Keefe said nothing.

The admiral waited just inside the doorway, almost as if he expected something from the priest. He alternated between meeting the man's eyes and looking away, hesitating just long enough for O'Keefe to realize that there *was* something he wanted. Like a child trying to ask his parents a favor, but afraid of being refused.

"Just a minute, Admiral," he said quickly, preventing the man from leaving. "May I ask you a question? To help settle a discussion Angela and I were having."

He decided to buy himself some time. Maybe he'd figure out what the admiral wanted. He moved away from the bed, crossing the room to stand closer to him. He had judged the man to be about his own age; but the age in his eyes was much older, as if the man had seen centuries more of life than O'Keefe would ever know.

"Sure. What?" Clearly, the idea of settling a dispute between the priest and the would-be angel appealed to him; especially, O'Keefe guessed, if that settlement came down against the angel.

"In the Navy," he started, "does the captain of a vessel always hold the rank of captain?"

The question puzzled Al. Dark eyebrows pulled together, and in a reflexive, habitual gesture, he shoved the cigar between his lips.

"No, not always. Why?"

O'Keefe turned his attention from the admiral for the moment. He looked back at Angela. "That's exactly my point."

"What point?" Angela demanded.

"You're not an angel. You're just a person—like me, or Al—trying to get rid of the dirtiness left on your soul. In your case, pride. And you've been given a second chance to do that."

Angela glowered and fanned herself furiously. "Jou have no right to tell me that I'm no angel!"

O'Keefe smiled. "And you," he said, "have no right passing yourself off as something you're not." He glanced back at Al. "It's like the difference between a captain in the Navy and the captain of a ship: it can be either a rank or a position."

"Yeah," the admiral chimed in, apparently enjoying the way this conversation was going. "You can be the captain of a ship and *still* be just a commander." Looking pleased with himself, he pulled a lighter from his pocket and held the flame to his stogie.

159

"Or," the priest continued, turning back to the woman, "you can be a captain of a ship and hold the rank of captain."

"So?" Angela shrugged. "What's that got to do with angels?"

"It's the difference between what you are and what you do. You may be a human acting like an angel. But you *aren't* an angel."

The dark anger on Angela's face brought a Cheshire cat grin to the admiral's.

"Humans have a body and a soul," O'Keefe said quietly. "Matter and spirit. Angels are pure spirit. Put another way, humans get a second chance; angels don't."

"What?" The admiral pulled the cigar from his mouth and leveled it at the priest.

With that word, O'Keefe's attention shifted.

"Haven't you ever said to yourself, 'If only I'd known, I'd never have done this or that'? Or done it differently?"

Al cleared his throat and shrugged. "I dunno. Maybe. Yeah. Well, who hasn't?" he demanded, jabbing the cigar forward.

"You can't see the future, can you? You do your best based on what you know at the time, the facts before you."

"Yeah, right." Al put the cigar back between his lips and let out his breath. "Right."

"You're limited by matter—by your body—"

"Hey! I got news for *you*, Father. This body ain't limited by—"

"By time," O'Keefe finished, ignoring Al's attempt to change the subject. "You can see only through the eyes of time. But the future is a foggy cloud. A mist. All you can do is guess what it will be like, what you will be like, what you want the future to be like."

He turned back to Angela. "It's not the same when you aren't constrained by time, is it, Angela? When the past and the present and the future merge together into one unending now? When time itself is nothing? If you could see the future, it would all be so clear, so easy, so beautiful."

Angela's eyes misted, and the hand that held her fan trembled for a moment, then dropped to her side.

"The angels, real angels, aren't bound by time. They know the future, the past, the present. To them, it *is* all one continuous now."

Beside him, he heard the admiral clamp his teeth on the cigar. It wasn't a sound one could normally hear.

"Every angel, from the moment of creation, knows the future. So for an angel, there is no second chance. All his choices and chances happen in one eternal, present moment."

"So that's it?" The admiral broke in again, his voice suddenly angry. "Forgiveness is based on the fact that we can't see the future? You're sayin' that *if* we knew the future—we couldn't be forgiven?"

O'Keefe turned back to him. Cigar smoke wafted around Al, and through the mist, he saw the ghost of a brokenhearted altar boy.

O'Keefe knew what Admiral Al had come here for. Not directly, not consciously. But timidly, like a frightened child.

He was looking for something he had once believed in.

"No. The angels know their past, future, and present as a never ending now. Those who choose to, live there. For those who don't, damnation is an eternal denial of the truth. They don't want to believe in who they are—or to accept it."

Al snickered. "That the *current* Catholic teaching?" he asked, and turned away. "I seem to remember somethin' about hellfire and unending torment when I was a kid."

"Think about it," O'Keefe said quietly. He decided not to point out that Al had just admitted to being what he'd denied earlier.

Al looked back, hesitating just long enough to give O'Keefe another opening.

"The Church teaches that Lucifer sinned by declaring himself higher than God. He didn't want to be the greatest of the angels. He wanted to be God. He wanted to be something he wasn't." He looked at Angela. "Isn't that an unending torment? Trying to be something you're not?"

The admiral had opened the door. He held the man's eyes. "And always knowing you're going to fail."

Let us then remember what the prophet says . . .
"In the presence of the angels I will sing."

**—THE RULE OF ST. BENEDICT:
CHAPTER 19**

CHAPTER
NINETEEN

December 25, 1998
Stallion's Gate, New Mexico

Ziggy was singing "Joy to the World" by the time Al reached the administrative offices where the three auditors were. The brief conversation with O'Keefe had left him unsettled. And he doubted that his meeting with the three women was going to leave him feeling any better. But if these women were as literal-minded as they seemed to be, he had to deal with this embezzlement issue head-on.

He'd collected the paperwork from his office and brought it with him. Without admitting it consciously, he'd almost hoped the priest might have an answer for him, some way out of this bind. If Angela had left the room, he might have explained the problem to the man, felt him out about what he had done.

But with Angela there, he wasn't about to discuss the issue. And, now that he thought about it again, he really didn't see what good talking to a priest would do, anyway. It had been a stupid idea.

He knocked on the door where the auditors were sequestered. There was no answer. He knocked again, but there was still no answer. He opened the door.

All three women had fallen asleep. Jenna and Christine had their heads on their desks, their arms folded under them for pillows. Kay sat on the floor, in a corner, her head lolled back against the walls, her legs curled under her. All three had been snoring when the door opened. All three woke the moment they heard the sound of Al clearing his throat.

"Sorry to bother you," he started awkwardly. The auditors woke by degrees. Kay was the first to fully regain consciousness and she stood, sweeping her hair back from her face, yawning, and straightening her suit.

"Admiral. I'm sorry, but—well, for us it's about two in the morning."

"Yeah."

As Jenna and Christine sat up, rubbed their eyes, and smoothed their clothing, he felt a certain pity for them. Six or more hours traveling from DC, then another eight locked in this room. And on Christmas!

"Look, I got guest rooms set up for you. Didn't realize how late it was until Ziggy—" He didn't finish. The women were glancing at each other, as if they had something to say. Whatever it was, Al guessed, it was going to be bad news.

"Did your programmer mention that we'd called DC?" Christine asked.

"Yeah." He took a deep breath and sucked on his cigar. By now, he'd eliminated all hope of a merry time with these three, so what the hell? He might as well not worry about offending them with cigar smoke. "And obviously, you don't know a joke when you hear one," he added, a snap to his words.

"We know a joke, Admiral," Jenna said. She stretched languorously, and Al was reminded of a cat: lithe and limber and. . . . He shook his head to clear the thought from his mind. "The problem is, $230,000 isn't a laughing matter. Smallwood is breathing down Senator Weitzman's neck about this."

"Oh, so now it's Weitzman's problem, huh? Since when did Weitzman decide this Project was worth losin' sleep over?"

The women looked at each other again and, as they had earlier, they congregated around Jenna's desk, leaning back against it, facing him. "Senator Smallwood's got some big trouble right now, Admiral. I don't know if you get the *Washington Post* out here, but he's all over the papers. Smallwood's suspected of diverting funds from some of the projects he has oversight of."

"Indictments are expected to come down against him in two days. Maybe less," Kay added. "So he's decided to divert some of the attention."

"Meaning?" Al asked.

"Meaning that he's tossed down the gauntlet," Jenna explained. "He's as much as told Senator Weitzman that if the indictments come down, the first thing he'll do is point out every irregularity in every project Weitzman's involved with. Including this one."

Al glanced from one of the women to the next, and then the third. Finally, it began to make sense. Joe Weitzman currently sat on several Senate subcommittees. The one that headed up this Project was only one. Another, Al knew, was the Ethics Subcommittee.

"Weitzman's pulling the plug on Smallwood, so Smallwood's planning a little political blackmail," Al muttered. He chuckled to himself and shook his head. "Merry Christmas after all!"

"This is no laughing matter, Admiral," Christine said.

"If Smallwood goes down in flames," Kay continued, "so does Quantum Leap. Or at least, it's going to suffer smoke damage."

"So what's your opinion? Is Smallwood guilty?"

The three women checked each other's reactions before saying anything. It was, finally, Jenna who answered him.

"He's got a son who's been in and out of jail and rehab clinics for the last three years," she said. "Apparently, the Senator's been—at least marginally involved in his activities."

"If Smallwood isn't guilty," Kay added, "why would he threaten to expose the Project?"

"If he *is* guilty," Al countered, "why would he threaten to point out a $230,000 problem to the press, when that's the kind of trouble he's trying to avoid?"

"Because there's a new Congress, a new Senate. A new regime, Admiral," Kay explained. She sounded, Al thought, a lot like Weitzman. "Public opinion tends to run against black-funded projects like this one. If they find out that two and a half billion dollars a year has been spent on a time-travel experiment they didn't even know existed—well, whether they're for it or against it, you can be damn sure it's going to capture more attention than the OJ trial three years ago. A lot more attention than one more corrupt senator."

Al winced. He'd done his time in DC, he remembered Pentagon politics. And politicians. He'd learned to live with them, even to suck up when necessary.

But he'd never learned to like them.

Still, very little surprised him anymore. Certainly not this.

"So you came out here expecting to find a discrepancy," he said. "Why'd you call Weitzman?"

"With what we found, we had no choice," Christine said. "We have orders, too, Admiral."

He sucked the cigar for a moment, regarding them evenly. They didn't seem to be antagonistic. If anything, they seemed to want to help. The question was, how much political blood did *they* have coursing through their veins?

"Rather than having Quantum Leap come out in the press, Senator Weitzman will close it down and conduct a private investigation. At least, that way, the whole project doesn't have to undergo a detailed investigation by CNN."

Somehow, Al thought, chewing idly on his cigar, Weitzman had a way of making even a gesture of support seem like an attack.

"Here." He tossed the sheaf of papers he'd brought with him on Jenna's desk, deciding that, of the three, his best shot was probably with her. She took them immediately and began riffling through them. The other two women looked over her shoulders.

"That oughtta explain it. All $230,647.15."

He turned to leave.

"Admiral." Jenna's voice stopped him. He looked back. All three women had trained their eyes on him. "You mentioned something about—guest rooms?" She smiled slightly.

He wondered briefly if there were any way he could pass his own quarters off as a guest room.

Saturday, April 1, 1995   11:30 P.M.
Windy Bluffs, Massachusetts

It was typical of Father Samuel to avoid a confrontation, thought Lillian Marco. After dinner, she had combed the guest house, the chapel, and every other public place at the monastery looking for him, but no one had seen him. He had hustled her off to her own room when she'd begun to cry, and promised he'd talk to her later. But when "later" finally came, he'd put her off again. Now that the rain had stopped, she sat in a chair on the front lawn of the guest house, sipping instant coffee and staring at the sky. She had tried to sleep; but for more than an hour, she'd listened to the low snoring of her son and had known that sleep would not be coming.

If there was one thing she'd learned about Father Samuel in the years she'd known him, it was that he hated emotions. He hated, most of all, emotional women. They were, to him, something so foreign that the sight of a woman in tears turned his stomach. At least, that was the impression he gave her.

So perhaps her emotional display hadn't been the best way to convince him to try to change his decision. And it certainly wasn't her normal way of approaching him. But the last few months had left her raw. Jack's death; having to drop her dream of finishing her doctorate; suddenly facing the reality of being a single parent. And then his bombshell last night.

Well, it had left her a little emotional. And it had been a long, exhausting drive up here from North Carolina, one she hadn't planned on making. Not until he'd come with the news that "in spite of all you've done for me in the past, I will no longer require your services."

He could have put it in a letter, she thought, but no, he'd flown all the way to Charlotte to tell her to her face. Why? To see her pain? To see her anguish? To share in her suffering?

She had lost her temper when Father Samuel came to see her. She had become enraged, accusing him of insensitivity, of unfairness, of a host of things. Some of them, in retrospect, were valid.

But some of them were born only of her pain, and they were, after all, unfair. When her tantrum had ended, and Father O'Keefe had left, she realized that Stephen had been watching and listening throughout.

She finished her coffee and put the cup in the grass at her feet. Then she stared at the stars. They were so bright, so fixed, so steady and unchanging. They were just about the only things in life that were.

A noise from behind startled her from her reverie. Lillian turned, seeing the shadow of her son in the doorway to the guest house.

"Stephen, you're supposed to be asleep."

The child walked toward her without actually seeing her; he was sleepwalking. Again.

She met him halfway across the lawn, moving him around the roots of the tree that spread out around him. She guided him back to the house, put him into bed, and curled next to him as he stroked her hair and went back into a deeper sleep from which he wouldn't wake until morning.

"Where's Daddy?" he murmured once.

"Daddy's gone to Heaven, sweetheart. You'll see him again someday." She kissed the top of his head and smelled baby shampoo. He curled closer to her, as if, for the moment, he wanted once more to be a part of her.

She held him, wishing the same thing.

The angel had appeared again. Sister Mary Catherine and Sister Mary Gertrude, leaving the Compline service, had seen him talking with Father O'Keefe. He appeared while the girl, Teresa, was there, but she seemed unaware of the apparition.

"Perhaps," Sister Mary Catherine whispered, breaking the night silence, "it's the girl's angel. Perhaps the angel has appeared for her."

Sister Mary Gertrude said nothing. They both stared at the spot, watching as the girl went back into the guest house. Several minutes later, with the light preceding him, the angel vanished.

"Should we mention it to Mother tonight?"

"Wait until tomorrow," Sister Mary Catherine urged. "Father O'Keefe felt the girl was in danger; if she's back here now, no harm will come to her overnight. We can tell Mother about it in the morning."

Silently, the two sisters moved off, walking back to their enclosure to pray about the sight they had seen.

But Sister Mary Catherine couldn't sleep. She could barely recite a rosary, though she knew that to remain in prayer after seeing such a sight was only right. Still, her mind was racing.

Something wonderful was happening at St. Bede's. The Lord never sent signs like that unless He was preparing to ask something heroic of those who saw the signs.

Would everyone eventually see the angel, Sister Mary Catherine wondered. Or would only a few of them witness the spectacular sight? Was he a messenger, preparing them for yet another visitation? Perhaps by the Blessed Mother herself?

The possibilities, endless and magnificent and exciting, passed through Sister Mary Catherine's mind for hours, until she felt she would burst from anticipation. Something exciting

169

was going to happen, and she wanted to be there, to be part of it, when it did.

Saturday, April 1, 1995   11:47 P.M.
Somewhere off Rte. 128, Northern Massachusetts

George had found a place to hide for the night. Backtracking almost an hour from the monastery, he'd checked into a small hotel, the kind he would *never* normally frequent. He hadn't seen the Ford Taurus again, but he didn't trust that he wasn't still being followed. He checked in under an assumed name and paid cash. It was the sort of place that didn't bother to question his lack of luggage.

His choices had become very narrow at this point. He couldn't go back to Boston without the drugs; and he couldn't go back with them, not without some assurance from Belluno that he would be given time to distribute the dope and get them their money.

An hour ago, he'd broken down and called his father, a long-distance call that really seemed to stretch the phone capacity of the hotel. After a fifteen-minute wait, he was connected to the house he had once called a home. But there was no good news to be had.

Not only was dear old dad playing the tight-assed politician that he'd been born to play, but he was also playing the righteous preacher as well.

As if the old fart hadn't been the one to get him started on the dope to begin with.

"But there is a time and a place for it, George," his father said, the pomposity of his words making George sick. "I've told you, I can no longer afford to support you or your habit. If you want to get help, that's different."

"I don't need help," George shouted. "I need $400,000!"

"You're on your own, George," the politician said coolly. "I'm sorry."

George had hung up on him, wondering if he'd be sorry when they found his son's mutilated body floating in Boston Harbor.

Probably not, George decided. What his father failed to understand—or maybe he did—was that the drugs weren't

170

George's problem. It was the money. And all the things that money could buy. The clothes, the car, the expensive dinners, the apartment on Beacon Hill. All the things he'd dreamed of since he was a kid. Things his father had always promised him—"one day."

Well, "one day" came along when George had finally wised up and realized Dad wasn't ever going to make it happen for him. George made it happen for himself. No more used cars and knockoff suits and eating out at fast food joints. No, when he got wind of Dad's nasty little habit a few years ago, he'd realized he had a golden opportunity to break free. And that's just what he did, working himself up the corporate ladder of the drug world. Not too high, of course. Not high enough to bring too much attention to himself.

Just high enough to pay for the things he loved.

For a while now, he'd even envisioned finding a nice girl, settling down, having a couple kids. But after the trouble Teresa had caused, he was beginning to think twice about that.

Lying on the twin bed, listening to the squabbling couple in one room and a moaning hooker in another, he began to realize that domestic bliss probably wasn't going to be part of his life.

So, once he got through the next twenty-four hours, he was going to have to ditch Teresa. Too bad, really. The girl had been a lot of fun.

Since he hadn't been followed, and since he was violating the "no smoking" sign posted in his room, the person knocking on the door must be the woman who had checked him in. He hurriedly stubbed out the cigarette on the sole of his shoe and kicked the butt under the bed. Not that he could do much to hide the smoke in the air.

"Yeah?" he called. He moved to the door; unfortunately, it didn't have a peephole.

"Mr. Smith," the wavering voice of the woman who had checked him in called, "I need to speak to you."

Faced with the inevitability of having to make nice to the old bitch now that he'd been caught, George opened the door.

"Mr. Smith, this man here says he needs to talk to you. About—a government matter." The elderly woman stepped aside, and George saw the man from the Ford, the glinting earring, the tattoo on his arm. . . .

"Oh, shit!" He tried to bolt from the room, but with

171

extraordinary grace and obvious foreknowledge, the man put his left foot out and tripped George. It would only have made him stumble momentarily under normal circumstances; but his foot was now so badly swollen, so painful, that he howled from the pain as his toes came into contact with the man's foot.

"Oh, dear," the woman moaned quietly.

"It's all right, ma'am," the very polite goon said, pushing George back inside his room. "I don't expect you'll be needed further." And with that, while the woman held a hand to her mouth in fear and surprise, the man closed the door and locked it.

"Now," he said, grabbing George's right arm and shoving him back onto the bed, "you and me are going to have a nice chat."

CHAPTER

TWENTY

December 25, 1998
Stallion's Gate, New Mexico

It might have been two in the morning for the auditors from the East Coast, but for Al Calavicci, it was just a little past midnight. He needed to check on Father O'Keefe once more. And Angela. He rubbed his eyes wearily as he rode the elevator back to the main level; any sleep he got tonight would be icing on the cake.

It was the coincidences that had begun to irritate Al the most; well, after Angela. But even she only added to his growing sense that there was something odd about this Leap, as if Someone had designed a collage of several of Sam's previous Leaps and put them all together into one. It left Al with a creepy, crawly sense of déjà vu that wouldn't go away. It crept up his spine and lodged in his brain, and couldn't be shaken.

From the moment he'd first seen Sam, it had been growing. But now, it was taking on a life of its own. Adding to the coincidences of the three Leaps Ziggy *had* correlated, there was the fact that Sam had Leaped, once again, into April first; and if ever the boogie man had a tendency to show up in a Leap, Al thought, it was on April first.

The lights in the Control Center had been dimmed when Al returned, a technological nod to the fact that it was night. Gooshie was under Ziggy's console again, apparently adjusting or fine-tuning something. And in the Waiting Room, what appeared to be a heated conversation between Angela and Father O'Keefe was in progress.

"Ziggy," he said, ignoring the sound of the Christmas music in the background, "what's Sam doin' now?" There was no answer, so he repeated the question. "Ziggy, what's Sam doing?—Are you listening to me?"

173

"Admiral, I'm quite capable of listening to you rant, playing Christmas carols, and keeping an eye on the changes you and Dr. Beckett are proposing to wreak on history." Ziggy's sudden haughtiness was almost a relief. It was better than having her pout in silent, sullen withdrawal.

"Well?"

"I cannot, of course, be certain unless you lock onto his brain waves, but I predict with 78 percent accuracy, based on a slight increase in his alpha-wave readings, that Dr. Beckett is sleeping."

Well, that was good news, Al thought. One down, three to go.

"Gooshie, soon as you've finished—whatever you're doin' there—" he said, waving his hand in the direction of the half-visible programmer, "why don't you get some sleep, too?"

"Uh, yes, sir," the man grunted from the floor. Al started up the ramp to the Waiting Room. "Oh, Admiral!" Gooshie hoisted himself up and brushed his coveralls off.

"Yeah, what?"

"Captain Davalos called, sir." Al winced without meaning to. "He's decided to stay over tonight at the Project, what with all the—well, unexpected guests."

Al grinned to himself; knowing Davalos, he should have expected something like that. "He got a bunk assignment for the night?"

"Yes, sir, he has one of the guest rooms."

"Let's hope it wasn't one of the ones I gave the auditors," Al muttered, and turned to pay a final visit to Father Samuel Francis O'Keefe.

"Jets! Jets, that's jus' what ees like!" Angela was waving her arms when Al walked in, and Father O'Keefe was actually smiling. Neither reaction was what Al had expected. Or, secretly, hoped for. It looked suspiciously as though O'Keefe and the angel were actually getting along.

"The choirs, they are so beautiful!" Angela continued, ignoring Al as she stepped closer to O'Keefe. "And esometimes, I get to sing with them, jou know?"

O'Keefe turned to Al, rose from his seat on the bed, and said, "Admiral, we have a problem."

"Yeah. Angela!" he agreed, shooting a quick, sharp look in her direction. "You finished with him, yet?" he asked, pointing with his final cigar of the night toward the priest.

"Oh, him and me, we are having a good time, jets? We are eschewing off the fat."

"*Chewing* the fat," Al corrected.

"Whatever!"

"Actually, Admiral, I've been informed that it's Christmas," O'Keefe continued, ignoring the sniping between Al and the woman who'd been keeping him company.

"Yeah. So?"

"Mass," the man said. "I must celebrate—or at the very least, attend—a Mass."

"Oh." Al shoved the stogie between his lips and had a strong, perverse desire to deny the demand outright. Fortunately, sheer cussedness wasn't needed for him to disapprove the man's request. Practicality, rules, regulations, and a host of other good reasons gave Al the answer he wanted.

"Well, sorry, Father, but I'm afraid we can't do that. See, you're not allowed outta this room—"

O'Keefe took a step toward Al. It was a silent, threatening gesture. "I am a Catholic priest," he said quietly. "And I take my faith very seriously. Now, if you're concerned about letting me leave here for—security reasons," he guessed, "I'll sign any papers you like that I won't mention anything I've seen here when you return me to—well, to wherever."

Al narrowed his eyes and tilted his head back. "Yeah, well, that's one concern," he agreed, "but not the only one. See, if Sam is ready to Leap and you're not here, well, we can't get him back." It was a simplified answer, not entirely correct because of its simplicity. But what the hell?

"There must be provisions," O'Keefe protested. Angela, Al noticed, was keeping her mouth shut. For once.

"Well, actually, no—"

"Admiral," O'Keefe started, moving closer again, "it's Christmas Day. Surely there must be a church around here somewhere that you could have me taken to—under armed guard, if necessary—just for an hour? One hour, Admiral. Is that so much to ask?"

"Chore," Angela piped up. "Jou know, there is a nice little Catholic church in Alamogordo. . . ."

"Angela!" Al interrupted. Nothing like giving away the location of the Project! What else had the woman told

175

O'Keefe, he wondered. He turned away from her once she looked safely silenced and faced the priest. "Look, I dunno where the nearest Catholic church is," he began.

"I told jou, there's this one in—"

"But the problem is still the same," Al cut her off. "We can't risk letting you leave the Project. I'm sorry."

The conversation was beginning to bother him, and he turned to leave.

"A portable altar, then?" O'Keefe asked quietly. The haughtiness had left his voice, and Al turned, suckered by the man's tone; he was practically begging.

"A what?"

"A portable altar," the man repeated. "One that's been consecrated. Priests in war often carry them so they can administer the sacraments before a battle. With a portable altar and—well, with some wafers and wine, I could celebrate a private Mass here."

Al met the man's eyes evenly. There was something in the priest's words, something in the way he was looking at Al, that made him cringe internally. He didn't show it; long years in the Navy—not to mention Vietnam—had certainly taught him how to hide the fact that he felt like the shish in the kabob.

"Look, Father," he said quietly, pulling out his cigar and noting that there wasn't much of it left, "it's after midnight. All the churches in this area are gonna be closed. And—well, people in this area aren't exactly aware of our existence to begin with."

"Priests *are* well known for keeping secrets, Admiral," O'Keefe reminded him.

"Maybe. But there's still the problem of finding a priest who's even *got* a portable altar, right?" He flailed his hands and waited for the man to agree. He didn't. "Besides, I got more'n enough to keep me busy without havin' to hunt down a stone slab with a bunch o' relics in it!"

"Would it hurt to try, Admiral? Just to try?"

Al took a deep breath and shut his eyes. The urge to yell, "Yes, dammit, it *would* hurt!" was almost overwhelming.

Instead, he said calmly, "I'll see what I can do." It was a truthful, noncommittal answer.

There wasn't *going* to be anything he could do. Between the time he got to bed tonight and the time he found himself back in the Imaging Chamber with Sam, he sure as hell wasn't going to be searching the streets of Alamogordo for a priest with a portable altar and a few extra Communion wafers.

Father O'Keefe held his gaze a moment, then nodded and said, very quietly, "I see." And Al knew he did.

He turned away and started for the door. "You comin'?" he called over his shoulder at the angel. "Or you gonna chew the fat with Father O'Keefe all night?"

"Oh, I can stay here, or I can go with jou," the woman responded, as if debating whether to have custard or pudding for dessert. Al slapped his hand on the scanner.

"Well, make up your mind," he ordered, turning to look at her. She was fanning herself and watching O'Keefe; the priest was watching Al.

"Hokay, well, I'll stay here for a while, then," Angela decided. "Samuel and me, we are getting to be good friends, no?" she asked cheerfully.

But O'Keefe didn't release Al from his gaze; the double image of the priest and Sam Beckett stared unblinkingly at Al as the door slid open.

"Was it the Catholic Church, Al? Or was it God?"

The question froze Al to the spot, his hand lifted to the cigar in his mouth.

"What?"

O'Keefe took two slow steps toward Al, then stopped and crossed his arms over his chest. "Was it the Church that let you down? Or was it God Himself? Clearly, it was one or the other."

"*Go to hell!*" was the phrase that rose unconsciously to Al's lips. He stopped it just before it rang through the Waiting Room. Somehow, even now, that just wasn't something you said to a priest.

"Why won't He listen to me, Father? It isn't fair! Poppa just came back! He said we'd be together again! He can't die! God can't let him die!"

"God's ways aren't our ways," came the uncomforting answer from the other side of the grille. *"When we ask God to hear our prayers, we cannot have selfish motives!"*

"What's selfish about wantin' God to heal my dad?"

"Keep your voice down, son. . . ."

177

Al shut his eyes and wiped a hand over his face. Then he turned.

"It was God," he answered. He took a deep breath, and it shook when he let it out. "It was God."

He left the room, escaping memories he wasn't about to start dealing with now.

Not now.

Mark Davalos had turned over the security detail to his shift replacement at ten o'clock. But instead of going home, he headed for the Project compound. There were spare rooms there, he knew; he'd slept over a few times. He flashed his badge at the kid standing guard at the main entrance and found his way to the lower level. He had a list of who was here, on duty or on call, and he knew which rooms were empty. He selected one of them at random, called the programmer in the Control Center, and told him which room he'd taken.

If Dr. Beckett had not Leaped earlier this afternoon, Mark might have returned home. But since Dr. Beckett was in the middle of a Leap, Mark had decided to hang around, just in case. There'd been enough strange happenings today to warrant it, he told himself.

He decided not to think about the fact that it was cheerier here than at home. At least, on Christmas.

No complaints, though. People who had dedicated themselves to this Project often didn't have time to dedicate themselves to anything else. That was the fact of it, and Mark had made his choice when he moved out here. Not that he didn't have friends, even family, back East, if he wanted to fly out there.

But it was hard to go home, where he couldn't discuss his job. And it was always a disappointment, somehow. The magic of Christmas was gone. It had been for decades.

Maybe if he'd had kids, he'd be able to bring it back. . . .

He fell asleep, dreamed about pudgy angels and beautiful auditors, and woke to the sharp whine of the internal monitor on the wall.

"Captain Davalos. Are you awake?"

He bolted upright; he'd heard that voice before, but not often. A soft, sultry woman's voice.

"Yes. Uh, what's wrong?" He rubbed his eyes, shook his

head, and ran his fingers through what was left of his hair. Then he glanced at his watch. It was just a little past midnight. Maybe there was some small celebration at the Project that he hadn't known about. . . .

"Admiral Calavicci would like to see you in his office. Immediately."

Scratch that thought!

He muttered a quiet curse, wondering whether it was his unauthorized stay-over or some new emergency that warranted the admiral's personal attention. With his luck, it could be both.

"On my way." He heard a soft click as the monitor shut off. He dressed in less than thirty seconds, and made his way up to the admiral's office.

The door was open, Admiral Calavicci was pacing, and his cigar was mostly gone. He looked up when Mark came in.

"Didn't know you were plannin' on takin' another shift tomorrow," he started without preamble. Mark smiled, recognizing in the man's brusqueness a kind of gratitude he wouldn't put into words.

"Well, sir, I thought—it might be wise to stay on duty."

"Hmm." The admiral pulled his cigar out of his mouth and stared at the burning end. "Listen, I got a question I wanna ask you. It's none of my business. . . ." He waved a quick hand to dismiss the question. "It's—well, it's kinda personal," he continued. The man looked as if he'd been dusted with itching powder. He paced almost uncontrollably, his hands making wild gestures that betrayed his anxiety.

"A personal question, sir?" Mark smiled, oddly pleased. In all the years he'd known the admiral, the man had never asked him anything personal; not unless it had a direct bearing on his work. This time, Mark knew, the question wasn't so much about him as about the admiral. Or some aspect of the Leap.

For several more seconds, the admiral paced. Then he stood behind his desk, straightened three piles of already straightened papers, and finally looked up.

"Sir?"

Calavicci took a deep breath and asked, "Are you Catholic?"

Mark glanced away; it was hardly the question he'd

179

expected. But then he nodded and said, "Yes, sir. Not—the best one in the world, by any means, but—yes."

"Hmm." Admiral Calavicci looked at him. "You, uh, you still—go to Mass?" he asked, gesturing again with his free hand. The cigar was almost gone now.

"Well, yes, sir, when I can. Sometimes I pull shifts here that—"

"Where do you go?" the admiral interrupted.

Mark shrugged and tried to keep a straight face, the import of what the admiral was asking him finally sinking in. After years—decades—of being a nonpracticing Catholic, it seemed that Admiral Calavicci was actually looking for a place to go to church. On Christmas! And *he*, Mark Davalos, was the man Admiral Calavicci had come to for advice.

"Well, sometimes I go into Alamogordo. But there's also a nice little church over near Tularosa," he suggested.

Admiral Calavicci nodded once and fiddled with a letter opener on his desk. He didn't quite meet Mark's eyes. Then he pulled his cigar from between his lips, glanced at the burning butt, and stubbed it out in his ashtray.

"You happen to know the priest at either o' those places? I mean," he added quickly, "would either of 'em know *you*?"

Mark considered the question. "Well, Father Joseph in Alamogordo."

The admiral nodded and let out a long breath. "I got a favor to ask you." He glanced at Mark. "A *big* favor. And—you're free to say no."

Mark felt a momentary thrill in the pit of his stomach. Something about the admiral's demeanor told him that "big" wasn't quite enough for what he was going to ask.

"Just say the word, sir."

The admiral smiled tightly and tilted his head back.

Mark braced himself.

CHAPTER
TWENTY-ONE

Sunday, April 2, 1995   1:05 A.M.
Somewhere off Rte. 128, Northern Massachusetts

Drugs, George decided, made strange bedfellows. Consider, for example, the man sitting across from him in this room right now. The man was playing solitaire, the deck of cards provided by the hotel manager, and periodically munching on a pizza he'd had delivered to the room about twenty minutes ago. Where in the hell the man had found a pizza delivery service out here at this hour was beyond George.

But then, maybe the pizza guy worked for the same people the man with the earring worked for.

"Frank Anderson, D.E.A.," the man had said, identifying himself with a badge the moment the door had closed on poor Mrs. What's Her Name. "You're in deep shit with Mr. Belluno, George. I'm here to give you a chance to dig yourself out. At least a little."

A little less than an hour later, the Drug Enforcement agent had made his point; and George had made a deal. He'd get the coke from Teresa, turn it over to the government, and have a little chat with them about what he knew of Belluno's organization.

Yeah, it was risky. But at this point, with a choice of dealing with the D.E.A. or Nicky, George decided on the D.E.A. After all, so far *they* hadn't smashed any of his body parts.

For the last half-hour, they'd been working out the plan. George told Anderson he'd take him to where the drugs were in the morning.

"My girlfriend's got them," he'd explained early on, almost sickened with himself for how quick he was to cave in. "She's at a monastery." At least, he rationalized, this guy wouldn't hurt her.

181

They'd find Teresa, explain the situation, and get the drugs back, nice and quiet. No one had to know she was involved, Anderson promised, and she wouldn't be charged. Belluno would never trace the drugs back to her because Belluno, the agent said, hadn't followed George. He was, according to the government's best knowledge, sitting in Boston, stewing and bitching about the fact that George was missing.

Nonetheless, the man insisted on keeping a watch overnight. And while George took a sponge bath of sorts, tried to rebandage his foot, and ate three pieces of pepperoni pizza, the man sat calmly at the desk in the room and played solitaire.

His win rate made George suspicious.

"So, I don't have to actually testify against this guy, right?" George asked, glancing through a magazine in the room. It didn't remotely interest him.

"Nope," the man said. He scratched the back of his neck and placed a black eight on a red nine.

"What if someone leaks what I say?" George pressed. "Or what if he gets word that—"

The man turned to him, very slowly, his eyes dark and bright at the same time. It unnerved George. "Look, you got two choices. It's me or it's them." He gestured with his thumb toward the door. "You want them? Go ahead, I won't stop you. But you'd better have damn good health insurance."

He turned back to his game, fingered the .38 Smith & Wesson in his holster, and placed another card.

George swallowed four ibuprofen tablets with a slug of beer the man had also ordered up, and flipped through the magazine some more. The problem with hotels this far down the evolutionary scale, he realized, was that most of them didn't have TVs in the room.

"So all the charges," George began after another minute. The man's silence was almost impermeable; it was hard to get up the courage to break through it. "They all get dropped, right?"

The man laughed quietly. "What are you, stupid? They get reduced, Georgie!" He turned again, swiveling in his chair. "We let you go completely, and Belluno's gonna know you talked." Then the man smiled and looked back into memory. "You do the crime, you do the time," he recited in a singsong voice.

He smiled so sweetly, so compassionately. George felt his skin crawl.

"Yeah, right," George murmured. "But—all we're talking about is possession, right? Six months? Maybe—parole, huh, 'cause it's the first time?"

"Maybe," the man cooed. George didn't like the sound of his answer.

"Maybe? I don't like 'maybe,' " he said. He dropped his legs over the side of the bed and sat there. He didn't want to stand on the bad foot unless he really had to. "You said possession, one count. No charges of dealing."

"Okay, okay! Possession. One count." The man was going to win another round of solitaire, George saw. Another round. . . . What was that? Four for the night so far? What were the odds of that?

George watched the man complete the game, then said, "How about poker? You play poker?"

The man turned, grinning. "Yeah," he said, eyeing George as if he'd just caught a rabbit in his headlights. "I play poker."

George limped across the room, pulled a chair from the corner, and drew it over to the desk. "I thought so." He nodded in the direction of the deck of cards. His heart was pounding hard against his chest. "Aces high, jacks wild. Deal."

The man scratched the back of his head and dealt the cards.

December 25, 1998
Stallion's Gate, New Mexico

Mark Davalos had a hard time feeling gloomy. With only the barest outline of what was going on in this current Leap, and a mission that seemed close to impossible, he was still having a good time.

After all, it *was* Christmas!

He drove through the desert, humming carols to himself along with the radio, noting every sight and sound along the way. The sagebrush, the rocks, the stars.

God, the stars were so bright tonight! He found himself looking up at them, then catching himself and turning his eyes back to the road.

It wasn't long, thanks to the use of the Project's high-speed car—and the fact that there weren't many police out tonight on these deserted roads—that Mark found himself at St. Jude's Church.

It had been a while since he'd attended midnight Mass on Christmas Eve, and this year wouldn't break that record. But he knew that Father Joseph would be up still. And he was pretty sure he'd have what Mark was looking for.

Or, rather, what Admiral Calavicci was looking for.

Christmas.

There were worse things Al had endured over the years. He kept reminding himself of that. Year after year, Christmas after Christmas, he replayed all the times in his life that had been worse.

Just to put the damned holiday into perspective.

But this year, it was harder. This year, all the reminders of how bad Christmas could be had come back to haunt him: old-fashioned priests who took themselves—and what they believed—seriously.

Angels from hell.

And a little girl he hadn't been able to save. Not forty-five years ago.

Maybe not three years ago.

What sleep he got was restless and tormented. That much, at least, was typical.

He woke from nightmares twice in the next four hours, willed himself back to sleep, and each time was awakened again.

No matter how much he tried to discount it, Christmas had a hold that he just couldn't shake. It wasn't a pleasant hold, either.

Memories of Christmases past haunted him like Scrooge.

Christmas at home, before his family had broken up. One Christmas in particular, when his mother flew into a rage because they were late for Mass: his sister, Trudy, couldn't find her shoes, couldn't figure out which foot to put each shoe on, and couldn't tie the laces once she did. It was a scene Al tried his hardest to forget; it was one of the few vivid memories he had of his mother.

Then Christmas at the orphanage in Philly. Paradoxically, one of the happiest memories. Sister Mary Something or Other dressed up as Santa and handed out gifts to each of the children. She was a young woman, and with the beard and pillow and red suit in place, her eyes had twinkled with joy as she watched the faces of the kids. He still didn't like to admit that he'd had a roaring crush on her. Sister Mary Something. He wished he remembered her name.

But that Christmas was overshadowed by dozens more, too many of them filled only with loss or solitude.

The dreams turned ugly then. He dreamed of coffins, of flower arrangements, of the smell of dead bodies. He dreamed of Christmas the year his father died.

The year God decided to stop listening.

Christmas was one holiday Al could do without. The Fourth of July was good. Patriotism, freedom, fireworks, and—when he got lucky—more fireworks!

And Thanksgiving wasn't too bad; at least there was usually a good meal in it for him, and lots of other people didn't seem to mind too much if they had to work overtime. After all, you could fix turkey and stuffing almost anywhere and call it Thanksgiving.

But Christmas? Albert Calavicci had never actually said, "Bah, humbug." But there'd been times he'd wanted to.

Eventually, he gave up on sleep. He took a long shower, dressed again in his uniform, and decided to check on the other inmates of Project Quantum Leap.

"What's the matter? Jou canno' sleep either?"

Despite her earlier choice to stay with Father O'Keefe, Angela was sitting in the Control Center when Al got off the elevator, reading one of Gooshie's technical manuals. Or at least leafing through it as if she were reading it.

"Just figured I'd check how things are goin'," he lied. The last person he'd admit Christmas jitters to was Angela. Or Father O'Keefe. The man was still sleeping, a peaceful sleep he'd managed to rob Al of several hours ago.

Admiral Calavicci nodded to Gooshie's shift replacement, a young technician Al knew had about half the credentials Gooshie had. That still made him more than qualified to watch over the computer and notify Al if anything happened; but it wasn't like having the familiar, sweating, bad-breathed programmer around.

Sometimes, Al admitted to himself, familiarity was better than decent breath.

Ignoring Angela for another moment, he went over to the console. Instantly, the young technician rose from his seat in the corner of the room, put down a manual he'd been looking through, and came almost to attention.

"Sir."

"Just checkin'," Al muttered, glancing at the displays. Currently, what brain wave activity Ziggy could monitor without Al in contact with Sam still showed him to be asleep. That was good. And so far, according to her other readouts, nothing earth-shattering had happened to change history. That could be good or bad.

"Gooshie tell you about her?" Al asked under his breath, barely gesturing with his chin to Angela. The woman looked up, as if she knew she was being talked about, and smiled.

"He mentioned she was a friend of yours, sir," the technician explained. "Said she was—" the man hesitated, cleared his throat and shrugged.

"An angel," Al finished for him.

"Well, yes, sir."

Al nodded and gave the man a half-grin. "You know how to put this thing on-line, right?"

"Well, of course, sir, I'm trained in all the necessary functions. . . ."

"Do it." Al turned away and glanced at Angela. "You just gonna sit there all night?" he asked.

He probably shouldn't have spoken to her. The woman put down the manual and stood. "Jou gonna go see Sam now?" she asked, moving toward him with the grace of a cloud—a thundercloud.

"I'm gonna check a couple things, that's all."

"I'll go with jou, hokay? I always wanted to see how these big machines work. Jou know, when I was alive, they had cars that—"

"No, it's not okay!" Al snapped. There was no need to check Sam because he was sleeping. And Al didn't really want to explain what he *was* doing. The last thing he wanted was company.

Angela stared at him for a moment, then resumed her seat. "Hokey dokey," she said. And when she picked up Gooshie's

186

outdated manual to flip through it again, Al felt as if a trap had been sprung; she gave in too easily.

"What, that's it?" Al demanded, a little disappointed. He crossed the room and stood over her. "Just 'hokey dokey'?"

"Chore." Then the woman laughed, a low, throaty laugh that Al remembered. "Jou got jour own business to take care of in the past, no?" And with that, and a too-innocent smile, the woman went back to her reading.

Al stifled a shiver, wondered if she really did know why he was going into the Imaging Chamber at this hour, and decided not to push the issue.

"I'm ready, Admiral," the technician said. Al took the handlink from the young man and strode up the ramp to the Imaging Chamber. Then, just outside the Door, he paused and looked back at Angela. She looked up, waiting, a kind of expectation and longing in her eyes that Al hadn't counted on.

Al ground his teeth, glanced at the technician, and sighed.

"Look, if you're comin', you'd better get your—you better get up here now," he said, inwardly cursing himself.

The plan for his off-hours visit was falling apart. He'd wanted to go back alone. He wasn't up at five in the morning because he was an early riser.

Well, maybe it was a stupid idea to begin with, right?

But even as one idea died, another started to take shape. Maybe Angela would be more cooperative if he took her back to the scene of the crime, so to speak. Maybe having her along wouldn't be so bad after all.

"Ho boy!" Angela grabbed her fan and scurried up the ramp faster than Al would have expected, given her size. She stood next to him, grinning broadly.

"Sir?" the technician asked, quietly but indirectly questioning Al's decision to take a guest into the Chamber.

Al smiled tightly at him and said, "It's Christmas, isn't it?" Then he turned to Angela. "When we're in there," he explained, "you'll only be able to see the past if you're in physical contact with me."

"Oh, I can see the past without jour help," Angela protested. "I jus' want to see the big machines!" Her voice rose with excitement, and even the technician winced.

"Yeah, well, we'll see about that."

Al opened the Door and stepped in. Angela followed. For

187

a moment, standing in the empty blue chamber, the angel turned around and around, her eyes and mouth open with wonder.

"Oh, is beautiful, no?"

Al felt a twitch at the corner of his mouth. "Yeah," he agreed, "it's beautiful." Then he spoke into the microphone that carried his voice back to the Control Center. "We're ready in here," he said. "Center me outside the monastery."

"Ho, boy!" Angela grabbed hold of Al's arm as the tornado of time descended around them. Al shut his eyes to diminish the visual impact.

"Oh, look! There's Mr. Nixon! There's John! I know her, she's the woman who works at the drugstore on Forty-third Street. . . ."

Angela muttered throughout the seconds it took to establish the contact. Her constant monologue on the history that swept around them began to give Al the same feeling that being caught in the visual typhoon gave him: he wanted to throw up.

"Save it, Charo, we're—" Before he could finish his sentence, reality stopped bouncing around him. He found himself outside the monastery, as he'd ordered. He and Angela appeared to be standing across the road that divided the monastery from the rocky coastline it bordered.

"Jou know," Angela mused, standing a few feet from Al and apparently still seeing what he saw, "I always wanted to see the world when I was alive." Then she chuckled. "I had to wait until I was dead!"

Al studied her for a moment, watched her moving through the Chamber without guidance, and felt a pang of envy. Then, following her as she strolled down the road and started to cross it, he said, "So this is where it happened, right?"

"What?" Angela turned to him and a car, sweeping down the road much too fast, sped right through her. Al opened his mouth to warn her, then shut it, realizing that this was how Sam must feel watching him pass through objects. Somehow, when it was someone else, it was a little different.

"This is where Teresa died, right?" Al gestured with the handlink in his palm, listening to the quiet squealing of the box.

"No, che died over there." Angela pointed behind Al, toward the cliffs. "Che fell over the cliff and went esplat." The angel shuddered. "It was very messy!"

Al looked backward and heard the sound of the water sloshing against the shore. It was a sound he knew well. "So what distracted you from saving her?" he asked, crossing the road toward the monastery's buildings. He followed Angela, hoping that her memory—and her willingness to tell him about the events he and Sam had to change—would be encouraged by being back here.

"Oh, jou know, that was the worst thing!" Angela's arms went up in an exaggerated shrug as she picked her way along the ground. It was, of course, a flat surface; but the visual effect seemed to be settling on her now, and she moved carefully along the holographic ground. Al watched, followed, and wondered if she'd trip on an insubstantial rock.

"What do you mean?"

"Oh, the little boy. I thought he was going to be killed." Angela was moving toward the main house. Al kept pace with her.

"What little boy?" Al asked, punching Angela's information into the handlink on the off chance that Ziggy could be coaxed out of pouting.

"Stephen Marco!" Angela turned around and waved her fan at Al. "That's why I'm here," she explained. "I got to make Father O'Keefe keep his mother on the translucent project."

"Translation," Al said, wondering, as he did, why he bothered. "Look, what does Father O'Keefe's translation have to do with Stephen Marco?"

Angela's eyes opened wide, and when she spoke, she did so slowly, as if she were talking to an idiot. "That is the reason I screwed up! Stephen was crossing this road, and I went to save him!"

And as if that explanation made everything clear, she picked her way along the path that led to the chapel.

CHAPTER
TWENTY-TWO

Teresa Bruckner had been dreaming about angels. Not your average, ordinary, haloed, winged angels. She'd been dreaming of angels with cigars, angels with fedoras, angels who took the place of her mother. Angels in flapper outfits, angels who sang off-key. Angels who came and went, who promised they'd come back—but didn't.

She woke, angry and sad, and then, when she looked around and realized where she was, she remembered George. And felt scared.

She didn't want to stay in that small cell of a room. It was decent enough, but it was plain and rather empty, like a hotel room. Sterile. Even the pictures on the wall—saints, she guessed—did nothing to relieve her fear or sadness. In fact, they just made things worse. How was it that all the saints looked so nice, so decent? Why couldn't just one of them be smoking a cigar and wearing a fedora?

She glanced outside; all that was visible this early was a hint of fog, a bluish mist that covered the grounds of the monastery like a cloak. She pulled on a jeans skirt and sweater, and dropped her feet into a pair of loafers. She wasn't sure where she was going or what she was going to do, but she wanted to get out of this cramped little room.

No one was up in the guest house. The doors along the hallway were shut, the lights were off. She crept down the stairs, listening to every creak of wood as she did, and unlocked the front door.

It was a brisk spring morning. When the sun finally came up and chased off the fog, it would probably be a nice day.

190

The rain had stopped but had left puddles that Teresa had to pick her way around. Not always successfully.

A light was on in the main house, off to the left of the front door. Teresa headed toward it, watched it grow brighter as she moved through the morning mist. There was a small wooden door on the side of the building that looked like a later addition to the house. A window that barely faced the road glowed from within, and Teresa put her face to the glass to peek inside.

It was a chapel, a very ornate chapel. The few times Teresa had been in a church—weddings, funerals, one or two baptisms—they had all been fairly barren and stark. This one looked like something out of the Vatican itself, and out of curiosity, she tried the door. It was unlocked.

A heavy scent of spicy smoke filled Teresa's nostrils the moment she stepped in. It wasn't unpleasant, but it was strong. She coughed quietly, unaccountably aware of the fact that, unlike other churches she'd been in, this one was used for one thing and one thing only. And though she certainly wasn't a Catholic, she recognized that this was a place those who came here obviously considered sacred. It demanded some respect.

She slid into a back pew, looking around her at the ornate lighting fixtures, the life-sized, gilt crucifix over the altar, the silver candlesticks, the deep purple cloths that draped the altar.

The same silence, the calm quietness that Teresa had sensed when she'd first arrived at the monastery, was here. It was peaceful, solitary. Even with a crowd in here, she thought, it would probably be the same.

After a few moments, she heard a noise, a throat being cleared. She looked around and saw, at the right front of the church, a second set of pews, separated from the others, at a right angle to the altar. A young nun was kneeling there, alone, a rosary in her hands. She looked at Teresa, smiled, and went back to her prayers.

Deciding that she probably shouldn't be here, Teresa stood to leave. As nice and peaceful as the place was, it probably wasn't right for her to be there. After all, she didn't believe in any of the things the chapel stood for, and she didn't want to distract the nun from what she was doing.

She was out of her seat, but not out of the pew, when the woman in the front of the church, who was watching her, gasped quietly. Fearing that she'd taken ill, Teresa moved toward her.

"Excuse me," Teresa whispered, approaching the nun slowly, "are you all right? Do you need some help?" The woman, whom Teresa remembered having seen earlier, had turned pale. Even in the dim candlelight of the chapel, it was evident.

"There," the woman whispered, pointing behind Teresa. "There! Do you see?"

Teresa turned around and stared at the door; she saw nothing out of the ordinary. "See what?" she asked.

"They're gone now," the young woman said. She finally looked at Teresa. "Two angels," she explained. "Dressed in white. . . ." Her voice faded off.

Teresa turned again, this time searching the entryway of the chapel. Without waiting for more from the nun, she ran to the back and pushed the door open, searching through the predawn mist to see if anything—*anything* that looked like an angel— was visible.

But except for the morning fog, there was nothing ethereal in sight.

Al followed Angela into the chapel without quite realizing it. Her last statement about Stephen Marco, whose mother O'Keefe was about to dump from his translation project, wasn't one he could ignore.

"All right, what are you talkin' about?" Al demanded. On the one hand, his revised plan—to get Angela to talk—seemed to be working. But he was sure as hell not going to carry on a conversation with her while she traipsed around the monastery.

It was only as she stopped and turned around to face him, her fingers to her lips to quiet him, that he realized where he was.

He took a deep breath and glanced around. The place looked eerily like the chapel in the orphanage in Philly. The place he'd gone to on his own volition, every day for almost a year, to plead for his father's life.

"I'm outta here," he said, and turned to leave.

"What's the matter?" Angela asked, spreading her arms as she looked around the room. "Is a pretty place, no?"

"No."

"Chore it is!" Angela protested. She walked up the aisle to the altar and, as Al watched in disbelief, she knelt and crossed herself. A moment later, she tried to stand. It was a losing battle. She reached out to grab one of the pews, but it of course passed through her. She put her hands on the floor to push herself up, but that didn't quite work either.

Finally, with a deep breath, Al strode over to her, grabbed her upper arm, and helped her. She latched onto him, half pulling him down as she got to her feet.

"Oh, jou know, is so much easier when jou don' weigh anything!" she complained.

"Yeah, well maybe you should've thought of that *before* you died," Al suggested. He let her go, and she brushed her knees and smoothed her dress.

"Well, before I died, I did no' know as much as I do now!" Angela snapped back.

"Like what to wear to a funeral?" he suggested, giving her dress a sour overview.

"This is no' what I wore to my funeral," she protested, a little hurt. "This is what I died in." And then, with a narrowed gaze and a wave of her fan, she added, "And jou better watch it, or jou're likely to die in jour underwear!"

"I don't think I have to worry about that," Al said quietly, lowering his voice and returning Angela's gaze. "If you hang around the Project much longer, I'm likely to kill myself!"

"Oh, jou could no' joke about something like that!" With a furtive gesture Al would hardly have expected, Angela crossed herself again.

Well, wasn't the world full of surprises tonight?

He started back to the door. He could have gone through a wall or a window, but years of avoiding such stunts for Sam's sake made him head for the nearest normal exit.

The noise behind him stopped him. Angela had started to follow, but she, too, turned as the side door from the sacristy opened.

Sister Mary Catherine stepped out, genuflected before the altar, and took a seat in one of the choir pews.

"We better get goin'," Al said, taking Angela's arm and steering her down the aisle.

"What's your hurry?" Angela slipped out of his grasp—

193

well, technically she yanked herself free—and stood her ground. "This is a good a place to talk, no?"

"No."

"What, jou scared of being here?"

"I am not *scared* of anything!" Al lifted his head and looked down on the woman. "It's just that a church isn't a good place to conduct business."

"Even when that business is saving someone's life?"

Al took two steadying breaths and said quietly, *"Especially* if the business is to save a life." He headed for the front door.

"I thought jou wanted to know about Stephen."

Baited, he turned. But as he did, he saw the front door open, and Teresa Bruckner stepped in.

"Teresa."

She didn't see him, didn't hear him. She was looking around the chapel, her braided hair askew, as if she hadn't rebraided it yet this morning. The look of wonder in her eyes was familiar, trusting.

God, how easy it had been to get wrapped around her little fingers, Al remembered. For the first time, he'd actually considered the pleasure a child of his own might bring to his life, instead of just thinking of the trouble kids would cause. He'd read to the munchkin while she held the book and begged him to read the same story over and over until even *he* had it memorized. . . .

"Inchworm, inchworm. . . ." He didn't realize that he was singing aloud. He watched Teresa take a seat in the back of the chapel and watched her. "Measuring the marigolds," he muttered. She moved with an innocence that, Al imagined, might still jump and play hide-and-seek with him.

He cautiously stepped closer.

"Seems to me you'd stop and see. . . ."

"Che canno' hear you," Angela whispered.

Al realized he'd spoken aloud. Embarrassed, he cleared his throat and wiped a hand across his eyes. A few hours of restless sleep hadn't done much to help, he discovered.

"It was kinda funny, you know," he muttered, still watching the girl. "Sam got to be her mother for a couple days, and I—kinda got to fill in for her. . . ." He stopped and shut his eyes. Another trap, he realized, had been sprung.

"I'm outta here," he said again, and this time, as he headed

194

for the back of the chapel, Angela followed him.

But as they reached the exit and Al started to go through the door, he heard a quiet gasp. Sister Mary Catherine was looking in their direction. Then she covered her face.

He glanced around. There was nothing alarming in sight.

Without another word to Angela, he left the oppressive, beautiful chapel—and all the memories—behind.

Sunday, April 2, 1995   7:15 A.M.
Somewhere off Rte. 128, Northern Massachusetts

Eight games out of eight. The D.E.A. agent won eight games of poker out of eight. That was more than luck, George figured.

So, after George had lost his Rolex watch, his Gucci bracelet, and the forty bucks in his wallet to the man, he suggested a game of blackjack. It was obvious that Anderson intended to stay up all night to guard George, and there was no way George was going to sleep with this man in his room. The .38 tucked in its holster was enough to keep George alert.

By the time the cold pizza was finished and the beers were gone and dawn had crept gingerly through the window, Anderson had become real chummy. He'd even helped George rebandage his foot, commiserating with him over the bloody stumps of his toes.

"Bad shit," the guy exclaimed softly. He bandaged the swollen appendages like a pro, and George thanked him for the help.

But the man didn't let George piss without company; and he didn't go himself unless George stayed within view. He was not a trusting man.

Now, after sixteen hands of blackjack, the man's unbeaten record still stood. George gave up, waving off the offer of another round.

"If I keep playing with you, I'm not going to have anything left to wear when we go out," he protested lightly. The man laughed and went back to playing solitaire.

Only one thing, George decided, made a man that good at cards, and it wasn't luck.

It was cheating.

The man cheated at poker. He cheated at blackjack. He even

195

cheated at solitaire! Not that George was about to call him on it; after all, Anderson was the man with the gun.

But as he sat on the bed, pretending to read a magazine that detailed the glories of the Gloucester area, he began to think.

Not that George knew a lot about such things, but he wondered: what kind of D.E.A. agent shows up without backup, without at least someone to spell him? What kind of D.E.A. agent cheats the man he's trying to make a deal with?

What kind of man cheats at solitaire?

The only answer, as far as George could figure it, wasn't one that made him at all comfortable.

Not at all.

CHAPTER
TWENTY-THREE

"Father? Father O'Keefe?"

Dim sounds beckoned Sam back to consciousness. But he wasn't sure he wanted to join them.

"Father, can you hear me? Father, please answer me! Please! Wake up!"

The sounds grew louder. There was a plea in the voice. A desperate plea.

But Sam wanted to stay where he was. He was floating somewhere dark, and he was getting closer and closer to one of his mom's homemade apple cobblers. Thanksgiving turkey. Polished silver. The best linens on the table, and candles. . . .

"Sam! Sam, wake up! I finally think I've got something useful here."

The harsh voice intruded, and he groaned. He didn't want to go back to that world. He knew that what was waiting for him there wasn't as good as what he had now.

Right now, he was very close to giblet stuffing and candied yams, mashed potatoes (with all the lumps) and green beans and cranberry sauce. . . .

"Father? Father, something incredible is happening! They're back, Father! They came back for me!"

Someone was calling him.

"Sam, wake up! Angela's finally coughed up something useful. Now, come on! Say bye-bye to dreamland! Come on, Sam, we got work to do!"

Someone needed him.

And as hungry as he was, as much as he wanted to go home and taste food that never tasted as good anywhere else, he knew he couldn't.

197

Not yet.

He opened his eyes.

Standing over his bed, hovering in a holographic shimmer, was the face of a thousand dreams, a thousand Leaps, a thousand lives.

"Sam?" Al leaned down, his face coming in close. "Geez, sometimes you sleep like a dead man!" The admiral, still in uniform, Sam noted, punched the glowing box in his hand. Then, with a grunt of disgust, he put it in his pocket. "Sam, Angela says the accident takes place sometime this afternoon. Problem is, she wasn't there for it—which is why Teresa died," he added bitterly.

Sam struggled to sit up. The scent of Mom's turkey stuffing, filled with sage and oregano, still lingered in his memory. Cranberry sauce and gravy and. . . .

"But according to her," Al continued, "we gotta keep Stephen Marco from crossing the road at the wrong time and gettin' killed, too. Looks like we got our work cut out for us today, Sam," the Observer concluded.

"Father O'Keefe! Are you awake?"

The knocking on the door and the voice from outside were still there. Sam had hoped it was a dream.

"Uh, yeah, I'm—just give me a minute," he called back. He glanced at the clock on the end table and groaned again.

He rubbed his eyes and reluctantly left the bed, aware of the hovering hologram next to him.

"Sam," Al said, persisting in his sudden streak of information, "according to Angela, Lillian's kid, Stephen, gets in the middle of a fight between his mom and Father O'Keefe this afternoon. He runs off and almost gets run over by a car." The man mimicked the zooming of an automobile with his hand. The gesture was too fast for Sam. "Angela was there, and she kept the kid from gettin' run over. But then she wasn't there when Teresa fell off the cliff."

Sam rubbed his face and tried to wake up. "Fell off what cliff?"

"Father O'Keefe? It's incredible what's happened!"

The voice outside the door, Sam remembered, belonged to Teresa Bruckner. But it was the voice on this side of the door that made it hard for him to get his bearings.

He staggered slowly to the door. If the horarium posted on

the wall was any indication, the entire monastic community was up and halfway through the early Mass. Vigils and Lauds, he saw, began at eight, as did breakfast for the guests.

Breakfast!

His stomach growled louder than it had in any recent memory. Not that memory was something Sam could actually count on.

"Al," he whispered as his verbal ability finally kicked in, "have I missed something? What's happened to Ziggy? Did you give her a new name?"

"What?"

"You keep calling her Angela." Sam opened O'Keefe's suitcase and pulled out a pair of blue jeans.

"Uh, Sam, no, not jeans," Al advised, shaking his hand at the choice. Sam looked at him through sleep-encrusted eyes. "It's Sunday, Sam," Al explained. "You gotta hear confessions and say Mass."

"What?"

"Look, that's not important right now. The thing is. . . ."

"Father O'Keefe!"

"Just a minute!" For the first time in *any* memory, Sam found himself wanting to tell everyone to shut up. He didn't, but he thought about it.

"Al, what are you talking about? Who's Angela? What's the matter with Ziggy? And how in—heaven's name am I supposed to do a Mass?"

Al let out a heavy breath and pulled an unopened cigar from his pants pocket. He unwrapped it, bit off the end, pulled a lighter from the opposite pocket, and began the lighting ritual. Sam dropped the blue jeans back on the bed and pulled out Father O'Keefe's second clerical suit.

"You don't remember Angela," Al started, "but she's an angel. She—helped us out once before."

"What?"

"Father O'Keefe? I really hate to bother you, but it's so great! They really came back!"

Sam half turned to the door. "Teresa, I'll—be there in a minute." He turned back to Al. "What do you mean she's an angel?"

"Look, that's not important," Al said. He pulled the cigar from his lips. "What's important is that she was here the first

199

time through, but she messed up and Teresa died. So—''

''Al!'' Sam cut him off as he pulled on a pair of black slacks. ''Are you saying you believe in angels?'' This Leap, Sam decided, was getting to be very strange.

Al narrowed one eye and tilted his chin upward. ''Let's not go into it, okay? The thing is, Stephen Marco and Teresa are both gonna be in danger at the same time.''

''Wait a minute!'' Sam sat back on the bed and pulled on the dark shirt. It was the collar—which he'd had trouble with last night—that he wasn't looking forward to. ''You said Father O'Keefe and Lillian Marco had an argument, right?''

''Yeah.''

''And then Stephen ran off and this—angel—kept him from getting run over?''

''Right. But Teresa—''

''Al, if *I'm* Father O'Keefe—sort of—then all I have to do is *not* get into an argument with Lillian Marco, right? Then Stephen won't run off and I can keep an eye on Teresa.'' He shrugged. It was amazing how simple some things seemed first thing in the morning.

Al, however, seemed doubtful. He pulled the handlink back out of his pocket and gave it a whack on the side. ''Damn!''

''Al, what is wrong with Ziggy?''

The admiral looked up from the box and gave Sam a long, evaluating stare. Then, with a sigh, he dropped his hand and said, ''I told you. We're having a disagreement.''

''About what?''

Several seconds passed. Al watched Sam as he struggled into the clerical collar and pulled on his shoes.

''About you.''

That got Sam's attention. The last vestiges of sleep dried up in an instant.

''What about me?'' He stood from the bed and waited.

Al shrugged. ''Oh, she's got some crazy idea about—well, the fact that—you hadn't—Leaped yet.''

It took a lot, Sam could tell, for Al to get that out.

''So?''

Al met his eyes briefly, then turned away and shrugged again. ''So, she thinks—if you—'' He looked back, desperation in his dark eyes. ''It won't work, Sam! Trust me!''

''What won't work?'' Sam wanted to draw his own conclusion about what Ziggy thought, but he needed to hear it from Al: he needed the statistical validation.

"Calling yourself, okay?" the man shouted. "Warning yourself! It won't work, Sam! You were too stubborn, too sure of yourself!" Cigar ash shot like firecrackers from the stogie and vanished. "You were so damned sure it was gonna work! Even when all the tests showed you it wasn't ready! Dammit, Sam, don't you think I tried to talk you out of it back then? Don't you think I *tried*?"

Sam turned away. The pain in Al's eyes—something he'd seen only once or twice in his life—was stark and despairing.

He only vaguely remembered that first Leap. Al showed up in a tux, half drunk, a little giddy, apparently excited by the fact that the experiment had succeeded.

They tried to retrieve him, but it failed.

And then Al showed up again. And again. And again. And again.

Al was there for every incarnation Sam took on: Kid Cody, the boxer who helped a group of nuns build their chapel. Frankie LaPalma, the Mafia hit man who fell in love with the wrong woman. Jesse Tyler, the elderly southern black man whose granddaughter nearly died from racial bigotry.

But one attempt after another to retrieve Sam failed.

Ziggy was imperfect; rules were broken; and, Sam realized, even the committee that had originally backed the Project wasn't completely supportive.

When had they given up trying to bring him home? Were they just waiting for God or Time or Fate to be finished with him and send him back?

"You sneaked into that damned Accelerator when I wasn't even there," Al said quietly, breaking Sam from his thoughts. "You risked everything without a shred of proof. All you had was faith. So what the hell do you think would happen if you actually heard your own voice on the phone, calling from the past to say, 'Hey, Sam! It's me, Sam!' You think that would *stop* you?"

Sam swallowed, his throat tightening. "I don't know," he said quietly. He turned away and saw himself; saw Father O'Keefe in his priestly garb, a man who had scorned his linguistics thesis, a man he had once looked up to.

He looked back at Al. "Why are you so certain it wouldn't?"

"I told you before," Al started. His voice was tired, defeated. "If you call yourself—if you *did* convince yourself not to step into the Accelerator—none of the people you've helped will be helped."

"But you're convinced it won't work," Sam countered. He grabbed Father O'Keefe's jacket and slipped it on. "So what's the harm in trying?"

Al didn't answer.

He opened the door. Teresa Bruckner was waiting for him.

"Father O'Keefe," the girl started, "I really didn't mean to wake you, but I just had to let you know what happened!"

"Maybe that's the harm," Al said quietly. Sam almost turned.

Behind Sam, the admiral had opened the Door to the Imaging Chamber. Sam heard the soft sigh as it slid open.

"You want the odds? Okay, here they are. Ziggy says there's a fifty-fifty chance it could work. And you'd never Leap. At least," Al said, just before he left, "not so you could save Teresa."

Sunday, April 2, 1995   8:13 A.M.
Windy Bluffs, Massachusetts

Mother Mary Frances sat alone in her office, pondering the beads of the rosary that traveled through her fingers. She was not praying, not exactly. She was contemplating, and the beads gave her fingers something to do. Forty years ago, she'd turned to them when she'd decided to enter the religious life; she had to find something to do with her fingers when she gave up smoking.

Last night, after Father Samuel had gone off to find his errant student, she'd called aside each of the sisters who'd claimed to have seen Sister Mary Catherine's apparition. Each of them, to her dismay, had said almost the same thing. They all saw a man, enveloped in a bright light, who appeared in the trees to speak with Father Samuel. He was dressed all in white. He held, they said, a rosary of many-colored beads in one hand, and a crucifix in the other.

All of them agreed that Father Samuel, when he noticed the

sisters, had moved farther away, as if they were not meant to see the apparition. And all of them declared that the appearance of—whatever it was—ended when a brilliant light engulfed the apparition and he disappeared.

But then, this morning, following the early Mass, Sister Mary Catherine had come to her. After Compline last night, she reported, she and Sister Mary Gertrude had seen the apparition again. An angel, speaking with Father Samuel in the presence of Teresa.

At least, Mother Mary Frances thought, if Teresa was back, the priest's mercy mission had been successful.

But Sister Mary Catherine's visions hadn't stopped there. When she was in the chapel early this morning, saying her private devotions, she saw the angel again.

This time, she claimed, there were two angels. Both of them were dressed in white. One appeared in the form of a man, one in the form of a woman.

No, she said, there was no light preceding them. No, the light didn't engulf them at the end. They simply vanished, she said, walking away.

Mother Mary Frances listened patiently to Sister Mary Catherine for more than half an hour. The young woman was certain they were angels.

But instead of only one apparition, now there were two. That, and the fact that the early-morning vision had not been heralded by a bright light, made Mother Mary Frances wonder. Generally, at least at first, visions from Heaven tended to be consistent; it gave the visionaries themselves a certain credibility.

"What about the rosary?" Mother Mary Frances asked, taking careful notes of what Sister Mary Catherine reported. "Did either of the—angels have one?"

"Oh, yes, the man, he had the rosary again. It was glowing, giving out a rainbow of colors! Oh, Mother, it was beautiful! Such a glorious sight—"

"What about the crucifix?" the mother superior persisted. "Did you see it?"

"No," the young woman answered. "He didn't seem to have it with him. But the woman, she had something in her hands. . . . But they were blurred, their images weren't clear. I'm sorry, Mother, I couldn't see what it was."

"Thank you, Sister," Mother said, dismissing the garrulous nun.

Now, pondering her beads, Mother Mary Frances was faced with the unpleasant possibility that her contemplative order actually had been blessed by an apparition. If that were the case, she would have to begin the official process of validating it. That involved letters to the bishop, investigations, representatives from Rome, and a host of other challenges to the validity of the claims.

And then, of course, there was the media. Television cameras, tabloid shows, scores of pilgrims, and the host of claims that would follow—healings, miracles—some legitimate, some not. Each of them, too, would have to be investigated.

The peace of St. Bede's would be shattered forever.

It was not, of course, Mother Mary Frances' prerogative to decide whether to involve diocesan and Vatican authorities. That decision, most likely, would be made for her. Either by Father Brenyzhov or by the apparition itself.

Seldom did an apparition appear to an entire group of people, then ask to be kept secret. Private revelations to individuals weren't uncommon. But once word spread around the monastery that there was an angel visiting—and during an oblate retreat, no less, when there were so many ways for the news to get out—it would be incumbent upon the apparition himself to explain what they were supposed to do about it.

Her first task would be to talk with Father Samuel. Each time the angel had appeared—with the exception of this morning—Father Samuel had been there.

She would have to begin with her former instructor. Her friend.

The man who'd agreed to give a retreat that, twenty-four hours after it should have started, hadn't yet begun.

CHAPTER TWENTY-FOUR

December 25, 1998
Stallion's Gate, New Mexico

A 63.8 percent probability that Dr. Sam Beckett had enough determination to undo the past now existed. That, between the third and fourth verses of "Jingle Bells," was Ziggy's latest way of hinting that she had been right about the purpose of this Leap.

Al ignored it, shoved the handlink in his pocket, and left the Imaging Chamber. One glance at Gooshie told him the news on this side of the Door was no better.

"What's up?" he asked, before the man could open his mouth.

"Well, Admiral, Father O'Keefe insists on seeing you right away. And, uh, the auditors have—well, I think they talked with Senator Weitzman again. Sir."

Al glanced at the Waiting Room and remembered various training exercises he'd gone through at the academy. Dealing with crises. Dealing with conflicting priorities. Dealing with fires on all decks at once.

Abandoning ship at this point, however, wasn't one of the viable options. So he resorted to a time-honored means of choosing which fire to put out first. He pulled a dime from his pocket. "Call it, Gooshie."

"Uh, sir?"

Clearly, Gooshie wasn't a gambler. Al handed him the dime and said, "All right, *I'll* call it. Heads, I deal with O'Keefe first. Tails, I deal with the auditors."

"Uh, sir, that's not very scientif—" Gooshie's voice died as he met Al's eyes. Silently, he tossed the coin and slapped it down on the back of his hand.

"Heads," he reported. He handed the coin back.

Al grimaced. "How 'bout two outta three?"

The Waiting Room was getting crowded. Angela had returned to the room after her trip through time with Al, and she watched as Mark Davalos and Father O'Keefe worked at setting up a makeshift altar.

"You got lucky, huh?" Al started, addressing Davalos as he entered the room.

"Well, in a manner of speaking, sir."

Mark Davalos was clearly having a great time. The chief of security had one of the more thankless jobs at the Project, sitting in the bunker on the edge of the compound, never really able to join in the work of the actual Leaps. Obviously, the task Al had sent the man on was being viewed as something of an adventure.

The portable altar, a stone slab about twelve inches long and ten inches wide, had been set on the card table Angela and O'Keefe had used earlier for a much more mundane purpose. Next to the table, on the floor, was a briefcase that probably held the rest of Father O'Keefe's required accouterments.

"Father Joseph was in the Navy back in Korea," Davalos explained. "A chaplain. He was allowed to keep his portable altar as a souvenir, I guess."

"Admiral, I need to speak with you about another matter of some importance." O'Keefe pulled himself away from the task of draping an altar cloth over the slab. Al turned to him. The look in his eyes told Al to anticipate another argument.

"Before you say anything else," Al said, hoping to hell the man wasn't going to complain about Davalos' choice of wine, "I'd like you to appreciate the fact that this guy just spent most of the night driving through the desert on Christmas to get this stuff for you. So if you've got any complaints about—"

"It's not this Mass I'm worried about," O'Keefe cut in. "It's the one I'm supposed to be saying at St. Bede's."

"Oh. Well." Al shrugged and let the fighting tension drain from his back and shoulders. "No problem. Sam's coverin' for you."

"He can't!"

Al stopped puffing and looked down at the man. "Wanna bet?"

"He isn't a priest." O'Keefe glared right back at him, unintimidated and uncompromising. "He can't celebrate the Mass, you know that."

Al met the stare. His mind raced back through decades of training, indoctrination, and catechism. The memory of O'Keefe's analogy of the bloodstain returned. So did the memory of the last time he'd entered a church as a believer—*before* his father died.

"Look." He pulled the cigar out and used it to make his point. "Far as we can tell, God's in charge of this experiment. And He made Sam a priest before. If it was good enough then—"

"Did he say Mass?" O'Keefe pressed.

Al had to think for a moment. As he recalled, Sam had Leaped in at the end of a marriage ceremony. He'd attended a funeral service, overseen by the priest he was there to save. And he'd volunteered for—but never actually went through with—hearing confession.

Unless the kid who shot him in the head at point-blank range in the confessional counted.

"No," Al admitted. "But he never got to hear confessions before, either. Guess there's a first time for everything."

"Confession? He's going to—No!" O'Keefe closed the distance between them and looked down on Al. "These are sacred mysteries," the man began slowly, using again the tone of voice that made Al feel like he'd just been caught downing the Communion wine in the sacristy. "They cannot be faked and they cannot be performed by someone who is not a priest. He cannot hear confessions! He cannot give absolution. It would be. . . ." The man paused, and chose his next words very carefully. "It would be a grave sin."

There were probably Catholics all over the world right now for whom those two words—"grave sin"—meant nothing. They'd gone out of favor in the late sixties, after all those new reforms that Al had watched from a distance.

But for Al, brought up on the old catechism, brought up in the land of night-black confessionals and Purgatory and mortal sins, the weight of those words made his stomach turn.

"What if someone in serious sin goes to him in the confessional?" O'Keefe pressed. "Their souls are in jeopardy, Admiral. Their *eternal* souls. You can't risk that!"

O'Keefe's eyes burned with intensity; Hell was licking at

Al's heels; and Angela and Davalos were waiting for his response.

He ground his teeth, cleared his throat, and found he couldn't look any of them in the eye.

"There's not much I can do about it," he muttered finally.

"That's not true," the priest whispered. *"There is always a way out. God never tests us beyond our ability to bear it."*

"So what's my way out this time, huh? Poppa's dead and no one around here gives a—hoot."

"There *must* be some way. Perhaps. . . ." O'Keefe's voice trailed off in thought. The voices in Al's head weren't so kind.

"Perhaps," the priest on the other side of the grille said quietly, *"you should consider faith."*

"You risked everything without a shred of proof! All you had was faith. . . ."

"Look," Al said, wiping a hand over his face to rid himself of the ghosts. "Sam's there to keep Teresa from dyin', okay? So whatever he has to do to keep that from happening, he'll do it. Sorry if that offends you, *Father,* but all we've got to go on is—"

Faith. . . .

He paused and lifted his chin. "Is the facts before us."

Al doubted that anyone had ever thrown Father O'Keefe's own words back at him before. The surprise in his expression, the half-opened mouth that shut wordlessly, the hand raised in a gesture that was never completed, told Al he had made his point. Good, bad, or otherwise.

This fire, Al decided, was out. He started to leave.

Almost unnoticed by the others, Angela was trying to hoist herself onto the table that doubled as a bed in the room; it was just a few inches too high for her, and he watched her embarrassing struggle for only a minute before crossing the room and hefting her up so she had a seat.

The woman beamed and fanned herself. "Oh, jou see! I knew jou could be a gentleman if jou tried hard enough."

Al scowled and turned away.

"Admiral?" Mark Davalos' quiet voice stopped him, and he looked back.

"What is it?"

Davalos glanced nervously at the priest before speaking. "Well, sir, I was thinking of—maybe a compromise? Something that might—well, I don't know if it would work or not, but—''

''Well?'' Al prompted.

Davalos glanced at Angela, then at O'Keefe. Both waited silently. He looked back at Al.

''Maybe, sir, we ought to discuss it in private,'' Davalos suggested. And Al almost smiled. There were some things Davalos had learned very well in the last twenty years: discretion was obviously one of them.

Sunday, April 2, 1995   8:07 A.M.
Windy Bluffs, Massachusetts

''I didn't see them myself, but Sister Mary Catherine—that's the nun who was there—she did. She said they were angels! Father O'Keefe, I really think they came back for me after all!''

Almost nothing about Teresa Bruckner resembled the young, frightened girl Sam had gone after last night. Or even the shy, cautious girl he'd seen yesterday afternoon in the guest house. In fact, had he not known better, he would have taken the bubbly, excited young woman who trailed after him as he made his way to the bathroom as an impostor.

But the wide-eyed wonder that her eyes had only hinted at yesterday—the large, joyous eyes he remembered from her childhood—sparked now with a renewed fire. Clearly, something had happened to wipe from her mind the very real danger she was in.

If only she'd slow down and explain it so that Sam could understand her.

''I'll—I'll just be a minute,'' Sam said, closing the bathroom door and taking a long breath. For a few moments, as Teresa had followed him down the hall, almost bouncing with excitement, he had wondered if Sister Mary Catherine had died overnight and been reincarnated. Teresa had been almost incoherent with elation for the last five minutes.

Once nature had been answered and Sam had splashed water on his face and run his fingers through his hair, he left the bathroom and found the girl hunched against the far wall, still animated with her news.

''Okay,'' he started. ''Now slow down and tell me what happened. Have you had breakfast?'' he asked on a hunch.

"No, not yet. I've been talking with Sister Mary Catherine—"

"Who'd have guessed?" Sam muttered.

"What?"

"Oh, uh, nothing, I just—" He grimaced. Suddenly the world wasn't as crystal clear as it had been when he'd solved the problem of preventing Stephen Marco's death. His stomach wasn't growling anymore; it was aching.

"Look, let's get some food, okay? We can talk on the way."

"Oh. Sure."

Sam started down the hall, glancing at the pictures that cluttered the wall. The building reminded him of his own home in some ways: walls covered with pictures of ancestors. Only instead of family portraits, this one had pictures of men and women dressed in long dark robes. Many of the artists had added the glow of a halo behind the saints they depicted.

Sam smiled to himself: to him, they looked as if they were either Quantum Leaping or in an Imaging Chamber.

"Well, it was really early," Teresa began. She was, Sam could tell, deliberately trying to relate her story more slowly. "I couldn't sleep, so I got up and went outside. There was a light on in the main house. . . ."

As she related her story, they left the guest house and crossed the lawn. A faint scent of bacon, carried on the brisk wind of the April morning, led him to the refectory.

By the time he got to the main door, Teresa had finished enough of her tale for Sam to realize that something odd was going on—something that had nothing to do with a drug-dealing boyfriend or a research assistant being fired from her job or a young boy who crossed the road at the wrong time.

"Angels?" He paused outside the door to the small building that held the food he desperately needed.

"Well, like I said," Teresa explained, crossing her arms to warm her hands, "I didn't see them myself. But Sister Mary Catherine did. And—well, I didn't tell you about this earlier, because I didn't want you to laugh at me—and, actually, I wasn't really sure myself—"

Sam waited out Teresa's hesitation. She pulled her braid around her shoulder and chewed it nervously. Sam was almost hungry enough to join her.

"There was this woman," Teresa said. "She came over to me Friday night, in the subway. And—she said she was an angel."

"Oh."

"No, it wasn't—well, she didn't look like an angel. But she knew things. About George and me. And—and the stuff," she added, glancing over her shoulder quickly. Sam looked, too, but no one was there. Everyone was inside, eating. Having breakfast. Enjoying a cup of coffee. Or maybe orange juice. . . .

"I didn't believe her, but when I was coming up here, she appeared again. She was on the road, and I picked her up. She knew—I think she knew all about what was going on. And— and she said I should tell you about it because—" She took a deep breath and shot out the final words rapidly, as if she were afraid of them. "She said you were here to help me."

Sam wrinkled his forehead and pushed his hands into the priest's coat jacket for warmth. "So what happened to her?"

Teresa shrugged and glanced into the distance, toward the cliffs. "She said she had to go check on someone else, I think. But she said she'd be back."

Sam nodded. Then he smiled and put a hand on her shoulder. "Well, she was right about one thing. I *am* going to help you. But first," he added, waggling a finger at her, the way he used to at his sister, "we need to get some breakfast. All right?"

Teresa allowed herself to be led into the building.

"It just seems strange, you know," she mused. "I kept praying that they'd come back to help me, and now Sister Mary Catherine sees two angels—it just seems a little coincidental, doesn't it, Father?"

Sam didn't answer immediately. "Well," he suggested finally, "maybe it isn't just—coincidence."

Teresa Bruckner's young, dark eyes brightened with hope. "You think so?" she asked. The quiet, awe-struck expectation in her voice was unmistakable. "Do you really think they came back? Like they said?"

Sam held his breath.

"They said—Al said—he'd come back. . . ."

"I don't wanna go. But—I'm gonna come back. I don't know when—but I'll come back."

211

"Promise?"

"I promise." And then he raised his hand and Teresa raised hers. Just before the light engulfed him, Sam saw their hands pass through each other: a promise made across time and space.

Would it break the rules to tell her? Ruin his chance to go home?

What harm would it cause to let her know that fourteen years of faith weren't in vain?

Would it be worse than letting her think that angels broke their promises?

"... but he promised. Do you think he kept that promise, Father? Do you believe that—maybe they came back after all? To help me out?"

Sam let out the breath he'd held. "Yeah," he said. He smiled and swallowed hard. "I think they did."

CHAPTER

TWENTY-FIVE

Sunday, April 2, 1995   8:25 A.M.
Somewhere off Rte. 128, Northern Massachusetts

"So, you think those nuns are up now?"

George had fallen asleep. Fortunately, no one had shot him, beheaded him, smashed his other foot, or otherwise harmed him while he nodded off. If there was such a thing as good luck, George figured, he was probably on the right side of it for the moment.

He rubbed his face and let out a deep, pepperoni-spiked breath. Frank Anderson, D.E.A. agent and card shark, was still sitting at the desk, another won game of solitaire spread out before him.

"Probably." First thing in the morning, talking wasn't George's strong point. Nor did he have any information about the habits of a bunch of repressed women who decided to spend their lives hiding away from the world instead of tasting its delights.

"I think so, too. Let's go."

With a groan, George rolled out of bed and gingerly set his foot on the floor. He'd unbandaged it overnight, and now, having been elevated, it wasn't quite as swollen. Still, the pain and pressure as he touched it to the floor were enough to make him groan.

Anderson watched him from the desk. George struggled to his feet, then limped to the bathroom and back.

"You want something for that?"

"What?"

Anderson's left shoulder went up and then down. He scratched his head. "I got some painkillers if you want one."

Painkillers, George decided, wouldn't be such a bad thing.

213

Not considering how he figured the day was going to go anyhow.

Even in the best of situations, there was going to be a fight. Probably crying. God, he hated it when Teresa pulled out the tears! How was a guy supposed to handle that, huh? And if she started yelling? If she got scared? If she was stubborn?

"What kind?"

Wordlessly, the man reached into his back pocket and pulled out a small prescription bottle. He tossed it across the room, and George caught it.

"Don't take more than two," the man advised. "They're pretty strong."

Fiorinal with codeine. The prescription label had Frank Anderson's name, and the drug had been bought recently. The warning on the bottle told him this drug could be habit forming and not to use it without being under a doctor's care.

It was exactly the kind of thing George had been dreaming of for more than a day.

"D.E.A. agents carry around narcotics all the time?" he asked.

Anderson chuckled. "Only when they got chronic sciatica," he said, rubbing his hip and leg for emphasis.

George dropped one pill from the bottle into his hand and swallowed it dry. "Thanks." He tossed the bottle back and stared at his foot. The toes were swollen, black and blue, twisted. And naked without the nails.

Just looking at them made them hurt more.

The bleeding had stopped, so he pulled a sock over his foot without rebandaging the toes, pressed his foot into his shoe, and waited for the narcotic to kick in.

"We'll take your car," Anderson said. He stood up and scratched his stomach. George began to wonder if the man had fleas. "We'll come back here after we get the dope."

George sighed. As badly as his foot hurt this morning, and as scared as he was of showing up in Boston without having made the sales, he was also reconsidering the deal he'd made.

Something about Anderson just didn't seem right. Maybe he'd watched too many movies. Or maybe he hadn't watched enough. But something just felt wrong. . . .

"Don't you have a partner?" George asked, limping toward the door.

"Nope." Anderson swept the deck of cards into a neat pile and put them into their box. "I'm on my own this time." He slapped an arm around George's shoulder. The unexpected weight put pressure on George's injured foot, and he gasped. Anderson didn't seem to notice.

"Agency didn't want to risk too many of us," the D.E.A. man said. He grinned.

George hobbled out of the room, and Anderson followed. Since neither of them had planned on spending the night there, neither of them had brought along anything that they had to collect.

As George checked out, Anderson watching him, his intuition grew stronger: something about all this just wasn't right.

But a drug fog, dulling the pain in his foot and the concerns in his head, began to drop. And he followed Anderson to the car.

Sunday, April 2, 1995   8:37 A.M.
Windy Bluffs, Massachusetts

The large dining hall where the guests of St. Bede's ate was set up as it had been when it was still a private farm. A long, wooden table centered the room, and benches took the place of chairs. A hutch against one wall held plates and cups and other dishes on open shelves. Drawers underneath held silverware. One corner of the room was given over to a double sink and drain, where the dishes were washed after each meal. Two large, industrial-size urns—one filled with hot water, the other with coffee—sat on the counter nearby so guests could help themselves.

The room opened to a sitting room, and many conversations that began at the table concluded over coffee on the sofas in the next room. There was a piano; some of their guests played quite well, giving impromptu concerts for anyone who cared to stay and listen. Around both rooms, paintings of saints blanketed the walls, interposed with pieces of cross-stitched art or paintings done by the sisters or friends of the monastery.

Mother Mary Frances was looking for Father O'Keefe, but she didn't see him when she walked in. But then, given her eyesight, he might have been there. She'd have to make the circuit of the room.

"Are you looking for someone in particular, Mother?"

215

Sister Mary Catherine, assigned to keep the oblates and guests company, rose from her seat near the end of the table and came over.

"Father O'Keefe."

Sister Mary Catherine shook her head. "I haven't seen him this morning."

"Thank you."

Mother Mary Frances nodded a greeting to the few guests who raised their hands in a quick wave; she couldn't make out many of them from the doorway, but she nodded anyway.

"Oh, uh, excuse me.—Uh, good morning, Mother."

She bumped into him just as she was leaving. The fortuitous nature of their meeting wasn't lost on her.

"Father Samuel! I was just looking for you. I wanted to know how you made out last night—"

"Uh, I—maybe we could—" He looked into the refectory. Despite what had appeared to be a successful venture last night, Father Samuel seemed acutely uncomfortable.

"Perhaps we should talk elsewhere." Mother Mary Frances started down the walk, back toward the main house and her office. There was no place quite as private. "Sister Mary Catherine told me that you brought Teresa back. I'm glad you found her. . . ."

Father Samuel, who had lingered at the door to the refectory, caught up with her on her way back to the main house.

"Sister Mary Catherine?"

Mother stopped and turned, pivoting on her cane. "Is something wrong, Father Samuel?"

He winced, she noticed, each time she called him that. And then he grimaced.

"Uh, well, no, not—" He let out a deep breath, awkwardly wringing his hands. It wasn't like Father Samuel. "Uh, no. I guess not."

She led him back into the main house, noticed him glancing longingly at the refectory, and realized that he probably hadn't eaten yet. She wouldn't keep him; but she had a serious matter to discuss.

Mother Mary Frances held the door to her office open until Father Samuel had followed her in, then shut it and went to her desk.

"There's something I needed to talk with you about, Fa-

216

ther," she began, before she lost her courage. "Several of the sisters here are reporting—well, I'm almost embarrassed to mention it, but—" She fiddled with her rosary, struggling for the right words. The last thing she wanted, if the sisters were mistaken, was for Father Samuel to think they were all a bit crazy. "Well, they believe they've seen—an angel. Or—something that appears to them to be an angel."

He cleared his throat. "I've—heard something about that," he muttered, not looking at her.

Apparently, despite her instructions, someone had begun talking about the apparitions.

"This angel—he didn't have wings, did he?"

Apparently, the stories had grown. Immediately, she felt foolish.

"No," Mother answered as calmly as she could. "He was dressed in white."

Father O'Keefe looked amused.

"And he carried a brightly colored rosary."

"A rosary," he repeated.

"And a crucifix."

This time, Father Samuel just nodded. A patient, disbelieving nod.

Mother Mary Frances paused, inhaled, and decided on the indirect approach. "Have you—seen anything like that?"

Father Samuel cleared his throat. "Uh, no, no, not that I can think of. But—I'll let you know if I do."

He rose, and Mother Mary Frances decided it was just as well to end the discussion. Apparently, if there were apparitions at St. Bede's, the sisters had been mistaken about one thing: Father Samuel knew nothing of them. Sister Mary Catherine's assertion that he seemed to be engaged in a heavenly conversation would have to be discounted.

So might the rest of the claims.

"Thank you, Father. I—trust you'll keep this business just between us for now. I wouldn't want the whole monastery in an uproar over what might turn out to be the product of a few vivid imaginations."

"Uh, no, right. I mean—I won't say a word."

He left, rather hurriedly, and Mother Mary Frances turned to the calendar on her desk.

April 2.

She wondered, just for a second, if her sisters might have been playing an April Fool's Day joke on her. It certainly wouldn't be beyond Sister Mary Catherine.

December 25, 1998
Stallion's Gate, New Mexico

Having agreed to the compromise Davalos had suggested to ease O'Keefe's ire—and with a feeling of molten lava forming in his stomach at the thought of going through with it—Al had sent the security chief back to the Control Center to begin the arrangements. Then he went on alone to deal with the auditors.

"All right," he started, marching into the room where the three gorgeous, untouchable auditors were waiting. "To paraphrase a great playwright, I have *tried* to be friendly, I have *tried* to be helpful, and I have *tried* to be cooperative. I don't know *what* it is you're trying to be!"

Kay Emerson, the brunette Brunhilde, stepped away from the desk she hadn't quite sat at, and answered his challenge with nearly the same irritation.

"We're *trying* to be efficient, Admiral. And effective. And we're trying to do that on very little sleep, two time-zone changes, and over a holiday we'd *like* to be spending with our families!"

"So welcome to Project Quantum Leap!"

The moment the words were out, he regretted them. Not only did they ring of self-pity, but they effectively solidified the barrier that had been growing between him and these women since they'd been here. Like an old song, an old record, he heard in his mind the resounding chorus that would follow that remark.

Christine Pike narrowed her eyes, smirked, and said, "We're here as a favor, Admiral. Not because we chose it."

Yup, Al thought. Same song, same record. Geez, if only women didn't have to make everything personal! At least—not right away.

It was time for a cigar.

"Okay, look," he started, using the conciliatory tone he'd learned years ago with one of his wives. He pulled a cigar

218

from his pocket. "I gave you all the invoices. So why the hell did you have to call DC again?"

"We didn't," Jenna Casper said. Her quiet voice was a welcome sign. "Senator Weitzman called us." She glanced at her companions. "You think we're up at this hour on our own?"

Al paused in lighting the cigar. "Sounded like *you* made the call."

"We had to call him back," Kay said. Then she cleared her voice. "Some of us are a little preverbal when we've had only two hours' sleep."

"Or three," Jenna chimed in.

Al smiled at her. Then he sucked in the first puff from his cigar.

"So why'd he call? And why didn't he call me?"

"He did," Christine answered. She ran her fingers through her long red hair. "Your programming friend said you were busy and couldn't be disturbed."

One for Gooshie, Al thought. He tilted his chin up. "So? What's the bad news?"

The women glanced first at each other, then at their toes. Al followed their gazes, and voted for Jenna's.

"Senator Smallwood's son was arrested last night. Again," Kay said quietly. When she looked up, Al stopped doubting the sincerity in her eyes. "He was high. He had drugs on him. And he tried to sell them to an undercover cop. Guess how many charges he was facing."

"*Was?*"

"They got him to deal," Jenna explained. She glanced at Kay before continuing. "He turned in his father."

Al's cigar smoldered, unnoticed and unsmoked, for several seconds. The ugliness of that statement—"*He turned in his father*"—kept him from responding for some time.

"Poppa?"

His father's gasping breath hurt just to listen to. Al closed his eyes and laid his head on the side of the bed, near his father's hand.

"Don't—worry," his father whispered. The words were slurred with pain. "Everything's gonna be fine. As long as—" His words were cut off by a long cough that ended only as blood dripped from the side of his mouth.

219

"Poppa?" He wiped the side of his father's face with his sleeve.

"Just pray for me." His voice was caught between a whisper and a groan.

"I will."

Al ran a hand over his face. "What the hell kind of a kid would turn in his own father?"

"Maybe the kind whose father got him started on drugs to begin with?" Jenna suggested.

He looked at her, then turned away. He wasn't sure, but he didn't want to take the chance that his memories were strong enough to be seen.

"His father got him started?"

"Back in the eighties," Christine said. "Then dad got elected and suddenly doing drugs wasn't good business any more. So he quit. But his son—well, George was dealing. You can stop buying, but it's a lot harder to stop selling."

"George?" Al asked. The memories began to retreat. Blissfully.

But the creepy coincidences of this Leap took their place.

"Senator Smallwood's son," Kay said. She fiddled with the calculator on her desk. "After his girlfriend died, he just— well, he went off the deep end. Using, selling, dealing. At one point, his father actually told the press that it was all *her* fault."

Al pulled the mostly useless handlink from his pocket and tested his intuition on the database that was currently humming along to Bing Crosby's "White Christmas."

"Trying to blame his son's problems on a girl who died," Kay continued. "If that isn't sick. . . ."

"George Smallwood." The name popped up on Ziggy's display, along with the lyrics for the second verse of "Winter Wonderland." He ignored the latter and waited for the rest of Ziggy's information. "*He* was datin' Teresa Bruckner."

"Teresa something, yeah," Christine agreed.

Jenna walked over and looked at the handlink that glowed in Al's palm. "Is that important?" she asked.

Al looked up and started to smile. "Maybe," he said. "If you believe in Santa Claus."

If a priest asks to be received at the monastery . . .
let him be allowed . . . to say Mass,
if the abbot bids him.

**—THE RULE OF ST. BENEDICT:
CHAPTER 60**

CHAPTER
TWENTY-SIX

December 25, 1998
Stallion's Gate, New Mexico

"Jou see the problem then, jets?"

Angela swung her legs back and forth, much like a child on a swing, her feet reaching only halfway to the ground from her perch on the Waiting Room table. O'Keefe, who was still trying to prepare an improvised altar for a Christmas Mass, listened, half-interested in what she was saying. He was beginning to tune her out.

"Yes, of course," he muttered, preparing the cruet of wine and another of water, not quite sure what he'd just agreed to.

"Then jou are going to keep Lillian Marco on the project, jets?"

Ah!

O'Keefe turned and looked at her. "Listen," he began, using his lecturing tone, "if you want to discuss theology, fine. Philosophy? Even the current religious fervor over reported angelic appearances—excluding this one—fine. But my translation project is no one's business. How I handle it—"

"Is going to ruin her life!" Angela dismounted from the table, the skirt of her dress hiked up momentarily by sliding down. O'Keefe averted his eyes.

"She's got a lot of talent, she's very gifted linguistically. I see no problems for her in finding another position somewhere." He looked back as Angela smoothed her dress. "But I can't afford to miss a deadline this big because of someone else's depression."

He didn't like this conversation. It had been hard enough to go to Charlotte in the first place, confront Lillian about her lack of performance. And, truth be told, he wasn't sure he

222

could find a replacement for her. Without her, the entire project fell on his shoulders.

That was one reason he had planned to hibernate at St. Bede's. At least there he could focus on his translation without being disturbed.

"Oh, jou won't make the deadline anyway!"

"What?"

Angela moved to his side and watched him set up the candles. "Jou are going to miss the deadline anyhow, so jou might as well have Lillian Marco—"

"I have never," O'Keefe interrupted, leveling a finger at her, "missed a deadline."

The woman laughed, deep in her throat. "Until now."

O'Keefe gave her his most imperious look. "Well perhaps if I'd made it to the monastery instead of being shanghaied here for two days—"

"It has no' been two days!"

"—I might have made it!" He turned, stared at the altar, and stifled the urge to express his actual feelings.

"Oh, jou no' have to worry too much," Angela said. "Not about jour project, anyhow." He glanced up. "Even though the Natural Endowment grant is pulled...."

"National Endowment."

"Whatever. Anyhow, some hotshot at Harvard decides to publish it anyway. It's still a *big* success!" She flailed her arms for emphasis.

O'Keefe sighed. "Fine. Then let's drop the subject."

"No, not until jou agree to keep Lillian Marco on the project!"

It was almost with relief that O'Keefe saw the Door open. The young man who'd brought him the altar reappeared.

"Captain."

"Father." The man shot a quick glance at Angela, but didn't address her. "I've worked out a compromise for you with Admiral—the admiral." Apparently, O'Keefe realized, security here required that no one be on a last-name basis.

"Are you sending me back?"

"No! Jou are no' finished here. And Sam still has to save Teresa...."

"I'm sorry, she's right," the captain confirmed. "But—

well, the admiral has agreed to let you be there. In a manner of speaking."

O'Keefe waited.

"See, there's an Imaging Chamber," Davalos explained. "It's how we contact Dr.—uh, Sam." Again, the last-name ban. "In there, as long as you're in physical contact with the admiral, you can see and hear the past. And—well, Sam can see and hear you."

O'Keefe's face wrinkled for a second; then understanding filled his eyes. "Then I could hear the confessions, not Sam?"

Davalos shrugged. "Well, Sam will still be there. No one will be able to see or hear you, though. Except the admiral and Sam. But," he continued, cutting off O'Keefe's attempted protest, "*you* would be able to see and hear them. And you could absolve them."

O'Keefe glanced at Angela; she was smiling and fanning herself.

"But neither Sam nor Al is bound by the seal of the confessional," he protested.

"Well, that's true, but. . . . " Davalos shoved his hands into his pockets. "Well, Sam loses parts of his memory when he Leaps. I don't think he'll even remember any of it."

"Oh, Sam is a good boy!" Angela added. "He would never tell what he hears in there."

The idea of having to go through another person—or two—to hear confessions was a terrible violation of the sanctity of the sacrament. But it was better than allowing those who came to St. Bede's for spiritual nurturing to be endanged by a false priest.

"What about Al?"

A wry grin and a half-grimace covered the captain's face. "Father, if there's anyone on this planet who knows how to keep his mouth shut, it's the admiral." The vote of confidence had a ring of personal experience to it.

O'Keefe sighed. "So he'll let me hear confessions."

"And celebrate Mass," Davalos added. He waited anxiously as O'Keefe considered the option.

Father O'Keefe pondered the choice a moment longer, relying on the acutely legalistic training he'd received as a Jesuit. It could be the first time technology and faith had ever walked this closely together, and the solution to the confession problem was, if risky, nowhere near as bad as the alternative. After all, people occasionally overheard others' confessions by accident, through proximity or voices that carried too far.

But the validity of a Mass said by a priest who was visible but separated by time and space had never come up in his studies.

"It would be a help to Doct—Sam," Davalos continued, trying to sway him into agreement. "He can follow your lead. And—the sisters won't become suspicious."

It wasn't, O'Keefe decided, an ideal solution by any means. But it might be better than nothing. After all, he rationalized, the Mass was a form of prayer. And prayer was *not* constrained by time and space.

As specious as he suspected the argument was, he nodded reluctant agreement. A gleam of pleasure flashed in Davalos' eyes.

"What do I need to do?"

"Admiral—the admiral will come back for you shortly. He'll take you in there."

"No, jou listen to Angela! We got to talk about Lillian Marco."

Fortunately, before Davalos had a chance to respond, the Door opened again and the admiral himself walked in. He opened his mouth to speak, but Angela got the first word.

"Jou tell him, hokay, Al? Jou tell Father Samuel what's going to happen to Lillian Marco if he dumps her off of this project."

"What?"

"It's a moot subject." O'Keefe turned back to Angela. "I've already told her I will no longer need her help."

"Oh, jou don' know it, but che is at the monastery right now! Right, Al?"

The admiral looked first at Angela, then at O'Keefe, and shrugged. "Yeah, right. Look, Angela, why didn't you bother to mention that Teresa's slimy boyfriend has a father who just happens to be on our committee?"

"Jou got a committee?" Angela fanned herself and smiled flirtatiously. "Can I meet them?"

Impatiently, the admiral waved an unlit cigar toward her. "Sure," he said. "Be my guest! Just take the first flight outta here for Washington!" He shoved the cigar between his teeth and sucked on it. "Look, why didn't you tell me about George?"

Angela shrugged nonchalantly. "I did no' know," she explained.

"What? Don't angels get some kind of briefing?"

"I told jou, tha's no' how it works!" She was becoming irritated. O'Keefe sighed and helped the captain pack up the altar. "I am jus' told what I am supposed to do, *si*?"

"Yeah, I see."

The angel narrowed her gaze. "Jou makin' fun of me 'cause of how I talk?"

"People!" O'Keefe interrupted. The squabbling was making it difficult to prepare for Mass. He held his hands up for a cease-fire. "This is getting no one anywhere. And I believe there *is* somewhere we need to go?" He posed it as a question.

"You're gonna do it?" the admiral asked. Something like dread was in his eyes.

O'Keefe shrugged. "It's better than nothing."

"No, no!" Angela put her hand out and grabbed the admiral's arm. He pulled it free. "No, first jou gotta tell him about Lillian Marco."

"Later, Charo."

"No, not later, now! Jou see, I got to get back to the monastery because—I promised Teresa I would come back." She batted her eyelashes at the admiral, just for a second, and O'Keefe had the distinct feeling a sharp knife had been delivered to some very soft flesh with those words.

Silent, giving the woman a venomous look, the admiral pulled the colorful box that he carried around with him from his pocket. It squealed like a mouse caught in a trap.

"Lillian Marco," he said quietly, reading from a small display. "Says here that after she left the Project she—" He stopped and looked up; first at Angela, then at O'Keefe. "She's hospitalized for severe depression. Tried to kill herself—maybe. Might have been an accidental overdose."

"You're making this up," O'Keefe protested. He grabbed the cruets of water and wine.

The admiral shook his head; the anger was gone from his eyes now. What replaced it resembled a very deep sorrow.

"She loses custody of her son. Next three years, he gets shuffled around to a series of foster homes. As of right now," he added, reading the last of the display and meeting O'Keefe's eyes, "the kid's in a home for juvenile offenders. Mom's in a psych ward." He sighed. "The kid's barely ten years old, and he's already got a record for shoplifting and larceny."

"Jou are no angel, Father O'Keefe," Angela said quietly. The entire room had suddenly become very, very quiet, O'Keefe realized. "But jou do get a second chance, jets?"

"Yeah," the admiral added, pulling the cigar from his lips and staring at it. "Don't I remember you sayin' something about the choices we'd make *if* we knew the future?" He gave O'Keefe a direct look, one that made O'Keefe feel small. "You're pretty lucky, huh? You got the chance to see it."

Sunday, April 2, 1995   9:10 A.M.
Route 128, Northern Massachusetts

It was hard for George to drive through the cloud of numbness that was engulfing his brain, and so, after about five minutes, Anderson took over at the wheel. He wore his gun in a holster on his left, so there was no chance for George to surprise him by grabbing it. Not that George was in any shape to grab anything at the moment.

"Don't go to sleep on me, now," the D.E.A. man commanded. He picked pepperoni, left over from the night before, from between his teeth. "You gotta help me find the dope when we get there."

"Teresa," George said drowsily. "She has it. Somewhere. She'll give it. . . ." His voice trailed off, and he stared out the window, watching the clouds pass above them, watching the trees pass beside them, watching the world tumble together like a kaleidoscope.

One of the last, foggy thoughts he had before he went to sleep was that he was either very sensitive to the effects of Fiorinal, or he'd been slipped something a lot more powerful.

Well, at least his foot didn't hurt anymore.

Sunday, April 2, 1995   9:10 A.M.
Windy Bluffs, Massachusetts

The road to breakfast, Sam discovered, was strewn with difficulties. After being waylaid by Mother Mary Frances, he

227

headed back toward the refectory, only to be caught by several oblates who wanted to discuss his book, *The Secret Language*, and the various points he made in it. Points they seemed to know more about than he did.

Politeness cost him an extra half-hour.

Finally, he made it inside the door, where the scent of coffee and doughnuts and coffee cakes renewed the call of hunger from his stomach. He watched as one of the other guests took a bowl from the hutch and filled it with cereal from a nearby sideboard. A small refrigerator contained milk and juices. Against the wall closest to Sam was the coffee urn, and he headed there first. It was a mistake. In retrospect, he should have made a mad dash for the muffins and coffee cakes on the table, and bolted.

"Sam! Sam, we gotta talk!"

Al Calavicci, still in uniform, startled Sam just as he reached for a cup near the coffee urn. Al was engulfed in the urn, and as Sam steadied his cup and reached out, the spout projected from the holographic image at the level of the man's belly button. It was an irritating sight.

"Al," he hissed, "do you mind?"

As if only then noticing where he'd materialized, Al looked at himself and chuckled. He moved out of the way, and stood behind Sam. "Sam, we got somethin' on this nozzle of a boy-friend Teresa's mixed up with," he said.

"Yeah, what?" Sam whispered. He made his way toward the dining table, where the pastries were. But there were also a number of other guests in the room, and several stopped their own conversations as they noticed him.

"You must be Father O'Keefe," one woman said. She brushed confectioner's sugar from her hand and clasped his as he reached for a muffin. "I'm Celia Thompson. This is my husband, Dan, and our kids, Dan Junior and Sheila." She pointed to two children across from her who were fighting over the last piece of strawberry strudel. Sam would have settled the argument for them, but he didn't have a chance. The moment the woman released his hand, the man next to her took it.

"Soon as we heard you were giving this retreat, well, we just knew we had to be here, isn't that right, Celia?" the man continued, taking over for his wife without missing a beat. She reached over to quiet the children by tearing the strudel in half and plunking a piece on each of their plates.

"Now, be quiet and eat. Your father and I are talking to Father Samuel," she chided, then turned back. "We read your book and we were so impressed! I mean, you really did a lot of research, didn't you?"

"Sa-am," the hologram beckoned. "Come on, we gotta talk!"

"Uh, well, yeah, I—I guess I—Could you hand me—" He reached in vain for the lone muffin in front of them—but a girl ran from the end of the table and snatched it.

"Really, the amount of work you must have put into that!" the woman cooed. "Here, please, sit down and talk with us!" She scooted to one side on the bench, her husband scooted to the other, and a small, tight space was cleared between them for Sam.

"Uh, well, I—actually, I have to—" he gestured vaguely behind him, toward the door.

"You gotta get outta here, Sam, so we can talk!" Al insisted.

"Oh, yes, I understand." The man glanced at his watch. "Hey, it *is* almost time for confession, honey. Come on, we'd better get going. You know, I lost track of time. . . ."

Sam saw another muffin at the end of the table. It looked as if most of the available food had been eaten by the time he'd arrived, but he wasn't giving up easily. He made his way to the end of the table and reached for the solitary cranberry muffin.

"Father O'Keefe!"

"Sam!" Al's voice had dropped to just above a growl. Sam ignored him, but the young, perky voice that called to Father O'Keefe was harder to ignore.

"Sister Mary Catherine." His fingers closed protectively around the muffin as he forced a smile and nodded at her. She was crossing the room from the sink, drying her hands on a dishcloth. She came up close to him and lowered her voice so she wouldn't be overheard.

"Father, I just wanted to tell you that, well, I mentioned to Mother what I saw yesterday."

"What you saw?" At the moment, nothing but the muffin in his hand mattered.

"Yes." Sister Mary Catherine cleared her throat and looked at him meaningfully. "In the trees?" she hinted.

Sam felt queasy; he'd thought the unfortunate incident by the side of the road had been forgotten. "You—told Mother Mary Frances—about that?"

"What's she talkin' about, Sam?" Al asked, suddenly interested. Sam grimaced and ducked his head.

"Well, I wasn't sure if I should, at first," Sister Mary Catherine confessed. "But, after all, I'd never seen anything like it before, and it was—well, it was so exciting."

Sam coughed. "Exciting?"

"Sam! What is she talkin' about? *What* did she see yesterday?"

"Well, Mother told me I shouldn't say anything to anyone else, but—this morning she said she was going to talk to you about it. Did she?"

"Uh, no, no. Listen, Sister." He licked his lips, suddenly dry, and cleared his throat. "Look, it was purely an accident. I mean, what you saw. So—let's forget about it, okay?"

"Forget it?" Clearly, the woman was disappointed. "But, Father it was—well, I was so inspired after I saw it. And none of the others sisters here has ever seen anything like it."

"Inspired?" Al repeated.

Sam's cheeks burned and he closed his eyes.

"Sister—"

"I was hoping that—well, that it would appear again."

"No!" Sam waved his hand and realized he'd inadvertently raised his voice with it. Al was giving him a look that was nearly as penetrating as Sister Mary Catherine's. "No, Sister, look, you really should—try to forget about it, all right?"

"Sam!" Al moved closer, poking the handlink with his finger. "You didn't!" he accused.

"It wasn't. . . ." He cut off his words and took a deep breath as Sister Mary Catherine began to look at him strangely. "It was *nothing*."

He shot a glare at the older man and saw the hologram giving Sister Mary Catherine an appraising look. "Geez, Sam, you Leap in as a priest and you're gettin' more action than *I* am!" the man complained, waving his cigar in a circle of defeat.

"If you say so." The young woman looked at the muffin

in his hand, tried to cover her disappointment, and said, "Oh, don't worry about cleaning up here, Father." She extricated the muffin from his grasp. "I'll take care of it. You'd better get ready for confessions."

"Sam, we gotta talk," Al reminded him, gesturing with his head toward the door. "You can pick up with Sister Mary Catherine later. Although," he added, shooting Sam a sour look, "I have to admit, I'm a little disappointed in you. A nun!"

Across the room, Sam noticed, Lillian Marco was finishing her breakfast, and he remembered he still had to talk to her. But the muffin, disappearing from view, was all Sam focused on. "Uh, Sister," Sam started, "would you—save that for me? For—after confession?"

The nun laughed quietly, her Ingrid Bergman laugh. "You mean after Mass," she said, and turned to put the leftovers in plastic wrap.

"After Mass?" Sam whispered. Watching numbly as the rest of the food was repackaged, wrapped, or refrigerated, Sam sighed and followed Al back outside. "After *Mass*?" he repeated to the hologram once they were outside, away from view.

"Well, let's see," Al muttered, glancing at the handlink. He shoved the cigar between his teeth. "Confessions start at 9:30—sounds like maybe *you* should be the one going—"

"Al! Nothing like that happened," Sam protested. But Al was apparently done with his teasing for the moment.

"Mass is at ten." He whacked the side of the box, as if to clear the display, and looked Sam in the eye. "With a group like this, you'll definitely be hearing confessions for at least half an hour."

Sam groaned and leaned against the side wall of the building. They'd moved into the relative protection of a few maples that grew nearby. From where he stood, Sam could see the walk that led to the chapel and the side of the main house.

"And I suppose it's against the rules to eat while you're hearing confessions?" he asked sarcastically.

Al looked puzzled, as if he'd never considered the question. He punched the handlink again, elicited a quick burst of what sounded like "The First Noel," and shook his head. "Well, it's close enough to the Mass that you might break the fast,"

Al said, as if that explained Sister Mary Catherine's abduction of his breakfast.

"Fast? You have to fast before Mass?"

"Well, only an hour. Hey!" Al added, waving the link for emphasis. "You should be happy. Back when I was growin' up, you had to fast from midnight the night before!"

Sam narrowed his gaze, and said, with all the heartfelt fervor he could muster on an empty stomach, "I did."

"Oh. Yeah." Al looked away, glanced at the link, and sucked his cigar.

"Look, what have you got on Teresa?"

Al pulled the cigar from his lips and looked at Sam. "Well, no thanks to Ziggy *or* Angela," he started, "I got the identity of the man Teresa's been seein'."

"Is he still alive?"

"Yeah, he's still alive." Al practically bounced with self-satisfaction.

"Well?"

"George Smallwood. As in Senator Bruce Smallwood's son."

Sam shook his head. "Who's Bruce Smallwood?" His blood sugar was at an all-time low. And while he knew it, it still didn't help his disposition much.

"That's right, you don't know him," Al muttered, twirling his cigar between his fingers. "He was elected to the Senate after you Leaped. He got himself put on our committee about a year ago."

"*Our* committee?"

"Our committee. He's the reason for the audit," Al explained. "He made a stink with Weitzman about the funds I've been transferring outta the motor pool. Weitzman knows about it; he's been winking at it this whole time."

"What funds?" Aside from monosyllabic responses, all Sam seemed to come up with were repetitions of Al's words. He was beginning to feel foolish.

"The funds," Al explained, gesturing, "that I have to pull outta the motor pool from time to time to keep Ziggy's research unit on-line. Anyway, that's not the issue." He waved it away with a swipe of his hand. "The issue is that Smallwood senior is in deep ca-ca right now for embezzlement and fraud.

And Junior is in deep ca-ca over a big bad drug problem. So what happens?''

"I give up." Sam shrugged. He was trying to keep the players straight at this point. Playing twenty questions was out of the question.

"Daddy sends auditors down to the Project and threatens to expose our improprieties unless the charges against him are dropped. Only before any of that can happen," Al said, giving Sam a look that let him know the punch line was near, "Junior gets himself arrested—again—on a whole slew of charges. Next thing we know, he cuts a deal and turns state's evidence against his daddy." Al raised an eyebrow and snickered. "Kinda brings a whole new meaning to 'dysfunctional families,' doesn't it?"

"Okay, let me get this straight." Sam paced in a small circle as he tried to untangle the story. "Smallwood's threatening to expose the Project unless the charges against him are dropped. But his son turns in enough evidence. . . ."

"For indictments. They're comin' out today. And when that happens, Sam, Weitzman's threatened to shut us down so the press doesn't get hold of any of this."

Whether it was hunger or fear, something in the pit of Sam's stomach began churning up bile. "Shut us—he wouldn't really do that, would he?"

Al shrugged. "I doubt it." He looked away. "But if the press gets wind of the Project, Sam, we're still gonna be in trouble."

Sam nodded, almost absently. "So—what does this have to do with Teresa's death?"

"Oh, that's the good part, Sam!" Al was suddenly enthusiastic again. "See, there isn't a whole lot on Teresa, but there's a whole busload of stuff on George." For emphasis, he pulled Ziggy's link back into view and punched it. It squealed, a curiously melodic sound.

"Right now, George is dealing."

"Yeah, we knew that."

"But it doesn't look like he started usin'—at least, not to any great extent—until after Teresa died. At one point," Al added, looking up, "he told one of the shrinks in a rehab hospital he was sent to that he got so depressed after she died that he stopped carin' about anything. He felt guilty about it. It ate him up.''

Sam took a long breath and glanced at his watch. He had less than ten minutes before he was supposed to be hearing confessions. "So if we save Teresa, George won't end up in trouble, is that what you're saying?''

"Pretty much.'' Al puffed on the cigar and stared at the smoke. "Apparently, a lot of what Daddy's been involved in had to do with covering up for his son. The more his son dealt and used, the more expensive it got and the more Senator Smallwood covered for him. Ziggy gives it an 89.5 percent probability that if we keep Teresa from dying, George's problem won't develop. And Daddy's problem won't develop. And—''

"And your problem won't develop,'' Sam finished.

"*Our* problem,'' Al reminded him pointedly. He waved the cigar to emphasize his point.

In the distance, a line of people had formed outside the chapel, waiting, no doubt, for the confessional to open.

"Okay, all right, so—I just have to save Teresa and—there won't be any threat to the Project, right?''

Al nodded slowly. "Right.''

"Well, what about the dope?''

"Well, after you get George out here,'' Al explained, "you sit him down and have a nice little talk with him. Convince him to turn the stuff over to someone. If he's willing to cut a deal that involves ratting on his own father three years from now,'' Al pointed out, "he might be willin' to cut a deal now to keep himself out of jail.''

"Or worse,'' Sam added, considering Teresa's fear.

"Or worse,'' Al agreed.

"Great.'' Sam moved toward the main house and heard the handlink squeal behind him. He turned around and waited until Al looked up.

"What?'' the hologram demanded. Sam shot a half glance at the main house, then looked back.

"Al, I—I don't remember much about—that last time— when I was a priest,'' he started. He gripped his hands, feeling suddenly quite nervous. "I mean, I don't remember—''

"Yeah, well, you didn't really have much of a chance to practice,'' Al muttered. Then he shrugged and looked away.

"Don't worry about it. We're gonna bring Father O'Keefe into the Imaging Chamber so you can see and hear him." He looked back, just for a second, and met Sam's eyes. "Like we did that time with Katie McBain, remember?"

Sam didn't, but he had to believe Al knew what he was talking about.

The admiral waved a hand in the air, a careless gesture that seemed forced. "All you gotta do is say what he says and do what he does." He punched the handlink, and the Door opened behind him. "It'll be a piece o' cake."

The Door shut, and Sam's stomach rumbled. "I wish it were," he said.

CHAPTER

TWENTY-SEVEN

December 25, 1998
Stallion's Gate, New Mexico

Of all the things in the world Al could think of to *not* look forward to, the compromise Davalos had proposed to O'Keefe had to be right up there with open heart surgery.

Minus the anesthetic.

Convincing the auditors to convince Weitzman not to act precipitately and shut them down before the Leap was over had to rank a close second. And in the next ten minutes, while Davalos and O'Keefe finished their preparations, Al had to do exactly that.

When he arrived in the administrative office, Jenna Casper was the first to look up from the papers Al had tossed on her desk earlier. With some food in their stomachs, which Al had seen to before returning to the Control Center, all three women seemed much more willing to listen to him. He hoped.

"So you've been transferring money from the motor pool to pay for the research unit and the Imaging Chamber?" A nice, straight approach. Al appreciated that. At least it showed they'd been doing their homework.

"Basically. Yeah." Al smoked his cigar without concern and leaned against the desk Kay Emerson had taken for herself. Across from him, Christine Pike was still leafing through the copies Jenna had made of the papers, still punching numbers into the calculator on her desk.

"It looks like this has been going on for some time," Kay commented. She spoke from behind him, and Al pulled himself up and turned to face her. She was rummaging through a few of the manila folders on the floor near her desk.

"Yeah. A while."

"Admiral," Jenna said, "according to these records, you've

been routinely running short of funds for research and imaging toward the end of each fiscal quarter.''

''Right.'' He smiled and stuffed the cigar back between his lips.

''As far as I can tell, this has been going on since—well, almost since the beginning.''

Al shrugged. ''We ran short before Sam Leaped, but we just had to sit on our hands and wait for the committee's next hearing to increase funding in that area. But once Sam disappeared,'' he continued, moving to Jenna's desk and noticing for the first time that she was wearing a lower-cut blouse than she had yesterday, ''then it became a matter of life or death.'' He risked giving her a more intense look, holding her attention while lowering his voice. ''We couldn't just sit around and twiddle our thumbs and hope Sam could figure out what to do on his own, now could we?'' He gave her a suggestive grin, and she blushed. He moved in for the kill. ''See, when Sam's Leapin', we can't lose contact with him or—''

''We've read your speeches to the committee, Admiral,'' Kay cut in. Jenna quickly looked away and fingered her blouse nervously. ''On the plane. Unfortunately, we all got airsick.'' Reluctantly, Al turned to her. Jenna had been captivated for the moment, but it was time to turn his attention to the new challenge.

''Then you've also read the committee's answer each time we asked 'em to increase funding in those areas.'' He snapped his cigar from his lips. '' 'No,' 'no,' and 'hell no.' '' The cigar punctuated his words, and Jenna flinched at the vehemence in his voice.

''Transferring money from one fund to another, Admiral, is still embezzlement,'' Kay said quietly.

''Weitzman's been lookin' the other way for three years,'' Al pointed out, his voice still quiet. ''Now, all I'd like is for him to keep a leash on Smallwood until this Leap is over.'' He looked at them in turn, holding Jenna's gaze the longest. '' 'Cause I got a hunch that once this Leap is over, Smallwood isn't gonna be a problem any longer.''

Jenna looked down, toyed with the papers on her desk, and said, ''You want us to call him?''

''Yeah. Figure you're probably more persuasive than I am,'' he added, letting his look do more than the words. Jenna caught on. But she glanced at the other women before saying anything.

"It *would* take at least four hours for an order from the committee to be implemented," she mused. She met his eyes. "Would that be enough time?"

Al glanced at his watch; according to Angela, Teresa died sometime this afternoon, Massachusetts Leap Time.

"That's cutting it close."

Kay shook her head. "I can call the senator," she said, "but it would help if I had something substantial to tell him. I don't imagine that 'the admiral has a hunch' will go over very well, do you?"

One side of his mouth crooked up. "No." He looked at the women. "But maybe if you told him George Smallwood is a critical part of this Leap—he might be convinced to pull some strings to keep the *real* embezzler quiet a little longer."

"If you're making this up, Admiral," Kay began.

"Lady," Al said, leaning a little closer, "I got way too much to worry about right now to have any time to make up stories. Even to cover my own butt."

Jenna muttered something under her breath that sounded like a compliment to that butt, and Al glanced at her curiously. Then he returned to Kay.

"Will you call Weitzman?"

The handlink in his pants pocket wailed but Al ignored it, holding Kay's gaze, willing her to cooperate.

"I'll call him," she agreed. "But no guarantees."

The link squealed again.

"Admiral," Jenna said, "I don't mean to be personal, but something in your pants wants attention."

Al stared, almost gaping, and heard the two other women in the room clearing their throats and snickering quietly.

Then he reached into his pocket and pulled out the colorful box. "Well, it isn't a banana," he reported, and enjoyed the responses.

He glanced at the display, realized his time here was up, and cursed softly. "Sorry, ladies. It's been fun, but I gotta go." He went to the door and waited for it to slide open. "When you talk to Weitzman, be sure to send him my regards."

The women exploded with repressed laughter as the door closed behind him.

Angela was saying her good-byes when Al returned to the Control Center. And although he knew she had claimed to be returning to the monastery, he was still a little surprised.

And, though he hated to admit it, disappointed.

"Can't you—hang around a little longer?" he asked, adopting as careless an attitude as he could. It wasn't easy. There were, as there had been at their first parting, tears in Angela's eyes; she wiped at them with her hand, trying to smile.

"No, I gotta go help out Sam now," she said.

Father O'Keefe and Davalos were in the Imaging Chamber, waiting for Al. Apparently she'd already said her farewells to them. Gooshie had crawled back under Ziggy's console, probably adjusting her for the increased energy this little stunt was going to require.

Al nodded and cocked his head to the side. "Yeah, well. Then I guess I'll see you there, huh?"

The angel sniffed. "I don't think so, Al." The rarity with which she used his name struck Al suddenly. He swallowed, his throat tightening a fraction.

"Well. . . ." He couldn't think of what to say.

"I'm going to miss you." The same bittersweet sadness that Al had seen before was in her eyes. And when she reached up and touched his cheek, he felt a powerful desire to give her a hug.

He resisted, cleared his throat, and cocked an eyebrow. "Yeah, like missin' a toothache."

She didn't answer him, but the look in her eyes didn't change.

"So this time—I'll forget about you?"

She shrugged and wiped a few final tears from her eyes. "That's the way it works, *si*?" She opened her purse and put her fan inside.

He smiled. "Jets," he answered.

She laughed. "Jou learn a little Puerto Rican English from Angela after all, huh?" Then she started toward the elevator. "I will no' forget jou, Al."

She got into the elevator and waved as the doors closed.

239

"Almost wish I could say the same," Al muttered, to no one in particular.

Sunday, April 2, 1995   9:33 A.M.
Windy Bluffs, Massachusetts

Depressed. That was how Teresa felt. After the exhilarating excitement of this morning, and even the acknowledgment by Father O'Keefe that her angels had returned, there had been no sign of them in the hours since. And no one else, no one but Sister Mary Catherine, had been there this morning.

Teresa hadn't seen them. No one else was saying anything about angels. And now, sitting in her room, alone except for the doll she'd salvaged from her childhood, she began to wonder if Father O'Keefe had just been humoring her.

She hugged her doll to her chest, clutching it as she had when she was a child, and stared out the window. The grounds were empty. No one was there. Everyone was probably in the chapel. Mass was supposed to start in half an hour. Confession was going on right now. And she was probably the only person at the monastery who wasn't there.

She had no yearning to go to a church service, especially not a Catholic one. They had a lot of strange rituals that she didn't understand; she'd feel foolish being there, and it wouldn't mean anything to her. It was just a lot of mumbo jumbo, like Kevin said. Magic, fairy tales.

"There are no such things as angels, munchkin. You just have to face up to that."

For a while, when she was little, after Sam and Al had gone, she and Kevin would talk about it. Just between themselves, of course. Kevin would tell her how Mom had laid into the two guys who'd kidnapped him. He'd tell her Mom could fight like a tiger. And Teresa would tell him—again and again— that it wasn't Mommy. It was the angel.

Eventually, Kevin got tired of trying to convince her she was wrong; and she got tired of trying to convince Kevin that she was right.

And then, when she was older, she began to wonder. If Sam and Al *were* angels, why didn't they come back to save her mother? Why didn't they return when she *really* needed them? Why did Al break his promise to her?

240

Until two nights ago, she'd given up believing in angels. She'd stopped talking about them. After all, people only laughed at her when she told them she'd seen an angel.

Everyone except Mom. Mom hadn't laughed. She'd listened, like she always did. And then she'd said, "Well, honey, I really don't remember it so well. But—if that's what you want to believe, you go right ahead. It certainly can't do you any harm. It's better than a lot of things people believe."

Hugging the childhood memory as close as she held the doll, Teresa realized that she didn't want to just sit here, waiting for something to happen. Maybe, maybe if the angels really were back, she'd see them in the chapel; after all, that's where they'd appeared to begin with, right?

The doll's head came off in her hands as she stroked its hair. She checked the stuffing, then put the head back on and laid the doll on the bed. She opened her suitcase and pulled out a clean set of clothes.

Mass, Schmass. Whatever it was, she would just sit through it.

Maybe Al and Sam would be there.

"Bless me, Father, for I have sinned."

Standing just outside the confessional, his hand resting lightly on Father O'Keefe's shoulder, Admiral Albert Calavicci shut his eyes when the first whispers sounded in the dark.

Of all the people Al had brought into the Imaging Chamber over the years—from Verbeena to Angela—O'Keefe was the only one who had had no reaction at all to the sensation of being swept through time. Al held off making physical contact with the priest until after he'd announced their presence to Sam, who was already in the dark, wardrobe-like box near the back of the chapel.

Al ducked his head through the wood and gave Sam brief instructions on how to operate the small, sliding panels on either side of him, through which he would speak to the penitents. Then he pulled back.

"Remember, Sam. Just repeat Father O'Keefe's words. Exactly as he says 'em. No paraphrasing. No improvising. Got it?"

He heard the tight breath Sam sucked in. "Yeah." And then he heard the first panel slide open.

He put his hand on Father O'Keefe's shoulder. "Here goes."

The past congealed around him; but O'Keefe didn't so much as breathe louder. He raised his right hand, made the sign of the cross in the air between himself and the imaged confessional, and whispered, "In the name of the Father, and of the Son, and of the Holy Spirit. Amen."

The moment it began, Al knew he had to get away.

But he couldn't leave. He couldn't walk out of the Chamber and leave O'Keefe to carry on without him.

He couldn't back down.

So, as he had done for most of his life, he shut his eyes and escaped into his own thoughts. He'd been doing it for so many years it was almost second nature.

"It's been three weeks since my last confession."

The words drifted through his thoughts, and Al tightened his concentration.

The auditors. He wondered if the auditors had gotten through to Weitzman. He wondered if they'd made the point about George Smallwood. He wondered if Weitzman had bought it.

He wondered if Weitzman was having a happy Hanukkah while the Project hung in the balance.

"For your penance," O'Keefe said quietly, "I want you to say three Hail Marys and three Our Fathers, meditating on the sacrifices our Lord made for us."

Sacrifices?

"*. . . He was crucified, dead, and buried. . . .*"

Ancient words from an ancient prayer interrupted Al's concentration.

Dead and buried.

Dead. And buried.

"Now, make a perfect act of contrition."

"*A perfect act of contrition,*" said Sister Mary Something, "*is when you're sorry for what you did, not because you're afraid of getting caught or being punished. But because you know that what you've done hurts God.*"

"*Sister?*" Al raised his hand and waited. She turned her gorgeous blue eyes on him. "*What if you really are just sorry 'cause you got caught? Or you got a whipping?*" Some of the

242

other kids laughed, and he smiled. His bottom, however, was still sore.

Sister shook her head and gave him a look. "That's an imperfect act of contrition." She walked down the aisle toward him. She leaned over his desk and he felt his heart flip-flop in his chest. Geez, she was pretty!

"It's better than nothing. But it's like washing your hands without using soap. They may be cleaner than they were when you started, but—" She paused and lifted one of his hands for inspection. "—you've still got the dirt under your nails."

He blushed. The other kids laughed. Sister Mary Something winked before she turned away.

"Oh, my God, I am heartily sorry. . . ."

Al opened his eyes and took a deep breath. His concentration was shot to—

". . . and I resolve, with the help of Thy grace, to amend my life, to sin no more, and to avoid the near occasion of sin."

He could almost smell the incense in the room. The dim candlelight was enhanced by the colored rays filtering through the stained glass windows at the back of the chapel. The Stations of the Cross—fourteen high points of Jesus' last moments on earth—surrounded him on the walls.

Surrounded.

That's how he felt. He was surrounded by the past, by *his* past. Surrounded by a God he wanted nothing more to do with.

". . . I absolve you of your sins, in the name of the Father, and of the Son, and of the Holy Spirit."

"Amen."

"Go in peace."

Peace? Al ground his teeth and closed out the images around him.

He heard Sam whispering the words after Father O'Keefe. Then he heard the small panel slide shut and the other one open.

"In the name of the Father, and of the Son, and of the Holy Spirit."

Al's left hand, shoved in his pocket, balled into a fist. It was starting all over again.

"Bless me, Father, for I have sinned." The voice in the box belonged to a child.

O'Keefe stepped closer to hear better: Al moved with him and found himself—and the Guest—nearly engulfed in old, oiled wood.

A wooden bench. Shiny white hallways. The sharp smell of rubbing alcohol. The rancid odor of the cancer that ate Poppa's body. The musky scent of incense and the sickly sweet smell of flowers.

"It's been three days since my last confession," the whisperer said.

"It's been two days since my last confession."

"Two days?"

The whispered sound of Sister Mary Something sitting next to him on the hard wooden bench outside his father's hospital room. The gentle clacking of the rosary beads trailing through her fingers. The muted sounds of the priest in the room behind them, giving his father the last rites.

"He's not really gonna die, is he, Sister?"

She put an arm around him and pulled him close. Her habit smelled of starch and incense. She didn't answer him. But she kept praying.

". . . . didn't mean to, but Joey said if I didn't, he'd tell Mom I broke the vase."

"Did you?" O'Keefe asked quietly. Sam repeated him.

"Ye-es," the boy reluctantly confessed.

"Then you need to tell your mother the truth, don't you?"

"She'll get mad at me!"

"Probably. But she'll probably be angrier that you lied than that you broke her vase."

"He lied to me!"

"Al." Sister Mary Whatever reached for him, but he pulled away. "You all lied!" The doctor, the priest, and the nun stood in the hallway, watching him. Inside, in the room where Poppa was supposed to get better, two guys in white coats were putting his body on a stretcher. They needed the bed for someone else; he heard them say that.

"Al, I know it hurts—"

"Get away! All of you! Just leave me alone!"

He ran down the corridor, past carts of useless medicine, past rooms that held more dying people, past men and women who lied and said they'd help Poppa.

He opened the first door with an exit sign and ran down

three flights of stairs, pushing the door at the bottom and finding himself outside. Only then did he know he was crying, when the bitter air slapped his face and he felt his cheeks burn with the icy sting.

He was in the back parking lot. There were only a few cars; not too many people wanted to work on Christmas.

He ran through the parking lot, slamming his fist on every car he passed, pounding sturdy metal with his flesh. Finally, when the knuckles of both hands were bleeding and the pain in his right hand told him he'd broken something, he sank to the ground, crouched against a car, and hunched over to cradle his hands against his chest.

"You bastard," he whispered.

The sky didn't open. Lightning didn't strike him down. His body wasn't instantly consumed by flames.

He raised his head and his voice. "You bastard!" he shouted at the sky. "He believed in You! I believed in You! And You killed him! You killed him!" His voice died into a sob and he gasped, breathless from running.

"Al."

Sister Mary Whoever found him there. Breathing hard, she wrapped her arms around him and pulled him toward her, toward the smell of incense and starch.

"He lied." It was hard to talk. It hurt so much. In his head. In his chest. In his stomach. It hurt. "He—lied to me. He said he would be—he'd be all right if I prayed for him." He gasped between words; he didn't want Sister to see him crying.

She didn't say anything. She just knelt on the ground next to him and held him and made quiet sounds in her throat. Maybe she was still praying.

"He broke his promise." Al struggled to stop crying. He tried to pull away, but Sister was stronger than he was.

"Your Poppa's in Heaven, Al. He's with God."

"No! He's dead! He's dead! He said we'd be together and—"

"Ssshh." The nun patted his head. "Your Poppa's gone to Heaven."

"What if he didn't?"

Hellfire. Eternal damnation. Unending torment.

With renewed fury, Al pulled away, stood up, and watched the young nun rise.

245

"What if he's in Hell?" he demanded. His eyes were burning. His hands shook. "Maybe he didn't make it! Maybe he died and went to Hell! I'll never know! Maybe he's burning in Hell right now!"

"Al, you have to have faith in—"

He started to leave. Sister's hand clamped down on his shoulder. Her fingers dug between bone and muscle.

"You prayed for him, didn't you?"

He wiped his face with his sleeve. The pain in his shoulder where Sister had grabbed him was almost a relief.

"I asked God—" he almost choked on anger—"to heal him. To make him better. But He let him die!"

Sister Mary Something released his shoulder and stood in front of him. "Everyone dies, Al. You. Me. The doctors in there." She gestured back to the brick building. "Everyone!" She gripped his shoulders with both hands. "Your Poppa believed that your prayers made a difference. Don't you think they did?"

He stared at her. Her eyes were so clear, so blue. Like the ocean. The world made sense to her.

But it didn't make any sense to Al. Not any more.

"No," he said. "They didn't! 'Cause Poppa still died!"

"Your Poppa is in a much better place."

Al pulled his shoulders back and swallowed hard. "I don't care if he's in a 'better place.' He's supposed to be here!" The first taste of bile, bitter and strong, rose in his throat. "He promised! He came back—and he promised we'd be together. He said we'd be like a real family! He said nothing would ever—" His eyes were filling up again; the cold air burned against the hot tears.

He took a deep breath and forced the pain down. "God doesn't care," he said. "He doesn't listen. Poppa would still be alive if He did!" He pulled free of Sister's grasp and clenched his hands. "I hate Him!" he screamed.

"Al. . . ."

"I hate Him!" Al swore again. "I hate Him! I hate Him! I hate Him!" He wouldn't cry: not any more. "I'm never gonna talk to Him again. Never!"

"Admiral!"

Al opened his eyes. His fingers were clenched tightly on Father O'Keefe's shoulder, white with tension, digging between bone and muscle. O'Keefe was in obvious pain.

O'Keefe stared at him as Al let out his breath and relaxed his grip.

"Now make a perfect act of contrition," O'Keefe said to the unseen penitent without releasing Al's gaze.

". . . a perfect act of contrition," Sam repeated inside the box.

"Oh, my God, I am heartily sorry. . . ."

Slowly, the images from Al's past began to fade. The sharp pain turned back to muted anger.

". . . and I absolve you of your sins. . . ."

One panel in Sam's box shut and the other slid open. A whispered prayer filled the silence.

"Bless me, Father, for I have sinned."

CHAPTER
TWENTY-EIGHT

Lillian Marco prepared to sit through the most excruciating Mass of her life. Father Samuel had made no attempt to speak with her this morning in the refectory. In fact, almost immediately after he saw her, he turned and headed out the door.

Her chance to keep her position with him obviously hadn't been improved by having driven all the way here to talk with him. Whatever heart the man had, she decided, didn't react to human compassion or suffering. Not even for her. Not even after five years.

She stopped hoping to talk with him before she left the monastery tonight. She decided, instead of begging him, to simply hold on to what was left of her pride. And she focused on her anger instead of the very disturbing possibility of being left without work—and therefore, an income—for some time.

There weren't, after all, many people clamoring for an Arabic translator these days.

The Mass began a few minutes late, and when it started, something seemed odd. Father Samuel appeared uncomfortable, as if he weren't used to the robes and cassock. He almost tripped twice during the processional.

The girl she had met yesterday, the one who'd received the phone call, came in at the end of the processional, looking unsure of herself. Lillian caught her eye and gestured her to the seat next to Stephen.

"Ever been to a Latin Mass?" she whispered as the girl accepted the invitation.

"No. Never been to a Mass at all."

Lillian was surprised, but said nothing. She turned her attention back to the altar and the focus of her irritation.

248

The sense that there was something odd occurring came again some moments after the Mass began. Not all at once, but with a slow regularity, several of the people in the congregation, and many of the sisters, let out quiet gasps and sank to their knees, their eyes fixed on the altar.

The only thing Lillian could figure was that Father Samuel was doing such a clumsy, inexpert job that everyone had gone to their knees to pray for him.

Teresa wasn't sure what was happening, but she was almost certain that this wasn't a normal Catholic service. Just minutes after she'd entered, several of the nuns in the stalls up front and to the right of the altar had let out quiet gasps and dropped to their knees. Some of the people in the pews had done the same. Others, still sitting, had looked around them, obviously as puzzled as Teresa was.

She had taken the seat near the woman who had brought her George's message. Her son squirmed unendingly. But Teresa was grateful for a familiar face in the middle of a very unfamiliar rite.

When the gasping and dropping started, she plucked up her courage and leaned over to the woman. "Are we supposed to kneel now?" she whispered.

The woman shook her head, glancing around her. "Not normally."

Behind them was one of the people who had responded as the nuns had; she was on her knees, her face covered, and she shook with tears.

"Excuse me," Teresa whispered, "what's wrong?"

"Can't you see them?" The woman looked up for a moment, then crossed herself. "There. On the altar. With Father O'Keefe."

Teresa looked back, fighting the growing hope in her chest. There were two altar boys, but no one else. Certainly the children hadn't caused this reaction.

"Who?"

"The angels," the woman whispered. "Two angels." The woman said nothing more to Teresa. She began a prayer Teresa knew as the Hail Mary.

But the woman was no longer Teresa's focus. The altar was. As hard as she tried, she couldn't see anyone there except

Father O'Keefe and the altar boys. But she believed she knew what the others saw.

Sam and Al *had* returned.

Sunday, April 2, 1995   11:15 A.M.
Windy Bluffs, Massachusetts

In retrospect, Sam thought, following Father O'Keefe through the motions of the Catholic priesthood had been one of the most memorable experiences of his life. He doubted that even with the Swiss-cheesing effect of Leaping through time, he would ever forget it.

Used to having Al coach and guide him through his more awkward moments, he found himself flustered in the presence of the priest. He remembered him not as a man of God but as a harsh, critical instructor. Throughout the half-hour of confessions and the hour of Mass, his stomach clenched in anticipation of the man roaring out that what he did was insufficient, incompetent garbage.

It didn't happen. But Sam was never sure that it wouldn't; not until it was over.

The makeshift altar that Al had set up in the Imaging Chamber was invisible to Sam, except for the few times that the priest touched it. Then, for a second or two, as Al's hand remained on the priest's shoulder, a folding table, covered with a white linen and set with candles and silver, appeared before the man. Only to disappear seconds later.

The most uncomfortable moment came at the point the missal in front of him labeled the Consecration. Though he went through the motions with Father O'Keefe, shadowing his actions and gestures, he had, by then, come to realize that what he was doing was intensely sacred to those who were watching him. And Sam Beckett was a fake, an impostor.

At that moment, though he didn't himself believe what everyone around him apparently did, he knew he was standing in someone else's place. He went through the ritual, saying words, making gestures, realizing with each Latin syllable that this was, for many in the room, the culmination of all they believed.

He felt small and guilty when he was done. And he wished,

even more than he had after confession, that he'd found some reason to back out of this. He didn't have to be a believer to realize that he had invaded something sacred to those who watched.

Al went through the ceremony of the Mass as he had gone through confession: a silent Observer, his only role to provide Sam with a window through time. But when Father O'Keefe lifted the consecrated Host to his lips, Al shook his head quickly at Sam and whispered, "Fake it."

His eyes were dark, his expression frozen and dangerous. What was going through his mind, Sam didn't even want to guess.

Father O'Keefe glanced first at Al, then at Sam. He said nothing.

Sam covered the wafer with his hand and pretended to eat it; but as he lowered his hand, he put the fragments back on the paten lying on the altar.

Al repeated his injunction when O'Keefe drank from the chalice. Obediently, Sam touched the cup to his lips and lowered it without tasting the wine and water mingled in it.

Someone served Father O'Keefe as an altar boy, but it wasn't Al. Throughout the unending hour, Sam had seen the priest respond to someone else, another person in the Imaging Chamber. But since he wasn't in contact with Al, the only glimpse Sam had of him was when Father O'Keefe offered Communion.

For less than a second, as the priest pressed the wafer into the man's palm, extended contact through Al made him visible. A naval officer. About Sam's age. Balding. Fleetingly familiar.

Then Father O'Keefe lifted another wafer and faced the admiral. "Corpus Christi," he said, and waited.

In the last hour and a half, through whispered prayers and dark confessions; through genuflecting and crossing himself; through incense and chants and hand-washing, Sam had begun to understand the power a faith like this could have over someone.

Even after he'd thrown it away.

It took only a second for Al to shake his head and refuse the wafer. But that second stretched back in time for hours and years and decades, like a deep scar.

Sam quickly turned away, not wanting to intrude on Al's decision.

Shortly after he'd begun the service, several nuns and a few of the congregation had dropped to their knees, whispering quiet prayers and covering their faces. A quick glance at Al and Father O'Keefe confirmed that this wasn't a normal response, but Sam ignored it: if his performance was that bad, he decided, maybe the extra prayers couldn't hurt.

As the sisters came forward to receive Communion, and the congregation filed up the center aisle to receive theirs, several of them continued to watch him warily. He tried to ignore the looks.

"Corpus Christi," he recited as he handed out the thin wafers to each. *The Body of Christ. . . .*

They looked just like little thin wafers. They felt just like little thin wafers. But after a dozen or so repetitions of that phrase, Sam began to wonder: If science and technology could allow him to transcend time and space and appear in the form of someone—or something—he wasn't, could God do the same?

The thought made him uneasy. But just in case, he handled the wafers carefully.

When the Mass ended, Al let go of Father O'Keefe's shoulder. For a second, the Observer remained as Sam waited for the altar servers and sisters to file out. Then, without a word, without a look, the admiral keyed the sequence into the handlink that opened the Door, and disappeared.

Sam expected it might be a while before he saw his friend again.

Along with several others in the congregation, Teresa lingered in the chapel after the service was over. She had strained, prayed, and begged to see the angelic apparitions so many others saw. But to no avail.

Finally, she left, disappointed but no longer depressed. She even hummed quietly to herself, a song Al had sung to her when she couldn't get to sleep.

She crossed the road, deciding to take a walk before returning to the monastery for lunch. She wanted to see the cliffs, the rocky shoreline that she and Father O'Keefe had wandered near last night in the rain. The path was still slippery but navigable. And it was as good a place as any to sit and think for a while.

She still wasn't certain what she was going to do about George and the drugs—she didn't want to leave him to the mercy of the men he worked for—but she wasn't quite as panicked about it now as she had been. She had a feeling that the answers were very close. Like the ocean. Eventually, everything would come clear. Something about this place just made her believe that.

"Hey! Jou better watch jour step!"

Teresa turned at the voice behind her and smiled. "Angela!" She waved to the woman who was, once more, stepping gingerly along the ground, her heels clicking on the stones, her ankles twisting with nearly every step.

"You should talk," Teresa chided the woman as she came up to her. Angela was panting.

"Jou chould no' be out here," Angela warned sternly. "This is a dangerous place!"

"Especially if you're wearing heels," Teresa pointed out. "Haven't seen you for a while. Where've you been hiding?"

Angela took Teresa's arm and began steering her back toward the road and the monastery. Sighing, Teresa gave in.

"Oh, in the future, about three years from now," the woman answered casually. "In a big blue room! Jou know," she added, clutching Teresa's arm more firmly after a misstep, "it was Christmas, but there wasn't very much Christmas jeer."

Teresa didn't bother to correct the woman's pronunciation; and she didn't try to follow what the woman said, either. Her mind was elsewhere. If Sam and Al had returned to help her, why had so many people been able to see them? She remembered overhearing part of their conversation years ago, when Al explained that only kids and animals could see them.

"The only one there who likes Christmas is the computer," Angela continued. They made it back to the road and waited for two cars to pass.

"The computer?" Teresa had lost track of the woman's monologue.

"Jets, a big colorful computer! They even gave it a name, can jou believe it?"

Teresa laughed. And then her laughter stopped. Down the road, well away from where the other cars were parked, away

253

from the dependencies, half hidden in the pines and maples that grew on this side of the road, was a brown car. From where she stood, she could see only the rear bumper of the car; but she could read the license plate.

George's car. He was here! And between the relief that it meant he was still alive and the fear of what else it meant, Teresa felt momentarily paralyzed.

"Something is wrong?" Angela stopped walking and followed her gaze, but Teresa looked away.

"No. No." She smiled at Angela and held onto her arm the rest of the way across the road. Then, releasing her, she said, "Look, I'm going to take a little walk. I'll stay away from the shoreline," she promised as Angela opened her mouth to make another motherly protest. "Promise. All right? Why don't you get some lunch?"

"Oh, I no eat."

Decency demanded that Teresa not respond to that.

"Okay, well, maybe there's someone who wants to take you on in Monopoly again," Teresa suggested. It was all she could do to keep her eyes from the car. All she could do to keep her hands from shaking.

"Oh, I don' know," the woman murmured. It was going to take some work to get rid of her, Teresa could tell. She shot a furtive glance at the car: there was no movement to indicate that George was planning to confront her right away. She had to take firmer steps to slip away from the eccentric woman so she could talk with George. Alone.

Not that she was at all sure what she was going to say to him.

She walked a few feet closer to the buildings, looking around for anyone who might be helpful. And found her.

"Sister! Sister Mary Catherine?"

The young nun, talking with a few of the other guests, looked up as Teresa and Angela approached. Apparently her timing was good: the others moved off toward the refectory, and Sister Mary Catherine lingered on the walk as they came over to her.

"Sister, have you met Angela? She's a friend of mine," Teresa explained quickly, shooting Sister Mary Catherine a significant glance. "We met on the way here—"

"No, we met in the subway, *si?*"

"Oh, right." Teresa smiled patiently at the woman. "Anyway," she continued, as Sister Mary Catherine extended her hand and shook Angela's, "Angela is an angel."

The young woman smiled indulgently and said, "I'm quite sure you are, Angela. Is this your first time at St. Bede's?"

"No, I really am an angel!" Angela protested.

Sister Mary Catherine hesitated for a moment, then turned to Teresa. "Did you. . . ."

"Not a word," Teresa promised, remembering Sister Mary Catherine's concern this morning that word about the apparitions might get around the monastery too soon. She hadn't considered Father O'Keefe a risk; after all, priests are supposed to keep secrets, right?

Sister Mary Catherine nodded and said, quite normally, "What kind of angel are you?"

"What?"

"Well, there are angels, archangels, dominions, principalities, powers, cherubim. . . ."

Teresa backed slowly away from the ensuing conversation and watched as the two walked along the path to the dining hall.

She sighed, then turned to the car in the trees. Still no movement, no sound.

Nothing to frighten her, she thought. So why was she frightened?

"Sam, Al," she whispered, "if you're really here again—" She paused, glancing at the sky, feeling foolish and childish. She hadn't tried talking to her angels since she was eight or nine. "Please help," she finished. And then she started for George's car.

CHAPTER
TWENTY-NINE

Sunday, April 2, 1995   11:20 A.M.
Windy Bluffs, Massachusetts

There was no escape. The only place to change out of the layers of medieval clothing Sam had been forced into was the small sacristy. And by the time he'd pulled off the stole and tunic, Mother Mary Frances was there. He felt momentarily embarrassed: after all, he was, in a sense, undressing. But she stood her ground, her cane clasped in both hands, and waited for his attention.

"Uh, Mother?" He wasn't sure, but the look on her face seemed to presage a disaster.

"Father Samuel," she began, "I've known you for almost twenty years. Longer," she corrected herself. Sam nodded, waiting, still half clothed in the ceremonial outfit. "Just between you and me, I've known you to be a bore, a stiff-necked intellect, a sourpuss, and an occasionally brilliant man."

Sam waited out what seemed to be the first honest evaluation he'd ever heard of his former teacher. But it surprised him: he'd never thought *anyone* would call Father O'Keefe a bore to his face!

"But I also know you to be a man who takes his calling seriously." The woman took a deep breath, apparently preparing herself for a confrontation. "That is why I'm shocked and dismayed by what has happened here."

Oh, boy.

Sam turned toward the wardrobe and placed his alb on a hanger. Sister Mary Catherine had said Mother Mary Frances was going to talk with him about the pit stop by the side of the road. And now, apparently, was the moment she had chosen to do so.

"Uh, Mother Mary Frances, I can explain," he started. He

256

swallowed a couple times, just to work up some moisture so his tongue would stop sticking to the roof of his mouth. "See, what Sister Mary Catherine saw. . . ."

"What Sister Mary Catherine saw," Mother interjected, "was quite surprising." Sam grimaced and couldn't meet her eyes. "But after I spoke with you this morning, I thought she might have been pulling a stunt," the woman went on, her voice dropping. "A very bad one at that!"

"This morning?" Sam remembered their conversation; it had had nothing to do with yesterday's untimely revelation.

"But now! Father," the woman said, moving closer in the already close room, her cane clacking on the tile floor, "even *I* saw something! I couldn't begin to swear to what the other sisters saw, but I saw something! Glowing, bright, it—it hovered around you the entire time you said the Mass!"

Sam sucked in his breath and realized he couldn't breathe out.

"You—saw. . . ."

"Angels, Father Samuel. Or some form of heavenly visitation. You tell me. The sisters have seen you speaking with the angel—for lack of a better word—since you arrived here. Twice last night. And then, this morning, two of them appeared to Sister Mary Catherine in the chapel. And now. . . ."

Sam winced, intuitively knowing what was coming.

"Father Samuel, the angels were there, on the altar with you! You could not have been unaware of them!"

"Oooh, boy."

Sam let out a breath and turned away. The strange behavior of the sisters and congregation during the Mass, he realized, hadn't been simple piety; it had been a physical impossibility.

Somehow, Sam realized, the sisters at the monastery were seeing Al!

The angel dressed in white? Al in uniform. The brightly colored rosary? Most likely the handlink. And the crucifix? That part, Sam couldn't quite figure out.

"Father Samuel, I don't understand! When I asked you about it this morning, you practically lied to me!"

"Uh, well, see. . . ." Sam twisted his hands. Under Mother Mary Frances' black-wimpled, glasses-thickened gaze, he *felt* guilty.

"Father, I can't keep this quiet any longer." The woman

257

was disappointed, Sam saw. She lowered her head and shook it. "If they had appeared only to you, or to a few of the sisters. . . ." She looked back at him. "But there were guests who saw them, Father."

How could they see Al? Or Father O'Keefe? And for that matter, could they see *him*?

He needed Al. He needed some answers before he tried to make up any for Mother Mary Frances. He unbuttoned his cassock and took it off, hanging it in the wardrobe next to the alb to buy himself some time.

"Father Samuel?"

"Kids and animals," he heard Al say. *"You know, they're pure of heart. They only see the truth. . . ."*

Could that be it, Sam wondered. Could it be that the sisters at this monastery were pure of heart? Like children?

Whatever the answer, denial of the apparitions certainly wasn't going to work. He cleared his throat and turned around. "Uh, look, Mother, I—" He closed his eyes and sighed. "Okay, yes, I know—you saw—something," he agreed. There was almost a look of relief on the woman's face. "But—well, it's hard to explain."

"Father," Mother Mary Frances said, her voice calm now, as if, having confronted the truth, she was better able to face it. "Just tell us, please. What is required of us now?"

"Required?"

"Should I call the bishop? Should I tell the sisters to—"

"Uh, no, no!" Sam took a step closer, trying to make the woman understand that publicity was definitely *not* what the "angels" would want. "Let's just keep it—quiet for now," he said. "And—I'll talk to the angels," he promised, almost choking on the word.

"I thought at first," Mother Mary Frances said, "that we weren't meant to see them. But then, this morning—well, if they hadn't wanted to be seen, this certainly was a bad place to show up."

"No kidding." Sam grimaced. "Well, they—" He shrugged and tried to cover. "You know how angels are," he tried.

Apparently, Mary Mother Frances didn't. She just looked at him.

"Father, this is a quiet, contemplative community. We live

by prayer and work, not by visions of angels and UFOs and all the other miraculous sightings the world relies on for *their* faith." She took a deep breath. "If this community is to become the next Fatima or Lourdes—I'd like some warning. That's all."

In the silence that followed, Sam heard three distinct bird-calls outside the chapel.

And that was the only thing he heard. No traffic, no crowds, no screaming, no crime. There was no smog here, no politics, no subways, no rush hours. There was only peace. And quiet. And the kind of solitude and silence most of those who lived with the traffic and subways and rush hours craved.

Mother Mary Frances, Sam could see, was very afraid of losing that.

He touched her shoulder, smiling as firmly as he could. "I don't think you have to worry," he assured her. "I have the feeling that—once the angels have done what they're here for—they'll leave you alone."

"What they're here for?" In her voice was a hint of hope.

"Uh, yeah." Sam dropped his hand and shrugged. "I—don't think they'll be around too much longer."

Mother Mary Frances looked at him. She almost smiled. And then she nodded.

"I'll make sure the sisters keep quiet about it, then," she promised. She turned, used her cane to find the doorway, and added, "But I can't make any promises about the guests."

She left, and Sam shut his eyes.

"Neither can I," he whispered, remembering that Teresa was once more among those who believed that he and Al were angels.

Sunday, April 2, 1995   11:35 A.M.
Windy Bluffs, Massachusetts

Lillian Marco looked for Teresa at lunch, but didn't see her. Stephen was being his usual self, running back and forth in the refectory, interrupting conversations, and generally trying to cope with twice the energy his small body could handle. Hyperactivity, Lillian had been told, often went hand in hand with high intelligence. Well, if that was the case, then Stephen's intelligence had to be off the scale!

"Stephen!" she called, as he raced toward the piano in the next room, determined to give a concert to an unwitting and unwilling audience. He turned.

"Yes, Mommy?"

"Why don't you go out and play?" she suggested. "Here's your jacket," she added, taking the windbreaker from the bench next to her. "Go see if Danny and Sheila want to play with you."

The boy took the jacket and said, "I don't want to play with a *girl*!"

"Fine, then play with Danny."

There were almost no safe places left in the world any more, but St. Bede's was still one of them, Lillian thought, watching her son leave the building. He slammed the screen door behind him. For Stephen, St. Bede's was a home away from home. He'd practically grown up here. Not only when his father had to come back to Massachusetts for work, but sometimes on vacations as well. They had had many happy weeks here, taking day trips to visit friends in the area and spending the evenings talking with the sisters about obscure, arcane areas of study that only a few people in the world seemed to care about.

Outside, Lillian knew, a dozen sisters and guests, like a second family, would keep an eye on Stephen. Just as Sister Mary Catherine had last night, bringing the boy back in to verify that he had permission to be playing outside.

And Stephen, after all these years, knew exactly where the best places to play were.

St. Bede's was one of the few spots left in the world where Lillian Marco could feel safe letting her son out of her sight.

CHAPTER

THIRTY

December 25, 1998
Stallion's Gate, New Mexico

Al Calavicci didn't have time for what he was feeling. He didn't have time to smash a fist into a wall, throw a book across the room, or yell at Gooshie. And he didn't have time to hate the consecrated, celebrated, wafer-thin God that O'Keefe worshiped. The improvised, holographic rituals that he'd taken part in were too much to deal with right now.

So was reliving his father's death all over again. And the death of everything he'd believed in up to that point.

He didn't have time for that. So after a moment, he took a deep breath and practiced what he preached: he straightened his uniform jacket, and went on with the show.

Gooshie was still looking nervously sweaty when Al left his office. Given his hasty exit from the Imaging Chamber, and the quick, sharp response he'd given when Gooshie had tried to speak to him, Al wasn't surprised. Even on the best of days, he could count on Gooshie to perspire under pressure.

"All right," he said, addressing Gooshie and glancing at the Waiting Room. Davalos was in there with O'Keefe. Al wasn't sure he liked that. "What's the scoop?"

"Uh, well, one of the auditors—Jenna, I think?" Al nodded him on. "She said they called Senator Weitzman, but—well, uh, they said—they think they were too late."

Whatever pain the last hour and a half had brought back for Al was quickly and mercifully dulled by the electric shock Gooshie's words gave him.

"Too late?"

Gooshie hunched his shoulders and nodded. "She said they—that I should tell you that—Senator Smallwood—" He cleared his throat, and Al waited. "He had a press release sent out as soon as his son was arrested." And from the console, where it had lain without Al noticing it, he handed the admiral a sheet of paper. "Here."

Al watched detachedly as his hand reached out to take the press release. He read it. He even knew, somewhere inside, what it meant.

The sounds of his father's agonizing death were still crying out in his mind. And the immense numbness that came from this news was doing its part.

But training took over. Al glanced at the release, at the words that exposed Project Quantum Leap to the world, and knew that very soon, the world was going to cave in.

It was either time to give up—or to start tunneling. Fast.

He strode up the ramp to the Waiting Room, slapped the scanner, and stepped in. Davalos and O'Keefe immediately stopped their conversation.

"Here," Al said, handing the paper to Davalos. "The prayer meeting's over. Get your ass back over to the security building. And get every damned security officer you can track down to give you a hand. I figure we've got thirty minutes before the local bloodhounds get hold of this and sniff us out. So be ready."

Davalos was a quick reader. He glanced over the document and looked up, his eyes wide and his expression appalled.

"I'll explain later," Al said. "Maybe," he added. With any luck at all, there was still a slim chance that he and Sam could stop this from ever happening.

Davalos didn't hesitate. He grabbed his cap from the table on his way out, stuffing the paper in his breast pocket.

"Mark!" Al called, just before he left. The officer turned, waiting for another order. Al tilted his chin upward and said, "Glad you stuck around."

Davalos nodded acknowledgment of the praise and left.

"What's wrong?" O'Keefe asked, the moment the Door had closed.

"Sorry, Father, I haven't got time to go into it." Al pulled the handlink from his pocket and jabbed it with his forefinger. But Good King Wenceslaus, looking out on the feast of Stephen, wasn't the information he wanted.

"Is there anything I can do?" O'Keefe asked quietly. The arrogance was gone from his voice.

"Sure," Al said angrily, stuffing the handlink back in his pocket. "Why don't you *pray*?" He hit the scanner on the wall instead of saying anything more.

"I remember him," O'Keefe said quietly. Al resisted the urge to turn around. "Sam Beckett, right? Physicist?"

Al shut his eyes and didn't answer.

"You know, I ran into him in North Carolina just before I took the plane back to Boston," the priest mused. And then, Al had to turn around.

"What?"

O'Keefe smiled, his gaze unfocused as he tried to recapture the memory. "We were at a coffeehouse. In Charlotte. He said he was working on a project—" The man's eyes suddenly focused. "Holography," he muttered. Then he looked around the room as if he'd just woken there. "*This* is the project he was working on, isn't it? He didn't want to talk about it. . . ."

Al hadn't thought about it before, but O'Keefe was probably right. Al had called Sam in North Carolina to tell him about the committee's ultimatum. It had brought him back to the Project on April Fool's Day—sooner than he'd planned.

"He said he didn't like to lose," O'Keefe continued, his voice still drifting in memory. "And he didn't like to quit." Then he smiled. "I guess he meant it."

Something in the man's words sent a shiver down Al's back. He ignored it. He ignored everything right now except what was needed to keep this Project functioning.

And to save Teresa.

Sunday, April 2, 1995   11:38 A.M.
Windy Bluffs, Massachusetts

"George?"

Teresa Bruckner approached the car slowly, quietly. She was far enough from the main buildings not to be seen, except by someone who was walking or driving past. The car had been deliberately half hidden, just enough of it exposed for her to see and recognize it. But not enough for most people to notice.

"George?" she called again. She moved closer, pushing

branches out of her way as she crept up the left side of the car. "George, are you—"

George was slumped on the passenger's side, his eyes shut, his head lolled to the left. His right shoe was on the seat next to him; his right foot was swollen and twisted.

"Oh, God! Oh, God!" Teresa pulled open the driver's side door and called to him. "George! George, can you hear me?" She knew enough to reach for his neck, to feel for a pulse. It was there, but it was so weak that she spent several seconds finding it. He was barely breathing.

"George! Oh, God!"

She started to back out of the car, to call for help. But before she could move more than an inch, a hand grabbed her around her waist, and another covered her mouth.

"All right, girlie," the voice said. "It's time to pay the piper."

She struggled frantically, but her assailant pulled her around and slapped her twice across the face. He didn't use his hands; he had a gun.

She tried to focus on the man who was hitting her; when she did, she recognized him. Grendel's Den. The subway. The convenience store.

"Al!" she called.

"Who's Al?" he asked, moving the barrel of the gun up under her nose and pushing her back against the car.

Teresa said nothing. He slammed the gun against her nose. She cried out.

"Okay, girlie, this is how it's going to go down," the man said, speaking slowly. "You're going to take me to the stash, and you're going to give it to me. Then, if you're a very good girl, I might just let you and your lover boy live out the day. How does that sound?"

"I don't—have—" Blood was trickling down her throat from the last blow. She swallowed, coughing and gagging.

"Oh, you've got it, girlie. Your little sweet-talker, here, told me. So let's go get it, right?"

He turned her, pulling her away from the car, using his gun hand to push the pine branches out of his way. He'd hidden there, she realized, in the clump of trees. Waiting for her.

How long? How long had he been waiting for her?

"Come on."

The man pushed her forward, and for just a second she was free. It was all the time she needed. She bolted, counting on the one thing her brain had registered: with all the potential witnesses here, he wouldn't risk shooting his gun.

But she wasn't quite fast enough. He caught up to her after only a few feet, grabbing her and tossing her onto the road. For a second she lay there, her face pressed against pavement, waiting for death. But he pulled her up, holding her close to him.

"That was your first stupid mistake," the man hissed. His breath smelled like pepperoni. "Try a second one, and I'll kill you." He pressed the gun to her ear. "But not too fast."

"Oh, God!" She started to cry, not wanting to, but too frightened to stop herself.

"Stop that! Stop it!" His arm tightened around her waist, choking the breath from her. She sniffed back the tears and tried to inhale.

After a moment, he loosened his hold on her. His fingers were curled around her arm, holding her tightly. But the gun disappeared from her head.

"All right. Now, where is it?" She hesitated, and he pressed the gun against her spine. "Where's the stuff, girlie? That's all I want, and you and your lover boy can go your own way. Now come on!" His voice lowered to an angry growl. "Where is it?"

"My room," Teresa whispered. She almost choked on the blood that was still drizzling down her throat and the terror that was creeping up her chest. "In the guest house."

"Okay," the man agreed. The pressure on her back disappeared. "Then like two good friends, we're going back there. Anyone asks about your face," he added, pushing her forward, toward the monastery, "you fell."

Teresa squeezed her eyes shut for just a second, pulling back the terror.

Al, she prayed. *Please be here! Please help me!*

"Sam, we got more important things to worry about right now than your stomach!"

With a sigh of irritation that bordered anger, Sam Beckett turned from the luncheon buffet the sisters had laid out for their guests in the refectory. Ham, potatoes, green beans, spinach, apple cobbler. . . .

Almost gingerly, Sam had made his way back here after his angelic discussion with Mother Mary Frances, keeping an eye out for anyone—or anything—that might deter him from his goal. He'd seen nothing. Even when he'd entered the dining hall and seen Lillian Marco, the woman had just given him a cool look and gone back to her food.

But as Al came up behind him once again, appearing without notice or warning, Sam was determined. This time, nothing was going to come between him and the basic sustenance he needed for life.

"Al," he whispered, grabbing a plate and heading for the ham, "in case you haven't realized it, I haven't eaten a thing— not even a wafer!—since I Leaped in here!"

Three or four people turned as he spoke, but then they all averted their eyes. And Sam remembered the other problem he had: some of these people might not just be watching him talk to Al, but watching Al talk back.

"Yeah, well, you're not close to *real* starvation yet," the Observer shot back. "Trust me, I know."

Sam looked at him and hesitated as he reached for the serving fork that lay next to the ham. Al's eyes were dark, ringed with exhaustion. And his face was gray.

"We got a big problem, Sam, and believe me, it's more important right now than a honey-cured ham!"

With a deep breath, Sam shut his eyes. He swallowed. He breathed out. And he looked at Al.

"Come on," Sam muttered, putting the plate down and leading his friend away from the crowd of feeding people.

They went outside, back to the small cluster of trees that edged the building. It was Sam who spoke first. "Al," he said, "the sisters can see you!"

Al's shoulders dropped two inches as tension gave way to puzzlement. His face wrinkled into a question and his mouth opened, but nothing came out. Sam shrugged and waved at the monastery grounds.

"I can't explain it," he said, "but some of the sisters here— including Sister Mary Catherine—can see you! They think—" He stopped and sighed. "They think you're an angel."

While Sam spoke, Al punched the handlink, then shook it.

Another melodic noise, what sounded suspiciously like "Silent Night," was squeezed out of the box. Al waited. Then he shook his head.

"Brain waves," he muttered.

"What?"

"Brain waves." The admiral looked up, ignoring the continuing sound that pealed forth from the caroling handlink. "Ziggy says their brain waves are all screwy."

Sam rubbed his eyes. His stomach was hurting. His blood sugar had plummeted. And his temper—usually something he never even noticed—was screaming.

"What do you mean, they're screwy?"

Al's temper, Sam noticed, wasn't much quieter. Al took a deep, frustrated breath. "Ziggy says a bunch of the sisters here have elevated alpha waves," he explained. "She says that happens in people who do a lot of meditating, and stuff like that."

"Or praying?" Sam suggested. Al scowled and shrugged.

"Yeah, maybe." Then he snickered. "So now we got a scientific way of tellin' who's prayin' and who's just saying the words, huh?" But as Sam considered that implication, Al continued, impatiently. "Sam, we got a bigger problem. Right now, we got reporters on the way to the Project to see if anything that Smallwood told 'em this morning was true."

It took a few seconds for the implication of Al's words to sink through Sam's starved brain. "He went public?"

"Before we could stop him. Time zones bein' what they are, he had a head start on us."

Sam turned away and stared across the road, toward the ocean. "How long do we have?"

"Maybe thirty minutes. Maybe less."

Thirty minutes. . . . "When is Teresa—?"

"Still don't know for sure. But sometime soon."

Thirty minutes, Sam thought. In thirty minutes or less, the Project might be exposed. Or shut down. And he would be trapped here, without help, without information, without a hope of ever going home.

He swallowed tightly, turned, and faced Al. It was now or never. God or Time or Fate—or pure coincidence—had brought him here for a reason. Maybe *this* was it.

"555-2231."

Al looked as if he'd just received a sharp blow to the gut.

His face went white; his stomach muscles tightened. He pulled his shoulders back as if he were preparing to return the blow.

"I remember the phone number, Al," Sam said quietly. "The only thing I *can't* remember is the area code."

Al stared, unblinking. "I thought we settled this."

Sam took a steadying breath and shook his head. "No. You just gave me the odds. *I'm* placing the bet." Even as he spoke them, the words rang in Sam's memory. He and Al had had this argument before.

"Teresa's gonna die."

"The Project's going to be shut down," Sam countered.

"*Not* if you save Teresa!"

"Not if I don't Leap too soon!"

"So the Project is more important than saving Teresa?"

"Maybe I still save her."

"You *won't* Leap!" Al stepped closer, very close. Sam could almost remember the smell of cigar smoke that clung to him. "You won't save anyone, Sam," he said. "You won't save Teresa! You won't save her brother. You won't save Jimmy or—" Al shut his eyes tightly. But before he did, Sam knew what he had seen in them. "You won't save Tom," he whispered.

Breathing got suddenly harder.

"Tom?"

"You wanted to save Tom," Al said, opening his eyes. They were dry now. "You were pushed by the committee, but the bottom line is, you wanted to save Tom." His hands didn't move. He barely opened his lips as he spoke. "And you did it, Sam. You made a choice, and you saved him. And a hell of a lot of other people, too. We didn't plan on changing the past, but—well, *Someone* did. And you volunteered."

"And I *don't* get a second chance?" Sam demanded. "Maybe a chance to still help them but—to go home, too?"

Al winced.

"You were wrong the last time, Al," Sam said more calmly. "You said I couldn't save Tom. But I did. Maybe—" He took a long breath. "Maybe I'm right this time, too."

Al turned away and punched the handlink. The opening notes of "Auld Lang Syne" devoured the silence: Should old acquaintance be forgot and never brought to mind?

Al ran his thumb and forefinger over his eyes as the Door opened. "505," he said.

"What?"

Al looked up.

"505," he repeated. "That's the area code."

Then his halo swallowed Al whole.

CHAPTER
THIRTY-ONE

Sunday, April 2, 1995   11:50 A.M.
Windy Bluffs, Massachusetts

Lillian Marco took advantage of Stephen's absence to go back
to her room on the second floor of the guest house and begin
packing. As much as she tried to keep the room neat while
she was there, Stephen always managed to create a mess.

She would leave tonight, she'd decided. After Compline,
when Stephen would be asleep. That way, she could drive
without as many pit stops, and get home sooner. And then?
Then, set about the task of checking through today's paper to
see what jobs there were. And do the same thing tomorrow.
And the day after that.

She was checking under Stephen's bed for a lost sock when
she heard the first sounds in the room next to her. It was odd
to hear anything; guests here were generally very quiet. What
she heard sounded like things being tossed around. Soft things,
like clothes and shoes.

She found the missing sock, put it in a bag of dirty laundry,
and continued packing.

"Bitch!"

She wasn't trying to eavesdrop; it was simply impossible to
avoid it. The walls in this place weren't made to accommodate
quarreling lovers or honeymooners.

The word was followed by a sharp sound that was clearly
a slap. Lillian cringed.

"It was there!" The wailing voice was familiar: Teresa. The
girl who'd sat near her today at Mass. The girl who'd gotten
the phone call last night.

Lillian heard more sounds, none of them pleasant, and
closed her eyes. Whatever was happening next door, she told
herself, it was none of her business.

"Who'd you give it to, you little whore? Huh? Did you already pass it to lover boy?"

Okay, that was it! The sisters, if they had any idea that someone was using language like that, would be offended. So, on the pretense of asking them to be quieter, she decided to go next door and see what was happening. Maybe her interruption would stop it.

She dropped two more socks into the laundry bag, then left the room. The hall was deserted; most of the guests were at lunch, and others had stayed at the chapel after the service, looking for the angels reported to have been there.

She knocked on the door next to hers and waited. There was thumping, a low grunt, and then the door opened a crack and the girl looked out.

"Oh, Teresa," Lillian said calmly. "It looks like you had an accident." Lillian's heart began pounding fast. The girl had been beaten, and half her body was hidden behind the door. "You fall?"

The girl's lip, cracked and dripping blood, trembled. She nodded. "On the rocks," she said. "I'm okay, though."

Lillian stared at the girl's eyes and could see terror in them.

"Anything I can get you? Some ice, maybe?" Lillian asked, keeping her tone calm. Whoever was in there with the girl had undoubtedly threatened her: maybe with a weapon that was stronger than the back of his hand.

"No," Teresa answered. She coughed. "Just—" She gave Lillian a sudden look, a look that was clearly a signal. "Tell Father O'Keefe I'm fine and—I'll see him later."

The door shut immediately. Lillian heard a scuffle and muted words. The man in the room with Teresa was keeping his voice down now.

Lillian's breath shook and she left the guest house, making her way across the lawn toward the refectory. She saw Stephen in passing; he was playing ball with several other children, some of them familiar, some not. But everything there was fine.

In the refectory, Father Samuel was standing before the baked ham—what was left of it—a plate in one hand, the serving fork in the other, his gaze wavering between the food and the small room where the phone was. The phone Teresa had used last night.

271

Of all the people to have to come to for help, Father Samuel was right down there on her list with Scrooge. But Teresa had sent a clear message; help, if it was going to come, should come from Father Samuel.

Perhaps, whatever the problem was, he already knew about it. Maybe that's why he seemed preoccupied with the small room by the front door.

"Father Samuel," she said, moving closer. She kept her voice low. An incident like this at St. Bede's wouldn't go over well.

He turned, startled from whatever thoughts had held him entranced. And when he saw her, he sighed, shook his head, and dropped the fork.

"Okay," he muttered, glancing upward as if he were addressing the Almighty. "I give up."

"Father," Lillian repeated more urgently, ignoring his bizarre behavior.

"All right, let's talk," he said, resignation in his voice. "This is about your job, right?"

"That girl," Lillian interrupted. "Teresa. I think she's your student?"

Instant wariness suffused Father Samuel's face. "What about her?"

"She's got some trouble. In her room," Lillian whispered. "There's a man in there with her and she—"

She didn't have the chance to finish. Father Samuel dropped his plate, and as it crashed on the floor, he ran from the refectory, his pace far faster than Lillian would have thought him capable of.

"Everything is okay?" A plump woman, dressed quite strangely, sat with Sister Mary Catherine at the end of the table. As Father Samuel bolted from the room, the woman stood and started after him.

"No, everything's fine," Lillian said. As much as she loved the people here, she didn't want anything to disrupt the quiet routine. And after this morning's apparent—if mild—hysteria during Mass, Lillian could only imagine what would happen if word of a domestic quarrel got around.

"It's fine, Father Samuel just had to go see someone."

"Where is Estephen?" the woman asked. Her anxiety, like her clothing, was inexplicable.

"Estephen?"

"Jour son! Where is he?" The woman almost pushed past her.

"He's playing out—back." Lillian shot a quick glance at Sister Mary Catherine for help. This woman was not one of the regulars at St. Bede's. So how did she know Stephen? And how did she know he was her son?

And why would she be concerned for *him*?

"Angela," Sister Mary Catherine said, joining them, "let's finish our coffee."

"No, I think I got to check on Estephen," the woman said. She tried again to move past Lillian, but maternal instinct snapped into place.

"Leave my son alone," she ordered. She left the refectory, deciding that, just to be on the safe side, maybe she should find Stephen and bring him back to their room. Sister Mary Catherine was doing her best to lead the woman away as she left.

December 25, 1998
Stallion's Gate, New Mexico

Al was still in the Imaging Chamber, staring at the hand he held out in front of him, noting with detached surprise that it was shaking.

He'd done it again, just like he had on that first Leap. He'd given Sam the one piece of information he needed to make a phone call, a call that could undo everything they'd worked so hard to accomplish.

But so what? After all, this *wasn't* supposed to be the way the experiment worked. Ziggy was right.

So what if Sam never Leaped? So what if he Leaped, and only observed? So what if Tom Stratton and Jimmy LaMotta and the sisters in Sacramento and Black Magic's niece—and Tom Beckett himself—never had their lives touched by Sam Beckett?

So what? What if they died, or their dreams died, or their families died? Sam deserved a second chance, right? After all, he'd stepped into the Accelerator without knowing what was going to happen to him. He deserved another chance to make

273

that decision, didn't he? That's probably what O'Keefe would claim: Sam Beckett was a human being, so he deserved a second chance.

And, dammit, Al wanted Sam home! Safe and sound.

He wanted Sam here, worrying about funding requests and particle acceleration and the Heisenberg principle. Not wondering if he was going to survive the next Leap. Or the next day.

But Al was also a Navy man. An officer. He knew the risks everyone faced when they walked into battle.

Sam had chosen his battle with the same gusto and fervor that Al had chosen his. And what counted in the end wasn't the sacrifice itself; it was whether the sacrifice had been worth something.

Was it all in vain? Or did any of it actually make a difference?

"Bless me, Father, for I have sinned. . . ."

Al curled his shaking hand into a fist and slammed it against the impenetrable wall of the Imaging Chamber, safe in the knowledge that no one outside that room would hear it.

"Admiral."

He sucked in a deep breath through his nostrils, but before he could answer, Ziggy continued, actually volunteering information.

"Teresa Bruckner is about to die. And Dr. Beckett is having some trouble locating her."

Al wiped a hand across his face, almost grateful for Ziggy's news. At least it meant he had something to do besides think.

"Gooshie! Center me on Sam," he ordered.

As time tore him from the present, he held his hand to his mouth and sucked.

His knuckles were bleeding.

Sunday, April 2, 1995   11:57 A.M.
Windy Bluffs, Massachusetts

Teresa wasn't sure which end of the world was up right now. The man with the earring and the tattoo and the gun had hit her so many times she couldn't see straight.

274

"You little bitch," the man swore once Lillian was gone. "You fucking little whore! Now where the hell is the dope?" He raised his gun, not to fire but to strike her. Teresa cringed in anticipation.

She clung to the doll she'd picked up from the bed while he'd searched her room. She stroked the hair on its head, cowering against the door, waiting for the gun to come down on her face again.

"It's gone," she whispered. "I swear, it's gone! Maybe someone found it." She was counting in her head: *one, two, three, four.* How long would it take Father O'Keefe to get here? Or Sam? Or Al? Or anyone?

Two and two are four. Four and four are eight. . . .

Her kidnapper grabbed her and pulled the door open. "Lover boy has it, doesn't he? You must've given it back to him *before* you went out to meet him, right?"

"No!"

He didn't listen. He dragged her through the door, no longer caring if anyone saw them. As he forced her ahead of him, she stumbled down the hall and out of the guest house, surprised that no one seemed to be around.

"Al," she cried. "Please be here!"

"Who's Al?" The man stopped and hauled her into the trees by the side of the house. "He the guy who's got the dope?"

"No!"

The man smacked her again, and her ears rang with pain. Then he pulled her back toward George's car.

She struggled to free herself. But with each twist of her body, with every wrench of muscle, she felt him tighten his grasp. And she felt herself growing weaker.

Then she stumbled, staggering from pain, and his hold on her loosened.

Something in her brain still worked. Something that told her both to run and not to endanger anyone else. She clutched her doll, the last symbol of her innocence, and ran across the road, toward the ocean, where all her problems would find an answer.

She knew he was following, but this time, despite the fact that her head and face were throbbing with pain, she had the upper hand: she had picked her way along these rocky bluffs twice. Once in the dark. She could do it a lot better than he could.

"Al!" she called once more, panting as she ran from her attacker. "Sam! Please! Find me!"

Sam made it back to the guest house within moments of Lillian's warning. But three guests on the way, each of them deterring him for only a few seconds to comment about the angelic apparitions this morning and to ask about their importance, had delayed him just long enough.

He searched the first floor rooms, not knowing which one Teresa had been assigned, and found several guests less than pleased by his abrupt interruption.

Then he tried the second floor. One room had been left open, and the moment Sam got to the doorway, he knew it was Teresa's: the sweater she'd worn last night was lying on one of the chairs.

"Sam!"

"Al!" Sam turned and realized, before he had to explain a thing, that Al already knew. "Where is she?"

"Ziggy's trying to get a focus on her, but—" He took a deep breath and waited. "Okay, here we go. She's headed for the cliffs, Sam. Same as before."

Sam headed out of the room. He was down the stairs and outside the guest house almost before he'd taken another breath.

"Father O'Keefe?" A curious, unconcerned voice called to him as he raced across the lawn in front of the guest house. "I wanted to tell you how much that sermon meant to me. . . ."

He was trapped by a series of cars on the road, and the nameless woman caught up to him.

"Look," he started breathlessly, "I can't talk right now. Sorry."

This was it. The moment he'd endured sleeplessness, hunger, and the interminable chattering of Sister Mary Catherine for. This was the moment he'd come to fix. And *nothing* was going to stop him.

"Sam! Over here!" Al was ahead of him, in the pines and maples by the side of the road. Sam ran toward him and saw the bumper of a car, almost hidden by the low-hanging pine

276

branches. Almost, but not quite. Al was peering inside, his face twisted. As Sam reached him, he saw why.

A young man with long hair tied into a neat ponytail was half sitting in the passenger's seat. One of his feet had been badly mangled.

"George?" Sam asked, pulling open the door. He felt for a pulse.

"Yeah," Al grunted. The handlink squealed. "He's been drugged," the Observer added quickly.

"Pulse is weak and thready. . . ."

"He's okay, Sam. Some kinda sleeping pill." Sam pulled away from the wounded, drugged man. He watched Al try to punch up data from the handlink and stared around him.

In the distance, he saw a movement.

"Over there!" He started off, tripping at first on the rocks, then beginning to get the feel of the uneven ground. He ran on, and as the trees that covered the roadside thinned and the ground became rockier, he saw her.

The man pursuing her, running a bit slower, was the man they'd seen at the convenience store last night. Teresa had been right: she *had* been followed.

He continued on, waiting until he was within voice range. The coast was only a couple dozen yards away. He heard the water, the gulls. And then he saw what Teresa apparently hadn't yet noticed: the ground dipped ahead of her, a sudden, sharp decline.

"Teresa, stop!" Al shouted. Once more, the Observer had positioned himself ahead of Sam. He was hovering in midair, over the edge of the bluff, his feet dangling just inches from the steep edge. But Teresa ran on. She ran awkwardly, her arms clutched to her chest, as if she were protecting something in her arms.

"Teresa!" Sam called. She didn't hear him. The sound of the waves, lapping beneath Al's feet, crashing against the rocks below, drowned out his voice.

He ran faster. The rocks were slippery with moss, worn smooth from eons of the water and wind. Sam tripped and caught himself.

"Teresa!" he called again.

"Teresa, stop! Stop!" Al was still in midair, flailing his arms, waving frantically at the girl. But whatever was driving her, she wasn't going to be stopped. Not even, Sam realized with a cold knot in his stomach, at the edge of the cliff.

The man following her, however, *had* realized where she was heading. He slowed his pace, finally stopping. He drew a gun and aimed it.

He said something to the girl, something the waves crashing in the background drowned from Sam's ears. But Teresa heard him.

She hesitated. Then she turned. The edge of the bluff was just behind her right foot. And as Sam watched, her mouth opened in a scream as she lost her footing.

She scrambled, trying to catch herself. Whatever she'd been clutching fell over the edge.

Just before she followed.

If we wish to arrive at humility,
we must erect a ladder such as Jacob saw
in his dream, by which angels appeared,
ascending and descending.

—THE RULE OF ST. BENEDICT:
CHAPTER 7

CHAPTER
THIRTY-TWO

Sunday, April 2, 1995   12:00 P.M.
Windy Bluffs, Massachusetts

"No!"

Al watched, frantic and helpless, as Teresa slipped backward over the edge of the bluff. The craggy face of the cliff was the only thing that saved her: she stretched her hands out as she fell and grabbed onto a sharp stone that jutted out and gave her a moment to hang on.

"Sam!" Al yelled. "Hurry! She's still here, Sam!"

The gunman who'd been chasing her was also still there, Al realized. And he was closing fast.

Panic spurred Sam on. As the man crept cautiously to the edge to see if his prey had died at the bottom, Sam rushed him from behind and grappled him to the ground. They rolled around for a time, each of them delivering and receiving a dozen or more punches and kicks.

Al looked anxiously from them to the girl, who was struggling to pull herself back up. She was begging, pleading with God: she wasn't ready to die. On that count, Al agreed heartily.

"Sam!" he called. "This is no time to be polite! Come on, Sam, Teresa's gonna die!"

Whether Sam heard him or not, Al wasn't sure. But a few seconds later, Sam delivered a painful and debilitating blow to the man's groin, and another to his eyes. And then, gasping and bleeding, he raised himself up just enough to deliver a final blow to the head that knocked the man out.

"Sam! Hurry up!"

Leaving his fallen victim, Sam Beckett turned, staggering from the fight, and headed toward the Observer.

"Careful," Al warned. "This place is slipperier than a virgin's—" He glanced at the collar on Sam's neck and didn't finish the sentence. It wasn't necessary, anyhow. Sam was carefully picking his way across the final feet of the bluff. The waves below Al slapped loudly against the rocks.

The tide was coming in.

. . . And now she had nowhere left to go. She was out of time, out of friends, out of family. And out of luck. And it had all happened so fast.

The world below her gaped and yawned, an ugly mouth with rocks for teeth. She was falling, her fingertips slipping on the precarious overhang she clung to, her body growing heavier as each second passed.

"Oh, God," she whimpered. "Please! I'm not ready to die!"

The rocks clasped in her bleeding fingers began to break loose. She slipped downward, her feet scrabbling frantically for a hold on something, anything, to keep her from plunging to the ground.

The cliff was dotted with trees, all too far for her to touch. Below her, a hundred feet or more, the earth was waiting; waiting to grasp her, cradle her, break her into a hundred pieces.

The world turned, and she felt herself slipping further.

"Please! Please, don't let me die!"

"Teresa! Hold on!"

"Father O'Keefe?"

He was here! He leaned over the edge of the cliff, lowering his hand for her to grasp. "It's okay," he assured her. "Come on, give me your hand."

"My doll," she whimpered. It was so silly: but it was the only thing she'd had that really reminded her of her mother. Of her childhood. Of Al, and Sam, and a world that made sense.

"Teresa, give me your hand!" Father O'Keefe's face was bloody, as she knew hers was. His lip was swollen, and there was a large gash over his right eye.

She reached for him, her fingertips bleeding and raw from having clawed at the rock. "My doll," she murmured.

It was down there, at the foot of the cliff. It had fallen when she'd heard the man yell that it was time to die. When she turned and lost her balance.

The doll's head had come off.

281

She felt Father O'Keefe pulling, trying to help her up. "I can't—"

She struggled for a hold with her feet, but the rocks slipped out from under her. And the waves below her were getting stronger.

"I *am* being careful, Al!" Father O'Keefe said suddenly, half turning his head away from her.

And in that instant, the world made sense again.

"Sam?"

The word brought his attention back, and she renewed her attempt to scramble up the cliff. But her attempts were working against him. The slope of the bluff and the laws of physics were pulling him down as she tried to come up.

"Come on, Teresa! You can do it!"

"I can do it, Sam," she said. One foot got a precarious hold, and she started to push upward.

He reached his other hand down to her. He was lying on the rocks on his stomach, and as he reached for her, she felt her foothold crumble beneath her, and heard the ocean lapping on the rocks.

The quick, jerking movements that she used to catch herself, to reach for Sam, were lost, and she felt herself sliding down.

"No!" he yelled.

A second later, both his hands gripped and pulled hard, almost yanking her arms out of their sockets. They pulled her upward as she clawed the crumbling rock. For just a second, she felt the strength of Sam's hands around her arms.

Sam!

She was sure it was Sam. And that knowledge was enough to make her pull harder.

But she pulled too hard.

It took less than a second for gravity to overcome him. It took less than a second for the rocks beneath him to crumble away. And it took less than a second for him to release her arms, deliberately, before he slid from the broken edge of the bluff.

"Sam, no!" She watched helplessly as he pulled his hands from her grasp and slid, rolling and tumbling most of the way, to the foot of the cliff.

"Oh, God, no! No!"

• • •

It was the one thing Al had most dreaded for the past three years. He watched in horror, watched Sam go over the edge of the cliff, watched him take the fall that had originally claimed Teresa's life. And he felt only one thing: utter fury.

Sam fell close to the edge of the cliff, not away from it. He grasped every hold he could along the way, desperately trying to break his fall. Trying to save himself. And that alone kept Al's heart beating when Sam landed at the bottom, on the rocky shore.

Al repositioned himself immediately. Sam's head was bleeding, and his entire face was covered with blood. His right leg was twisted at an unnatural angle.

"Sam!" he called. There was no answer. "Sam, come on! Sam!" He reached his hand out and watched it slide through the figure of his friend.

"Oh, God," he whispered. He shut his eyes tightly. "God, no! Not now! Not this time! Dammit, not this time!"

Above him, three years and a hundred feet away, Teresa was still clinging desperately to life, her cries audible over the incoming tide.

"Angel of God, guardian dear. . . ."

"Teresa!"

"To whom God's love commits—" She slipped. "Al!" He heard her gasping breath, her frantic plea as she struggled to keep her precarious hold. "Please! Save me! Please!"

Al shuddered. His mind churned, a violent upheaval, like vomiting from the outside in. He shut his eyes and felt time collapse around him.

"Okay," he whispered. "You win. But this time—You owe *me*." He took a shaky breath and lowered his head, trying to remember the words.

He touched his forehead, chest, left and right shoulders, and whispered through his teeth, "I believe—in God. . . ."

A gasp drew his attention. Al opened his eyes and saw Sam's chest move; in and out. And in. And out.

"Sam!" If he could have remembered how to cry for joy, Al would have. But the moment was lost. Teresa slipped again, the rocks beneath her fingers crumbling as she continued to grasp them.

"Sam, wake up! Wake up, Sam!" He didn't. "Come on, Sam!"

"Ever this day be at my side. . . . Al! Please help me!" Teresa called, her voice shattered by the tide. It was moving in fast, and Sam was on the verge of being drowned by it.

Help, if it was going to come, was going to have to come now.

And the only help either one of them had was a hologram, trapped in the future, crouched in the Imaging Chamber.

And then it came together. The whole damned Leap!

He was an angel, right? The sisters could see him! All those Leaps when animals and kids and loonies saw him had a reason now.

They all had a reason!

"Sam," he said, bending low in case the unconscious man could hear him. "I'm gonna get help, Sam. I'm gonna get the sisters. You wait right here," he added, ignoring the absurdity of his own words. He stood and entered a new set of coordinates into the handlink. "I'll be right back, Sam. You hold on, okay?"

There was a small groan from the man on the rocky shore. Al decided to believe that he knew help was on the way.

Stephen Charles Marco had slipped away from his mother again. She was talking to someone, so he went back to playing in the field. That's when he heard the noise. He ignored it at first. The baseball he'd found in the basement of the guest house was a lot more fun.

Then he heard more noises. The kind of noises his mom always told *him* not to make. Noises that would make people think you were in trouble.

He grabbed the baseball and decided to see what was going on. St. Bede's was a nice place, but sometimes it got boring. Maybe something interesting had finally happened.

Sister Mary Gertrude was in front of the main house, pointing, talking to the other sisters.

"There! There he is!" She dropped to her knees and crossed herself. "Tell us what you want!"

"I see him!" another sister said. And she, too, fell to her knees.

Stephen looked in the direction they were pointing, but all he saw were trees and rocks and the road.

284

"He wants us to go with him." Sister Mary Catherine, who had just come out of the refectory with a big woman he'd never seen before, was staring at the same spot the others were. "He's telling us to follow him!"

She started across the road. The others went with her. All except the big woman.

Stephen looked at the baseball in his hand. And he looked at the sisters. Well, between the two, the baseball was more fun. He turned away and decided that whatever was going on was just for grown-ups.

"The angel!"

It was Sister Mary Michael, the old nun who always liked him. She smelled nice, like incense and starch. She was leaving the main house. But when she got to the road, she stopped. Then, with a small gasp, she too, crossed.

Well, Stephen decided, maybe there was something worth seeing over there after all. An angel!

He started across the road, tossing the ball in his hand, wondering what an angel looked like.

A moment later, he was thrown to the ground, a heavy weight on top of him.

"Jou chould look where jou're going!"

The baseball rolled out into the road and was crushed under the tires of a car he hadn't seen coming.

CHAPTER
THIRTY-THREE

The most extraordinary thing, as far as Al was concerned, was how calm and efficient the sisters of St. Bede's were when confronted with a crisis. Not one of them fainted from shock. None of them screamed at the sight of Father O'Keefe's—Sam's—bleeding body. And from the moment they saw Al, they followed without question, those who *could* see him calling out to those who couldn't.

Faith alone did for some what sight did for others.

By the time they reached the cliff where Sam and Teresa waited for salvation, nearly the entire monastery, including several of the guests, had followed.

Retrieving Teresa took almost no time. Three men who had come for the retreat formed a chain, holding onto each other and providing enough weight to overcome the gravity that had pulled Sam over.

The girl was crying, her hands were bloody, and her face was a mess when they finally drew her to safety. But she was all right.

While the rescue of Teresa had been going on, the sisters of St. Bede's had proved to be far more resourceful than Al had expected. Three of them, listening closely to words he had to repeat several times before they understood him, realized that the man lying unconscious several feet from the edge of the bluff was *not* the man they were there to help. The gun, lying nearby, finally helped them understand. One of them pulled off her scapular, the long cloth she wore over her habit. She kissed it reverently, and glanced skyward.

"Forgive me, Father," she whispered, then tore it in two lengthwise, and with the help of two others, tied the man's hands and feet.

The other sisters, who had seen Sam and heard Teresa's pleas for him, removed their own scapulars. As Al watched, they tied them together and lowered the length of strong, cotton cloth to the bottom of the cliff.

"Geez! Were you all Girl Scouts, or what?" Al asked. Two of them looked at him and smiled. The others concentrated on their task.

One of the men who had helped rescue Teresa used the makeshift rope to rappel down the cliff.

"Don't worry," one of the sisters said. She glanced around her, including Al in her gaze. "He's a professional."

Al hadn't even considered being worried about the rescuer: he was too busy being worried about Sam. It had been more than fifteen minutes since Sam had fallen. And when Al had returned, he still hadn't moved.

He watched the man who descended the black rope crouch beside Sam. Al stayed where he was, begging Ziggy for information, glancing at Teresa as she huddled in the arms of the man who had pulled her from death, and watching the rescue he himself could do nothing more to help.

"Has anyone called 911?" he asked suddenly. Ziggy had finally coughed up some data, and what it told him wasn't promising. Everyone who wasn't involved in the rescue looked at him, but it was clear they had trouble hearing him. Alpha waves, Al decided, must not be too strong during an emergency.

"Nine. One. One," he repeated, more slowly. Nearly fifteen women and two men were on their knees in front of him, crossing themselves, praying their rosaries, and obviously hearing very little of what he said.

"Call—an—ambulance!" he shouted. Two of them seemed to hear him; but it was a voice from the edge of the cliff that translated his words.

"Get an ambulance!" Sister Mary Catherine, half bent by the side of the cliff, watching as a second man was lowered to Sam's inert body, turned to the others and shouted the command. "Hurry up! He's alive!"

"Yeah, he's alive," Al repeated. He swallowed a lump as large as a grapefruit and turned to the young woman. "Sister, can you hear me? Please! Let me know if you can hear me!"

"I hear you," she whispered. She was concentrating on holding her part of the scapular rope that the second man was descending.

"Okay, then listen carefully," Al said. "Where's the nearest hospital?"

"Forty minutes from here," she said. "But it should only take the ambulance fifteen to get here." She didn't even look at him. Her face was twisted into a mask of exertion as she and the string of sisters pulled against the weight of the rescuer who dropped to the ground beside the first man.

Al punched the data Ziggy had asked for into the handlink; apparently, the Massachusetts databases were still off-line. He read the results and felt sick to his stomach.

Below him, the two men were tying Sam into a makeshift hoist made of more scapulars, wrapping the physicist in a shroud that they were preparing to raise by the same rope they'd used to get down.

But if Ziggy was right, it was going to be a futile effort.

"He's got a concussion, Sister," Al said, leaning closer to the nun to make sure she heard him. "Fifty-five minutes is too long. He's not gonna make it."

"Oh, yes he is." Sister Mary Catherine grunted as she and the other sisters began pulling on the scapulars that slowly lifted Sam. Al looked down, just for a second, and saw that Sam was regaining consciousness.

"Sam!" he called. There was no response.

The slow, methodical lift continued. Sam's limp body bumped against the face of the bluff, against rocks that had already broken his bones and bruised his body.

Al closed his eyes: the ascent was almost as hard to watch as the fall had been.

"Mother!" Sister Mary Catherine called. Al opened his eyes and saw Sam's body, inches from the ground. Almost within touching range. . . .

"Yes, Sister?" Al turned and saw Mother Mary Frances.

"Father O'Keefe took my keys to the car," Sister Mary Catherine said. "Do you have the spare set?"

Mother Mary Frances nodded to one of the other nuns, who went running back to the monastery.

"They're in my office. Sister Mary Gertrude is going for them now." The woman hesitated, trying to see through her thick glasses. "Is he—?"

"We don't have time for an ambulance, Mother," Sister Mary Catherine said. "The angel told me. We have to get him to the hospital ourselves."

"Lord, have mercy," Mother Mary Frances whispered, crossing herself as she spoke.

Al watched as the last few inches of rock were covered. The sisters, keeping a relatively safe distance from the crumbling stone, reached out, and six sets of hands pulled him up and over the ledge.

"Al?" Sam murmured.

It was the sweetest sound the admiral had ever heard.

"Right here, Sam."

"Al?" Sam opened his eyes and looked around him. "Al?" he asked again.

"It's all right, now," Sister Mary Catherine said. But as she worked with the others to release Sam from the black rope and to send it back to retrieve the others, Al felt another knot twist his guts.

"Sam! Sam, can you hear me?"

"Al?" Sam muttered again. His eyes weren't focused.

"Sam, can you hear me?"

"Is Al your angel?" Sister Mary Catherine asked, lowering her voice a fraction. Sam tried to swallow, and moved his head against the hard ground. It was as close as he could come to a nod.

"He's here," Sister Mary Catherine reassured him. And then she looked at Al and smiled. "He's right here."

"I—can't see him," Sam said. "Al!"

"Al's here."

Al turned.

Teresa pulled away from her comforter and came to Sam's side. She knelt next to him and took his hand. "I can't see him, either," she said, "but I know he's here." She looked around her, looked at the crowd that had gathered to help her, the men and women who had come to save them. Her eyes teared, and she sniffed. "He kept his promise after all," she whispered again, meeting Al's eyes without knowing it.

Sister Mary Catherine oversaw the ride to the hospital; Mother Mary Frances deferred to her youth and her expertise with the Grand Prix.

Sister Mary Gertrude brought the car to the site of the accident, and Sam was carefully carried over and loaded in. He was still slipping in and out of consciousness.

"The police are on the way," Sister Mary Joseph reported. "I called the ambulance for that man in the car."

"Good idea," Al muttered.

He watched as Teresa was taken to the teal-colored Grand Prix and helped into the front passenger's seat. Despite the trauma she'd been through, the pain she was in, the girl chuckled as she saw the car.

"It's the same color as Al's fedora."

Sister Mary Catherine accepted a rosary from Mother Mary Frances before setting out on her journey. Then she turned the key in the ignition and took off, almost—but not quite—fast enough to dislodge Sam from the back seat where he'd been laid.

Al followed along, positioning his image out of Sister Mary Catherine's view. But Sister Mary Catherine and the monastery and the car and Sam began to fade from view: the image winked out for a second, then came back.

"You gotta talk to him, Sister," he reported, glancing at the information in his handlink. "He's got a concussion. You gotta keep him awake. Talk to him!"

"Father O'Keefe?" the woman called from the front seat. "I had a couple questions about this morning's homily. Father?"

"What?" Sam murmured.

"Well, you were discussing the differences between the old Latin Mass and the new Mass," the nun continued. "I was wondering what your view was about the earlier reforms that permitted the Mass to be said in other languages. For instance, do you think that. . . ."

As Sister Mary Catherine talked, Al glanced at the handlink. According to Ziggy, the concussion was interfering with Sam's ability to see and hear the Observer. And for Al, the effect was growing.

It was Havenwell all over again.

Head trauma after all.

The image of the car, speeding down Route 128 at 80 miles an hour, faded out again.

"Sister!" Al ordered. "Keep talking to him! You can't let him fall asleep!"

He wasn't sure if Sister Mary Catherine heard him. But he heard her ask Sam a question, and he heard Sam mumble a reply.

Just before the image died.

CHAPTER

THIRTY-FOUR

Sunday, April 2, 1995   12:50 P.M.
Windy Bluffs, Massachusetts

The world was fading in and out for Sam Beckett. Sometimes he was with it, feeling the pain in his body. Sometimes he wasn't. And he liked that.

"Father! I asked you a question!"

He knew the voice, and he groaned. Sister Mary Catherine.

"I'm sorry, what?"

"I was asking what your opinion was of the liturgical reforms after the First Vatican Council. Actually, I think they simply purified the rite back to its original form, don't you?"

Everything hurt. And some of it hurt badly. Every time he took a breath, hot pain shot through his chest. And his right leg: he thought it was broken.

"What happened?" He was in a car. Sister Mary Catherine's car? He tried to sit up, but the first stab of agony in his head convinced him to stay where he was.

"You fell off the cliff trying to save Teresa. Al says you're going to be all right, but you've got a concussion, so I have to keep you awake by talking to you. But you have to talk back, too, otherwise I won't know if you're awake, right? Anyhow, Teresa's right here with us. . . ."

"Where's Al?" He remembered the fall, the terrifying plunge to the bottom of the bluff. He didn't remember much else, though. Like how he'd gotten back up.

"He's right here," Teresa's voice said. She leaned back and touched Sam's arm. Her hand was bleeding. "He got the sisters to come and help us."

Her face was badly bruised. Blood seeped down her chin and from her nose.

"They called the police to pick up that guy who came after us."

"What about George?"

Teresa turned back to stare out the front window. "I don't know."

"Actually," Sister Mary Catherine said, "Al's gone right now, but he said to tell you that someone called Ziggy says you'll be fine. Who's Ziggy?"

"Hard to explain," Sam said, wondering how much the sisters had been told or guessed or knew of the truth. At the moment, he didn't much care. All he wanted to do was sleep. He shut his eyes. Then Teresa put her hand on his arm again and gently shook him.

"You can't go to sleep," she said. "Come on! Stay awake."

Sam wasn't sure how long the drive to the hospital took, but he struggled to remain alert until they got there. Sister Mary Catherine not only managed to talk to him the entire time, but she also managed to toss in a few questions to make sure he answered her. He had no idea what he said or what she talked about. But he had the feeling that he was probably talking a little more than he should have about who he and Al really were.

Sister Mary Catherine told Teresa to stay in the car with Sam while she ran into the emergency room and got help. And as professional hands removed Sam from the back seat of the Grand Prix and wheeled him in on a gurney to begin examining him, he watched Sister Mary Catherine wrap a protective arm around Teresa and take her in.

He smiled; she couldn't be in better hands, he thought.

December 25, 1998
Stallion's Gate, New Mexico

The blue walls of the Imaging Chamber were the same. The handlink in Al's hand was the same. But things at the Project had changed in the last hour. Drastically.

Without leaving the room, Al knew that the auditors were gone. More correctly, thanks to Sam's success in 1995, they'd never been here. The disturbing reality of a changing reality made Al's head swim for a moment, as if he were waking from a bad dream.

According to Ziggy, George Smallwood was on his way to the hospital right now, along with a couple police officers. The man who'd been responsible for sending Teresa and Sam over the cliff was a narcotics agent named Anderson who worked for the D.E.A. Ziggy found records of the man's trial that indicated he'd gone bad about a year before and started working his own deals with the kingpins, taking a juicy cut for himself. He faced a very long time in prison.

For George, the ending was a bit happier. Though he spent some time at Walpole, the experience apparently scared him straight. As of today, he'd been clean and out of the drug business for three and a half years.

His father was not under investigation.

The media were not on the way to the Project.

And for the moment, at Project Quantum Leap, there was peace on earth.

Al punched up the latest data from Ziggy, waiting for an indication that she could regain a lock on Sam's brain waves. She was amazingly confident that the disruption was only a temporary, traumatic reaction to the fall.

But Al waited, pacing the empty blue room, unwilling to leave. Despite the many successes of this Leap, he felt depressed.

He never got a chance to say good-bye to the auditors, especially Jenna, the blonde bombshell he'd figured was warming up to him.

And it was still Christmas.

And Ziggy was still predicting a possibility that, even after all that had happened, Sam *would* make the phone call.

"Admiral," Ziggy said, as Al once more tried to get a lock on Sam, "I have told you. I believe it will be at least an hour before his brain waves settle back to normal. May I suggest that you leave the Imaging Chamber? Father O'Keefe is requesting an audience."

Al sighed quietly. As if he needed the aggravation.

"All right," he acceded. He slapped open the Door and left, turning over the handlink to Gooshie.

O'Keefe was pacing around the table in the Waiting Room,

his arms crossed, his head down. He looked up when Al walked in, his face wrinkled with puzzlement.

"What's up?" Al asked.

"Lillian Marco," he said. "I—Angela said she was at the monastery. She must have gone there because of her job." He stopped pacing and stared at Al. A very troubled look. "I've always lived a predictable life, Admiral. Well planned, well thought out. Secure. Uneventful. Until yesterday, I never really considered—"

He stopped. Al waited. "I never considered all the things that could go wrong." O'Keefe narrowed his eyes and drew his lips tight. It took several seconds before he spoke again.

"I could see them, Admiral. At the Mass." He shook his head and took a step to the side, no longer meeting Al's eyes. "Lillian and Stephen. Five years now she's been working with me. And all that time, all I was concerned about was making the deadline. All those years," he whispered, "all I cared about was my Projects."

Al shut his eyes and took a long drag on his cigar.

"But if this trip into the future has taught me one thing," O'Keefe continued, his voice regaining a modicum of its familiar assurance, "it's that people are more important." The priest in Sam Beckett's form clasped his hands behind him and assumed the air of a lecturer. "I want Lillian to come back to work for me," he said.

Almost, Al smiled.

"Angela says I miss the deadline anyway, so—well, maybe I'll miss it by less with Lillian helping me."

Al shook his head, amused by O'Keefe's near confession. "That's still the Project talking," he said.

O'Keefe scowled. But at the moment, that look no longer held the force it once had. It was the memory of Sam's eyes, searching blindly for him as he stood only inches away, that tore his conscience.

One phone call. Just one call, and maybe none of this would have happened.

None of it.

"You're right," O'Keefe said. Al tilted his head. "I want Lillian to finish this job with me. Regardless of the deadline. Or the outcome."

Al shrugged. "Well, she's still at the monastery. With any

294

luck, you'll be back there in time to tell her yourself.''

O'Keefe nodded. "I'll tell her," he agreed. "But—just in case—will you have Sam tell her she's got her job back? In case I *don't* get there in time," he added, a wry expression on his face that told Al he was beginning to get a taste for the unpredictability of his situation.

"Yeah, I'll make sure Sam tells her. Once he's able to,'' he added.

"Is he all right?''

Al let out another breath. The adrenaline that had kept him going through the crisis at the cliff was slowly dissipating. And he was beginning to feel his age. "He'll be okay," he said, waving off the man's concern. "Look, is there anything else?''

O'Keefe met Al's eyes for a moment, then tilted his head to the side. "I don't know. *Is* there anything else?''

Once again, Al felt the skewering effect of the priest's gaze, like an insect caught on a pin in a scientific collection.

He took a deep breath, remembering his prayer at the foot of the cliff.

Then he remembered all the unanswered prayers at the foot of the altar.

He shook his head. "No.'' He turned and hit the scanner by the door.

Suddenly, Father O'Keefe's words hit him, and he whirled. "Wait a minute! Angela? You *remember* Angela?''

"Well, she's—not exactly easy to forget.'' The man raised an eyebrow for emphasis.

"But we're not—supposed to. . . .''

He strode quickly from the Waiting Room and went to the console. "Gooshie, do you remember Angela?''

The man made a face. "How could I forget *her*?''

Al shook his head.

"Admiral,'' Ziggy broke in, "I've located Dr. Beckett.''

"Thought you said it was gonna take an hour,'' Al snapped, grabbing the handlink Gooshie held out for him and starting back up the ramp. There were days when it felt as though all he did was walk up and down these damned ramps!

"Well, uh, the new extender we put in yesterday? It works better than I thought,'' Gooshie explained. He patted the top of the console gently, as one might pet a dog.

"Great. Then center me on Sam.''

Mother Mary Frances was quick to bring the monastery of St. Bede's back under control. The police took statements from everyone who had one to offer—shooting rather cynical looks at each other each time the angels were mentioned, and finding great amusement in the means by which the nuns had restrained the girl's pursuer.

The ambulance removed Teresa's boyfriend with a police escort. And the sisters were busy untying their scapulars and quietly comparing exactly how much of the angel they had been able to see and hear. Their experiences ranged from seeing only a vague, hazy image, as Mother Mary Frances had, to actually being able to make out the man's face.

"He was wearing a uniform," Sister Mary Gertrude said. "It wasn't a robe, it was—a *naval* uniform."

"And it wasn't a rosary," Sister Mary Joseph clarified. "It looked like a bunch of—well, glowing Legos."

Mother Mary Frances let them talk among themselves for a while, realizing that after this much excitement, they needed time to calm down. But she listened carefully to the altered details of the apparition and wondered what, exactly, *had* happened here. Personally, she doubted that angels wore naval uniforms during their appearances.

Several of the oblates and other guests had remained near the spot, praying. It would do no harm, Mother Mary Frances thought, as long as the site didn't become a regular spot for miracles.

"Excuse me, Mother." She turned to see one of the men who had gone down the cliff to bring Father Samuel back. She'd never seen him here before.

"I can't thank you enough for your help this afternoon," she told him.

"Aw, it was nothing. Listen, I found this down there," the man said. "I think that girl dropped it when she fell."

He handed Mother Mary Frances a doll. The head was separated from the body. Both were hollow.

"This was inside it when I found it." The man handed her a plastic bag filled with white powder.

"Oh, dear," Mother sighed. "Why didn't you turn this over to the police?"

The man shrugged and cocked an eyebrow. "Well, with all the other problems this afternoon, you probably didn't need the papers reporting that there were drugs at the monastery, did you? And—my guess is that it would be pretty easy for this to just—wash out to sea?"

Mother Mary Frances considered the possibility. If Teresa had the drugs, she might be charged with possession. On the other hand, it was probably evidence in a crime. And yet, if she turned in the bag now, it would probably mean that federal agents would be back here, combing the grounds for any other drugs. But still. . . .

"You know," Mother Mary Frances said, "my eyesight is terrible. I can barely see what's in this bag." She squinted through her glasses. "But whatever it is, it looks like it's gone bad." She handed it back to the man. "Would you throw it away for me?"

The man took the bag and headed off.

"You're a stranger here, aren't you?" Mother called.

"Yes, ma'am." The man turned and laughed. "Call me Malachi."

Mother Mary Frances smiled as he turned toward the cliff. Then she remembered her Hebrew: Malachi meant "my messenger."

She shook her head and felt her way back toward the monastery with her cane. "Angels and strangers," she muttered, glancing toward Heaven. "Guess You were right about being ready to entertain them. Can't tell one from another these days."

Sunday, April 2, 1995   2:36 P.M.
Danvers Hospital, Massachusetts

"Well, George strikes a deal with the D.E.A.," Al said, pacing at the foot of Sam's hospital bed. "Ziggy doesn't have a lotta details on that, but he does six months at Walpole, then he's out."

"And still straight?"

Al grimaced. "Well, except for a couple of his toes."

Sam's head was swathed in bandages. An IV dripped a mild

297

painkiller into his system. And his right leg, in a cast, was propped on several pillows. He looked awful, Al thought; but he looked a hundred times better than he had when he'd been lying at the bottom of the cliff. The memory still made Al shiver.

"Do he and Teresa get back together?"

Al shook his head. He was indulging in an especially fine cigar, a brand he saved for special occasions. "Nope. Teresa testifies on his behalf, but after he goes to jail—well, nuthin' lasts forever, right?"

"Probably just as well," Sam said. "What happens to Teresa?"

Al shook the handlink, frustrated by Ziggy's sudden silence. "Damn thing," he muttered. He looked at Sam and sighed. "She says there's no data on Teresa," he explained, waving the link in the air. "Maybe she became a professional student, huh?"

Sam looked as if he didn't buy that, and winced as he tried to rearrange himself on the bed. "So?"

"So what?"

Sam shrugged, a gesture that cost him. He grimaced. "Why haven't I Leaped?"

"Are you up for some company?"

The door behind Al opened, and Teresa Bruckner stood in the doorway. There were bandages on her face and hands, but she looked remarkably happy.

"Teresa!" Sam grinned as she stepped in. Sister Mary Catherine followed, her hands folded under her recovered—but wrinkled—scapular.

"How are you feeling, Sam?" Teresa asked, sitting gingerly on the side of his bed and giving him a very long, very knowing look.

"Uh, better," he said, shooting a wary glance at Al. "Since when do you call a priest by his first name?" he asked.

Teresa shrugged and smiled, then glanced at Sister Mary Catherine. "I don't."

"Would you prefer 'Dr. Beckett'?" Sister Mary Catherine asked, smiling mischievously.

"Sa-am?"

The physicist ignored Al, wrinkled his forehead, and sniffed the air as if he smelled something.

"Oh, hi, Al." Sister Mary Catherine turned and looked at the hologram. "You're beginning to fade."

"He's back?" Teresa asked, glancing eagerly around the room. "Al?"

"Sam, what's goin' on here?" Al demanded. He wasn't very happy about this development.

"I don't know," Sam muttered. Then he turned to the nun. "Uh, Sister—"

"You were talking your head off for a while," Teresa explained. "On the way to the hospital? Even Sister Mary Catherine couldn't get a word in edgewise."

"And what—did I say?" Sam asked.

"Oh, you told us about the Project and Al and the time machine and Ziggy and the Waiting Room and the Imaging Chamber. And you told us about how Father O'Keefe threw your thesis on the ground, and how your mother made the best cobbler in Indiana, and then you told us about. . . ."

"I get the picture," Sam said, holding up his hand to stop Sister Mary Catherine's blow-by-blow recounting of his indiscretion. He glanced at Al, who checked quickly on the figures; what were the chances that Project Quantum Leap was going to be exposed now?

"And—you mentioned something else." Sister Mary Catherine pulled one hand from under her scapular and held something out for Sam.

It was a hot dog. A cheap, vending-machine hot dog, sold at an exorbitant price. No onions; but there *was* mustard.

"The doctors will kick us out of here if they find out we brought that to you," she said quietly. "So eat fast!"

Sam needed no more urging. He lifted the nitrate-laden food to his lips and sank his teeth into it.

"And I thought angels didn't eat," Teresa said. Al chuckled.

"Well," Sam started, still waiting for a sign from Al. But the admiral just shook his head and shrugged. Sam took another bite.

"Everything's still here," he answered. "Doesn't look like they talked to anyone."

"We didn't—we didn't mean to deceive you," Sam started. He wiped grease from the hot dog off his lips. "It was just the best explanation we could come up with at the time."

Teresa considered his answer for a moment, then put her hand out and took his. "At least you kept your promise. I would have died if you hadn't, wouldn't I?"

Al saw Sam looking to him again. He shrugged. What the hell? They already knew just about everything else, right?

"Yes," Sam said. "You died." The hot dog was almost gone.

"Wow!" Sister Mary Catherine let out a little whistle.

"Sorry, but what I can't quite figure," Al said, half addressing Sister Mary Catherine, wondering if she could still see him, "is how come you two *believed* what Sam said."

Sister Mary Catherine looked surprised. "Why shouldn't we? We believe in angels."

"Yeah, but Sam and I *aren't* angels. That's the point! We're just—" Al stopped, and almost chuckled as he heard himself about to give one of Father O'Keefe's speeches. "We're just human beings," he said quietly, looking away. "Gettin' a second chance."

Sam paused in his ravenous eating and stared at him, but Al avoided the physicist's eyes.

"There are different kinds of angels, Al," Sister Mary Catherine said. "The word comes from the Hebrew, you know. It means 'messenger of God.'" She turned to Sam. "I'd say that description fits you two to a T."

Sam smiled, then looked down. Al grimaced. He wasn't sure he agreed with Sister Mary Catherine on that one.

"Anyway," the woman said, perking up. "I called the monastery to let Mother Mary Frances know that you're all right. And guess what? Ours wasn't the only miraculous rescue today. You know that woman, Angela?" She half turned to Teresa. "That friend of yours?"

"Oh, yeah." Teresa laughed. "The other angel."

"Angela?" Sam asked.

"Well, in all the excitement while we were heading toward the cliffs, Stephen Marco decided he'd come along, too. He almost got hit by a car, but Angela saved him." She shook her head in quiet amazement. "I must say, it's going to seem very boring around here after you leave."

Al punched the handlink.

"What's wrong?" Sam asked.

"Well, it just doesn't figure," Al explained. "See, we're all supposed to forget Angela when she's finished doin' whatever she does. But—we all still remember her.''

''Maybe she isn't finished, then,'' Sister Mary Catherine suggested. ''Anyway, I need to get back to the monastery.''

Teresa stood and turned to her. ''You mind if I check on George before we go?''

Sister Mary Catherine shrugged. ''I guess a few more minutes won't hurt.''

Teresa stood by the side of Sam's bed for a moment longer, looking at him wistfully. ''I guess I won't see you again?''

''I—don't know.''

She looked around. ''Is Al still here?''

''Yeah,'' Al muttered. He stepped a little closer.

''He's here,'' Sam said, swallowing a mouthful of meat.

''It occurred to me that—well, you two probably never get any thanks for what you do. So—thank you for saving my life.'' She turned back to Sam. ''Thank you for saving my brother's life.'' Her eyes misted, just slightly. ''And on behalf of all the people who'd tell you if they could: thanks.''

''Sam,'' Al said, swallowing tightly. ''Do me a favor, huh?'' He stepped close enough to the bed to be within reach, and lifted his hand, palm outward.

Sam smiled, and put the last two inches of his hot dog on the bed beside him. ''Give me your hand, Teresa,'' he said, and the girl came closer. He took her bandaged hand, held it up, and guided it until it was just touching the image of Al's.

''Bye, Teresa,'' the admiral whispered.

''He said good-bye,'' Sam told her. He released her hand.

''You know what I wish?'' she asked. Sam shook his head. ''I wish I was still innocent enough to see him again. Just once.''

Al ran a hand over his face. He thought it'd be easier to say good-bye this time.

Teresa leaned down and gently kissed Sam on the cheek. ''Maybe when you get home,'' she said, ''you can give me a call.'' She smiled at the remnants of Sam's hot dog. ''Maybe we'll have lunch.'' She tried to lighten her voice, to lighten the moment. But two tears rolled down her face. She brushed them away, then turned and left.

Sister Mary Catherine watched, looking from Sam to Al, then back.

"Uh, Sister," Al said. She looked up, but Al's image was apparently blurred. She didn't quite meet his eyes. "Give Lillian Marco a message, would you? From Father O'Keefe."

"Father O'Keefe?" the nun asked.

"Yeah. Tell her she's still got a lotta work to do on his project."

Sister Mary Catherine smiled. "I'll tell her." Then she turned to Sam. "We'll all be praying for you, Dr. Beckett," she said. "And for Al." She touched the physicist's hand in a final farewell, and left.

For a moment, neither Al nor Sam spoke. They didn't look at each other. They stared at the door, each caught up in his own memories. Then Al took a deep breath.

"So," he started, punching the handlink for something to keep his eyes on. "You got any phone calls you wanna make?"

There was a phone next to the bed. Sam could pick it up right now, Al thought, before he Leaped.

Sam didn't answer right away.

Finally, Al looked up. Sam smiled at him, then picked up the last of his hot dog.

"And miss out on all this excitement?" he asked. Al let out a sigh, and Sam swallowed the last of his first meal in more than a day. "Besides," Sam added, his voice more philosophical, "if I called now, it would feel too much like quitting." He shook his head. "I don't like to quit."

Al chuckled. "That's just what Father O'Keefe said about you."

And with a look of puzzlement on his face, Sam Beckett Leaped.

EPILOGUE

December 25, 1998
Stallion's Gate, New Mexico

Whatever it was that was coming upon a midnight clear, Al Calavicci didn't plan to wait up for it. He glanced at his watch; it wasn't exactly time for bed, but he was beat. And he'd learned long ago to catch a nap—or anything else he could catch—whenever the opportunity arose.

He'd spent the last hour with what he called "post-Leap cleanup," covering for Tina's absence by helping Gooshie backup Ziggy's data. He'd taken a few minutes to change out of his uniform and indulge in a little whimsy: he put on the teal fedora he'd worn when he and Sam had first Leaped into Teresa Bruckner's life. Sort of a commemoration of this Leap, too.

Gooshie was still fiddling with Ziggy, apparently using the time to work on maintenance. Or maybe, Al thought, he just preferred her company.

"I'm goin' to my quarters, Gooshie," he announced as he punched the button for the elevator.

Gooshie didn't even bother to look up.

But before the elevator arrived, Ziggy caught him. "Admiral? Your security officer would like to speak with you. He says it's urgent."

Al furrowed his brow. "What the hell . . . ?" He went back to his office and picked up the phone. "Calavicci."

"Admiral, we've got—well, I think we have a security breach."

"A breach?" His stomach twisted. Dammit! Sister Mary Catherine or Teresa must have talked after all!

"I think you'd better come out here, sir. This is going to require your personal attention."

303

"Shit." He ran a hand across his face and thought rapidly. "Have you notified Weitzman?"

"Not yet, sir."

"Well, get him on the phone. Let him know we may need some backup. I'll be there in five minutes." He hung up, grabbed two cigars, and left the room. "Gooshie," he called, crossing the Control Center quickly. "Davalos says our security's been breached. I want you to secure everything from here."

"A security breach?" Gooshie's alarm was as visible as his perspiration. "Admiral, how could—"

"We were found out," Al explained, jabbing an unlit cigar in the air. "Remember?"

"Oh."

Al left, wondering how bad the damage was. Maybe Davalos was overreacting, he thought. But then again, maybe he wasn't.

The ride to the security office seemed to take a lot longer than five minutes; in point of fact, he made it in just under four.

The security chief's car was there, but no others. The swarm he'd expected was missing.

Davalos was waiting outside the adobe building.

Puzzled, Al got out of his car and saw a remarkably silly grin on Davalos' face. "They're inside, sir," he said, stepping aside to let Al precede him.

"They?"

Davalos didn't answer. He just stood there, grinning like a cat on a canary diet.

Al spared him a momentary look, then went in. This time, Davalos didn't follow.

"Ees a surprise, no?" Angela stood up from the chair, fanned herself, and smiled. "Jou are surprised?"

But Al's mouth wasn't working. Not yet.

Next to her, looking only slightly older than she had the last time he had seen her, was Teresa Bruckner. The cuts on her face, the bruises, were gone. The bandages on her hands were gone. And her hair was cut very short. But the childlike wonder in her eyes was still there.

"You're wearing the fedora!" were the first words out of

304

her mouth. And it was only then that Al realized he was going to have to breathe or lose consciousness.

"Teresa!"

Without thinking, he stepped forward, grabbed her, and pulled her into a tight embrace. The warmth of her body surprised him. The feel of it surprised him. In the whole history of the Project, he'd never had a chance to actually touch one of the people Sam had helped.

He held onto her, maybe a little too long, and felt his eyes burn. Then he let her go, wiped a hand across his face, and said, "You look great, munchkin."

Teresa laughed, her eyes sparkling with emotion. She wiped them quickly, and Al turned back to Angela. The woman was looking remarkably pleased with herself. And Al couldn't blame her.

"We didn't forget you," he told her.

Angela shrugged. "No, I was no' finished," she explained. And then, with a low, throaty laugh she said, "I got to bring Teresa here. Jou were surprised, jets?"

"Yeah," he admitted. "I was surprised."

"And," Angela continued, "I got an especial bonus this time."

"A bonus?" Al asked. His voice was thick, and he cleared his throat.

"Jets. Father O'Keefe, he is the one who told me how to do it. Jou see, no one remembered me because I was too vain, and so I had to do the good things without getting credit for them. But this time, I did such a good job, *jou* get to remember me." She smiled very sweetly at Al.

He narrowed his gaze. "Wait a minute," he said. He poked the cigar at her. "You're tellin' me that for *your* reward, I won't *ever* be able to forget you?"

Angela laughed. "*Now* jou understand what penance is."

He glowered at her, but his heart wasn't actually in it.

"Al, I brought you something." Teresa pulled his attention from the gloating angel. From the chair she'd been sitting in, she picked up a small box. It was wrapped in Christmas paper, tied with a red bow.

Torn between finding a suitable response to Angela's last statement and the gift-wrapped box, he chose the box. He pulled the ribbon off and tore the wrapping away. Two sets

305

of eyes eagerly watched as he opened the shoe box and pulled out a doll.

"In case you ever have trouble getting to sleep at night," Teresa explained. "It doesn't sing to you or anything, but—" She waited uncertainly for his reaction. "It's the one I had—"

"The head comes off, right?" he asked tightly, looking up from the toy. Teresa beamed. Al took a deep breath. "I thought this went into the ocean."

"One of the men who helped in the rescue found it." She glanced at Angela and blushed. "It's where I'd hidden the dope," she confessed. "Mother Mary Frances gave it to me when I went back to the monastery. I guess the dope washed away. They never found it."

"No loss there," Al mumbled. He cleared his throat and stared at the doll. There was a bandage on the head, just as there had been the night he'd sung Teresa to sleep.

"Well, what are you gonna do when you can't get to sleep at night?"

"Oh, I don't—" She hesitated and glanced at Angela. Then she smiled. "I don't have that problem any more."

He looked at the doll, knowing how much it meant to her, and wished he had something to give her in return.

"Well," Teresa said. She glanced at Angela. "We'd better be going."

"Now?" Al asked.

For a moment, Teresa looked uncomfortable. Then she smiled. "Well, Angela has another assignment and I'm—going home."

Al nodded. "California?"

Teresa shook her head and gave him a long, wistful look. "No. Somewhere much nicer." She closed her eyes, then turned to Angela. "Ready?"

"Look, wait a minute," Al said, stepping in front of them. "It's Christmas, right? How 'bout we at least go out, get some dinner or somethin'?"

"Oh, no, I don't eat—"

Teresa stopped her words with a look that told Al she had never meant to say what she had just said.

Al swallowed the premonition. He stared at the young woman, stared hard. But the look in her eyes told him that she'd meant what she'd said.

And *he* knew what that meant.

Ziggy's silence about Teresa's future suddenly made sense.

"Teresa?" She looked away. "Teresa, no!" He reached for her, but she pulled away.

He was damned if he'd cry. But dammit, it wasn't fair! It just wasn't fair!

"Teresa, no!" He dropped his hands to his sides, shaking. "No, we saved you!"

"Yes, you did." The girl's eyes filled, and her nose reddened. "It was the wrong time three years ago, Al," she said. Her voice broke. "I had no idea how wrong until—" She rubbed her eyes and forced herself to meet Al's. "We all die sometime, don't we? The important thing is to be prepared. You and Sam gave me a second chance. If I'd died three years ago, I never would have made it."

"Made it?" Al demanded, his teeth barely parting. He couldn't breathe. Rage was building in him, a rage he hadn't felt since. . . . "Made *what*? Teresa, you had your whole life ahead of you! You could have been another Nobel scientist or a teacher or—dammit!"

"I decided to stay with the sisters," Teresa said quietly. And then she smiled, a genuine smile. "Between you and Sam and Angela—well, *I* wanted to do something that would last, too."

For a moment, Al couldn't bring himself to look at her.

"Oh, it was no' supposed to be like this!" Angela exclaimed. "This was her final wish, Al! Come on, jou chould no' be sad for her!"

He ground his teeth and looked at the young woman. Her eyes were calm, peaceful.

"How . . . ?" He breathed out. "When?"

"Last night," Teresa said. "Cancer. Like my mom." Then she glanced at Angela, very quickly, as if for permission. And when she turned back, she said, "Like your dad."

Al's gaze sharpened. "How did you know about . . . ?"

"You prayed for him," Teresa said quietly. "He never would have made it if you hadn't prayed for him."

Al opened his mouth, then shut it. And then, glancing once

more at Angela, he asked, very carefully, "He made it?"

Teresa smiled. "Merry Christmas, Al."

For a second, the world stopped turning. The past, the present, and the future combined into one unending now.

"If you could see the future," Father O'Keefe's voice said, *"it would all be so clear, so easy, so beautiful."*

"Everything's going to be all right," Poppa promised. *"As long as you pray for me."*

Al closed his eyes tightly. Was that, after all, what his father had meant? Not that the cancer would leave; but that Heaven would wait?

Could it all have been that simple?

He sucked in a deep breath and pulled the fedora from his head. He turned it over in his hands, looking at it.

Remembering.

"Two and two are four. Four and four are eight. . . ."

The pain that Al had harbored for so long started to slip away.

And if Teresa's peace was any indication, there didn't seem to be a damn thing left to be angry about, either.

"Here." He handed the hat to Teresa. "To remember me by." Then he smiled. "Merry Christmas, munchkin."

Teresa laughed, the high-pitched, gleeful laugh she'd had as a child, and put the fedora on her head, tapping it down with her fingers.

"Cutting edge stuff," she said. "How do I look?"

Al swallowed and thumbed the side of his nose. "Like an angel," he said.